Chapter One

"Wrong Tools, Right Man"

If Claire Maddox had known the village ht have rethought the heels. They were lovely h⟨ ⟩ff in a sale she absolutely hadn't needed to w⟨ ⟩or gravel driveways, winding bridle paths, ⟨ ⟩as pretending to be.

She stopped outside the gate of what was, allegedly, her charming rental cottage. It leaned slightly to the left. A tile slid from the roof with a soft thunk, and somewhere inside, a pipe was either hissing or sobbing. Claire couldn't decide which was more relatable.

Still. Fresh start.

She tucked her hair behind one ear, straightened her posture, and hoisted her suitcase over the gate with more optimism than upper body strength. This was what she wanted. No more London drama. No more men who said things like *"It's not cheating if it's emotional growth."*

No, this was Ashford Vale. Birds chirping. Cakes cooling on windowsills. Community. Thatched roofs. Possibly a cat named Mr Tiddlywink.

She dragged the case up the front step and gave the door a hopeful knock. Then a firmer one. Then a frustrated one with her forehead.

"Alright, alright—don't break the thing," came a voice from behind her.

Claire turned. Slowly.

And there he was. Flannel shirt, scowl for days, forearms that looked like they could lift her entire London flat, and the expression of a man who did not enjoy being interrupted by... anything, really.

"You're Claire," he said, like it was a crime.

She smiled, all teeth. "That's me. You must be Mr Mercer?"

He didn't confirm it. Just unlocked the door with a grunt and pushed it open.

It smelled of damp plaster and... possibly regret.

She stepped in, the heels clicking bravely on worn wooden floorboards. The walls were half stripped, a ladder leaned in the corner like it had given up midway through, and the kitchen—such as it was—featured a kettle from the 1950s and a fridge humming in a tone that sounded vaguely threatening.

"So," she said, injecting cheer into the gloom like a scented candle in a bin fire, "cozy!"

He arched an eyebrow.

"This place needs more than a lick of paint," he said. "It needs a miracle. Or a demolition team."

Claire set her suitcase down. "I'm an interior designer."

He looked at her heels, her London curls, her polka-dot blouse. "Of course you are."

She squared her shoulders. "I'll make it work."

"You shouldn't even be here. It's not ready."

"It's a rental," she said, pointing at the printed confirmation in her handbag. "And I've come a long way. Surely there's a bed?"

"There's half a mattress," he muttered. "And a ceiling that leaks directly onto it."

Claire brightened. "So not *directly* uninhabitable."

He stared at her. "You plan on staying?"

She nodded. "Just for the night. Maybe two."

He rubbed a hand over his jaw, sighed like a man counting to ten internally, then finally said, "You got any idea what you're doing with a sledgehammer?"

She hesitated. "Is that the one that looks like a cartoon mallet?"

He sighed again. "Right. No."

But when she walked over to a crumbly internal wall and tapped it with her knuckles, eyeing it thoughtfully, something shifted in his posture. Just a little.

"I'd get help," he said, gruffly. "Before you electrocute yourself. Or flatten the place."

"I can handle it," she replied, planting her hands on her hips. "I may be from London, but I'm not completely useless."

The smile he gave was brief. Disbelieving. But maybe—*maybe*—not entirely unamused.

"I'll be back in the morning," he said. "To make sure the roof hasn't fallen in. And maybe to bring a proper tool."

Claire looked down at her heels.

He was already walking away. "And trainers. You're going to want trainers."

Claire stood in the half-lit cottage, alone now except for the groan of the pipes and the slow drip-drip-drip of something—somewhere—inside the walls. She exhaled through her nose.

"Charming," she muttered, tossing her handbag onto the nearest surface (which turned out to be a paint-splattered stepladder).

Still, she was here. She'd committed. A whole year, according to the lease—signed after two glasses of Sauvignon Blanc and a Google image search of "English countryside escapes."

She turned in a slow circle, taking it all in: warped floorboards, a fireplace boarded up with what looked like an old cupboard door, and wallpaper that was less "vintage floral" and more "ghosts of mildew past."

And yet... it had good bones. Somewhere beneath the damp and the dust and the disdain of one Jack Mercer, this place had potential. So did she.

She reached for her phone to take a photo—before, obviously. She needed a dramatic "after" someday—and realised she had no signal. Not even a bar. Brilliant.

The rest of the evening was spent in a strange ballet of semi-survival: finding the least creaky spot on the mattress (which was, admittedly, generous to even call a mattress), boiling water for tea using the ancient kettle and a plug socket that sparked ominously, and lighting a candle she'd brought from London that smelled of lemongrass and denial.

By 10 p.m., wrapped in two cardigans and one questionable blanket, Claire lay on the mattress in the corner of the bedroom and stared at the cracked ceiling. Outside, an owl hooted. Something scuttled in the attic. Possibly a mouse. Possibly a ghost.

She'd wanted peace, hadn't she?

Well. She'd found it.

And a man with forearms like Greek sculpture and the warmth of a fridge.

Morning arrived like a slap.

Claire woke to a cold nose—*not hers*—nudging against her cheek. She blinked blearily, rolled over, and came face to face with a Labrador.

"Um—hello?"

The dog, entirely unconcerned, gave a tail thump and a sniff, then plopped down beside her as if this were entirely normal.

A voice followed. "Hope you don't mind. He has no boundaries."

Claire sat up so quickly her neck crunched.

Jack Mercer stood in the doorway, mug in hand, expression unreadable.

Claire tried to rearrange herself into dignity, which was difficult while wrapped in a floral blanket and wearing one sock.

"I—um. Good morning?"

He walked in like he owned the place. Which, technically, he probably did.

"Brought coffee," he said, setting it down on the windowsill. "Can't have you taking a crowbar to the electrics without caffeine."

She blinked. "I wasn't going to—"

"Yet," he said, deadpan.

Claire narrowed her eyes, then took the mug. It was surprisingly warm. Strong. A little too bitter. Just like the man who brewed it.

"You're chipper this morning," she said.

Jack glanced around the room. "You stayed the night. Figured you weren't a total flake."

Claire tilted her head. "So that's progress?"

"You didn't run off to the train station sobbing about country spiders. That's more than most."

Claire sipped. "Is that a compliment?"

"Don't get used to it."

But there was a flicker at the corner of his mouth. Not a smile, exactly—but not entirely not one either.

He showed her around the cottage properly that morning, albeit with the air of someone giving a warning rather than a tour.

"This wall's non-structural," he said, tapping it with a knuckle. "But behind it? Probably old wiring. Watch your step in the kitchen. Floor dips near the fridge. And the bathroom—well. Don't expect miracles."

Claire followed, nodding and taking notes on her phone. She didn't catch every detail, mostly because she kept watching the way he moved—confident, capable, and completely immune to small talk.

"How long have you lived here?" she asked, as they stood in what used to be the dining room.

He shrugged. "All my life."

"And you're a... handyman?"

"Among other things. Builder. Joiner. Plumber, if I have to be. It's a small town. You do what needs doing."

"Jack of all trades," she said, smiling.

He gave her a look. "That supposed to be funny?"

"A little."

He didn't smile, but he also didn't frown. Which, Claire suspected, meant she was winning.

They lingered in the dining room—or what would *be* a dining room once it had walls, flooring, and didn't echo quite so much. A long table could go beneath the window, Claire thought. Mismatched chairs. String lights over the beam. Maybe one of those antique sideboards with charmingly sticky drawers.

Jack, however, was staring at the peeling wallpaper like it had personally offended him.

"You going to paint everything white and grey like they do on telly?" he asked, arms folded.

Claire glanced at him. "Not everything. I like colour."

He snorted. "Yeah, I clocked that. Red heels on a gravel track."

"They made a statement."

"They made blisters."

Claire grinned, but it faded quicker than she meant it to. There was something about the silence here—thicker than London's. No sirens, no phones pinging, no constant need to pretend she was fine in front of people who never really saw her.

Jack must've noticed the shift, because he asked, almost too casually, "So. What're you running from?"

Claire blinked. "Excuse me?"

He didn't even flinch. "Nobody moves to Ashford Vale in January for the scenery. Not unless they're escaping something."

She opened her mouth. Closed it. Then looked out the window, where fog curled around the hedgerows like secrets that hadn't made up their minds yet.

"I wasn't... running," she said eventually. "I just needed... out."

Jack said nothing.

Claire sighed, the sound catching in her chest. "My ex and I—we shared a flat. And a business. Well. *His* business. I was the 'branding consultant.'" She made air quotes with more venom than expected. "Turns out, he was also sharing himself with our receptionist. And possibly our accountant."

Jack made a low sound in his throat. Disapproval, maybe. Or something quieter.

"I didn't cry," Claire added quickly. "Just packed up my stuff and left."

"You should've cried."

She blinked at him. "What?"

He looked over, steady. "Sometimes crying's the bravest thing you can do. Doesn't mean he deserved your tears. Just means you're human."

Claire stared at him.

It was the first time she'd heard warmth in his voice. Not just gruff sarcasm or local suspicion—but real, lived-in empathy. The kind that didn't ask for explanation. The kind that had probably come from somewhere painful.

She cleared her throat. "What about you?" she asked. "Why so cheerful all the time?"

Jack's jaw shifted. "My wife died six years ago. Heart condition. Sudden."

The words dropped like stones between them.

"I'm—Jack, I'm so sorry."

He gave a tight nod. "Yeah. Well. You don't get a say in that sort of thing. Just wake up one day and there's more silence than you know what to do with."

Claire looked at him—*really* looked this time.

Not just at the scowl or the flannel or the stubborn crossed arms, but at the man underneath. The quiet in his voice. The shadows behind his eyes. The softness he'd never admit to.

"That must've been…"

"Hell," he said simply. "Especially with a four-year-old who still asked when Mummy was coming home."

Claire's breath hitched.

"She's eleven now," Jack said, a little more quietly. "Lily. Bright kid. Smarter than me."

"Does she live here with you?"

He nodded. "Most days. My sister helps out. I work early mornings and late afternoons, so she's usually at school when I'm not on site. You'll probably meet her soon. She'll ask a thousand questions."

"I like questions."

"Be careful. She'll take that as a challenge."

A small silence stretched out between them. It wasn't awkward this time—just thoughtful. Shared.

Then Claire said, "Thank you."

Jack frowned. "For what?"

"For telling me. And for the coffee. And… for not letting me accidentally demolish this place in my sleep."

He grunted. "I might still let you. Entertainment value."

She smiled, and this time, it lingered.

Outside, the clouds were beginning to thin. A smudge of sunlight reached through the cracked window and lit the corner of the room—the one she'd already decided would hold her reading chair. Jack noticed the light, too.

"Needs new windows," he said.

"Everything needs something," she replied.

He looked at her again. "Yeah. But some things are worth fixing."

And before she could answer, before she could let that comment warm her too much, he was already walking out the door.

Claire changed into trainers, pulled her hair into a ponytail, and told herself she was absolutely not shaken by anything Jack Mercer had said—about his wife, or her shoes, or the roof. Then she zipped her coat and set out to meet the village.

Ashford Vale greeted her like a postcard that had been accidentally left out in the rain. Pretty, but soft around the edges.

There was a crooked sign for the high street, two ducks waddling defiantly across the lane like they owned it, and a red telephone box that had been repurposed into a mini free library—currently offering a warped copy of *Eat Pray Love*, a local church newsletter from 2012, and, inexplicably, a packet of dried lentils.

The bakery came first.

A pale blue door with a hand-painted sign above it: **"The Flour Pot – Est. 1967."** Warmth and cinnamon spilled from its open window like something from a daydream.

Inside, a woman was balancing a tray of iced buns while trying to stop a small dog from licking the display case.

"Sorry!" she called. "He's not meant to be in here, but he has abandonment issues. Like me, really."

Claire laughed, stepping in. "He's got good taste."

The woman looked up, brushing flour off her apron. She had curly red hair tied in a cheerful scarf and eyes that crinkled at the corners when she smiled.

"You're new," she said, pointing a wooden spoon like a wand. "You must be the one renting Maple Hollow."

"Is that what it's called?"

The woman winced. "Bit optimistic, calling it a hollow. More like Maple Hole."

Claire laughed again. "Guilty. Claire Maddox."

"Ellie Harper," she said, shaking hands. "Baker. Owner. Local gossip sponge."

Claire instantly liked her.

"You settling in alright?" Ellie asked. "I heard Jack Mercer nearly bit your head off."

"He was... reserved."

Ellie snorted. "That's Jack for you. He's got the personality of wet cement until you get past the surface. Then it's just slightly drier cement, but with a heart buried in it somewhere."

Claire accepted a bun wrapped in paper. "Is this a peace offering?"

"It's a 'welcome to the village, I hope you survive your walls collapsing' bun."

Claire took a bite. It was warm and soft and made her eyes sting, just a little.

"Wow," she said. "I'm not sure if I'm going to cry or propose."

Ellie winked. "You wouldn't be the first."

After the bakery, Claire wandered down the lane past a florist's shop spilling with marigolds and a bookshop that looked like it had never once alphabetised anything.

A man with salt-and-pepper hair and a mischievous grin appeared in the doorway just as she slowed to peek inside.

"You can come in," he said. "We're not contagious. Not anymore, anyway."

Claire hesitated, then stepped over the threshold. The bell above the door gave a half-hearted jingle.

"I'm new," she said, immediately regretting how obvious it sounded.

"Thought so. We don't get many new faces unless someone dies or gets divorced. Welcome to Ashford Vale. I'm Caleb."

"Claire."

He nodded, then gestured to a precarious stack of novels. "Organised chaos. Like the rest of the village."

A cat appeared from nowhere and climbed onto the till.

"Oh, hello," Claire said.

"That's Edith. She runs the place. I just pay the heating bill."

Claire picked up a second-hand copy of *The Secret Garden* with a faded cover. "This place has charm."

"Careful," Caleb said. "That's how they get you. First it's a dusty bookshop, then you're enrolled in the Christmas panto and judging the bake-off."

Claire smiled. "Is that a threat or a promise?"

He grinned. "Bit of both."

By midday, Claire had met five villagers, been offered three scones, warned twice about "the goats near Old Mill Farm," and invited to a community meeting about the pub's new dartboard.

She found herself on a bench near the village green, unwrapping the rest of her bun from Ellie's bakery and watching a group of teenagers kick a football around a leaning goalpost. The sun broke through the clouds for just a moment, warming the back of her neck.

It was nothing like London.

There was no rush here. No pressure to be dazzling, or sharp, or perfectly on time. Just a strange, unfamiliar stillness.

Claire closed her eyes for a moment and let it in.

Peace.

Not permanent, maybe—but real.

And she didn't know it yet, but in that moment, Jack Mercer was standing on the scaffolding just beyond the church roof, watching her from a distance. He didn't know why. Or what that twist in his chest meant. But he'd never seen anyone eat a bun like it might save their life.

The pub was called **The Crooked Hare**, though the sign swinging above the door looked more like *The Disinterested Rabbit*. The painted animal leaned sideways with one ear half missing and an expression that said, *I've seen things and I no longer care*.

Claire pushed open the door and stepped into warmth and wood polish. It smelled of chips, old ale, and Sunday roasts that had seeped into the floorboards years ago and never quite left.

A low fire crackled in the grate. Mismatched tables filled the front room, and every chair seemed to have a dent that belonged to someone specific. Locals turned to look at her—not rudely, just... with interest. As if she were the news.

Behind the bar stood a woman in her sixties with silver-blonde hair and a posture that said she'd once managed a team of soldiers and could do it again with one hand.

"You're the London girl," she said, before Claire could even open her mouth.

Claire blinked. "Guilty."

"Thought so. You've got the look. That sort of *'Where's the oat milk and why does my phone say emergency calls only'* panic in your eyes."

Claire laughed. "It's been... a morning."

"Well, welcome to Ashford Vale. I'm Mags. I run this circus. You'll get used to it. Eventually."

Claire stepped up to the bar. "Do you do food?"

"Till three," Mags said. "Then we go suspiciously quiet till the menfolk remember they've forgotten dinner and panic order pies at half six. Fancy something now?"

"I'll take whatever's hot."

"You're in luck. Barry left his sausage and mash untouched when he ran off to chase his dog. Again."

Mags disappeared into the kitchen with a muttered, "He owes me three forks."

Claire sat at a high table near the fire and tried not to look like someone who wasn't sure of the etiquette—pubs in London were either gastropubs filled with Instagram influencers or aggressively ironic. This felt like... *home*. A bit wonky. A bit odd. But real.

A man two stools down raised a pint in greeting. "You're the one in Jack's cottage?"

Claire turned. "Apparently that's my defining trait today."

He grinned. "Don't mind Mags. She's better than she looks."

"I thought she looked great?"

"Exactly. Terrifying."

Claire laughed, properly this time. The sound bounced off the beams overhead and seemed to settle in the corners like it belonged there.

"I'm Dean," he said. "Firefighter, part-time pastry delivery boy, full-time dad."

"Claire. Designer, part-time crisis manager, occasional life imploder."

Dean gave a half-salute with his pint. "We'll get along."

Mags returned with a plate of sausage and mash and a jug of gravy that looked older than Claire's entire lease agreement. She set it down with authority.

"There," she said. "Get that down you before the village decides you're too thin to survive a winter here."

Claire smiled. "Thank you."

"Don't thank me. Just eat it and don't redecorate my toilets with some rustic Pinterest vision, alright?"

"Understood."

Mags moved off, muttering about someone who still owed her for the 2014 darts tournament.

Dean leaned closer. "You've landed at an interesting time."

"Oh?"

"Jack doesn't usually *do* tenants. Or visitors. Or conversation."

Claire stabbed a piece of sausage. "So I've gathered."

"But you got a coffee out of him," Dean said. "That's practically a marriage proposal."

Claire blinked.

He laughed. "Kidding. Mostly."

The door swung open again and a gust of wind blew in a woman with wet curls, a tray of mail, and an expression like she'd just had a conversation with a goose that refused to move.

"Sorry, sorry!" she called. "The green bin blew over and I got hit by a circular for chimney sweeps and three pensioners' birthday cards."

Dean waved. "Hey Beth."

The woman—Beth—dropped her tray on the bar and peeled off her coat. "You're new," she said, pointing at Claire. "You have that *'what have I done with my life'* look."

"Does everyone here come with psychic abilities?"

Beth smiled. "Just pattern recognition."

"I'm Claire. Just moved into Maple Hollow."

"Oh, Jack's place." Beth raised her eyebrows. "Brave."

"Is that the general consensus?"

Beth slid onto the stool beside her. "He's a good man. Just... quiet. Still half in the past. Most people don't realise how lonely he's been."

Claire paused, fork hovering mid-air.

Beth added, "But Lily's brought a bit of light back. His daughter. She's lovely. Reads upside down and knows every bird call in the hedgerow."

Claire smiled slowly. "Sounds like someone I want to meet."

"Oh, you will. She has a radar for new people and a passion for asking questions like *'Do you believe in ghosts?'* in the middle of perfectly normal conversations."

Dean raised his glass. "To Ashford Vale: where the pubs are warm, the builders are broody, and the ducks have territorial issues."

Claire clinked her lemonade to his pint. "Cheers to that."

By the time Claire reached Maple Hollow again—boots muddy, cheeks flushed, and half a sausage roll from Mags tucked in her coat pocket for later—the sky had turned the colour of over-steeped tea.

A curl of smoke drifted from the chimney, which was odd, because she hadn't figured out how to light the fire without setting off every smoke alarm in a ten-mile radius.

She pushed open the front door slowly.

Jack was kneeling on the hearth in his usual flannel shirt, coaxing flames into reluctant life with an air of grim determination. Across the room, a girl—maybe ten or eleven—was curled in the battered armchair with a book nearly the size of her head.

The girl looked up.

"Hello," she said. Not shy. Not bold either. Just... curious.

"Hi." Claire shut the door behind her, suddenly aware of how loud her entrance had sounded. "You must be Lily."

Lily nodded, eyes wide and owl-bright. "You're the lady who sleeps in the house with no proper walls."

"That's me."

Jack stood, brushing ash off his knees. "Lily, this is Claire. She's going to be staying here while the roof figures out if it wants to collapse."

Lily tilted her head. "Do you believe in ghosts?"

Claire blinked. "That's... a bold opening."

"She does this," Jack muttered.

"I've decided this house has a ghost," Lily said solemnly. "I heard footsteps last night. And it smelled like lavender and sadness."

Claire raised her eyebrows. "That might've been my candle."

"Oh. Or that."

Jack gave her a look, as if to say *welcome to my world*, and headed into the kitchen, where the ancient kettle was already rattling like it was having an emotional episode.

Lily closed her book. "Are you scared of being alone?"

Claire hesitated. "Sometimes."

The girl nodded like this was a perfectly acceptable answer. "Me too. But not when there's books."

Claire smiled. "Good philosophy."

Lily stood, moving with the gangly grace of someone caught halfway between childhood and the edge of something else. "Do you like it here?"

Claire looked around. At the uneven floors and dusty corners. At the flickering fire Jack had somehow coaxed to life. At the girl in mismatched socks who asked questions like she was writing a story in her head.

"I think I might," she said quietly.

Jack returned with three mugs—one for each of them, and one for the fireplace, which still hissed like it had personal objections to being helpful.

They sat together—Jack on the floor near the hearth, Lily curled back into her chair, and Claire cross-legged on the threadbare rug—drinking tea that tasted slightly of smoke and old ceramic.

For the first time in weeks, Claire didn't feel like she had to *perform*. No fake smile. No perfectly phrased email. No anxious wondering whether someone was about to tell her she wasn't enough.

Just heat, and quiet company, and a girl who thought ghosts might live in the walls.

After a while, Lily leaned against her father's arm and whispered something. He ruffled her hair, and she yawned with theatrical flair.

"Bed," Jack said. "Now."

Lily rolled her eyes but obeyed. As she passed Claire, she added, "If you hear scratching in the walls, it's either the ghost or a squirrel with anger issues."

"Thanks for the warning."

She padded off, leaving Claire and Jack in a room that suddenly felt a little fuller than it had before.

He didn't speak right away.

Then: "She likes you."

Claire raised her brows. "Is that unusual?"

"She doesn't like most people."

"She's got good instincts."

Jack almost smiled. Almost. "You heading back to London anytime soon?"

Claire looked into the fire. "No. I don't think I am."

And for the first time since she'd stepped off the train into a world of crumbling plaster and flannel-shirted frowns, she meant it.

Chapter Two

"Plaster Dust and Bribes"

Claire woke to a drip landing squarely on her forehead.

She blinked at the ceiling. It blinked back with a damp stain the shape of a fox, possibly mid-sneeze.

"Well," she muttered, "good morning, Ashford Vale."

The rain was pattering steadily on the roof above, and her hair was definitely frizzing in defiance. She swung her legs out of bed—or *off mattress scrap*, to be precise—and padded toward the kitchen, her slipper catching slightly on a nail that jutted up like it had a personal grudge.

She'd made a to-do list the night before, written on the back of a takeaway menu and now pinned to the wall with a fork:

- Call hardware shop
- Find decent coffee

- Clean the kitchen (without dying)
- Unpack box labelled "Optimism"
- Don't cry

She boiled the kettle (which screamed like a kettle in a horror film) and stood sipping lukewarm instant coffee while eyeing the half-stripped living room.

It looked worse in daylight.

Then again, she probably did too.

Still—today was about progress.

She pulled on a hoodie over her pyjamas, laced her boots, and grabbed the one weapon she felt vaguely competent wielding: a tape measure.

An hour later, she had managed to:

- Measure three walls
- Fall through one floorboard
- Knock over a tin of paint dust older than democracy
- Discover a family of spiders living behind a fuse box

And not once had she screamed. Not loudly.

She had, however, screamed *internally* when the front door creaked open and Jack appeared—again—without warning.

"You planning to live in that jumper all week?" he said by way of greeting.

Claire looked down. The jumper in question read *"Renovation? I Hardly Know Her!"* in flaking gold letters.

"Yes," she said primly. "It's part of my brand."

Jack walked in, surveyed the room like a general appraising a battlefield, and rubbed the back of his neck.

"You got a plan?"

"Of course."

She held up a slightly smudged drawing of what was either a floor layout or a schematic for a theme park.

Jack squinted. "Is that... a disco ball?"

"Optional."

"Right."

He folded his arms, still somehow managing to take up most of the oxygen in the room.

Claire put her hands on her hips. "Look, I know I'm not exactly your ideal co-worker, and I might not know how to use half your tools—"

"Not *half*."

"—but I've got vision. I see what this place could be."

Jack looked at her, not unkindly. "It'll take more than vision to stop that bathroom from giving someone tetanus."

Claire smiled. "That's why you're here."

He grunted. "Don't make me regret it."

She didn't answer. But she did hand him a bribe: a warm cheese scone from Ellie, wrapped in napkin and hope.

Jack took it. Didn't thank her. But also didn't not-thank her.

They worked in parallel after that—Jack pulling down the last of the ruined drywall while Claire swept up plaster shards and occasionally ducked when something creaked alarmingly.

Every so often, they'd exchange brief words. A practical question. A dry remark. But slowly, something shifted. Not quite ease—but a lack of tension. A working rhythm.

Until, of course, Lily burst in just before lunch, rain dripping from her coat and a half-finished sketch in hand.

"Dad!" she cried. "Edith the cat stole my toast again and Mrs Renfrew says you haven't fixed her bird feeder and also—who's been drawing fairies on the village noticeboard?"

Jack looked up from the wall he'd just split with a crowbar. "Breathe, Lil."

Lily turned to Claire. "Was it you?"

Claire blinked. "I haven't been near the noticeboard."

"Hmm." Lily peered at her as if she was still guilty of something. "You look like someone who draws fairies."

"I'll take that as a compliment."

Lily climbed onto the only stable chair left and studied the room like an interior designer possessed. "This place is chaos. I like it."

"Thank you."

"But it needs a nook. For reading. And snacks."

Claire smiled. "Deal."

Jack glanced between them, shook his head slightly, and returned to his crowbar. But his mouth curved just enough to suggest he wasn't entirely annoyed by either of them.

That afternoon, as the rain turned to a damp mist and Claire's once-white trainers took on a permanent shade of despair, she sat with Lily on the doorstep eating slices of apple and planning where the "nook" should go.

Jack worked silently nearby, his movements precise and practiced, like someone who didn't need to think about what came next—he just knew. And Claire couldn't help but wonder what it would be like to know something, or someone, that well.

But then Lily offered her half a biscuit and asked, "Do ghosts get bored?"

And just like that, the heaviness lifted again.

The knock came just after four.

Three precise taps on the door—neither hesitant nor urgent—followed by a pause and a polite, almost sheepish cough.

Claire wiped her hands on a tea towel, dust still clinging to her sleeves, and opened the door to reveal a woman in her mid-thirties with a clipboard, a fountain pen, and a knitted poncho the colour of rhubarb crumble.

"Claire Maddox?" she asked, voice soft but certain.

"That's me."

"Beatrice Fairweather. I run the Ashford Vale Events Committee. Don't let the title fool you—it's mostly me and three pensioners who argue about bunting. I heard you moved in. Welcome."

Claire blinked. "That's... incredibly organised of you."

Beatrice smiled with the faint air of someone who had colour-coded her spice rack by both region and emotional association. "We take our community very seriously. And we were hoping you'd like to be part of the Spring Fête Planning Meeting."

Claire tried not to visibly recoil. "Spring...?"

"Fête. With an accent."

"Ah."

"It's still three months away," Beatrice added cheerfully. "But we like to get ahead of things. You never know when someone will demand a maypole or bring back the cheese rolling. Last year's Bake-Off ended in scandal. We had to ban Susan from using mascarpone."

Claire nodded as if she understood any of that.

"And," Beatrice continued, flipping to a fresh page on her clipboard, "we're holding a little 'Welcome to Ashford' drinks gathering at the pub tonight. Informal. Unless you count the quiz round. Which Mags takes very seriously."

Jack, now behind Claire and holding a hammer like it had personally offended him, muttered, "You'll regret it if you win. Mags once threw a pickle jar at a bloke for misquoting Shakespeare."

Beatrice beamed. "Ah! Jack. Still grumbling, I see."

"Still clipboard-wielding," he replied.

Claire looked between them, amused.

Beatrice turned back to her. "You don't *have* to come. But people are curious. And you might get a few friendly questions. Or minor interrogation."

Claire hesitated.

On the one hand, she had dust in her hair and a to-do list longer than her arm. On the other—she'd spent years making excuses to avoid things, and all that had got her was a dodgy breakup and an overpriced coffee habit.

So she smiled. "I'll come."

"Lovely!" Beatrice looked delighted, ticking something off with the flourish of someone born to tick things off. "Eight o'clock. Pub quiz theme is 'Curious Creatures and Local History.' Do brush up on your ferret knowledge."

With that, she swept away, poncho flapping gently behind her like a soft woollen cape.

Later, as Claire stood brushing her hair by the cracked mirror in the bathroom and wondering whether "pub casual" in Ashford Vale meant jeans or a tactical cardigan, Jack passed by the doorway.

"You don't have to go," he said. "They'll still consider you a local if you just survive the winter without crying in public."

Claire smiled at her reflection. "Too late on that front. I teared up during Ellie's cinnamon roll."

Jack leaned on the doorframe. "Fair. That's her signature weapon."

He watched her for a moment, not speaking. Then: "You'll do fine. You're not what I expected."

She turned. "What *did* you expect?"

He didn't answer straight away. Then, gruffly: "More flounce. Less grit."

Claire shrugged. "I'm full of surprises."

"Yeah," he said, almost to himself. "You are."

Claire stood at the bathroom mirror with a hairbrush in one hand and a damp flannel in the other, giving herself the kind of pep talk usually reserved for job interviews and emergency flatpack assembly.

"You are capable," she murmured. "You are independent. You are not going to spill anything down yourself within the first five minutes."

The mirror, cracked in the top corner like a spider had whispered a secret into it, was not particularly encouraging.

Still, she'd done her best. A soft green jumper, freshly de-fluffed with a roll of tape and optimism. Black jeans that hadn't been paint-splattered—yet. A quick swipe of mascara that hopefully said *friendly and mysterious* rather than *flustered raccoon*.

She stepped back from the mirror and assessed. Not bad. A little tired around the edges. A bit of flour still in her hair from Ellie's surprise pastry delivery. But human. Present. Here.

And then—

"You missed a bit."

Claire jumped.

Jack was in the doorway, leaning just far enough against the frame to look casual and just close enough to cause a flutter beneath her ribs.

"Missed what?"

He reached over, thumb brushing gently against her temple. "Bit of dust. Or possibly a dead moth. Hard to tell in this place."

Claire laughed despite herself. "You do wonders for my confidence."

Jack's expression didn't change much, but his eyes warmed at the corners. "You don't need confidence. You've got nerve."

She hesitated. "Is that a compliment?"

"Getting there."

She turned slightly, catching his reflection in the cracked mirror behind her. It was strange seeing him like this—half in shadow, sleeves pushed up, hair still damp from the rain, looking more real than he ever did mid-grumble and hammer swing.

And yet somehow... gentler.

"Will Lily be at the pub too?" Claire asked.

"She's sleeping at my sister's tonight. Movie night. They'll eat too many crisps and fall asleep halfway through something animated."

Claire smiled. "That sounds... nice."

Jack nodded, then reached out to straighten the collar of her jumper. It wasn't crooked. Not really. But he adjusted it anyway.

"There," he said, voice low. "Ready to face the wolves."

Claire swallowed. "That's what we're calling your neighbours?"

"You haven't met the twins yet. One of them once stapled Beatrice's bunting to the church door."

Claire snorted. "I'm beginning to think this whole village runs on cake and mild anarchy."

Jack didn't disagree.

He stepped back, as if catching himself, and gave her a quick once-over. Not rude. Not lingering. Just... seeing.

"You'll do," he said.

Claire crossed her arms. "Charming."

He started to turn away, then paused—just briefly—and added, without looking at her, "For what it's worth... I'm glad you stayed."

And then he was gone. Just like that.

Leaving Claire standing in the bathroom with a fluttering in her chest and the distinct sense that something had shifted—but she wasn't quite sure what.

The Crooked Hare was already humming by the time Claire stepped inside.

A wave of chatter, clinking glasses, and the low thump of a badly-tuned pub piano hit her like warm velvet. Fairy lights were strung along the rafters in defiance of seasonal trends, and someone had placed a giant stuffed badger wearing a crown on the bar. No one seemed to be questioning it.

Claire spotted Ellie first, waving enthusiastically from a table by the window already half-covered in empty pint glasses and a small knitted banner that read *Team Crumble Rises Again*.

"You came!" Ellie called. "We've got a seat, and a pen, and a secret weapon—Beth memorised all the mammals of the Peak District in Year Ten!"

Beth gave a modest shrug. "We weren't allowed smartphones."

Claire slipped into the empty seat between Ellie and a cheerful man with eyebrows like startled caterpillars, who introduced himself as Gary-from-the-post-office-and-sometimes-sausage-rolls.

Beatrice swept past the table with a clipboard and a bell. "Five minutes to quiz start! Round one: Curious Creatures! Round two: Local Legends! Round three: Mags's Surprise."

From behind the bar, Mags raised an eyebrow. "Let's just say there's a cheese round and you're not ready for it."

Claire's team erupted in groans and mutters of "not again" and "at least no stilton this time, please."

She was halfway through her first sip of cider when Jack arrived.

Not dramatically. Not loudly. Just... there.

He didn't sit at their table. Instead, he nodded a brief greeting to the room, said something quiet to Mags behind the bar, and took a place at a small table near the fireplace with Dean and two men who looked like they'd once wrestled sheep competitively and won.

Claire tried not to stare. She mostly failed.

Jack caught her eye once. Just once. But it was enough to make her heart do a slow, ill-timed flip in her chest.

The quiz began in the usual village fashion: chaotically.

Beatrice read the first question like it was a royal decree. "Round One, Question One: What is the gestation period of a hedgehog?"

"Three weeks," whispered Beth confidently.

Gary leaned in. "I think it's shorter if it's cold."

"Gary, they're not kettle noodles," Ellie whispered.

Claire bit her lip to keep from laughing.

Question after question followed—everything from "Which bird can fly backwards?" (Beth said hummingbird with a reverent sigh) to "How many legs does a woodlouse have?" (Ellie guessed too many and lost all confidence in her own legs afterward).

Across the room, Claire caught Jack watching their table.

He didn't smile. But he didn't scowl either. And when she held up her team's answer to *"What was the name of the rogue goat that shut down the Ashford market in 1997?"* and mouthed *"Was it Trevor?"*—Jack nodded, almost imperceptibly.

It *was* Trevor, apparently. And he had a criminal record for carrot theft.

By Round Three—Mags's infamous "Surprise Cheese Round"—things were less about points and more about dignity. Which, Claire discovered, vanished quickly once you were blindfolded and asked to identify obscure cheeses by smell alone.

"I think this one's... a foot," Claire said, gagging slightly.

"Double Gloucester," Beatrice corrected. "But I'll allow 'foot'."

Someone started playing *Wonderwall* on the pub piano. Mags yelled, "Not again, Steve!" and threatened to throw a coaster.

Claire leaned back in her seat, breathless from laughter, eyes dancing.

She hadn't felt this light in years.

Not since long before London, or Alex, or the realisation that she'd been living someone else's version of a perfect life.

Now here she was, elbow-deep in cheese and goat trivia, being teased by strangers who already seemed to know how she took her tea.

And watching Jack Mercer quietly watching her.

As the quiz drew to a close (Team Crumble Rises Again came second, beaten only by Mags's team of ringers), Claire gathered her things and stepped outside for a breath of cool air. The night smelled of woodsmoke and damp hedges.

The door creaked open behind her.

Jack.

Of course.

"Good quiz," he said, hands in his pockets.

Claire smiled. "I now know more about regional goats and cheese than any normal person should."

They stood there for a long moment. Not speaking. Just... existing. Together. The kind of quiet that didn't demand anything.

Then Jack said, almost too casually, "You fit here."

Claire looked at him. "You don't think I'm too... much?"

He shook his head. "I think you're just enough."

And for a moment, with the stars peeking out through mist and the sound of laughter still drifting from the pub, Claire Maddox wondered if maybe—just maybe—she'd come home.

They didn't say much on the walk back.

Jack offered to walk her—gruffly, like it was more about storm drains and uneven cobbles than concern—but Claire accepted without teasing him for it.

Ashford Vale at night was hushed, the streets lit by old-fashioned lamps that flickered slightly as if they hadn't decided whether to commit to modern electricity. A cat darted across the lane. Somewhere in the dark, an owl hooted once, mournfully.

Claire tucked her hands into her coat pockets and tried not to feel too content. Which, of course, made her feel it more.

"You always walk this route?" she asked, mostly to fill the silence.

Jack shrugged. "Used to. With Lily. After dinner. Before it all got too cold and dark and full of GCSE panic."

"She's great."

He gave a quiet smile. "She is."

They paused outside Maple Hollow.

Claire half-expected him to mumble a goodbye and disappear like he always did, but instead, he lingered a beat longer.

"If you need anything," he said, not quite looking at her, "just yell. Or throw something. I'm usually around."

Claire tilted her head. "And here I thought you were allergic to being helpful."

He looked at her then—really looked.

"I never said I wasn't helpful," he said. "Just cautious."

And with that, he was gone.

Claire watched him walk away, hands still in his pockets, head ducked against the breeze. Then she let herself inside, kicked off her boots, and stood in the middle of the half-ruined cottage with a strange little smile tugging at the corner of her mouth.

It wasn't a life yet. Not quite. But it was something. A start.

She exhaled, long and quiet.

Then went to bed with the sound of quiz-night laughter still echoing faintly in her ears.

Chapter Three

"Tea Leaves and Trouble"

Claire awoke the next morning to two things:

1. The smell of toast that she definitely hadn't made, and
2. A child humming what sounded suspiciously like *"Bohemian Rhapsody"* off-key in the hallway.

She sat up, blinked at the watery sunshine spilling through the cracked curtains, and padded into the kitchen—where Lily was buttering toast with great purpose and wearing a dressing gown roughly five sizes too big for her.

"Morning," the girl said brightly, as if this were a normal occurrence.

Claire blinked. "Um. Hello?"

"I let myself in. Hope that's okay."

Claire looked at the door, then back at Lily. "Did your dad—?"

"He said I could come say hi while he's fixing a chimney down the lane. Also, I brought tarot cards."

Claire blinked again. "That escalated quickly."

Lily held up a very bent deck of cards. "I'm practising. Beth says they're for entertainment purposes only, but the last time I pulled one for her, she got offered a free quiche. So."

Claire pulled on a jumper and made tea. "You don't waste time, do you?"

"Nope." Lily shuffled the cards with alarming confidence. "Now pick three."

Claire humoured her, selecting three cards and laying them down on the kitchen table—next to the burnt toast, an open bag of jelly babies, and a small hand-drawn map of *"Haunted Spots in Ashford Vale."*

Lily turned over the first card. "The Tower. That's bad."

Claire frowned. "Great."

"But wait—then The Fool. New beginnings."

"Well, that sounds more promising."

"And then..." Lily flipped the final card. "The Lovers."

Claire choked on her tea. "Excuse me?"

Lily gave her a wise look far too old for her age. "That one always turns up when people act like they're *not* in love but clearly *are*."

Claire laughed, shaking her head. "You are trouble."

"I know," Lily said cheerfully. "Want a jelly baby?"

The jelly babies had just begun disappearing in earnest when there was another knock at the door—this one fast and flurried, like someone who knocked with their whole personality.

Claire opened it to find a woman in a raspberry beret, floral gumboots, and a high-vis cycling vest standing there with a basket full of mismatched muffins and a clipboard clipped to a clipboard.

"Claire Maddox?" she chirped.

"Yes?"

"Frances Brewster. I'm on the Sustainability Subcommittee of the Ashford Vale Neighbourhood Harmony Circle."

Claire blinked. "That's... a long title."

"We used to be the Green Friends but someone complained it sounded like a lizard cult. Anyway—welcome! I brought low-waste muffins and a reusable door hanger."

She handed Claire a piece of laminated cardboard that read *"YES TO SPONTANEOUS BISCUITS, NO TO DOORSTEP EVANGELISM."*

"Thanks... I think?"

Frances peered inside. "Is that Lily Mercer eating jelly babies?"

"It is."

Frances beamed. "Then you've already made friends with the village's unofficial Youth Council. Good. That saves me a meeting. Now—just a quick note to say you're invited to Compost Thursdays, Knit for Bees night, and the monthly Silent Dog Walk."

"The what?"

"We walk our dogs. But silently. It's very restorative."

Claire nodded slowly, wondering if she was still asleep.

Frances leaned forward, eyes glinting. "And between us, Mags says she saw you *looking* at Jack Mercer like a woman with good taste and worse impulse control."

Claire nearly dropped the muffin basket. "I—what?"

"Don't worry," Frances said, patting her arm. "It's not a crime. Just a warning. He's emotionally constipated, but he can lift things. It's a trade-off."

And with that, she turned on her heel and pedalled away on a bicycle entirely covered in fairy lights and what looked like hand-crocheted streamers.

Claire shut the door slowly.

Lily looked up from the table. "I like her. She made me a hat once."

"Of course she did."

The day settled after that.

Jack popped by briefly with a spare fuse and a vague mumble about the boiler, but left again before Claire could ask whether he was emotionally constipated or just professionally abrupt.

Lily vanished to her aunt's with a wave and an apple tart she claimed she'd bartered from Ellie using only compliments and a drawing of a frog on a unicycle.

And for a few glorious hours, Claire had peace.

Until she didn't.

It started with a hiss. Then a pop. Then a sound like a goat sneezing into a pipe organ.

Claire looked up from her phone. The ceiling groaned.

"Oh no."

And then water—*actual, unapologetic water*—burst from the pipe behind the kitchen sink and sprayed across the entire room like it had something to prove.

Claire shrieked and grabbed the nearest thing—a frying pan—to try and shield herself, as though this were some kind of plumbing duel.

Water hit the toaster. The ceiling. The back wall. The floor.

Claire grabbed her phone, already sloshing through puddles. "Call Jack," she muttered. "Call the man. Call—"

But before she could press the button, the door banged open.

Jack stood there, dripping slightly from the rain, toolbox in hand.

He stared at the chaos.

Claire pointed helplessly. "It *attacked* me."

Jack blinked. "Did you touch the stopcock?"

"I didn't touch *anything!*"

He exhaled through his nose like someone preparing to wrestle a bear, crossed the room in three quick strides, and yanked the stopcock under the sink with a firm twist.

The pipe sputtered.

Then silence.

Only the slow, damp plink of water dripping off the table edge.

Claire stood in the centre of it all, hair soaked, jumper clinging to her like a regret, holding a frying pan like a shield.

Jack stared at her.

And then—*actually smiled.*

Not a smirk. Not a twitch. A real, reluctant, *blasted-by-hurricane-Claire* kind of smile.

"Not quite the Pinterest renovation you had in mind?"

Claire let the pan drop with a wet clatter. "It's *possessed.*"

Jack crouched beside the burst pipe, rolling up his sleeves. "More like sixty years of poor maintenance and blind optimism."

"Same."

He looked up at her. "You okay?"

Claire nodded. "Fine. A bit... damp. A bit humiliated."

He shook his head, unscrewing part of the pipe. "Nah. You handled it."

"I brandished a frying pan."

"I've seen worse."

They worked side by side after that—Jack replacing a section of the pipe, Claire mopping the floor with towels that smelled faintly of the previous tenant's perfume and despair.

At one point their hands brushed. Just for a second.

Neither of them said anything.

But neither of them moved away, either.

The worst of the chaos was over.

Jack had replaced the pipe with the kind of no-nonsense efficiency that made Claire feel both very safe and mildly inadequate. The leak had stopped. The water had been banished. The toaster, miraculously, had survived.

Claire was sitting on the floor, her back against the cabinet, sleeves pushed up and a towel over her knees like she was in some kind of domestic therapy group.

Jack sat opposite, elbows on his thighs, twisting his wrench idly in his hands. The only sound was the drip of the last puddle into an old biscuit tin and the occasional sigh of the kettle as it reheated for the third time that day.

"Thanks," Claire said eventually. "Again."

Jack gave a slow nod. "Not your fault."

"I know. But if I don't say thank you, I'll feel like a freeloader."

He glanced at her. "You're not a freeloader."

She raised an eyebrow. "You did just save me from being eaten alive by rogue plumbing."

"True. But you didn't scream. Or run."

"I *did* wave a frying pan."

He smiled—just a little. "Better than most."

There was a pause. Not awkward. Just quiet.

Claire pulled her damp hair into a bun and stared at her knees. "I think part of me thought this would be... easy."

Jack didn't interrupt.

"I had this whole image in my head," she continued. "You know? Moving somewhere small. Cozy. Fixing up a cottage. Maybe growing herbs in a windowsill. The full romcom montage."

Jack made a noise—something between a laugh and a grunt.

Claire looked up. "What?"

"Just picturing you with a watering can and one of those wide-brimmed gardening hats."

"I'd wear it with dignity."

"You'd terrify the roses."

She laughed. "You know, you're very good at insulting people without actually sounding rude."

Jack shrugged. "Skill. Took years."

Another pause.

Then—quieter—Claire said, "Do you miss her?"

Jack looked at her then. Not startled. Just... still.

"My wife?"

Claire nodded. "You don't have to answer."

He didn't for a long moment.

Then: "Every day."

His voice wasn't broken or soft or tragic. Just... steady. The way a person sounds when they've carried something heavy for a long time and know all its corners by heart.

Claire swallowed. "I'm sorry."

"She was the one who wanted to move away. Start over somewhere else. I kept putting it off. Work. Money. Lily was still small." He paused. "And then suddenly... there wasn't time anymore."

Claire looked at him, really looked—at the man who always fixed things, who never said much, who carried his grief like a second skin.

"Do you ever wish you'd gone?" she asked.

He shook his head slowly. "No. I just wish she'd stayed."

A silence bloomed in the room.

Not heavy. Not uncomfortable.

Just true.

Claire reached across the narrow space and touched his hand. Just once. Lightly.

Jack didn't move away.

Outside, the rain had stopped. The clouds were parting just slightly, and somewhere beyond the fogged-up windows, birds were beginning to sing again.

In the stillness of the kitchen—water-stained, a bit broken, but slowly coming back to life—something shifted between them. Not loud. Not dramatic.

But real.

And perhaps—just perhaps—the start of something neither of them had planned.

By early evening, the cottage had dried out—more or less.

Claire had managed to change into fresh clothes, hang two soggy towels over the radiator, and coax the fire into a soft, steady crackle. A second-hand radio hummed low in the background, the sort of mellow folk music that always sounded vaguely like someone had recorded it in a wheat field.

She was curled on the armchair with a chipped mug of peppermint tea, blanket around her knees, and the half-finished plans for the living room spread across the coffee table. Her hands smelled faintly of soap and wood polish, and her muscles ached in that oddly satisfying way that meant she'd actually *done* something.

It was the first time in weeks she'd let herself just sit.

No emails. No frantic to-do lists. No ex-boyfriend messaging her vague apologies at 1 a.m.

Just the sound of rain ticking gently on the windows and the occasional soft groan from the house as if it, too, was finally exhaling.

A knock came.

Not loud. Just a quiet, two-tap rhythm against the door.

Claire stood, blanket still draped over her shoulders like a shawl, and opened it to find Jack on the step. His hair was damp again, curls brushing his collar, toolbox gone, but hands still in his jacket pockets like he wasn't quite sure why he was here.

She tilted her head. "Back for round two?"

He didn't smile, but his voice was softer than usual. "Just wanted to check you weren't electrocuted."

"Still alive," she said, holding up her tea like proof.

Jack glanced past her shoulder at the faint glow of the fire, the papers, the general air of "lived-in chaos" she'd made her own.

"Looks warmer in there than it does in mine."

Claire stepped back. "Come in, then. I promise no more surprise plumbing."

He hesitated only for a second. Then nodded and stepped inside, bringing a trace of cool evening air with him.

He didn't sit right away. Just wandered the edge of the room, eyeing the exposed beams and half-planned sketches with that builder's gaze—half critical, half curious.

Claire poured him a mug of tea without asking and passed it over.

He took it. Sipped. Didn't comment.

They sat in silence for a while. The kind of silence that felt... earned.

Then Claire said, "Is it always like this here? This quiet?"

Jack leaned back, one ankle resting on the opposite knee. "Sometimes. Depends on the ducks. And Frances's schedule."

Claire smiled into her mug. "I like it. I think. I mean, it's slightly terrifying, but in a nice way."

He glanced at her. "You've lasted longer than most."

"Most what?"

"People who move here thinking they'll 'find themselves.'" He made air quotes with one hand. "Usually lasts until the WiFi goes down or they realise the corner shop doesn't sell almond milk."

Claire laughed. "I'm more of a builder's brew type, actually."

Jack looked at her again. Really looked.

And maybe it was the firelight, or the softened edges of a long day, but something flickered in his eyes—something not quite guarded, not quite open.

"I think you're braver than you let on," he said quietly.

Claire blinked. "That's... unexpectedly kind."

"Don't get used to it."

"Noted."

But her heart had already tucked the compliment somewhere safe.

They talked a little after that. Not about big things. Just... stories. Lily's obsession with badgers. The time Jack fell through a client's greenhouse roof and landed in a rhubarb patch. Claire's disastrous first attempt at wallpapering, which ended in her gluing her phone to the skirting board.

And all the while, the fire burned low, the tea cooled, and the world outside faded into mist and moonlight.

Eventually, Jack stood.

"I should go," he said. "Lily'll expect breakfast that doesn't involve me burning toast again."

Claire followed him to the door. "Thanks for coming by."

He paused on the step. Looked at her.

Then said, quietly, "It's nice. Talking."

She nodded. "It is."

He didn't kiss her. Didn't touch her hand. Just... held her gaze for a second too long.

And then he was gone, boots crunching softly against the damp gravel.

Claire stood in the doorway for a moment, watching the fog roll in over the hedgerows, and let the warmth in her chest linger.

Not everything had to happen all at once.

Some things, she was learning, were better when they unfolded slowly.

The next morning, Claire woke to sunshine.

Not the bold, golden kind that poured across bedsheets like a film montage—this was more of a tentative drizzle of light, the sort that peeked shyly through clouds as if unsure whether it had permission to be here.

Still. It was enough.

She dressed in a thick jumper and jeans, tugged on her battered boots, and opened the back door to the garden she hadn't properly looked at yet.

It was… overgrown.

There were weeds climbing over what might once have been a path, a half-rotted bench sagging beneath a wild tangle of ivy, and something that looked suspiciously like a shopping trolley hiding under a hydrangea.

Claire stepped outside and breathed it in.

Cold air. Damp earth. The faint scent of woodsmoke drifting from somewhere nearby.

The garden was chaos—but it had charm. Like a friend who turned up late, brought biscuits, and spilled tea everywhere but made you laugh so hard you didn't mind.

She walked a slow loop around it, imagining fairy lights strung across the fence, maybe a little herb patch by the kitchen window. A place to sit with coffee and feel like she hadn't made a terrible life decision.

"Someone had big plans," came a voice from over the fence.

Claire jumped. Nearly fell into a compost bin.

A woman with short grey curls, bright blue glasses, and a paint-splattered scarf leaned over the fence, smiling.

"Don't worry, love. Everyone forgets the back garden their first week."

Claire laughed, brushing herself off. "I've just discovered it. It may take a while to recover."

"I'm Jean. Two doors down. I've lived here since the last ice age. You must be the London one."

Claire considered resisting the label, then gave up. "Claire Maddox. And yes. The one with the broken plumbing and overly ambitious Pinterest board."

Jean grinned. "Excellent. You're just what this street needed."

An hour later, Claire was back inside attempting to tackle the kitchen cupboard doors (which didn't so much open as wheeze and fall sideways) when her phone buzzed on the counter.

Ellie Harper:

URGENT. Need hands. Scone disaster. You like apricots?

Claire stared at the message, then at the cupboard door now sitting at a worrying angle.

Claire:

I have hands. And a vague memory of apricots. On my way.

The bakery smelled like comfort and chaos.

Ellie stood in the middle of it all, apron dusted with flour, a tray of misshapen scones cooling by the window and a look of mild panic in her eyes.

"Thank god," she said. "I accidentally doubled the batch. My maths is fine, my measuring jug is not. I need boxes packed, a label written, and moral support."

Claire rolled up her sleeves. "I'm your girl."

Half an hour later, her hair smelled like cinnamon and she had officially named the misshapen ones *'rustic-style artisan splodges'*. Mags popped in for a crumpet and left with a paper bag of gossip. Beth arrived with a list of overdue library books and stayed to re-label the fig and almond traybakes using calligraphy and mild judgement.

Claire laughed more in one hour than she had in a month.

And when the bell above the door rang again, she didn't even look up—just called out, "We're all out of common sense but the lemon tarts are still warm!"

A quiet voice answered. "I'll take two lemon tarts and a bit of whatever that is."

She turned.

Jack.

Looking slightly windblown. Holding a broken measuring tape. And watching her with that unreadable expression that always seemed one blink away from a smile.

Claire blinked. "You buy pastries?"

He shrugged. "Lily bribed me."

Ellie handed him a box. "Don't tell the others. He's got a weakness for lemon."

Jack took it, nodded to them all, and—on his way out—tapped the edge of Claire's elbow as if to say, *See? You belong here.*

She felt the warmth of it long after the bell had stopped ringing.

By the time Claire returned to Maple Hollow, the clouds had rolled in again—not with menace, but with the lazy indifference of weather that couldn't decide what it wanted to be.

She carried a bakery bag under one arm, her jumper dusted with flour and her fingers still faintly sticky from an emergency lemon drizzle repair. The house greeted her with its usual groan and creak, but she swore it sounded slightly more welcoming now. Or maybe she was just imagining it.

She set the bag on the counter, kicked off her boots, and paused by the little table in the corner—the one she'd cleared off yesterday in a fit of optimism.

There was still a stack of paperwork to go through. Old documents. Receipts. Notes scribbled by a former tenant who seemed to have an unhealthy obsession with comparing teabag brands.

She thumbed through a few pages, half-listening to the soft tick of the kitchen clock.

And then, tucked between a recipe for onion marmalade and a receipt from a garden centre dated 1994, she found it.

A postcard.

Faded around the edges, ink bleeding slightly from damp. The picture was of a cottage by the sea—whitewashed walls, blue door, geraniums in pots along the sill.

On the back, in small, looping handwriting:

"One day, I'll live somewhere small and quiet, where the tea is hot and the neighbours don't know your star sign before they know your name. Until then—plant something that doesn't bloom fast. It's worth the wait."
—M.

Claire held the card for a long moment.

She didn't know who M was.

But she liked them.

She tucked the card into the inside pocket of her notebook, where she kept the scraps of things that felt like they meant something, even if she couldn't explain why.

Outside, the wind picked up just enough to rattle the old windowpanes. Inside, the kettle began its low, familiar rumble.

And for the first time since arriving, Claire didn't feel like she was passing through.

She felt—just a little bit—*rooted*.

Chapter Four

"Tea, Trepidation, and a Sheep Named Graham"

Claire had only been awake for ten minutes when the doorbell rang.

Which was impressive, considering she wasn't entirely convinced the doorbell worked. It sounded less like a bell and more like someone poking a kazoo underwater.

She padded barefoot to the door, still in a hoodie and pajama bottoms with foxes on them, and opened it to find Beth standing there—library tote over one arm, clipboard under the other, and an expression that suggested Claire had committed a minor crime by not being ready for the day.

"Oh," Beth said brightly. "Good. You're in."

Claire blinked. "It's… 8:03."

"I know. This is the time of day when things get done. Also, the community centre is too cold to loiter in, so I'm making the rounds early. Here."

She handed over a sheet of paper that looked suspiciously like a rota.

"What is this?"

"You've been added to the *Ashford Vale Village Spring Fair* planning team. Everyone takes a shift. Don't worry, it's nothing difficult."

Claire stared. "It says I'm in charge of the 'Children's Craft Corner and Livestock Liaison'."

Beth nodded cheerfully. "Just a few glue sticks and one sheep named Graham. You'll be fine."

"I haven't even *met* Graham."

"He's moody but photogenic."

Claire opened her mouth, closed it again, then exhaled slowly. "This feels like entrapment."

"Welcome to Ashford Vale."

Later that morning, Claire wandered down to the bakery with a distinct sense of impending chaos and a mild resentment toward animals with names.

Ellie was already behind the counter, wrestling with an industrial-size piping bag and humming along to a playlist titled *'Kitchen Confidence & Cake-Induced Power'*.

"You've got your face on," Ellie said, glancing up.

"My what?"

"Your *'I've been roped into something against my will but will probably end up enjoying it and making a Pinterest board about it later'* face."

Claire slumped onto a stool. "Children's craft corner. And sheep management."

Ellie winced. "Graham?"

"Apparently he bites."

"You'll want to keep biscuits on you. He respects snacks."

Claire groaned. "I moved here for peace and scones. Not ovine diplomacy."

Beth appeared behind her, startling both. "Also, Jack's been assigned the marquee tent and stage setup."

Claire straightened slightly. "Oh."

Beth sipped her tea. "I thought you'd like to know. Although he *did* request to be moved to electrical setup instead."

Claire's shoulders sank. "Ah."

"Could be he's just busy," Ellie offered quickly. "Or allergic to bunting. I think one of his eyebrows twitched during last year's tinsel incident."

Claire smiled weakly. But the seed of doubt had been planted.

Maybe she *had* imagined something. Maybe that quiet moment by the fire, the shared tea, the way he'd touched her elbow in the bakery—maybe that had just been… kindness. Jack's version of polite.

Or maybe this was what happened when you got a little too comfortable in a village where everyone saw everything and nothing stayed just yours for long.

That afternoon, Claire took the long route back to Maple Hollow, past the cricket green and down toward the river. The hedgerows were beginning to bud, and the ducks looked smug about it.

She stopped by the little bench on the footpath, the one that faced the water, and sat with her scarf tucked tight and the wind in her hair.

She'd known, deep down, that this whole thing was a leap.

A cottage that barely held itself together. A village full of people who already had their rhythms. A man who'd clearly learned to protect his quiet like a castle wall.

But she was here.

Still standing. Still planting roots, however clumsily.

And if it turned out Jack Mercer was more cement than softness—well. She'd built around worse foundations before.

The village hall smelled of poster paint, tea bags, and ambition.

Claire stepped inside hesitantly, clutching a half-full packet of glitter pens, two glue sticks she found in the bottom of a drawer, and a vague hope that the children of Ashford Vale wouldn't eat the art supplies.

Beth was already there, organising the chairs into aggressively neat rows. Frances was decorating a cardboard sheep with real wool and muttering about "textural authenticity." A small child in wellies was licking a glue stick in the corner and looked delighted with himself.

Claire approached Ellie, who was wrangling a pile of mismatched bunting like it was trying to escape.

"I can't tell if we're setting up for a craft event or a low-budget music festival," Claire said, eyeing the glittery signage.

Ellie grinned. "Bit of both. And the twins are building a cardboard castle. With fire exits, apparently."

Claire set down her things and rubbed her hands together. "Alright. Let's try not to glue anyone to anything important."

The plan was to keep her head down. Help with the prep. Avoid emotional thinking.

Which was going quite well until the door opened.

And in walked Jack.

Claire looked up, blinked—and nearly dropped a pack of googly eyes into a tub of paint water.

He stood in the doorway for a moment, scanning the chaos with the faintly overwhelmed expression of a man who could build a roof blindfolded but had no idea how to operate a glitter gun.

Claire recovered first. "You're not electrics."

Jack gave a non-committal shrug. "Frances bribed me with flapjacks. Said they needed extra hands."

Frances waved from across the room. "And I told him you were woefully under-glittered."

Claire folded her arms. "So you came all this way to rescue me from pipe cleaners?"

"I came," he said, "because I said I would help."

He moved toward her then, sleeves rolled up, tool belt slung around his waist like he was preparing for a full-scale craft-related incident.

Claire handed him a pile of foam animal cutouts. "Do you know what to do with these?"

"Burn them?"

Claire grinned. "Close enough."

The afternoon was a mild disaster in the best possible way.

One child stuck three pom-poms to their forehead and claimed to be a unicorn. Someone knocked over the juice table. Beth accidentally glued her sleeve to a tablecloth and calmly declared it "mixed media."

Jack, to everyone's surprise, was *excellent* at corralling chaos.

He herded glitter-wielding children like a sheepdog with power tools. He tied bunting without swearing (aloud). And when Graham the sheep made an unscheduled indoor appearance—led by a seven-year-old holding a leash made from three skipping ropes and a sense of destiny—Jack caught the animal's lead with one hand and calmly walked it back outside without blinking.

"You're unnervingly good at this," Claire said, watching him tie Graham's rope to the bike rack.

He shrugged. "Animals make more sense than people."

"I'm starting to think that includes me."

Jack looked at her for a long moment. "Not really."

Claire opened her mouth, but he was already walking back into the hall.

By the end of the afternoon, the floor was sticky, the crafts were half-exploded across four tables, and Claire had glitter in her eyebrows. But somehow—miraculously—it had worked.

The kids had laughed. The grown-ups had survived. And Jack had stayed.

As they packed up the last of the mess, Claire reached for a roll of tape at the same time he did. Their hands brushed. Just for a second.

And for the second time that day, he didn't move away.

Claire pretended not to notice the way her hand still tingled from where it had brushed Jack's. She bent to collect a runaway roll of crepe paper and tried to focus on anything other than the warmth still humming between them.

Jack, for his part, was now deep in conversation with a boy about eight years old, who was explaining in great detail how glitter was "probably made from unicorn toenails."

Claire caught Jack's deadpan reply: "That checks out."

She smiled despite herself.

He didn't even try to be charming. He just... was. In that gruff, dry, completely unpolished way that made her want to simultaneously hug him and roll her eyes.

Ellie sidled up next to her with a box of leftover craft materials and a not-so-subtle smirk. "So. That was unexpected."

Claire glanced sideways. "What was?"

"Oh, I don't know... Jack Mercer turning up to a glitter explosion with flapjack and casual heroism. That moment with the sheep rope was frankly cinematic."

"He didn't even look fazed."

"He never does," Ellie said. "Which is half the problem."

Claire gave her a look.

Ellie continued. "People think that means he doesn't feel anything. But Jack? He feels everything. Just very, very quietly. Like a kettle on low."

Claire laughed softly. "Do you all take turns delivering cryptic metaphors about him?"

Ellie shrugged. "Beth's got a poem about his eyebrows. Frances has a theory he's part Viking. I just like to meddle."

She handed Claire the last box. "Don't overthink it. He's here, isn't he?"

Claire nodded slowly. "He is."

Outside, the sky had dipped into early twilight—the kind where the sun still brushed the edges of the fields with soft gold, but the air had turned sharp enough to hint at coats and scarves and soup waiting at home.

The craft supplies were packed away. The children had dispersed, some still wearing glitter like war paint. Mags had commandeered two plastic chairs and was now deeply engrossed in a debate with Frances about whether the raffle should include a live chicken this year.

Claire picked up the last box and turned toward Jack, who was crouched by the church fence, adjusting a stubborn string of fairy lights someone had insisted be tested "for tone."

She cleared her throat. "Need help?"

He looked over his shoulder. "These lights hate me."

Claire joined him, resting the box against her hip. "Most things with personalities do."

He gave her a sideways look. "I walked straight into that."

She offered a grin. "And you didn't even flinch."

They worked side by side again, untangling cables and muttering about extension leads, and somewhere between the knots and the silence, Claire said quietly, "Thank you. For coming."

Jack glanced at her, one hand still holding the lights. "I said I would."

"I know. But... still."

He didn't answer right away. Then he said, low, "It's easier when you're around."

Claire's heart did something entirely inconvenient.

Then Mags shouted something about a runaway raffle chicken and they both stood up too quickly.

Claire blinked. "Did she say chicken?"

Jack sighed. "You learn not to ask."

"*I need everyone's attention immediately!*"

The voice rang out across the church green like a town crier who'd just discovered TikTok. Heads turned. Paintbrushes froze mid-rinse. Mags paused mid-argument with Frances, holding a raffle ticket aloft like it might double as legal tender.

Lily Mercer had arrived.

She strode across the grass with the energy of someone who had just staged a coup in Year 6 and was now issuing official policy. Her coat flapped open, revealing a glitter-covered backpack, a clipboard under one arm, and a rolled-up poster tucked like a scroll into the other.

Jack muttered under his breath, "Oh no."

Claire looked amused. "That one's yours?"

"She's been planning something," Jack said darkly. "She's been *quiet* all week. It's always a trap."

Lily reached the makeshift craft tent podium (an upside-down bucket) and climbed on with theatrical flair.

"I," she declared, "am proud to announce the formation of the *Ashford Vale Young Investigators League*."

Beth, who'd just re-entered the green carrying a tray of leftover biscuits, froze. "Oh no. Not this again."

Lily unrolled her scroll with a flourish. "Membership is open to anyone under the age of fourteen with a keen eye for detail, a working knowledge of biscuit incentives, and at least one functioning torch."

Claire leaned toward Jack. "Should we be worried?"

He sighed. "Last time they tried to arrest the vicar for hiding jam."

Lily pressed on. "Our mission: to uncover the *hidden mysteries of Ashford Vale*. Is the post office haunted? Is Graham the sheep really just a clever man in disguise? What does Mrs. Prendergast keep in her enormous handbag?"

"She does have a suspiciously shaped thermos," Ellie whispered.

"First meeting is tomorrow," Lily continued. "Code name: Operation Scone Shadow. Please bring your own torch and a statement of intent. And if anyone sees Mr. Hargrove's missing wheelbarrow, please report immediately."

She stepped off the bucket and curtsied.

Claire applauded. Jack did not.

"You're not encouraging this?" he asked her as Lily jogged off to recruit new members using what appeared to be personalised badges.

"I am *absolutely* encouraging this," Claire said. "She has a clipboard and everything."

Jack muttered, "She was supposed to be revising for spelling tests."

Claire handed him a ginger biscuit. "She's clearly spelling *adventure*."

As the chaos mellowed back into its usual low thrum of village oddities and overlapping conversations, Ellie appeared at Claire's side with a cup of tea and her signature I've-thought-of-something face.

"I have an idea," she said.

"Oh no," said Jack.

Claire smiled. "Let's hear it."

Ellie looked positively delighted. "You're both clearly more useful than half this village's able-bodied adults. So. I propose a *co-coordinator* system."

Jack narrowed his eyes. "What's that when it's at home?"

"You," Ellie said, pointing at him, "handle anything involving drills or tarpaulin or children with ambition. And *you*," she added, turning to Claire, "handle the things that require... tact. And colour palettes."

Claire raised a brow. "So you want us to run the fair?"

"No," Ellie said. "Just the parts that matter."

Jack looked like he wanted to protest. But he didn't.

Claire, watching him, bit back a smile. "We'll consider it."

"Excellent," Ellie said, already walking away. "You start on Monday."

The sky had begun its slow dip into dusk, softening the edges of the rooftops and tinting the clouds with a warm, pale apricot.

Claire and Jack walked side by side down the lane, past the bakery's shuttered windows and the empty bench outside the post office, which now wore a paper sign that read *"Reserved for Scone Shadow Agents Only."*

Neither of them spoke right away.

Claire kicked a pebble along the path, hands in her coat pockets. "She's... something else."

"Lily?" Jack nodded. "Yeah. I don't know whether to be proud or install CCTV."

"She's brilliant," Claire said. "Wild, but brilliant."

Jack gave a small smile. "Her mother was the same."

Claire glanced sideways at him.

It wasn't often he brought up Lily's mum. And when he did, it was always in the kind of tone people used when handling something precious but breakable.

"She used to write lists in the middle of the night," Jack continued, voice soft. "Ideas. Trips we never took. Names for chickens we didn't own. Just... thoughts she didn't want to forget."

Claire smiled. "Sounds like my kind of woman."

"She'd have liked you."

Claire blinked. "That's... kind of a big thing to say."

Jack shrugged, not meeting her eyes. "She had a good read on people."

They walked in silence for a few more paces, their boots crunching on the loose gravel, the smell of woodsmoke drifting faintly from someone's chimney nearby.

Claire exhaled slowly. "It's strange. I've been here... what? A week? And already I feel like I've accidentally joined a slightly unhinged cult. But in a good way."

"That's Ashford Vale," Jack said. "There's a form somewhere. Probably in Beth's filing cabinet."

Claire gave a quiet laugh. "You know, I used to have this very firm idea of what my life was supposed to look like. Clean. Stylish. Predictable."

Jack glanced at her. "And now?"

She kicked the pebble again. "Now I know what it's like to be attacked by plumbing and asked to supervise livestock with googly eyes. So. Not quite what I had in mind."

He didn't smile, but there was something in the set of his shoulders that softened.

"You're handling it," he said.

Claire looked up. "Am I?"

Jack stopped walking. Turned to her.

"You didn't run. That's more than most."

And there it was again—that quiet steadiness in him. Like he wasn't trying to impress her, or comfort her, or say the perfect thing. He was just telling the truth.

Claire nodded, unsure of what to say. So she said nothing.

They walked the rest of the way back to the cottage in silence. Not awkward. Not uncomfortable.

Just... companionable.

And when they reached the gate of Maple Hollow, Jack lingered.

Only a moment.

Then he gave a small nod. "See you Monday."

Claire smiled. "For tarpaulin and tact."

He didn't quite smile back. But his eyes did.

And then he turned and walked away, hands deep in his pockets, coat collar turned up against the cooling breeze.

Claire watched him go, then turned toward the cottage with something warm and hard to name settling in her chest.

The cottage was quiet when Claire stepped inside.

Not the eerie kind of quiet, but the comforting sort—the kind that wrapped around her like a blanket after a long day in a too-loud world.

She clicked on the lamp in the corner. It flickered once, then glowed a little too yellow, casting the room in a warm, tired sort of light. The fire hadn't been lit, but the air still held the scent of the last one—woodsmoke, dust, and something vaguely sweet, like dried lavender from a drawer long forgotten.

Claire kicked off her boots, peeled off her coat, and padded into the kitchen in search of tea and normality.

As she waited for the kettle to do its slow, prehistoric wheeze, she looked around the space again—really looked. The cupboards had dents. The walls had stories. The corner by the back door still held the faint imprint of the boots Jack had kicked off the day of the plumbing incident.

And on the sideboard, behind a half-empty jar of screws and a chipped enamel teapot, was a narrow drawer she hadn't noticed before.

It didn't look like it wanted to be opened.

Naturally, she opened it.

Inside was a bundle of old paper tied with twine, delicate with age and slightly curled at the edges. Not letters, exactly—but notes. Lists. Scribbled ideas. All in the same looping hand she recognised from the postcard she'd found before.

"Things I Would Plant If I Had Braver Soil."
– Peonies
– Gooseberries
– A fig tree, against the odds
– Something that surprises me

Claire sat down slowly, unfolding another page.

"Things I'd Say If I Didn't Care What People Thought."
– "I'm lonely."
– "I miss who I used to be."
– "I want someone to stay."
– "I'm tired of being fine."

She ran her fingers over the paper, careful not to smudge the faded ink.

There was no name. No date. Just the words—and the distinct feeling that someone had once sat in this exact kitchen, searching for courage they weren't sure they'd find.

Claire tucked the bundle back into the drawer gently, as if closing a small secret.

She didn't know who had written the notes.

But she knew what they meant.

The kettle clicked off behind her, forgotten.

She sat for a while longer in the quiet, listening to the tick of the old clock above the pantry, and wondered—just for a moment—what someone might one day find in *her* handwriting, left behind in a drawer no one meant to open.

The next morning began with toast and the realisation that she'd somehow used hand soap on her face.

Claire stood at the kitchen sink, blinking into the cold morning light, wondering if "mild tangerine stinging" counted as a skincare regime.

Outside, the frost still clung to the grass like it didn't want to leave. Her breath fogged the window as she peered out, cradling a lukewarm cup of tea and debating whether it was a dressing gown sort of day or a pretending-to-be-functional jumper situation.

Then came the knock.

Three short taps. Familiar by now.

She opened the door to find Jack standing there, one hand on the porch post, the other holding a folded newspaper and what looked suspiciously like... a cinnamon bun.

Claire blinked. "Is that... for me?"

"No," he said. "It's for Graham the sheep. He's very into seasonal pastries."

She took it with a grin. "I knew I liked him."

Jack didn't say anything. Just glanced past her into the house. "You free this morning?"

"That depends," she said cautiously. "Does it involve livestock or more glue guns?"

"No livestock," he said. "No glue. Just timber. Thought you might want to pick out the new joists for the hallway floor—since you'll be the one walking on them."

Claire blinked. "You're letting me choose structural wood?"

"You get veto power on grain and colour. I draw the line at anything 'statement.'"

Claire mock sighed. "There goes my neon parquet dream."

Jack half-smiled. "Get your boots. We'll be back before Lily's school bell."

The timber yard was only ten minutes out of the village, tucked behind a farm shop and a line of hedges that looked like they'd seen things.

Claire hadn't expected to enjoy it.

She thought it would be cold and grey and full of men who made her feel like she should apologise for existing.

But instead, it was... oddly soothing.

Stacks of planks in neat rows. The scent of cedar and sawdust in the air. A kettle boiling in the corner of the shed with three mugs labelled *"tea"*, *"also tea"*, and *"builder's orders."*

Jack moved through the space like he belonged to it. Not showing off—just comfortable. At ease in a way she hadn't really seen before.

He paused at a rack of floorboards and looked over at her. "Well?"

Claire stepped forward and ran her hand along one of the smoother planks. "That one's nice."

"White oak. Clean grain. Good finish."

She nodded, then glanced at him. "It's very... straight."

Jack gave her a sidelong look. "It's a piece of wood."

"Still. Couldn't we go slightly less predictable? Something with a knot? A bit of drama?"

He exhaled like she'd just suggested installing a disco ball but obliged. "How about this one?"

It had a swirl near the centre—like the wood had once decided to change direction just for fun.

Claire smiled. "Perfect."

He studied her for a second. "You really see things differently, don't you?"

She shrugged. "I just think flaws make things more interesting."

There was a beat of silence, soft and heavy between them.

Jack looked down. "I'll get it cut to size."

As they drove back through the village, the bakery came into view with a new chalkboard sign outside:

OPEN
PASTRIES | GOSSIP | POSSIBLY BOTH AT ONCE

Claire laughed. "Ellie's had caffeine."

Jack glanced at her. "Do you always narrate the world like it's part of a novel?"

"Probably," she said. "Do you always act like you're the one character who refuses to admit he's in one?"

He didn't answer, but the corner of his mouth tugged just enough to count.

Back at Maple Hollow, the hallway was an echo of itself—boards removed, tools lined up, and dust floating in the light like it had nowhere better to be.

Claire stood barefoot at the edge of the gap, mug in hand, peering down into what looked like the remains of a tiny shipwreck beneath the floor.

"This feels symbolic," she said.

Jack knelt beside the joists and pulled on his gloves. "How so?"

"Taking something apart. Getting to the bones of it. Fixing what you can't see first."

He gave her a look. "It's floorboards."

Claire smiled into her tea. "It's always more than that."

Jack didn't argue. But he didn't dismiss her either.

He showed her how to line up the new boards—where to place them, how to mark for the cuts. His movements were steady, sure, always three steps ahead.

Claire knelt beside him, pencil tucked behind one ear, tongue poking out slightly as she measured with careful precision.

"You don't need to try so hard," Jack said eventually.

"I like getting it right."

"You already are."

She looked up. "What?"

Jack met her gaze. "Getting it right. Being here. Doing this."

Claire opened her mouth, but no words came out. Just warmth. Rising in her chest like the fire she hadn't lit yet.

They worked in silence for a while after that. Not tense—just focused. Comfortable. And when Jack leaned past her to reach the tool bag, his arm brushed hers. He didn't move away.

Claire could feel the heat of him. The steadiness.

The part of him he didn't say out loud.

By late afternoon, the first new board was in place. Smooth, golden, with a visible swirl right in the centre—like a knot, or a fingerprint, or a tiny storm frozen in timber.

Claire ran her fingers over it. "See? Character."

Jack sat back on his heels. "It's not perfect."

"That's why it's right."

He looked at her then. Not just at her face, but through it, almost. Like he could see every layer she wasn't saying.

She wasn't sure what would happen next.

A word. A touch. A shift.

But instead, Jack stood, brushed dust from his jeans, and said, "I'll be back tomorrow. We'll finish the run before the rain hits."

Claire nodded, her voice caught somewhere behind her heart. "Okay."

He didn't say goodbye. He never really did.

But at the door, he paused.

And without turning around, he said, "That postcard you found. With the fig tree."

Claire froze. "How did you—?"

"I wrote it. Years ago. Before everything."

Then he left.

And Claire stood in the hallway, hand resting on the still-warm floorboard, heart tilted sideways.

Outside, the first drop of rain hit the window.

And inside, for the first time in a long while, she didn't feel like something was ending.

She felt like something had just begun.

Chapter Five

"Special Delivery (and Mild Existential Panic)"

Claire was just finishing her second cup of tea—and third biscuit, though who was counting—when the knock came.

It wasn't Jack's knock. Or Lily's. Or Mags' "I'm-not-waiting-you-have-five-seconds" knock.

It was a stranger's knock.

Brisk. Professional. Slightly smug.

She opened the door to find a courier standing on the step, scanning something on his device with the disinterest of someone who had long ago stopped being surprised by life.

"Claire Maddox?"

"Yes."

"Delivery from London. Sign here."

She signed, confused. Then watched as he wheeled a suspiciously large box through the gate and onto the path.

"Have a nice day," he said, already turning.

The van drove off. Claire stared at the box.

It was tall. Marked FRAGILE. And had her old address scribbled out in felt-tip beneath the courier label.

A small envelope was taped to the side.
From: Kayleigh xx

Claire's stomach dropped slightly.

Kayleigh had been her flatmate for two years. Friend-ish. Brand loyal. Never met a neon accent wall she didn't love. The kind of person who called everything "a journey" and said things like "just be a vibe" without irony.

Claire peeled the envelope open.

Thought you'd want your old "work stuff." It was taking up space in the coat cupboard and getting dusty. Hope the sticks-and-mud renovation is going well! Call me when you're ready to talk real jobs again.

Also, I kept the velvet blazer. It looked better on me. ☕

Kay x

Claire stared at the note for a long second.

Then at the box.

Then—without opening it—dragged it into the hallway and kicked it soundly in the side.

Later, after she'd made tea strong enough to qualify as a health hazard, she opened the box.

Inside was everything she thought she'd left behind.

Design boards. A box of business cards from her freelance branding days. A sample book full of luxury paint swatches in colours like *Moonlight Whisper* and *Rich Divorcee*. A broken ring light. A bottle of champagne with a post-it still stuck to it: *"Pitch night—drink if we win!"*

They hadn't.

Claire sat on the floor in her too-big jumper, legs crossed, flipping through a sleek magazine portfolio full of crisp white spaces and polished gold fixtures. Rooms she'd helped style. Places that had no people in them.

She looked around at her own cottage. At the scuffed skirting board. The paint-splotched windowsill. The hammer lying beside the hallway floor she'd started rebuilding with Jack.

This place wasn't perfect.

But it felt more real than anything in that box.

An hour later, she hauled the box up into the spare room. Not to throw it away. Not yet. Just... upstairs. Out of reach.

She was tying her hair up when her phone buzzed.

Ellie:

Can you come now?

Don't panic.

Okay maybe panic slightly.

The bakery smelled like something had exploded. In a festive, cinnamon-scented way.

Claire pushed through the back door and found Ellie kneeling beside a very large, very broken mixing bowl, surrounded by what looked like a snowdrift of flour and a deeply unimpressed cat.

"I dropped the holiday order dough," Ellie said, voice tight.

Claire blinked. "Holiday order?"

"Four dozen cardamom buns. Due in three hours."

"And the oven?"

"Still works. But the universe is definitely laughing."

Claire didn't hesitate.

She rolled up her sleeves.

"Right," she said. "Let's save Christmas. Or Thursday. Whichever comes first."

They worked fast. The kind of messy, elbow-deep baking frenzy that left Claire with flour in her eyebrows and icing sugar on her jumper. Ellie muttered to herself like a war general. Claire accidentally used salt instead of sugar once and was quickly removed from any measuring duties.

But the kitchen filled with warmth, and laughter, and the scent of something golden and alive.

Just as they pulled the first tray from the oven, the door creaked open.

Jack.

He stood in the doorway, clearly mid-job, with paint on his forearm and sawdust in his hair.

Claire looked up. "We're accepting volunteers. Must have excellent wrist strength and no fear of pastry."

He looked amused. "I heard there was panic."

"I may have screamed," Ellie admitted. "Once."

"Twice," said the cat.

Jack stepped in and picked up a piping bag without comment.

Claire tried not to watch him too closely. Tried not to notice how normal it suddenly felt, the three of them standing there like this had always been part of her life.

But somewhere, beneath the cinnamon and the panic, something inside her shifted.

And she wasn't sure if it was a beginning or a warning.

By the time the final tray of cardamom buns came out of the oven, the air was thick with heat, sugar, and the kind of quiet triumph that only came after a mild crisis narrowly averted.

Ellie collapsed onto a stool with a dramatic sigh. "Remind me never to agree to a bulk order while slightly tipsy and emotionally manipulated by pensioners."

Claire slid a tray onto the rack. "What did they offer you?"

"A promise that Mags wouldn't sing at the spring fair this year. I was blinded by hope."

Jack was still at the far counter, piping the last batch with unnerving precision. Claire watched him squeeze a perfect swirl onto each bun, methodical and focused, as if this were just another kind of carpentry.

"You're very calm under pressure," she said, leaning beside him.

"I've had to rebuild a roof in a hailstorm with a raccoon watching. This is easier."

Claire laughed. "I forget how weird your life is."

Jack finished the last bun and turned slightly toward her, his sleeves rolled up, a smear of flour across his forearm, and that unreadable look in his eyes again—like he wanted to say something but was still sanding down the words.

"I saw the box," he said quietly.

Claire blinked. "What box?"

He wiped his hand on a tea towel. "The one from London. It was by the door earlier."

She froze. "Oh. Right. That."

"You okay?"

There was something in the way he asked it—casual, quiet—but with the weight of someone who would listen if she cracked.

Claire nodded. "Yeah. It just caught me off guard. That life feels like... someone else's now. But there it was, turning up on my doorstep. With passive-aggressive sticky notes."

Jack didn't smile. But he didn't look away either.

She added, more softly, "I don't want to go back. Not really."

He studied her for a moment.

Then said, "Good."

That was all.

But somehow, it felt like a door had opened just a little.

Claire reached for the piping bag, but he still held it.

Their fingers touched. Just briefly. Warm and dusty and unintentional.

Except—maybe not entirely unintentional.

Neither of them moved right away.

Claire looked up.

Jack was already looking at her.

And then—

"I should clean the trays," he said, stepping back suddenly.

Claire blinked. "Right. Of course. Yes. Clean trays. Essential."

He turned to the sink.

She turned to the buns.

Neither of them spoke for a minute.

But the kitchen felt different now.

Not awkward.

Just... quieter.

Like it was holding its breath.

The door to the bakery burst open with all the subtlety of a jazz band falling down a flight of stairs.

"*I have news!*" came Lily's voice, full of purpose and dramatic intent.

Ellie groaned from her perch at the back table. "Not again."

Jack looked up from the sink. "What now?"

Lily stomped in, hair windblown, cheeks flushed, clipboard under one arm and a suspicious-looking thermos under the other.

"Scone Shadow has officially uncovered our first mystery," she announced.

Claire blinked. "You named your club *Scone Shadow*?"

"It was that or The Crumb Files."

Claire nodded. "Good choice."

Lily pointed at her clipboard. "We have three working theories about Mrs. Renfrew's missing hanging basket. One involves squirrels. One involves witchcraft. And one involves Mags."

"I'm going to need a stronger biscuit," Ellie muttered.

Jack handed Lily a clean tea towel without comment, clearly long-accustomed to his daughter's flair for disruption.

Lily took it, wiped her nose, and turned to Claire with a sudden, laser-focused shift in tone. "Also, you've been acting strange."

Claire blinked. "Excuse me?"

"You and Dad. You're both twitchy. And you paused for *exactly 1.7 seconds* too long when he handed you that piping bag."

Claire flushed. "I—what?"

Lily nodded solemnly. "That's how people act when they've either committed a crime together or accidentally had a romantic moment."

Jack coughed. Loudly.

Ellie made a noise that might have been a laugh disguised as a sneeze.

Claire attempted dignity. "Lily, not everything is a conspiracy."

"It's not a conspiracy," Lily said, taking a bun from the cooling tray. "It's *science*. I read body language now. It's a skill."

Claire gave her a narrow look. "Have you been spying on us?"

"Not *spying*. Observing. For example—" Lily turned to her father— "you only use your quiet voice when you like someone."

Jack raised an eyebrow. "I have one voice."

Lily smirked. "Not when Claire's around."

He stared at her.

She stared right back.

Claire buried her face in a tea towel and whispered, "I take it back. This *is* a conspiracy."

Eventually, after Lily had been bribed into silence with two buns and a promise of a future "interview series" for her newsletter (Claire feared the headline already), the kitchen calmed again.

Jack was washing up.

Ellie had disappeared into the front of the shop.

Claire leaned against the counter, arms folded, and glanced toward the back door, where Lily was sitting on a crate, scribbling furiously into her notebook.

"She's relentless," Claire said.

Jack nodded. "She gets it from her mother."

Claire looked over at him, softening. "That's not a bad thing."

Jack didn't answer right away. Then: "No. It's not."

And even though he kept his eyes on the dishes, Claire saw the corner of his mouth curve.

Claire left the bakery just as the afternoon was starting to soften into something golden and low.

The sky had settled into a pale blue, the kind that made the whole village feel slightly watercoloured. A breeze nudged at her coat, and somewhere in the hedgerows, a bird was doing its best impression of a car alarm.

She walked the long way back.

Not intentionally. She just... didn't quite want to go straight home. Not yet.

Her hands were still dusted faintly with flour, and her jumper smelled like sugar and something warmly spiced. Her heart, though—her heart was less settled.

She kept thinking about the way Jack had looked at her when she'd mentioned not wanting to go back to London. Not surprised. Not smug. Just... like he understood.

And then, of course, the piping bag moment.

It had been nothing.

Except it hadn't been.

Claire kicked a pebble into the grass, frowning at the vague sense of tilt in her chest.

She wasn't someone who usually second-guessed herself. She made decisions. She took action. She used to design entire brand campaigns on two hours of sleep and half a packet of peanut M&Ms.

But here, things felt... slower. Softer. Like everything she said and did *meant* something. And the way Jack had quietly stepped back, after standing so close—*that* meant something too.

She turned onto the lane that led to Maple Hollow, boots crunching on gravel, hands deep in her pockets.

The cottage came into view, small and crooked and quietly waiting.

It didn't look like a project anymore.

It looked like hers.

She paused at the gate.

In the stillness, she could just hear laughter echoing back from the bakery—Ellie and Lily, probably, plotting new ways to mortify Jack.

Claire smiled, then sighed, then stood a moment longer.

Because it was getting harder to pretend that something *wasn't* happening.

That this wasn't starting to matter.

That *he* didn't.

And that—perhaps—Ashford Vale wasn't just a temporary pause in her life.

It might be where the real part began.

By the time Claire got home, the sun had dipped behind the rooftops, painting the sky in soft strokes of lavender and peach. The lane was quiet, the kind of quiet that made you walk slower, like it would be rude to disturb the hush.

She turned up the garden path to Maple Hollow, her boots crunching on the gravel, still smelling faintly of cardamom and woodsmoke.

Then she saw it.

A folded note.

Tucked just behind the handle of the front door, held in place with a small pebble.

No envelope. No address. Just her name.

Claire — scrawled in neat, practical handwriting she recognised immediately.

Jack.

She stood there a moment, hand on the note, heart doing something slightly irrational for someone holding stationary.

She read it there, standing in the fading light.

The timber came in. Left it around the side. Thought you might want to pick the finish for the bannisters before I cut.

Also — you did good today.

– J.

That was it.

No flourish. No unnecessary words.

But it settled into her chest like something warm and quiet.

She folded the note and slipped it into her coat pocket, fingers lingering.

Then she let herself inside.

The hallway was still mid-renovation. The tools were lined up beside the wall. The light flickered when she switched it on. And the house smelled like old plaster and new beginnings.

She made a cup of tea. Sat by the fire.

And pulled the note out again.

Just to read it once more.

Because maybe, she thought, that's how something starts.

Not with grand gestures.

But with a knock on the door.

A piping bag.

A note held down by a pebble.

And someone who shows up when you're not even sure you asked.

Chapter Six

"Tea Before Trouble"

Claire woke to the sound of something thudding against the front door.

Not knocking.

Not polite.

Just a *thud*, followed by what might have been a muffled expletive and the unmistakable sound of someone stepping in what could only be jam.

She pulled on a cardigan, padded downstairs, and opened the door.

There, standing on the step with one sock slightly askew and a large tupperware box clutched like a holy relic, was Mags.

"Oh," Claire said. "Good morning?"

Mags scowled. "It's barely morning. It's criminal. And Frances made me carry this because she claims she's allergic to elderflower now, even though she drank two glasses of elderflower gin at the Harvest Dance and tried to kiss the postman."

Claire blinked. "Is that... cake?"

"It's a peace offering. Or a bribe. Or possibly both. There's a situation."

Mags pushed the container into Claire's hands like it might explode.

"Council meeting's gone sideways," she muttered. "Beth's threatening to resign from the fête planning committee unless someone else handles livestock this year. And now Frances is demanding we put poetry on the bunting."

Claire frowned. "Poetry?"

"'Seasonally-themed haikus,'" Mags quoted grimly. "About sheep."

Claire paused. "And this involves me... how?"

Mags stared at her. "You're new. You're efficient. You don't frighten small children or vicarage pets. That makes you perfect."

"For what?"

"For *managing it*, obviously."

And with that, Mags turned and stomped off down the path, muttering something about "the last time I trust a woman with a glue gun and a dream."

Claire stood there, cake in hand, pyjamas hidden under her coat, blinking into the cool morning air.

Then she looked down at the tupperware.

Inside was a square of what looked like sponge cake, but with suspiciously green icing and—unless her eyes deceived her—a delicate drizzle shaped like a chicken.

She sighed.

And put the kettle on.

Claire had just finished her second slice of suspiciously green chicken-drizzled cake when the doorbell rang again—less of a ring, more of a wheeze followed by what sounded like someone poking a wasp with a spoon.

She opened the door expecting Lily.

Instead, it was Beth. Clipboard. Boots. Purpose.

"I'm so sorry," Beth said, in a tone that meant *I am not sorry at all*. "But we've had a small problem with the fête committee."

Claire braced herself. "Smaller than sheep-themed haikus?"

"Barely. But significantly stickier."

Beth handed her a flyer.

SPRING FÊTE PRIZE DRAW

WIN A CUSTOM CAKE DECORATED BY A LOCAL "CELEBRITY"

(*Note: By "celebrity" we mean "someone the village quite likes right now."*)

Claire stared. "Oh no."

"Oh yes," Beth said, cheerfully ruthless. "You were nominated. By Mags. After she saw your iced buns at the bakery."

"Ellie iced the buns!"

"You held a piping bag. That counts."

"I'm not a baker!"

Beth patted her arm. "Perfect. That'll make the winner feel like they're part of something raw and vulnerable."

Claire spent the rest of the morning in a fog of flour-related dread, trying to plan how one might design a cake that screamed *vaguely competent romantic interloper with limited skills and a fondness for cardamom*.

It didn't help that Jack didn't appear.

Not at the door. Not on the lane. Not even a text about wood finishes or sheep-proof fencing.

And for reasons Claire didn't entirely want to examine, it bothered her more than it should.

By late afternoon, she'd tried to distract herself with emails, wallpaper samples, and a YouTube tutorial that confidently declared *"fondant is your friend"*—which was a lie, obviously.

The house felt too quiet.

The fireplace wouldn't light properly.

And the silence she used to crave now felt like it echoed.

Then, just as the sun was dipping low over the hedgerows, the door creaked open again.

"Dad says we're avoiding you," Lily said, standing in the doorway with a crumpled notebook and half a jam tart.

Claire blinked. "You are?"

"Emotionally," Lily clarified. "Not physically. He's on the roof of the vicarage. But I could *feel* the avoidance."

Claire laughed. "Is this a Scone Shadow update?"

"Sort of," Lily said. "But also, you looked like someone who needed a truth biscuit."

She handed Claire the tart.

Claire sat on the step and took a bite.

"Do you think he's—" she paused. "Is Jack okay?"

Lily nodded. "He does that sometimes. Pulls in. Doesn't mean he doesn't like you."

Claire smiled faintly. "That obvious, is it?"

Lily looked at her with the unflinching honesty of someone unburdened by adult subtlety. "You *both* have faces like people in a book who don't know they're the main characters yet."

Claire blinked. "That's... incredibly insightful."

"I read a lot," Lily said, hopping down the step. "Also, you smell like fear and sponge cake."

And then she was off, notebook in hand, jam tart trail in her wake.

Claire stood alone for a moment longer.

She looked at the empty lane.

The fading light.

The door that hadn't opened today the way she'd wanted it to.

And told herself it was just a day.

Just one day.

But still—she felt it.

The shift.

The almost.

The quiet space that someone had filled and now hadn't.

Claire was halfway through rewriting her to-do list for the fourth time—having scratched off *"try fondant again"* with decisive rage—when a text pinged.

Ellie:
Emergency committee meeting. Church hall. Now-ish.
Wear something fleece-lined. Beth has opinions.

Claire sighed, found her boots, grabbed a cardigan that smelt vaguely of scones, and trudged out into the early evening mist.

The church hall was already buzzing when she arrived—string lights flickering overhead, chairs in disarray, and the comforting scent of something baked and questionably labelled wafting in from a side table.

Mags was setting up a flipchart with the solemnity of a general going to war. Frances was arranging biscuits by emotional tone. Beth had colour-coded agendas.

Claire took a seat near the back and tried to disappear into her scarf.

And then Jack walked in.

No warning. No slow-motion fanfare. Just... there.

He gave a polite nod to the room, then spotted Claire and paused.

She straightened a little.

But instead of coming over, he veered toward the opposite side of the hall and began inspecting the broken window latch like it was the most fascinating piece of hardware in existence.

Claire stared down at her notebook.

Wrote the word *fencepost* four times without meaning to.

The meeting began in its usual swirl of overlapping announcements.

"First item," Beth said crisply. "The poetry bunting is a go. Each stallholder must now contribute a haiku."

A groan rippled across the room.

Mags muttered, "I'm not rhyming anything with sheep again."

"Second item," Frances added, "the Spring Fête poster has been finalised. And yes, before anyone asks, I did use clip art. It's retro now."

Claire risked a glance at Jack.

He was staring out the window.

His jaw was set in that way that made her stomach tighten—like he was doing everything not to look back at her.

Half an hour later, after mild uproar over whether or not the coconut shy should be "less coconut, more vegan-friendly," Beth called for a five-minute break.

Claire slipped outside for air.

The lane was dark now, moonlight scattered on the rooftops, and her breath formed little clouds in front of her face.

She wasn't upset, exactly.

Just... off balance.

She leaned against the stone wall, arms crossed.

"Cold out," came Jack's voice.

She turned.

He stood a few paces away, hands deep in his pockets, shoulders hunched slightly against the chill.

"I didn't know you'd be here," she said.

"Ellie texted. Said they needed someone to check the electrics."

Claire nodded. "Right."

A pause.

Then: "You've been... quiet."

Jack didn't respond straight away.

Then: "I'm not great at... this."

She frowned. "At what?"

"Whatever it is this is becoming."

Claire blinked.

Oh.

There it was.

The thing neither of them had said.

The thing she'd been wondering about since the piping bag and the note and the way her chest lifted every time she thought she heard his footsteps.

She cleared her throat. "Jack—"

"I like you," he said, before she could finish. "That's the problem."

She blinked again. "That's a problem?"

"I don't have room for it," he said quietly. "I thought I did. I thought... but Lily. Work. The house. And then there's you. And I don't want to mess it up by not knowing how to do it right."

Claire stood very still.

A breeze lifted the edges of her scarf.

Then she said, "I'm not asking you to know how."

He looked at her then. Really looked. And for a second, she thought maybe he'd say something else—reach for her, close the distance.

But instead, the church door creaked open and Mags barked, "If you're not back in your seats in sixty seconds, I'm assigning someone to write a limerick about jam!"

Jack exhaled. "Duty calls."

He turned, walked inside, and left Claire standing in the moonlight.

Alone.

But not quite the same.

The next morning, Claire stirred her tea three times before realising she'd forgotten to add milk.

She blinked down at the mug, vaguely offended, then poured it away and started again.

The cottage was unusually quiet. Or maybe she just felt unusually loud inside her own head.

Jack's words from the night before were still echoing.

"I like you. That's the problem."

Well.

There was a line, if ever she'd heard one.

It hadn't been cruel. Or cold. Just... honest. Hesitant. Like someone holding out a hand and warning you not to take it.

So she wouldn't.

She wouldn't chase it.

She wouldn't text.

She wouldn't wander up to the workshop "just to ask about doorframes."

She wouldn't—

A knock at the back door interrupted her thoughts.

Claire opened it, braced for Mags with a haiku emergency.

Instead: Lily.

Clipboard. Chewed pencil. Biscuit.

Claire smiled. "You again."

"Dad's at the shop picking up nails and pretending to care about screw gauge debates," Lily said, breezing past her and into the kitchen like she paid rent. "Thought I'd come do reconnaissance."

"On me?"

"On the vibe," Lily said, climbing onto a stool. "And because you always have the good biscuits."

Claire slid her a packet.

Lily opened it, took one, and then fixed her with a far-too-knowing stare.

"You're being quiet," she said.

"I'm not—"

"You didn't make a joke about my spy socks," Lily said, pointing to her feet.

Claire blinked. "Are those... ferrets in trench coats?"

"Exactly. And not even a snort. Very suspicious."

Claire sighed, leaning against the counter. "It's just one of those days."

"You're upset with Dad."

Claire hesitated. "No. I mean—not *upset*. Just... adjusting."

Lily swung her legs under the stool. "He does that sometimes. Pulls away when things get real."

Claire nodded slowly. "He said he didn't know how to do this."

"He says that a lot," Lily said, then added with all the bluntness of a ten-year-old philosopher, "but he usually figures it out eventually."

Claire didn't reply.

Instead, she walked to the window, watched the garden for a moment.

The frost was lifting.

Sunlight was catching on the weeds.

And even the broken corner of the shed looked a little gentler in the light.

Back at the table, Lily took another biscuit and said, more softly now, "You make things nicer."

Claire turned.

"For him," Lily clarified. "You make things... less grey."

Claire swallowed. "Thank you."

Lily nodded. "Just don't go all weird and distant now. I like you. And if this turns into another *'she moved away because of adult emotional awkwardness'* story arc, I'm going to be very cross."

Claire smiled. "I'll try not to ruin the narrative."

"Good," Lily said. "Now. Want to help me design a logo for Operation Suspicious Bunting?"

It was mid-afternoon when the knock came.

Just two quick taps on the door. Familiar. Functional.

Claire was in the middle of sorting a drawer full of loose screws, old receipts, and a mysterious key that fit nothing she owned. Lily had gone off to interrogate the vicar about "suspicious hymn choices," leaving the house pleasantly calm.

She opened the door.

Jack stood there, toolbox in one hand, a length of timber tucked under his arm.

His expression was unreadable—but then, it usually was.

"Thought I'd drop this off," he said. "Bannister rail. It's pre-sanded. Just needs fitting."

Claire nodded. "Thanks."

An awkward beat passed.

Jack cleared his throat. "I was going to message but figured I'd be passing anyway."

She stepped aside. "Come in, if you want."

He followed her into the hallway, setting the timber down against the wall with careful precision.

She stayed by the door, arms loosely crossed.

"So," he said after a moment. "The council meeting was... something."

Claire gave a small smile. "I hear the jam limerick was a highlight."

He huffed out a breath that might've been a laugh. "Frances hasn't forgiven me for voting against her composting limerick."

"Tragic," Claire said mildly.

Jack looked at her then. "Claire—"

"It's fine," she said, too quickly. "You were clear. It's all fine."

He blinked. "That's not what I—"

"You don't have to explain," she said, voice light, almost cheerful. "Honestly. You're busy. Lily. Work. Joists. Emotional insulation. I get it."

He winced. "That's not fair."

Claire tilted her head. "No. But it's not untrue."

He looked down, scuffed his boot lightly against the floorboards they'd installed together just days ago.

"I just needed space," he said finally. "I didn't mean to hurt you."

"You didn't," Claire said, with a smile that didn't quite reach her eyes. "Like you said—there's no room for it."

Jack looked up sharply. "That's not—"

"It's alright," she said again. "I've survived worse than being liked cautiously."

Another silence settled between them.

The one she hated now. The one that used to feel safe.

Jack looked like he wanted to say something else—but instead he just nodded.

"I'll be back next week to help with the upstairs landing."

Claire nodded. "Sure."

He picked up the empty mug on the side table—the one he'd used last week—and rinsed it in the sink without asking.

Then he left.

Quietly.

And Claire, standing in the doorway, felt the house grow colder in his absence.

Claire stayed by the door long after it clicked shut.

She could still hear the echo of his boots on the gravel, fading slowly down the lane. The mug sat clean on the drying rack. The bannister rail leaned quietly against the wall, waiting.

She wasn't angry.

Not really.

But there was a bruise blooming somewhere behind her ribs. Not sharp. Just sore.

She turned to go back into the kitchen—and then she saw it.

A folded piece of paper, tucked under the bannister rail.

She bent, picked it up, unfolded it slowly.

It was a sketch.

Rough pencil lines, faint and unfinished.

A bannister—her bannister—but with delicate curves carved into the side. Not just practical. Beautiful. Thoughtful. Something someone had imagined her holding on to, every morning.

At the bottom, a few words in Jack's compact handwriting:

"Just an idea. If you want it to feel like yours."

Claire stood there for a long time, the paper warm in her hand.

Then she smiled.

Small.

Quiet.

But real.

Chapter Seven
"Muffins, Messages, and Maybe"

Claire woke to the smell of cinnamon.

At first she thought she'd dreamed it—something about cardamom buns and a Scandinavian village where everyone spoke in puns. But no. It was real.

The scent drifted faintly through the house, curling under doorways, winding up the stairs.

She blinked at the ceiling, listened for movement, and found... silence.

And then her phone buzzed.

Ellie:

Left something on your doorstep.

Also: emergency muffin situation. Not mine. Yours.

Explain later. x

Claire sat up, hair lopsided, one sock still somehow on, and padded downstairs in her pyjamas and a cardigan that might once have belonged to a man named Dennis.

The front door creaked as she opened it.

There, on the step, sat a brown paper bag.

Warm. Aromatic. Handwritten note pinned to the top:

"Because you looked like someone who needed a muffin and a reason not to run. – E."

Claire carried it inside like it might contain treasure. Or maybe it did.

She sat on the kitchen stool, unwrapped the muffin—still soft, golden, the top gently caramelised—and took a slow, thoughtful bite.

It tasted of cinnamon, ginger, and something faintly citrusy—like sunshine had decided to come in disguise.

And as she chewed, the knot in her chest loosened, just a little.

She was halfway through the muffin and contemplating whether "muffin as emotional metaphor" was too cliché to write in her journal when her phone buzzed again.

Beth:

Can you make the 11:00 planning session at the community garden?

Bring gloves. And possibly biscuits. Someone will cry, and it's Frances's turn.

Claire stared at the message.

Then down at the muffin.

Then back at the message.

It was the kind of morning where part of her wanted to crawl back into bed and hide from everything she didn't quite understand yet.

But it was also the kind of morning where the sun was doing that soft, filtered thing through the window. Where the tea was still warm. Where someone had *thought about her*.

And that, she realised, was worth stepping outside for.

Even if she didn't have all the answers yet.

Even if Jack hadn't shown up with another note.

Even if her heart still tilted sideways when she passed the bannister rail.

She wrapped the rest of the muffin in napkin, found her boots, and packed a tin of emergency biscuits.

Just in case.

The community garden was a glorious mess.

There were carrots growing in places no one remembered planting them, a slightly lopsided compost bin that leaned like it had secrets, and three retired teachers arguing over whether rosemary was a herb or "more of a shrub with ideas above its station."

Claire arrived at five minutes past eleven, holding a tin of biscuits and a vague sense of apprehension.

Beth greeted her with a nod. "Perfect timing. Frances has already cried. About the mint."

Claire blinked. "What did the mint do?"

"Outgrew its boundaries," Beth said grimly. "Philosophically and literally."

Ellie waved from across the plot, holding a trowel like a wand and wearing a gardening apron with the words *"I Dig You"* embroidered across the front in glitter thread.

Claire joined her near the raised beds.

"Why are we all here again?" Claire asked.

"Beth wants to redesign the plot layout before the open day," Ellie said. "Mags says the current layout is historically accurate and therefore sacred. Frances wants to install a poetry pergola. Also there's a bee."

Claire looked around. "One bee?"

"No," Ellie said. "*The* bee. His name's Howard. He's built a nest under the potting bench and now we're morally obligated to work around him."

Claire took a deep breath. "Right. So this is normal."

"By Ashford Vale standards? Absolutely."

The next hour passed in a blur of spades, string lines, biscuit negotiations, and a short-lived campaign to name every worm they found.

Claire found herself kneeling beside a raised bed with Beth, tying string around a sagging tomato plant.

"I saw the sketch," Beth said quietly.

Claire looked up. "What sketch?"

"The one Jack left. The bannister. It was... thoughtful."

Claire nodded, fingers pausing on the knot. "He's good at quiet gestures."

Beth smiled. "That man could rebuild your entire house and apologise for it."

Claire laughed, a soft, surprised sound.

Beth added, "He's scared. Doesn't mean he's not trying."

Claire didn't answer. She didn't know how to.

And then—just as she reached for the watering can—a familiar voice behind her said, "You're drowning that rosemary."

Claire turned.

Jack.

Standing a few feet away, sleeves rolled, shirt slightly rumpled, holding a battered toolbox and a potted lavender plant that looked mildly offended to be involved.

Her stomach fluttered in a way she refused to acknowledge.

He gave a half-shrug. "Beth asked me to reinforce the shed door."

Beth, several metres away and suddenly very busy not looking in their direction, called, "It was either you or Graham the sheep. And Graham doesn't have thumbs."

Jack stepped past her toward the shed, brushing slightly against her shoulder.

Claire didn't say anything.

But she didn't move away either.

They worked side by side for the rest of the afternoon.

Not talking much.

Not not-talking either.

And when he passed her the trowel, their fingers touched for a moment too long.

And when he asked, "Can you hold this for a sec?" it wasn't about the trowel.

And when she said "Okay," it wasn't just about the shed.

Jack disappeared into the shed with his usual quiet efficiency, and Claire tried very hard not to watch him the entire time.

Instead, she pretended to be very invested in the relocation of a mislabelled rhubarb plant that turned out to be chard. Or possibly beetroot. No one was entirely sure.

Frances had begun arranging her haiku drafts along the compost bin with thumbtacks and great drama.

"Do you think 'compost dreams' is too intimate?" she asked the air.

Mags muttered, "Only if it involves actual imagery."

Claire tied back a rogue strand of hair with the elastic around her wrist and wiped her hands on her jeans.

Beth sidled up with a mug of tea and an expression that said *I am saying nothing but I am saying everything.*

Claire took the mug.

Beth nodded towards the shed. "He's still here."

Claire didn't look. "I noticed."

Beth took a sip from her own mug. "Still being the emotionally elusive, mildly tortured village artisan of your dreams?"

"Definitely more plaster dust than poetry at the moment," Claire murmured.

"Poetry's overrated," Beth said. "You want someone who knows how to fix a door *and* apologise before you ask."

Claire nodded slowly. "Yeah. Well. He's got the door bit nailed."

Eventually, Jack reappeared from the shed, wiping his hands on a rag, and walked back toward the group.

Claire stayed kneeling beside the bed of basil and carrots, brushing dirt from her fingertips.

"You're not very good at hiding when you're thinking," Jack said quietly.

She looked up.

"I wasn't hiding," she said. "I was gardening. That's what people do in community gardens, traditionally."

He crouched beside her, resting his arms on his knees.

"Right," he said, gently. "That's why you just replanted three carrots into the herb bed."

Claire looked down. Sure enough—three proud orange tips now stood like confused sentries next to a patch of mint.

"Well," she said. "They're adaptable."

Jack gave the smallest of smiles.

Then: "I meant what I said yesterday. I just didn't say it well."

Claire turned toward him, heart flickering. "Which part?"

"The bit about not knowing how to do this. About needing space." He exhaled. "I've spent so long holding things together—Lily, work, the house—I forgot how to let anything in that doesn't need fixing."

Claire didn't speak.

Jack looked at her. "You don't need fixing. That scares me more than anything."

Claire's throat tightened. "You could've just said you like me and left it at that."

"I do."

There it was again.

Simple.

Spoken like a fact he was only just starting to let himself believe.

Before she could answer, a sharp cry echoed from the far corner of the garden.

"HOWARD'S BEEN COMPROMISED!"

They both turned.

Lily sprinted toward them, waving her clipboard wildly.

"What?" Claire stood, brushing off her knees.

"The bee!" Lily said breathlessly. "Howard's nest has been invaded. The twin boys were poking it with a stick and now he's fled! We have a pollination emergency!"

Mags appeared behind her holding a trowel and a very unamused expression. "This is exactly why bees shouldn't be made honorary garden committee members."

Ellie called across the beds, "We need backup pollinators!"

Beth sighed and pulled out a bag of dried lavender. "I knew this day would come."

Claire and Jack exchanged a look.

Then both stood, without speaking, and joined the others in the chaos.

Half an hour later, the crisis had passed.

Howard had been coaxed back toward his corner with a trail of sugared water and a stern talking-to from Frances.

The twins were reprimanded and then fed a calming biscuit.

Lily had updated her bee security protocols with dramatic flair.

And Claire and Jack found themselves side by side near the shed again, arms brushing slightly as they passed out juice boxes.

Neither of them said anything.

But the silence didn't feel heavy this time.

It felt like... something new.

Something starting.

The sun had dipped behind the treeline by the time the last wheelbarrow was returned and the final rogue child was reunited with a mildly exasperated grandparent.

Howard the bee had resumed his grumpy buzzing under the potting bench, and the lavender bed had been ceremonially named *Pollination Square* with a cardboard sign Lily had coloured in biro.

Claire sat on the low stone wall at the edge of the plot, legs stretched out, sleeves pushed up, a flask of lukewarm tea balanced on her knee.

Ellie dropped beside her with the weight of someone who had used every emotional tool in her kit that day—clipboard, sarcasm, biscuits.

They sat in companionable silence for a minute.

Then Ellie said, "You've got that face again."

Claire didn't look over. "What face?"

"The one where you're pretending everything's fine when you're actually running a full Shakespearean monologue in your head."

Claire smiled faintly. "I'm a designer. I have layers."

Ellie nudged her shoulder gently. "Want to talk about it?"

Claire exhaled. "Jack."

"Ah." Ellie nodded, as if she'd just named the weather. "That old drama."

Claire was quiet for a second longer. "I like him."

"I know."

"But I also don't know what I'm doing."

Ellie sipped her tea. "That makes two of you."

Claire turned to her. "He said he doesn't know how to let things in that don't need fixing."

"That sounds like him," Ellie said. "Tragic. Honest. Mildly infuriating."

Claire smiled again, but her voice was softer now. "I don't want to push. But I don't want to be... background either. An afterthought. Or worse—some quiet chapter he never really opened."

Ellie looked at her then. "You're not a chapter, Claire. You're a whole bloody book."

Claire blinked.

"And not one of those sad literary ones where everyone stares at rivers and regrets things. You're a good book. Funny. Warm. Messy. Makes people feel better just by being around."

Claire's throat tightened.

"You think he sees that?" she asked.

"I think," Ellie said gently, "he's terrified he already does."

They sat in silence for a while after that.

Just the sound of birds in the hedges and the occasional distant rustle of Mags lecturing the compost pile.

Then Claire said, "Thanks."

Ellie shrugged. "You're one of us now. Comes with the biscuit therapy and unsolicited life advice."

Claire bumped her shoulder lightly. "Is there a membership card?"

"No," Ellie said. "But there is a rota for tea duty. I'll sign you up for Thursday."

The sky had turned a soft, sleepy shade of mauve by the time Claire said her goodbyes and left the garden behind.

Her boots crunched on the gravel lane as she walked, the familiar route from the church hall to Maple Hollow stretching out ahead like a path she'd always known, even when she hadn't.

The village had quieted for the evening. A few windows glowed amber behind curtains. Someone had just lit a fire—she could smell it on the breeze, that sweet tang of woodsmoke curling between the hedgerows. A dog barked lazily in the distance. And the last of the crows skimmed the treetops like punctuation marks at the end of the day.

She passed the old postbox where Lily had once taped up a sign declaring it "an interdimensional portal for secret missions." It was still slightly wonky, still smeared with crayon at the base.

Claire slowed a little.

Her legs were tired, but it was that good kind of tired—the kind you earned from digging into garden soil, from laughing without planning to, from staying longer than you'd meant to.

She tucked her hands into her coat pockets, feeling the folded edge of Jack's bannister sketch still resting there, as if it had a heartbeat of its own.

She didn't take it out.

She just held it, lightly.

And for the first time since he'd said *I like you. That's the problem,* she didn't feel bruised by it.

She felt—oddly—calmer.

Because at least he'd said something.

Because he hadn't disappeared, not really.

Because she was still here. And so was he.

She passed the bakery, lights off now, the blackboard out front already wiped clean for tomorrow's optimism.

She imagined what it might say.

Muffins. Mistakes. Magic. Repeat.

Claire smiled to herself.

Not everything had to be certain.

Not everything had to be finished.

Some things just had to keep growing.

By the time Claire reached Maple Hollow, the sky had deepened to the colour of early plum jam. That soft, quiet blue-purple that always made her think of old books and dusk-kissed secrets.

She pushed open the garden gate, its familiar creak sounding less annoyed than usual, and stepped onto the gravel path.

The cottage windows glowed gold. She hadn't left any lights on.

Her steps slowed.

Not fearful. Just curious.

She turned the key in the door—still locked—and stepped inside, the warm hush of home wrapping around her like a cardigan.

The hallway smelled faintly of paint and lavender.

Then she saw it.

On the kitchen table.

A small, square tin.

Not new. The kind with worn edges and a painted robin on the lid. One she vaguely remembered from the tall cupboard above the pantry—where everything from expired cocoa to mystery screws lived in long-forgotten harmony.

It hadn't been there that morning.

She walked over, lifted the lid.

Inside: a handful of items, nestled carefully.

- A folded, faded photograph of the cottage in winter—snow on the windowsills, a wreath on the door.
- A small velvet pouch with a broken brooch inside—gold filigree in the shape of a thistle.
- And a note. In tidy, looping handwriting.

"For whoever finds this: This house has always been kind. Even when we weren't sure we deserved it. May it be kind to you too. – M."

Claire stared at the note, heart softening in her chest.

She didn't know who *M* was.

But she suddenly felt less alone.

She set the tin gently back on the table, then put the kettle on without thinking.

As the water bubbled, she glanced around the kitchen. The bannister sketch still sat tucked under a magnet on the fridge. A reminder. Or a maybe. Or both.

And there, propped beside the bread bin, was a small folded scrap of paper she hadn't noticed earlier.

Another note.

Jack's handwriting, unmistakably him—compact, slanted, slightly too neat for someone with sawdust in his eyelashes.

"Fixed the pantry door. It doesn't groan anymore, but it might still sigh if pushed too hard. Like the rest of us."

Claire blinked.

Then smiled.

It wasn't flowers. Or grand gestures. Or apologies.

But it was something.

It was his version of presence. Of saying, *I see you. I was here.*

She poured the tea, still holding the note, and leaned against the counter as the kettle ticked and the warmth filled the room.

Outside, the wind stirred the leaves. Somewhere, a fox barked in the lane.

Inside, the cottage sighed. Quietly. Kindly.

Just as promised.

The morning arrived on tiptoes.

Sunlight filtered through the curtain in slow, syrupy streaks, and Claire lay there blinking at the ceiling, still unsure if the note from Jack—*about sighing pantry doors and maybe-something feelings*—had been real or just something her tired brain had cooked up alongside the dream where she'd been married to a hedgehog who made jam.

She stretched, padded downstairs, and had just turned on the kettle when the front door **banged open** like a plot twist.

"CLAIRE," Lily called, "I'm invoking the Clause!"

Claire froze. "What clause?"

Lily appeared in the kitchen doorway holding a clipboard and a half-eaten crumpet. Her plaits were wonky. Her T-shirt read **BEES OVER BOYS** in glitter pen.

"The Emergency Tea & Intervention Clause," she said, as if it were obvious. "Section four. Subsection vibe check. You're not allowed to mope in flannel without external supervision."

Claire blinked. "I'm not moping."

"You're emotionally simmering," Lily said, walking straight to the cupboard and pulling out mugs like she owned the place. "It's worse."

Claire gave a slow smile. "Did you make this clause up just now?"

"I have a legal team," Lily said. "They're very reasonably priced. Mostly accept chocolate buttons."

Claire laughed, the sound catching her by surprise.

Lily handed her a mug and leaned against the counter. "Beth says you're glowing in a brooding heroine sort of way. Ellie says you're in the 'what does it mean?' stage. And Mags says if you don't kiss him by Tuesday, she's going to write her own fanfiction and publish it in the parish newsletter."

Claire nearly choked on her tea.

"She's got a following," Lily added solemnly.

There was a beat of quiet between them then.

Claire stared into her tea, the steam curling like a question mark.

Then she said, softly, "He fixed the pantry door."

Lily raised her eyebrows. "That's basically a love confession in DIY."

Claire laughed again, warmer now.

And somewhere deep down, past the panic and the paint fumes and the part of her that still didn't trust good things to stay—she felt something shift.

Not everything had to be solved today.

Some things just had to start.

Chapter Eight

"The Committee of Slightly Overexcited Villagers"

Claire had precisely three bites left of her toast, a cup of tea cooling by the window, and a tentative plan to spend the morning quietly reworking the Moonlight Market flyer layout.

That was, of course, when the doorbell rang.

Three times.

In rapid succession.

She opened the door to find **Frances** standing there in a paisley scarf the size of a tent and a clipboard clutched like a holy relic.

"Planning meeting," Frances declared.

Claire blinked. "I thought the planning meeting was tomorrow."

"It was moved forward by unanimous decision," Frances said, brushing past her. "Well. I decided. That's still a kind of unanimous."

"Unilateral, maybe," Claire murmured.

Frances had already made it to the kitchen and was rearranging the salt and pepper shakers for "a more dynamic feng shui."

"You have ten minutes," Frances added. "Bring pens. And opinions."

By the time Claire arrived at the **village hall**, the mood was somewhere between "mildly chaotic school fundraiser" and "early stages of a rebellion."

Ellie was pinning revised posters to the noticeboard using sparkly push-pins that matched her earrings. Beth was organising tea trays with a look that said she'd rather be regrouting her bathroom. Mags was sharpening pencils like she meant it.

And **Jack** was already there.

He stood off to one side, arms folded, eyes flicking between the growing stack of floral-themed bunting and the half-crushed pile of "historically accurate" village signage.

Claire's stomach did something deeply unhelpful.

He hadn't noticed her yet.

She adjusted her scarf unnecessarily and sat beside Ellie, who handed her a biscuit without looking.

"Planning agenda," Ellie whispered. "One: stall layout. Two: insurance for the Morris dancers. Three: someone vandalised the mock-up for your new bannister."

Claire blinked. "What?"

"Come and see."

The committee had stored her **sketch and the first prototype section of the bannister**—a charmingly curved segment with painted woodland creatures and vines—at the back of the hall near the coat rail.

Only now…

Claire stared at it.

Someone had added **googly eyes** to the fox. The deer was wearing lipstick. And a squirrel was now holding what appeared to be a lightsaber.

"It was like this when we opened up," Beth said diplomatically.

Jack stepped in, mouth twitching. "Might be Lily. Or the twins. Or possibly Frances in a moment of creative expression."

"I added nothing," Frances huffed. "Except vision."

Claire put a hand over her mouth. She was laughing before she realised it.

And Jack—well, Jack was watching her now.

Quietly.

Warmly.

"It's fixable," he said.

Claire looked up. "You're not just saying that because you want to repaint the squirrel with a hammer this time?"

He smiled. "No promises."

The meeting descended from there into arguments about bunting lengths, the price of homemade chutney, and whether or not Graham the sheep could be "officially designated a community member."

By the end, Claire had agreed to redesign the stall map, Jack had volunteered for gatepost duty, and someone—possibly Lily—had taped a post-it note to Claire's back that said BANNISTER QUEEN.

The committee meeting, as most Ashford Vale committee meetings did, eventually began to resemble less a structured gathering and more an interpretive dance of paperwork, biscuit crumbs, and mild emotional outbursts.

Someone had brought flapjacks. Someone else had *forgotten* to bring the laminated emergency evacuation map for the fête, which triggered a 15-minute debate about whether or not the cricket pavilion was technically flame-retardant. (It wasn't. And no one wanted to test it.)

Claire had given up trying to take coherent notes after Mags started drawing battle plans for the tea urn queue.

"I just think," Mags said, stabbing her biro into the paper, "if we deploy the shortbread *here*—and I do mean *shortbread*, not those sad chocolate digestives—then we can funnel foot traffic away from the raffle table and reduce queue congestion."

Beth muttered something about tactical scone deployment under her breath and began sketching her own alternative route in the margin.

Meanwhile, Frances had declared herself "Director of Ambiance" and was insisting the bunting should follow a colour story based on the four seasons.

"It's July," Ellie pointed out. "We're only *in* one season."

"That's such a *linear* way to see time," Frances said gravely, as if she'd just returned from a monastery in the Alps.

Claire watched all of it unfold with a strange, growing fondness. This village, these people, their eccentric chaos—it was all beginning to feel oddly... permanent.

She didn't quite belong yet.

But maybe she was learning how to.

When the noise had dulled to its usual end-of-meeting grumble, Claire quietly slipped out the side door of the hall, letting the cool midday breeze wrap around her.

The stone bench just outside, beside the hydrangeas that bloomed whether anyone asked them to or not, was bathed in soft shade.

She sank onto it, grateful to be still for a moment.

And then—

Jack stepped outside.

He didn't say anything at first. Just sat beside her.

Not too close.

Not far away either.

He held out a paper cup with tea in it—lukewarm, possibly over-steeped, with a single soggy custard cream perched on the rim.

Claire took it.

They sat in silence for a while.

Birds chirped indifferently from the hedge.

The door behind them creaked open, then shut again. Distant laughter spilled from inside.

Claire glanced at him.

"You were brave in there," she said lightly. "You volunteered to man the gate like it was a noble calling."

He gave a dry smile. "I figured someone should stand between Frances and the compost queen from the next village. Apparently, there's been tension."

"She tried to poach Lily's jam stall last year," Claire said.

"That explains the warning sign on the preserves table."

Jack took a sip of his tea and glanced sideways at her. "You seemed... more relaxed today."

Claire thought about the morning. The laughter. The googly-eyed squirrel.

"Maybe I am," she said.

Another pause.

Jack looked down at the cup in his hands. "I don't always know how to say things right."

Claire glanced at him again, gently. "You could start by not saying them like an apology."

He looked over then. Really looked.

And for a moment, the sounds of the village fell away—the committee voices, the sheep in the field beyond, even the ridiculous rustling of Frances' scarf flapping dramatically from the windowsill.

It was just the two of them. On a bench. In the shade. Sharing a slightly rubbish cup of tea.

"I like being around you," he said finally. "Even when it's complicated."

Claire's heart thudded once.

Then twice.

"I like it too," she said quietly.

And then—

Lily crashed through the side gate dragging a fold-up banner and what looked like half a disassembled sandwich board.

"WE'VE LOST THE RAFFLE PRIZES," she announced, breathless. "Frances is blaming solar flares. Ellie's blaming Mags. Mags is blaming capitalism."

Jack stood slowly. "Duty calls?"

Claire smiled. "You did say you were brave."

He gave her a mock-salute and followed Lily back inside, the sandwich board clattering behind them like a clumsy promise.

Claire stayed where she was for a moment longer.

Cup in hand.

Sun warm against her shoulder.

And a feeling—small but unmistakable—beginning to root somewhere beneath her ribs.

By the time Claire got back to Maple Hollow, the sky was buttercream gold and the birds were having animated conversations in the hedgerows.

She kicked off her boots at the door, dropped her bag by the bannister—now blissfully squirrel-free—and padded into the kitchen.

The house was quiet in that soft, settling way cottages seemed to have. Like it knew how to breathe with her now.

She filled the kettle, opened the window a crack, and stood there for a minute with her hands wrapped around the worktop, watching the wind move through the trees like it had secrets to tell.

Then something caught her eye.

A small, flat package.

It had been slipped through the letterbox and now rested on the welcome mat, tied with rough string and a single red thread.

She picked it up, half expecting a flyer or another overenthusiastic village leaflet about organic quiche ethics.

But no.

No label.

Just her name, written carefully on the front in blocky, carpenter's pencil script.

Inside: a thin wooden tile, sanded smooth. A test panel, she realised, for the bannister.

And burned into the corner—neatly, almost shyly—was the outline of a fox.

No googly eyes.

No lightsaber.

Just a fox. Curled into itself. Content.

She ran her fingers over it.

No note.

But it didn't need one.

She'd just set it down on the kitchen table when the front door banged open again.

"CLAIRE."

She didn't even jump this time.

"In here," she called.

Lily burst into the kitchen carrying a clipboard, a bag of marshmallows, and what looked like a partially dismantled wind chime.

"We're having a crisis," she said.

Claire raised an eyebrow. "Of course we are."

"Beth's oven has exploded," Lily said gravely. "Mags is refusing to host. Ellie's trying to make bunting out of toilet paper and it's not *aesthetic*. Therefore, you have been democratically elected host of the Moonlight Market prep evening."

Claire blinked. "By who?"

"Me," Lily said, and plonked the marshmallows on the counter. "Now. Where's your hot chocolate pan and are you emotionally prepared for Frances to bring four types of chutney and a grudge?"

Claire just smiled, moved to the cupboard, and reached for the cocoa.

"I suppose I should hoover the sofa."

"Too late," Lily said. "I already put a glitter bomb under one of the cushions. For morale."

The evening was loud, ridiculous, full of cinnamon sticks and badly folded flyers and one near-disastrous incident involving a cat and Mags' mulled wine jug.

Claire stood in the kitchen at one point, marshmallow stuck to her elbow, glitter in her hair, watching Lily argue with the tea caddy and Ellie trying to staple paper lanterns to the curtain rail.

And in that moment—absurd, messy, real—she thought:

This.
This is what it means to stay.
This is what it feels like to belong.

It was after nine when things began to wind down.

The paper lanterns—slightly wonky, one featuring what could only be described as an interpretive hedgehog—had finally been hung. The last of the flyers had been stacked with only minor glitter incidents. And Frances had declared the evening a "creative triumph" before slipping out into the night with three jars of chutney and a leftover cinnamon stick.

Claire was rinsing mugs when she heard the knock.

Not the doorbell—just a quiet tap at the kitchen door, the one that faced the garden.

She wiped her hands, crossed the floor, and opened it.

Jack stood there, hands in his pockets, eyes soft.

"Sorry to drop in," he said. "I saw the cars. Thought maybe you were hosting some sort of glitter-based summit."

Claire smiled. "Close. Moonlight Market planning. Marshmallows were harmed."

He glanced past her at the kitchen—Ellie laughing in the background, Lily climbing onto a stool to hang something above the sink, probably illegally.

"Looks like it went well," he said.

Claire leaned against the doorframe. "Mostly. We lost a ladle, two teaspoons, and possibly Beth's faith in humanity."

He held out a small brown paper bag.

"Thought you might need this."

She took it. Warm. Heavy.

Inside: still-warm cheese scones. Four, perfectly imperfect, slightly floury, and clearly homemade.

Claire looked up at him.

"I owed you," Jack said, rubbing the back of his neck. "For the pantry door. And the fox. And the squirrel. And… probably just in general."

Claire felt the corners of her mouth lift.

"You didn't have to."

"I know."

A pause.

Lily appeared behind her with a sparkly headband and a serious expression.

"Tell him if he wants to help, he can assemble the paper moons. We have glue sticks. And ambition."

Claire looked back at Jack.

He smiled.

"I can handle ambition," he said.

And just like that, he stepped inside.

Not loudly. Not formally.

Just… as if he'd always known his way around.

Chapter Nine

"In Which Glitter Is Declared a Controlled Substance"

Claire woke to the sound of… bells?

Not delicate, Christmas-style ones.

Big ones.

Possibly cowbells.

She rolled out of bed, padded to the window, and peeked through the curtain.

Lily was in the garden.

Wearing a cloak.

Holding a clipboard.

And ringing a bell the size of a dinner plate.

Behind her, two teenagers Claire vaguely recognised from the jam stall were attempting to assemble a folding table using only one leg and, inexplicably, a garden rake.

Claire opened the window.

"Lily?"

"PREP DAY," Lily bellowed.

Claire winced. "It's seven forty."

Lily checked her clipboard. "Exactly. We're on Schedule B: Optimistic Chaos."

By 9 a.m., Maple Hollow was a **festival-in-progress**.

Fairy lights were being tested and promptly tangled. Mags had roped off a "hot beverage zone" and was refusing to allow anyone in without a temperature-appropriate drink. Frances was leading a séance for "positive market vibrations," and someone had spray-painted a smiley face onto the compost bin.

Claire found herself in charge of tablecloth logistics, lantern stringing, and, by accidental volunteerism, the *Bake Sale Stall of Destiny*, which Ellie had labelled with a glitter pen and no regard for spacing.

Jack arrived mid-morning with a toolbox, two planks of wood, and the expression of a man who had accepted his fate and chosen power tools.

"Frances wants a photo booth backdrop built 'with the energy of Jane Austen and mild danger,'" he said, glancing at Claire.

She blinked. "How are you still surprised?"

"I'm not. I'm just documenting the escalation."

Lily, meanwhile, had taken over the front green with the force of a small but determined dictator.

"We need a hay bale throne," she said, pacing in front of the raffle table like a general surveying a siege.

"Why?" Beth asked.

"For the Raffle Regent, obviously."

Claire raised an eyebrow. "That's not a thing."

"It is now," Lily declared. "Tradition starts somewhere."

"Should I be worried that you have a tiara?" Ellie asked.

"No," Lily said. "You should be worried that I have *two*."

An hour later, there was glitter in the tea urn, jam on someone's dog, and Frances was trying to negotiate a truce between the cheese stall and the ethically-foraged honey vendor over pitch proximity.

Claire stood in the middle of it all, holding a basket of mismatched bunting triangles, wondering how it had come to this.

Jack appeared at her side with a handful of zip ties and a calm expression.

"Still want to run?" he asked.

Claire looked around.

At the chaos. At the ridiculousness. At the people who somehow, inexplicably, had become *her* people.

"No," she said. "I think I want to build a hay bale throne."

Jack passed her the zip ties. "Let's make it magnificent."

By late afternoon, Ashford Vale had reached peak transformation.

The cricket pitch was no longer a pitch but a weaving maze of stalls, fairy lights, chalkboards, and bunting that obeyed no known pattern of logic or symmetry. Paper lanterns bobbed in the trees. Battery-powered candles flickered in old jam jars. The Bake Sale Stall of Destiny had been upgraded—without Claire's input—to include a foam sword, a plaque made of shortbread, and a crown of ribbon rosettes.

"I can't even tell if we're fundraising," Ellie muttered as she stapled a sign to the cider barrel. "Or accidentally starting a midsummer cult."

Claire was trying to string battery lights around the hay bale throne—which now had **cup holders**, thanks to Lily—when someone handed her a cup of tea she hadn't asked for.

She turned.

Jack.

He didn't say anything. Just held the cup out, that usual calm behind his eyes, like the whole world could fall down around them and he'd still remember how she liked her tea.

She took it, their fingers brushing briefly.

Then Lily crashed past them wearing the larger tiara, trailing a line of bunting like a comet.

"We need more signage!" she shouted. "Beth's written 'Hot Soup' but it looks like 'Rat Soap' and I refuse to be sued again."

Claire blinked. "Again?"

"I said *refuse!*" Lily vanished into the crowd.

Jack watched her go. "I thought Max Mayhem was chaotic."

Claire smiled. "He has nothing on Lily."

As twilight settled in and the first stars began peeking between the clouds, something shifted.

The lanterns came to life all at once—soft glows blooming through the branches, catching in the jar lights and fairy strings like a village holding its breath and exhaling joy.

Music started—accordion and fiddle and something vaguely resembling rhythm.

Children ran with glow sticks. Mags served cider like it was a matter of pride. Frances gave an impromptu reading of her war-time romance novella beside the raffle prizes, two of which were mystery jars no one wanted to touch.

Claire stood behind the bake stall, now manned jointly by Ellie and a highly excitable spaniel, and looked out at the whole glowing, glorious, nonsense-filled market.

And felt it again.

That strange, fizzy sense of **this is mine now**.

Not bought. Not planned. Just… grown into.

Jack reappeared at her side with a string of unlabelled raffle tickets and a look that said *don't ask*.

"They made me the backup caller," he said.

"You going to wing it?"

"I might make up some winners."

Claire laughed, warm and open.

"Be careful," she said. "Frances has a gavel."

Jack leaned a little closer.

"I'll behave," he said, quietly, just for her.

And for a moment, there was only the sound of laughter, the glow of lanterns, and something unspoken settling gently between them—comfortable, tentative, and entirely theirs.

The raffle was always destined to go wrong.

It began smoothly enough. Frances climbed onto the hay bale throne wearing her *Raffle Regent* sash (hand-lettered in glitter by Lily), and Mags rang a ceremonial cowbell borrowed from the WI cupboard.

"Welcome," Frances announced, "to the most prestigious raffle Ashford Vale has hosted since 2003, when we accidentally gave away Barry's campervan."

Someone in the crowd shouted, "It wasn't an accident!"

Barry, from the cider stall, lifted his tankard solemnly.

Claire stood wedged between Ellie and Beth at the edge of the green, raffle ticket curled in her hand, the scent of cinnamon and patchouli thick in the air. Someone had just set off a single sparkler, which fizzed out halfway up and nearly lit the sandwich board.

Frances flourished the first ticket. "One-two-three… seven!"

Silence.

Jack, standing to her left with the backup caller list, leaned over. "You're reading it upside down."

Frances squinted. "Ah. Four."

A cheer rose from the hot drinks queue, where Lily sprinted forward in triumph.

"I claim the scented candle of mystery!"

"It smells like feet and ambition," Ellie whispered.

The rest followed in quick, chaotic bursts: someone won a scarf that might have been a tea towel, two jars of Frances' *Experimental Autumn Pickle*, and a broken yo-yo no one remembered donating.

At one point, Mags swapped tickets mid-call to ensure Beth got the deluxe biscuit tin, and no one challenged it because she was holding the gavel.

Then the music started.

The band—half local folk group, half Ellie's cousin with a ukulele—struck up a tune that veered between jig and pop cover depending on how many ciders they'd had.

Lily had roped Jack into dancing within seconds, dragging him into the makeshift circle with gleeful abandon.

Claire laughed, trying to sidestep her way out of the crowd, only to be caught by Ellie's hand.

"Oh no," Ellie said. "No escape. We're embracing our rural chaos."

And before Claire could argue, she was twirling in a lopsided loop of villagers, skirts spinning, lights flashing, laughter bubbling like kettle steam.

The grass was uneven, the music slightly off, and at least one man was trying to dance with a wheelbarrow.

It was perfect.

When the music paused for a breath, and people began stumbling off in smiling clusters, Claire stepped back toward the bunting poles, breathless and warm.

Jack appeared beside her, hair tousled, cheeks flushed, sleeves rolled just a little higher than she remembered.

He looked at her like maybe—just maybe—he was trying not to say something that would change everything.

So instead, he said, "Not bad for a village that once set fire to its own maypole."

Claire laughed again. "I'm beginning to understand the appeal."

Jack opened his mouth to reply—

—and just then, the hay bale throne collapsed in slow motion under Frances, the raffle board, and one very confused golden retriever.

Claire gasped.

Jack winced.

"Don't worry," Lily shouted from somewhere near the cider tent. "*This is exactly how I wrote it in the script!*"

The market roared with laughter, and someone restarted the music.

The market ebbed slowly, like a tide of fairy lights and tired feet.

Children were collected, dogs rounded up, stalls packed with the satisfying clink of tins and folded bunting. The cider barrel had been declared empty and sacred in equal measure. Someone had misplaced their left shoe and found it again in the biscuit tin.

Claire sat at the edge of the green, shoes off, toes digging into the cool grass, a paper cup of tea in her hands and a stolen moment of calm in her chest.

The lanterns still glowed above, dimmer now, flickering slightly in the breeze like tired stars.

She didn't realise Jack was beside her until he sat down with a quiet exhale, long legs stretched out, boots scuffed, hair falling into his eyes in a way that looked wholly unintentional and somehow still unfair.

They didn't speak for a while.

Didn't need to.

Around them, the village folded itself into dusk, and the crickets started up, and somewhere—probably Lily—someone played a soft, meandering tune on a melodica.

Claire took a sip of tea.

"It wasn't perfect," she said, watching the last of the glow sticks blink out on the grass.

Jack shook his head. "Not even close."

"But it was good."

He turned to look at her. "It was yours."

She blinked, surprised.

"You think?"

He nodded slowly. "You were everywhere. Bake stall. Bunting. That poor, doomed throne. And everyone looked at you like… like you'd always been here."

Claire looked down at her tea, suddenly finding it difficult to look at him.

"That's new," she said softly.

He didn't push. Just let it sit.

Then, a moment later, he reached into his coat pocket and pulled out something small. Folded. Paper.

He handed it to her without ceremony.

She unfolded it.

A tiny sketch. Done in pencil. Quick, but thoughtful.

Her. Laughing. Holding a cupcake. Lily in the background, mid-gesture, looking triumphant.

It was ridiculous.

And lovely.

Claire's chest tightened.

"Is this…?"

Jack rubbed the back of his neck. "Lily told me I needed to start carrying a notebook. In case of 'moments worth remembering.'"

Claire smiled, tucking the sketch gently into her coat pocket.

"I think she's right."

The silence between them softened again, less like absence and more like understanding.

"Thanks for staying late," she said.

Jack looked sideways at her. "I wasn't going to leave before the hay bale made its final stand."

Claire laughed. "We'll need a new one next year."

Jack paused.

Then—casually, carefully—

"I'd like to be around for that."

Claire turned, heart doing that slow, fluttery thing again.

He didn't push. Didn't look away.

He just let it sit there.

Like a promise left gently on the table, still warm.

And Claire, for the first time in longer than she could remember, let herself believe in the idea of next year.

The walk home was quiet.

Not silent—Ashford Vale was never truly silent—but *quiet in the right ways*: the soft scuff of her boots on the lane, the rustle of trees shaking off the heat of the day, the occasional echo of laughter still drifting from the green like leftover music.

Claire had tucked the sketch into the inside pocket of her coat, right next to her heart, and she hadn't stopped thinking about it since they'd left the grass behind.

It wasn't just the drawing itself, though that had surprised her—the way Jack had caught her smile, caught *her*, in just a few quick pencil lines. It was the gesture. The quiet offering. The thought that someone had seen her and decided she was worth capturing.

That hadn't happened in a long time.

She passed the post box, the low stone wall, the garden with the slightly judgmental gnomes, all bathed in the soft silver of a village falling asleep under its own fairy lights.

Maple Hollow waited for her, its porch light on—flickering slightly, as usual—and the faint scent of old lavender wafting through the open upstairs window.

She pushed the gate open slowly, boots crunching the gravel path, and stood for a moment just before the door.

Inside, the cottage would still be holding the echo of laughter from earlier. Glitter on the rug. Maybe a marshmallow stuck to the kettle. A ribbon hanging from the bannister like it had wandered away from the party and forgotten what it was doing.

But out here—

Claire closed her eyes and breathed it in.

The air. The calm.

And under it, the realisation she hadn't quite let herself name yet.

She was home.

Not visiting.

Not surviving.

Home.

The word settled somewhere low in her chest, warm and strange and just a little terrifying.

She pulled out the sketch again before unlocking the door.

Held it in both hands. Smiled to herself in the quiet.

And for the first time in years, Claire didn't feel like she was carrying everything alone.

The cottage greeted her the way it always did—softly.

She stepped inside, shutting the door behind her with that familiar click that sounded more like a sigh than a latch. The hallway lamp was still on, casting a warm golden halo across the faded rug. One of Lily's posters had peeled slightly from the bannister and now flopped cheerfully like a paper flag of victory.

Claire toed off her boots, dropped her coat gently over the armchair, and walked into the kitchen.

She meant to go straight upstairs.

She really did.

But instead, she found herself reaching for a small wooden picture frame from the second drawer—the one that held batteries, mystery keys, and an unopened pack of novelty candles from Christmas.

She dusted it off with her sleeve, smoothed the corners of the sketch, and slid it inside.

Then, after a moment of consideration, she placed it—carefully—on the shelf above the kettle.

Not too prominent.

Not hidden either.

Just there.

Quiet. Constant.

Like the memory of laughter you didn't realise you needed.

She turned to head upstairs, only to pause.

Something was different.

A smell—faint, warm, not hers.

Cinnamon?

She frowned, crossed to the pantry, opened the door—

And there, tucked neatly on the middle shelf beside her half-used teabags and the disaster jar of quinoa, sat a small paper bag.

Inside: two cheese scones.

Still warm.

Still flour-dusted.

And a note.

"In case the raffle snacks didn't survive the glitter fallout."
– J

Claire smiled, slow and surprised and entirely undone.

She left the bag where it was for now.

Then turned off the kitchen light, the little frame catching the last glow of it on its way out.

Upstairs, the window was open to the night air.

And the cottage—her cottage—exhaled once more around her, quietly happy to have her back.

Chapter Ten

"Tea, Toast, and Trouble Brewing (Probably)"

The morning tiptoed in like it knew the village was tired.

Sunlight stretched gently across the windowsill, warming the teacup from the night before and catching in the dust motes that danced like lazy confetti in the air. Somewhere nearby, a pigeon cooed with the self-importance of someone who hadn't spent the evening constructing a raffle throne out of hay and poor decisions.

Claire sat at the little kitchen table in her pyjamas, wrapped in a cardigan that still smelled vaguely of bonfire smoke and cinnamon, cradling her mug like it held the secrets of the universe.

The scone from the pantry was on a plate.

Mostly uneaten.

She wasn't entirely sure why.

There was just… something about it she wasn't ready to disturb. Not yet.

She took another sip of tea, let her thoughts drift like steam from the mug—

—and then the door banged open.

"CLAIRE."

Claire didn't flinch anymore.

"Well," she said. "That's ominous."

Lily charged into the kitchen wearing a neon hoodie, leggings with tiny foxes on them, and the expression of someone who'd already had two coffees and possibly a sugar high.

"I bring urgent matters of state," she announced, dropping her rucksack on the floor and pulling out a clipboard, a thermos, and what might have been a sock puppet.

Claire raised an eyebrow. "We're doing sock diplomacy now?"

Lily waved the clipboard. "No time. Crisis. Well, minor situation. Well… evolving situation."

Claire blinked. "Which is it?"

"You're being evasive," Lily said, accusingly, pointing the thermos at her like a gavel. "Which means something *happened*."

Claire looked down at her tea.

Lily gasped. "You *didn't* kiss him, did you?!"

Claire nearly snorted tea through her nose. "What—Lily!"

"You had a moonlit moment! There were scones involved!"

"It was a raffle," Claire said weakly. "And maybe one and a half moments."

"Moments are how it starts," Lily said, flopping into a chair and immediately spilling half the contents of her rucksack across the floor. "Next thing you know, you're sharing jam and arguing about tile grouting. That's how Frances and Brenda got together."

Claire stared. "Frances is with Brenda?"

"They're in 'early murmurs,'" Lily said, making air quotes. "We're very happy for them. Now—"

She slapped a fresh flyer onto the table. It was a draft for the village newsletter.

Claire glanced at it.

Then looked again.

The headline read:
BANNISTER LOVE BLOOMS IN THE DARK

Underneath was a frankly worrying doodle of two foxes snuggling under a bannister archway.

"I'm sorry, what?" Claire said.

Lily looked far too pleased. "Frances wrote it in a burst of inspiration. I told her it needed more emotional peril, but she said your eyes did all the heavy lifting."

Claire dropped her head to the table with a groan.

"Can I veto this?"

"No," Lily said cheerfully. "It's already been approved by the unofficial newsletter subcommittee, which is mostly me and Mags after cider."

Claire groaned again.

"But on the plus side," Lily added, "everyone now agrees you and Jack are the slow-burn romance of the season."

Claire lifted her head slowly. "There's a season?"

"Spring was Barbara and the postman. Summer's yours." She beamed. "Congratulations."

After Lily left—socks, flyers, and declarations of "emotional peril" trailing behind her like confetti—Claire stood in the centre of the kitchen with her hands on her hips.

"I am," she said aloud, to no one, "a grown woman with things to do."

The cottage, predictably, did not disagree.

She made a list.

It was neat, bullet-pointed, entirely sensible:

- Hoover the stairs
- Tidy the garden shed
- Re-measure bannister angles (no emotional layering)
- Order more tea
- Absolutely **do not** reread the note from Jack or touch the framed sketch

Then she ignored the hoovering entirely and went to the garden shed.

The shed, she reasoned, was safe. It was practical. It had cobwebs and questionable paint tins and that broken folding chair she still hadn't managed to part with. A shed did not make one question their emotional trajectory or whether pencil sketches could be flirty.

She shoved the door open and immediately sneezed.

Right. The lavender sachet Mags had insisted would keep away "unhelpful spirits."

She ducked past the drying herbs, pulled the light cord (which worked on the third try), and set about reorganising the shelves.

She was halfway through stacking empty terracotta pots into some semblance of order when she noticed something tucked behind the watering can.

A strip of wood.

No bigger than her hand. Smooth. Pale. Sanded to perfection.

And drawn on it—in faint pencil—was a tiny fox.

Different from the first one. This one was mid-leap. Wild and joyful.

Her breath caught.

It hadn't been there yesterday.

Her hand curled around it without thinking.

It wasn't signed.

Didn't need to be.

She stood there for a long moment in the stillness of the shed, surrounded by garden tools and the smell of earth and sawdust.

Then, slowly, she smiled.

Because no matter how much she told herself she was focusing on *practicality* today, some stories didn't wait politely in the background.

Some quietly built themselves, one sketch at a time.

Even in sheds.

Even in her.

Claire didn't mean to go into the village.

She was just popping out for more tea.

And possibly bread.

And maybe a new sponge because the old one had started looking at her like it had been through three world wars and a jam stall.

She absolutely wasn't hoping to run into anyone. Least of all anyone who sketched foxes on bits of wood and made scones and smiled like he had *no idea* he was slowly lodging himself under her skin like a splinter that didn't hurt.

She was fine.

Completely fine.

The village, of course, had other plans.

As she turned the corner by the post office—carrying a paper bag, a box of lemon biscuits (on offer), and two more things she hadn't intended to buy—Claire almost collided with a ladder.

More specifically, the ladder's owner.

"Careful," came the voice. Calm. Familiar.

And definitely from Jack.

He stepped down from the second rung and caught her arm automatically, steadying both her and her precariously balanced lemon biscuits.

Claire blinked. "You again."

Jack smiled. "It's a small village."

She glanced up at the ladder. "Painting something?"

"Frances wants the postbox arch to be 'more festive.'"

Claire looked. Someone had already attached paper sunflowers and a felt squirrel.

Jack followed her gaze. "I've stopped asking questions."

"I've stopped expecting logic," Claire said.

They both smiled.

Then didn't move.

Not quite yet.

Jack tilted his head slightly, eyes scanning the top of her bag.

"Are those the biscuits Mags pretends she hates but secretly hoards?"

Claire held them closer. "They were on offer."

He nodded. "Always the best excuse."

She glanced at him—t-shirt dusty, jeans smudged, that relaxed, *just-here-to-fix-things* kind of presence that made her want to hand him a list and also maybe a key.

Claire cleared her throat.

"I found the sketch," she said.

Jack's expression didn't change. But something in his shoulders shifted—like a breath half-held.

"In the shed," she added. "Was that... on purpose?"

He looked at her, quiet again.

"I didn't know if you'd find it," he said eventually. "But... I hoped."

Claire's fingers tightened slightly on the bag.

There were a dozen things she could say.

None of them fit in a village street with bunting tangled in the telegraph pole and a sheep currently escaping the petting zoo behind them.

So instead, she said, "You're getting glitter in your hair again."

Jack raised an eyebrow. "Not again."

She reached out before she could stop herself, brushing a piece of gold fleck from the top of his ear.

Their eyes met.

Just for a moment.

And then—

"CLAIRE!" came a voice from somewhere near the bakery. "IS IT TRUE ABOUT THE FOXES?"

Claire sighed.

Jack grinned.

"I should get this ladder back before Frances asks me to install bunting on the bus stop."

Claire stepped back, smiling despite herself.

"I'll see you later?"

He nodded. "You will."

And he meant it.

She walked away with lemon biscuits, tea, and the quiet knowledge that—somehow—the shed, the sketch, and the street with bunting now all carried the same name in the back of her heart.

Jack.

Claire made it exactly twenty-seven feet down the high street before she heard it.

The unmistakable voice of **Mrs. Trish Lovelace**, owner of **"Trinkets & Treasures (Home of the Hand-Poured Candle and Mild Judgement)"**.

"Claire darling!" Trish called from the doorway, already armed with a clipboard and what looked suspiciously like a weekly rota for volunteer jam tasters.

Claire tried to turn it into a nod-and-smile situation.

Trish was having none of it.

"You'll be popping in, won't you? I've just had a fresh delivery of lavender-scented fox coasters and we're all pretending it's *not* related to recent events."

Claire sighed. Then smiled. Then surrendered.

The bell above the shop door tinkled merrily as she stepped inside.

The scent hit her instantly: part rose petal, part optimism, part something dangerously close to a cinnamon explosion.

Trish leaned across the counter like she was about to sell Claire either a candle or state secrets.

"So." She tapped her pen twice against the till. "You and Jack."

Claire blinked. "We—what?"

"I'm just saying," Trish said, with all the innocence of a woman who once planned an entire bake sale to investigate a new couple, "it's refreshing to see two people who clearly hate the fuss but are quietly radiating mutual admiration under the bunting."

Claire flushed. "There's no bunting involved."

Trish raised a single eyebrow.

Claire cleared her throat. "I was just buying biscuits."

"Oh, I know," Trish said. "And Jack was just installing decorative archwork with a power drill and a wistful expression. Completely unrelated."

Before Claire could formulate a coherent defence, the shop bell jingled again.

Ellie walked in.

Saw Claire.

Paused.

Grinned.

"Well, well, well," she said. "Fancy seeing you here, *Bannister Queen*."

Claire covered her face with both hands. "I'm going to move. To a cave. Maybe open a jam stall in the Hebrides."

"Too late," Ellie said, plucking a candle from the shelf. "You're local folklore now. People are shipping you like you're a Regency drama with hand tools."

Trish beamed. "Would you like the fox coasters gift-wrapped?"

Claire groaned. "I'm not buying the coasters."

"They're scented with possibility," Trish said brightly.

Ellie held one up and sniffed it. "Smells like trouble and romance."

Claire turned on her heel, biscuits under one arm, dignity escaping through the keyhole.

"I'm leaving," she said.

Ellie followed. "Good luck. The allotment ladies are already calling him 'the Fox Whisperer.'"

Claire didn't stop walking.

By the time Claire reached Maple Hollow again, the sun had begun its slow, golden slide behind the rooftops, and the air held that soft, almost-forgotten chill that hinted September was somewhere in the wings.

She paused at the gate, shifting the paper bag in her arms—tea, biscuits, an accidental jar of ginger curd, and **one** fox coaster she swore Trish must have slipped in while she wasn't looking.

The cottage looked just as she'd left it.

And yet, as she pushed open the door, something felt… different.

Not wrong. Just… new.

She stepped into the hallway, placed the bag carefully on the console table, and froze.

There. Leaning against the bannister post.

A **tin of wood polish**.

Next to it, a folded cloth.

And a note. Just one word, in the same pencil-line print she recognised now without question.

"Trust."

That was it.

No explanation.

No name.

Just that.

Claire stared at it, heart thudding softly in her chest like it hadn't quite caught up with the rest of her.

She reached down, picked up the cloth.

It smelled faintly of cedar and something she couldn't name—something warm.

The bannister gleamed.

Not overly polished. Not showroom perfect.

Just… better.

Seen. Tended to.

Like it mattered.

She sank onto the bottom step and rested the cloth on her lap, fingertips brushing the grain of the post.

He hadn't stayed.

He hadn't needed to.

The gesture said enough.

Claire sat there for a long while, the sounds of the village softening outside, the kettle ticking in the background, the scent of polished wood curling through the hall like a memory.

And when she finally moved, it was only to take the coaster from the bag and place it—quietly, without comment—on the table beside the sketch.

Chapter Eleven

"Unexpected Guests & Unavoidable Dances"

Claire was halfway through her second slice of toast, considering the logistics of replacing the hallway mirror (currently cracked and held together with hope), when someone knocked on the door.

Not the usual Lily-knock, which sounded like a jazz drum solo.

This was polite.

Pointed.

Possibly carrying paperwork.

She opened it to find **Cynthia Grainger** standing on the step in an immaculately pressed linen coat and the kind of expression that could curdle milk at fifty paces.

Claire blinked. "Cynthia."

"Claire." A stiff nod. "You're looking well. I suppose the bannister incident worked out in your favour."

Claire opened her mouth, unsure whether to thank her or question the phrase *bannister incident*, but Cynthia steamrolled ahead.

"I'm here in my capacity as Chair of the Autumn Harvest Ball Committee."

"Oh," Claire said cautiously. "That's… a thing?"

"It is *the* thing," Cynthia said crisply. "The single most important event on Ashford Vale's social calendar, second only to the rogue peacock incident of 2017."

Claire nodded as if this made sense.

"We've reviewed the decorating proposals," Cynthia continued, flipping open a folder. "And, regrettably, your name was put forward."

"Regrettably?"

"Apparently you have—" she made a face "—an *eye*."

Claire wasn't sure whether to feel flattered or vaguely endangered.

"I was told to formally invite you to join the décor subcommittee," Cynthia went on. "There will be bunting. And a *theme*."

"A theme," Claire echoed.

"Rustic regency," Cynthia said, as if daring her to laugh. "With optional woodland accents."

Claire blinked again.

"And of course," Cynthia added, almost as an afterthought, "you'll be expected to attend. It's a *dancing* event. Bring a partner if you like. Or don't. Though I understand you've already become—how shall I put this—*attached* to one of our more elusive tradesmen."

Claire flushed. "That's not—"

"Lovely," Cynthia said, snapping her folder shut. "I'll see you Thursday at the hall."

And with that, she turned and walked off, coat swishing, not waiting for agreement.

Claire stood in the doorway holding her toast, speechless.

Behind her, Lily—who had apparently let herself in via the back door again—appeared holding a tea strainer and a look of glee.

"Did I just hear *Rustic Regency*?"

Claire groaned.

Lily grinned.

"Oh, we are *absolutely* making you a corsage."

Claire shut the cottage door behind her with a thud, dropped the lemon biscuits on the table, and immediately covered her face with both hands.

She let out a sound somewhere between a sigh and a groan.

"Rustic. Regency," she muttered into her palms. "With woodland accents. That's not a theme. That's a fever dream."

She peeled her hands away and stared at the note Jack had left yesterday on the bannister post.

Trust.

Trust what, exactly? That Cynthia Grainger wouldn't dress her up like a Brontë sister and parade her past the raffle stall? That no one else in the village would refer to her as *emotionally attached to a tradesman* in broad daylight?

The door creaked open behind her.

"Don't panic," came Ellie's voice, far too cheerful for someone who'd just walked in uninvited. "I brought snacks and emotional detachment."

Claire turned as Ellie held up a packet of Percy Pigs and two tubs of hummus, like she'd been shopping for someone having a full-blown identity crisis in a cardigan.

"What's happening to me?" Claire asked, half-laughing. "Last week I was designing flyers. Now I'm being invited to balls like it's a Jane Austen reboot and people are naming me after foxes."

"Oh, honey," Ellie said, flopping onto the sofa. "You're not being invited. You're being *cast*."

Claire blinked. "Excuse me?"

"You're part of the local narrative now," Ellie said, poking her with a stray breadstick. "You've got a bannister, a backstory, and brooding man energy. That's how it starts. First the newsletter, then the themed dancing event. Next thing you know, Mags starts referring to you and Jack as a 'unit.'"

Claire buried her face in a cushion. "Stop talking."

The back door slammed open.

"Am I too late for the spiral?" Lily appeared in a cloud of ribbon scraps and possibly cider. "I brought a trial corsage. Smell it. It's fennel and ambition."

Ellie looked at Claire. "You were saying?"

Claire groaned again. "I'm not wearing a corsage."

"You say that now," Lily said, already unwinding the twine. "But wait until you see the matching epaulettes."

Claire was still protesting the idea of fennel-scented accessories when Lily plopped down next to Ellie, kicked off one trainer, and pulled a folded piece of paper from her pocket like it was an afterthought.

"Oh, right," she said, waving it. "I also came because of this."

Claire eyed it warily. "If that's another flyer about your moonlight poetry slam, I'm still recovering from the last one."

Lily grinned. "It's not poetry. It's better."

She smoothed the paper out on the table between the hummus and the fox coaster.

Ellie leaned forward. "What am I looking at?"

"It's the preliminary stall map for the Harvest Ball," Lily said, tapping the little grid at the bottom with wild enthusiasm. "Look! They've added a feature wall."

"A what now?" Claire asked.

"For photographs," Lily said. "Rustic backdrop, hay bales, fairy lights, maybe a fake sheep if Frances can source one."

Claire squinted. "And this affects me how?"

Lily tapped again. "Because you've been put down as 'Joint Design Lead' on the visual concept."

"What?"

"And," Lily added, completely ignoring the growing horror in Claire's voice, "Jack's been listed as your co-lead. Because, and I quote from Cynthia's notes, 'those two seem to work with wood and longing looks.'"

Claire froze.

Ellie started laughing so hard she nearly dropped her hummus.

"I didn't agree to this," Claire said, trying very hard not to sound like someone who had just mentally run through every moment she and Jack had been in the same room since the raffle.

"You didn't have to," Lily said cheerfully. "Cynthia says 'you're the face of local charm now,' which I think is code for *you're doomed.*"

Claire stared at the map, then at the scribbled names beside the staging area, her own written next to Jack's in someone's extremely aggressive cursive.

"She's matchmaking," Claire said faintly. "With plywood and mood boards."

"Frances says it's all very 'slow burn-y,'" Lily offered, reaching for a biscuit. "And if you two don't at least kiss by the backdrop unveiling, she's threatening to add dramatic voiceover narration to the slideshow."

Claire dropped her head to the table again.

Ellie patted her shoulder. "Look on the bright side. At least you're not designing it with Barry from the cider stall."

"Barry's got a lovely eye," Lily said.

"For disaster," Ellie muttered.

Claire groaned into the tabletop. "I'm never going outside again."

Claire managed to escape Lily and Ellie after promising—under duress and with half a biscuit as collateral—that she would *at least* glance at the Harvest Ball mood board Lily was creating out of magazine clippings, Pinterest screenshots, and something that might once have been a wedding invitation.

"I need to breathe in a room that isn't full of stationery aggression," Claire muttered to herself as she pulled her coat on.

The truth was, she needed air. And not just the crisp autumn kind. She needed *space*—from bunting, from fox-themed assumptions, from being *the face of local charm*, and most of all, from the slow, certain way Jack had begun to settle under her skin.

She headed toward the village shop for milk, telling herself it was just a walk.

Just a walk. Nothing emotional.

Just milk.

Naturally, the shop was closed.

A note on the door read: *"Gone to collect Nigel's new prescription. Back in 15-ish. Or whenever the pharmacist stops arguing about goats."*

Claire exhaled, turned to leave, and promptly bumped into **Bev Withers** from the flower stall, who was carrying a bucket of dahlias and the kind of expression that meant Claire wasn't going anywhere quickly.

"Oh good, Claire," Bev said, thrusting the bucket toward her. "Hold this."

"I—what?"

"I need to move the other half of the display but I've put my back out wrestling a trellis and Trish says you have good flower-holding arms."

Before Claire could dispute this sudden new identity, the bucket was in her hands.

"I'm just going to—"

"Don't move. You'll ruin the line."

Claire stood on the corner, holding dahlias, trying not to let the water slosh on her coat.

And that was when she heard the voice.

"I'd say that's a strong look for you."

She didn't even have to turn.

Jack.

Of course it was Jack.

She looked over her shoulder.

He was leaning against the gatepost outside the butcher's, arms folded, casual as you please, like this was just another moment in a long, ongoing joke only they were in on.

Claire raised her eyebrows. "If you say 'florist's assistant is your true calling,' I'm throwing a gerbera at you."

He walked over, took the bucket from her without being asked, and shifted it easily to the table Bev had been eyeing from across the road.

"You weren't supposed to do that," Claire said.

"She was going to make you hold it for another fifteen minutes."

"She also called me the Bunting Whisperer last week."

"I heard," Jack said. "Lily's trying to make it stick."

Claire huffed a laugh despite herself.

They stood there for a moment, watching Bev fuss with her sign, arguing quietly with herself about the placement of a chalkboard heart.

Claire glanced sideways. "You heard about the Harvest Ball thing, didn't you?"

Jack gave a small, guilty smile.

"You're listed as my co-lead."

"I am."

"And you didn't object?"

He turned to her fully then, something quiet and steady in his expression.

"No," he said. "I didn't."

She swallowed, looked away.

He let the silence stretch, not pushing.

Then he added, lightly, "Though I'm still unclear on the role of faux woodland accents in a Regency theme."

Claire laughed, surprised by how quickly he could unspool her tension like that—like it was easy.

"You know they've made a photo wall?"

"I've heard."

"And apparently we're designing it."

"Apparently."

Claire folded her arms, narrowed her eyes. "If you bring back the squirrel, we're done."

Jack pretended to think. "What if the squirrel wears a cravat?"

"No."

"Tiny top hat?"

"Still no."

They began walking without deciding to, falling into step down the high street as the village settled into late afternoon rhythms: dogs barking, the occasional clang of a teacup, someone setting up fairy lights for no immediately clear reason.

It felt... natural.

Too natural.

Claire tried to remind herself that just because Jack knew how to walk in comfortable silence didn't mean anything. That just because he knew how she took her tea, or when not to talk, or how to leave sketches in sheds—none of it meant he wanted anything more.

She glanced up at him, only to find he was already watching her.

Not intensely. Not dramatically.

Just... seeing her.

Like he always had.

She looked away, heart thudding in a way she was really beginning to resent.

"Walk with me to the green?" he asked suddenly.

Claire hesitated. "Why?"

Jack shrugged. "I want your opinion on something."

She squinted. "Does it involve glitter?"

"No."

"Paper lanterns?"

"No."

"Bunting?"

Jack smiled. "Trust me."

The words hit her like a pebble tossed into a still pond.

She exhaled.

And nodded.

They walked without speaking at first.

Not because there was nothing to say—but because the silence was comfortable. Familiar. A kind of quiet that padded gently between them, like an old cat curling up in a sunlit window.

Claire kept her hands tucked in her pockets, eyes on the road ahead, vaguely aware of the way the leaves were beginning to crisp at the edges. September had always been her favourite month. That halfway place between summer and autumn—still warm enough to hope, cool enough to breathe.

Jack walked beside her like he always did: unhurried, solid, a quiet presence who didn't fill silence for the sake of it.

She hated how much she liked that.

They passed the post office, where someone had placed a pot of chrysanthemums outside the door, and a chalk sign reading *YES, WE STILL SELL STAMPS, JANET.*

Claire caught herself smiling at it.

Jack noticed. Of course he did.

"You're smiling," he said, voice soft.

"I am," she admitted.

He didn't ask why.

Just let it sit.

They turned onto the path toward the green, the trees overhead dappling the ground with patches of light. Somewhere in the distance, a dog barked. A child laughed. The kind of sounds that didn't ask anything of you—just reminded you that the world was ticking on.

Claire glanced sideways.

"Is this what you thought your life would be?"

Jack raised an eyebrow. "That's a heavy question for someone who just came out for milk."

She gave a half-laugh. "Sorry. I don't know why I asked."

He shrugged. "It's fair."

They walked a few more steps before he answered.

"No," he said eventually. "Not exactly. But… I think I'm okay with that."

Claire turned toward him a little. "You think?"

He smiled wryly. "Some days more than others."

She nodded. "Yeah. Same."

They reached the low stone wall by the green. Jack slowed, let his hand skim across the top of it. Claire did the same, her fingers brushing faint moss.

It was nothing. It was everything.

She found herself speaking before she could talk herself out of it.

"You know, when I moved into Maple Hollow, I thought I'd stay for a month. Maybe two. Just enough time to clear it out. Fix a few things. Sell it on."

Jack nodded slowly, watching her.

"And now?"

Claire looked away.

"I bought more tea yesterday," she said. "In bulk."

He smiled.

Not wide.

Not smug.

Just quietly.

Like he understood what that meant.

Like he knew it was more than tea.

The light was shifting now—brushing the tops of the trees in gold, warming the edge of the path where the late wildflowers still clung on.

Claire stopped walking.

Jack did too.

She looked at him.

"This thing you want to show me," she said, voice lighter now, "it's not another fox sketch, is it?"

He shook his head. "No."

"Good. Because I think Lily's started a fan club."

Jack smiled again. "Don't worry. This is… something else."

She tilted her head. "What kind of something?"

He didn't answer.

Just looked at her.

And for a moment, Claire had the oddest feeling she was standing on the edge of something—not frightening. Not even unexpected.

Just… new.

She drew a breath.

"Okay," she said. "Show me."

Claire followed him across the green.

The sun had dropped just enough to throw long shadows from the trees, and the grass was scattered with the first fallen leaves—gold, brown, that almost-rust colour that made you want to knit things and bake cinnamon scones.

They veered off the path, toward the far corner where the old garden wall stood crumbling beneath a crooked row of apple trees.

Claire hadn't been this far since the Moonlight Market. It was quieter here, the village sounds dampened by hedgerows and the low hum of bees still clinging to the last of the summer wildflowers.

Jack stopped near the wall, where someone had propped a few wooden boards against a tree.

Claire's brow furrowed.

"What's this?"

Jack picked up one of the boards—clean, sanded, the wood pale and fine-grained. Not scrap. Chosen.

He looked down at it. Then back at her.

"I had an idea," he said. "After the raffle. And the dancing. And… everything."

Claire arched an eyebrow. "That's a lot of inspiration from one hay bale collapse."

He smiled faintly.

"I thought this space could be something more," he said, turning slowly to gesture at the corner of the green—the shaded curve of land, the apple trees, the quiet.

"Like what?"

"Something permanent," he said. "A bench. A little trellis maybe. A proper seat under the trees. For after markets. Or just… when someone wants five minutes away from the bunting."

Claire looked around.

It was a funny little patch of land—slightly uneven, always a bit too shady for the flower stalls, mostly forgotten.

But standing there now, with the late sun catching the apples and the wind tugging gently at the leaves, she saw it.

Saw what he saw.

"It'd be nice," she said softly. "A bench here."

Jack nodded once.

"I started sketching it out," he added. "I was going to build it anyway. But… then I thought maybe you'd want to help."

Claire looked at him sharply.

"You want me to help with woodworking?"

He grinned. "No saws. Just… design. Finish. Maybe the paint."

She narrowed her eyes. "What colour?"

"You pick."

Claire hesitated.

It was such a *small* thing. Just a bench. Some wood. A patch of grass no one else had looked at twice.

But it felt like something else.

Like an invitation.

Not just to help.

To belong.

To stay.

She swallowed.

"Okay," she said.

Jack looked at her. That calm, steady way that made her heart do annoying things.

"Yeah?"

She nodded. "But if you make me use glitter varnish, I'm reporting you to Cynthia."

He laughed.

The sound settled into her like warmth after a long walk.

They stood there for another few seconds—nothing dramatic. Just sunlight, breeze, apples falling quietly onto soft grass.

But something had shifted.

Claire didn't know what it would become.

But for the first time, she wanted to find out.

Jack crouched beside the pile of boards, ran a hand along one of the smoother planks like he was checking it for secrets.

Claire stayed standing, arms loosely folded, pretending she was watching the trees and not the way his sleeves had rolled up just past his elbows, or the small half-smile that tugged at the corner of his mouth when he was concentrating.

"So," he said, glancing up. "Rustic? Clean lines? Elaborate gothic?"

Claire arched a brow. "Are you mocking my style?"

Jack shrugged. "You do own five jars of buttons."

"Those are curated."

He looked impressed. "Didn't know buttons could be curated."

"There's an art to it."

"Of course there is."

He stood slowly, brushing sawdust from his hands. The movement was quiet, casual, and for some reason, Claire felt every second of it.

She looked away.

"I'm not good at this kind of thing," she said.

Jack tilted his head. "Benches?"

She gave him a look.

He smiled. "You seem to be doing just fine."

Claire exhaled, stepped toward the low wall. Sat on it. Picked up an apple that had fallen nearby—small, blushed red at the edges, not quite ripe.

She turned it in her hands. "I wasn't meant to stay here."

"I know."

"I was going to sell the place. Move on. Go somewhere with… Deliveroo and public transport."

Jack smiled faintly. "We have a bus. Technically."

"It only runs on Tuesdays and gives up halfway to the garden centre."

He laughed.

Claire looked down at the apple, thumb tracing a faint nick in the skin.

"But then the bannister broke. And Lily arrived. And the whole place got glittered. And…"

She trailed off.

Jack sat beside her.

Not close enough to touch. Just close enough that she could feel the heat of him. The solid presence. The quiet *there-ness* that had always made her feel… less alone.

"Now I'm designing benches," she finished softly. "Apparently."

He didn't say anything.

Just sat with her.

Let it be what it was.

The trees rustled softly above them. A bee bumbled past. Somewhere in the distance, a kettle whistled from an open kitchen window.

Claire turned to look at him.

He wasn't watching her.

He was watching the corner of the green, measuring something only he could see.

And something about that—about the way he was always *building* something, even when no one noticed—made her chest ache in a way she didn't quite know what to do with.

So she said, "I vote for clean lines. And a curved backrest. And if you sneak in a fox carving, I will know."

Jack smiled without turning. "I'd never."

She smiled back.

And neither of them moved.

Because sometimes, in a Jenny Colgan kind of world, the biggest moments are the ones where nothing happens at all.

Claire walked home with the apple still in her hand.

She hadn't meant to keep it. Had picked it up without thinking. But it sat there now, warm from her palm, the skin flushed as if it had overheard something personal and didn't quite know what to do about it.

The lane back to Maple Hollow was quiet.

Not the kind of quiet that feels empty—but the kind that holds its breath. That carries things. Breezes and secrets and the smell of something baking three doors down.

She let her pace slow as she passed the crooked fence by the library garden, where someone had strung little solar lanterns between the railings and forgotten to take them down since midsummer. They flickered faintly in the afternoon sun, tiny spheres of gold in a world that hadn't asked for them but didn't seem to mind.

Claire ran her thumb over the apple skin again.

That *look* Jack had given her—not dramatic, not heavy. Just… *intentional*. Like she wasn't passing through this village. Like she was part of it now, in ways she hadn't agreed to but couldn't seem to undo.

The thought was both comforting and terrifying.

She reached the cottage, pushed open the gate, and stepped into the soft quiet of home. The light was slanting across the porch tiles, turning the dust motes into tiny constellations. The front garden still smelled faintly of rosemary and warm stone. Someone—probably Lily—had stuck a "Coming Soon: Rustic Romance!" flyer through the letterbox.

Claire rolled her eyes and picked it up on the way in.

The hallway greeted her with its usual mess: one boot lying sideways, a scarf that had detached itself from its hook, a teacup on the windowsill she didn't remember putting there. The sketch from Jack was still on the shelf, angled slightly askew. She reached out and straightened it, almost without thinking.

Then she went into the kitchen, placed the apple gently on the windowsill, and filled the kettle.

The silence settled around her like a cardigan—familiar, worn in, quietly kind.

She opened the back door to let the breeze in.

And stood there.

Just stood.

Breathing.

Letting the air move through her. Letting herself feel whatever it was that had stirred under the apple trees. Not certainty, exactly. But something *else*. Something that felt like a *beginning*, but not in the way she'd expected.

She made her tea. Added honey. Stirred slowly.

Then, without thinking too hard about it, she reached for the little pad she kept in the drawer next to the teaspoons—the one with coffee stains and recipes scrawled in the corners.

She flipped to a blank page.

Picked up a pencil.

And started sketching.

It wasn't perfect. The lines were off. The curve of the bench didn't sit quite right at first. But her hand kept moving.

A seat. Under apple trees.

Wide enough for two.

With clean lines and just a hint of something curved near the armrest—maybe a nod to the bannister, maybe just… comfort.

She drew quietly for a long while.

The kettle clicked off again behind her.

The village rolled on outside.

But Claire stayed right there, at the kitchen table, drawing something she hadn't known she needed to draw until she did.

And when she finally put the pencil down, there was a small smile at the corner of her mouth she didn't bother to hide—even though no one was watching.

Claire sat at the table long after the sketch was done.

The pencil lay beside it, slightly smudged at the tip, and her teacup had grown cold. But she didn't move.

The kitchen was lit only by the soft spill of afternoon sun curling in through the open back door. It touched the tablecloth. The mug. The edge of her paper. Everything just slightly glowing.

She wasn't used to this. Not this kind of stillness.

In London, everything had been fast, busy, directional. You were either going somewhere or catching up from being behind. There were never these long silences that didn't ask anything of you. That didn't require an answer or a performance.

She stood, finally, with a stretch that pulled at her shoulders and made her remember she hadn't eaten lunch.

She set the sketch aside and crossed to the pantry.

She wasn't sure what she was looking for—maybe something edible, maybe just distraction. But her hand reached automatically for the top shelf, behind the cereal boxes she hadn't opened since the week she moved in.

And there, tucked into the narrow sliver between a long-forgotten tin of lentils and a packet of custard powder that might pre-date the internet… was a small envelope.

Claire frowned.

It was yellowed slightly at the edges. Folded once, neatly. No stamp. Just a short name in fading blue ink.

Rosie.

Her breath caught.

She pulled it down carefully, wiping her hands on her jumper first like it might be fragile.

The flap wasn't sealed.

Inside was a note.

Written in a hand that looked like it had once been elegant but had grown shaky toward the end. There were faint tea rings on the paper, as though it had been read and re-read many times in the past.

Rosie,

Don't forget the apples. They're nearly ready. You always did say they tasted best just before the leaves turned. If I'm not back by Thursday, start the jam without me—but for heaven's sake, let the sugar boil longer this time. No one likes a runny batch, no matter what Mags says.

P.S. If you find the squirrel, it wasn't me.

– A.

Claire stared at it.

It was nothing. And also everything.

A life. A moment. Captured in the curl of a letter R and a gentle joke about jam. A friendship maybe. Or something more. She didn't know.

But it felt like a window into the house's heartbeat. Into the lives that had passed through it long before her, laughing in the kitchen and boiling sugar too fast and blaming mysterious squirrel appearances on each other.

She smiled without meaning to.

Then folded the letter carefully and sat back down at the table.

She looked again at the bench sketch. Then at the envelope.

Then, without quite knowing why, she flipped the page and began a new drawing.

This one was smaller. Looser.

A shelf.

A window.

Two jam jars and a kettle in the background.

And a tiny squirrel sitting smugly on the bannister post.

By the time she'd finished, the light had shifted again, angling low across the kitchen floor in a long golden stripe. Dust motes turned to glitter. Somewhere in the village a clock chimed five.

Claire stood again, slower this time, and reached for the radio.

She flicked it on, let it murmur through the cottage like company.

Then she made toast, cut it into triangles, and spread it with far too much butter.

And she sat by the window, the newly found letter beside her and her sketchbook open, and thought—not for the first time—that maybe she'd never meant to stay here…

But maybe the house had meant for her to come.

She didn't expect to fall asleep.

But sometime after the toast and the squirrel sketch, sometime between the third cup of tea and the slow jazz drifting from the radio, her eyelids grew heavy and the kitchen wrapped itself around her like a blanket.

Claire stirred just as the light began to fade fully from the window. The air had turned cooler, the radio had clicked off, and the shadows in the hallway had grown long and a little uncertain.

She sat up slowly, her neck creaking in protest, her hands still curled near the edge of the sketchbook.

The house was quiet again. Not hollow—but waiting.

Claire stood, stretched again, and padded into the hall to switch on the little lamp by the stairs. Its glow was soft, familiar, amber. The bannister gleamed slightly in the light, that subtle sheen from Jack's polish still catching at certain angles like it had been tended to by someone who cared.

She ran her fingers along the wood as she passed.

Upstairs, she changed into her oldest jumper—the one with the stretched sleeves and a neckline that had given up—and pulled her hair into a loose knot.

She didn't plan on going back down.

But the cottage pulled her back toward the kitchen anyway. One of the back windows had been left slightly open, and a breeze carried in the faintest trace of woodsmoke from a neighbour's stove and the first stirrings of village night.

She poured one last cup of tea. Didn't heat it. Just let it be warm enough.

And then, as if the moment had been waiting for her, she turned to head back through the hall—

And saw it.

There, tucked into the edge of the front door's letterbox flap, barely poking through, was a folded piece of card.

No postmark. No envelope.

Just her name. Scrawled in the same pencil-sharp, slightly rushed handwriting she was beginning to recognise too well.

Claire
Underlined once.

She opened it slowly.

Inside, written across the centre of a repurposed blueprint sketch—one of Jack's, she realised, for a trellis design she'd teased him about two weeks ago—was a short note:

If you're free tomorrow afternoon, I'll be on the green.
Bring the squirrel sketch.

– J.*

Claire stared at it.

It wasn't a declaration. Wasn't a plan.

Just… a nudge.

An invitation.

A step.

She folded the note carefully. Slipped it into the back of her sketchbook. Then turned off the kitchen light, the last of the dusk falling gently behind her.

Upstairs, Maple Hollow felt still and sure. The kind of stillness that didn't feel lonely anymore—just lived in. Full of stories. And maybe, if she was brave enough, room for a few more.

Claire climbed into bed and pulled the blanket up to her chin.

And somewhere between the note and the apple still on the windowsill, she let herself wonder—not what would happen next.

But what she wanted to.

And that—at last—felt like a beginning.

Chapter Twelve

"Tea First, Everything Else Later"

Claire woke to the sound of birds and a floorboard creaking—possibly from the house settling, possibly from a ghost with opinions about wallpaper. Either way, the room was full of early light, and the smell of September was creeping in through the cracked window: apples, damp grass, and the faint trace of woodsmoke from somewhere down the lane.

She blinked up at the ceiling for a moment, disoriented in that half-second before your brain remembers where you are, and then exhaled slowly.

Still here.

Still in Maple Hollow.

Still, apparently, a person who received cryptic notes from carpenters about squirrel sketches.

She rolled over, hugged the blanket a moment longer than she meant to, then finally climbed out of bed and shuffled down to the kitchen in wool socks and a cardigan that had definitely seen better days.

The kettle took its time. The old toaster, as usual, refused to cooperate without a little verbal encouragement and one strategic elbow bump. But eventually, she stood at the window with a slice of toast in one hand and her first mug of tea warming the other.

The apple from yesterday was still on the sill. It looked slightly more smug this morning.

Claire narrowed her eyes at it. "Don't start."

The apple said nothing.

Which, frankly, was the bare minimum.

She sat at the kitchen table, pulled the sketchbook toward her, and flipped to the bench drawing.

She didn't change anything.

Just… looked.

Took in the way the lines curved, how her hand had unconsciously followed the shape of that quiet corner of the green. She'd drawn it soft. Welcoming. A place to rest without being watched. A place where things didn't have to be said out loud to be understood.

She touched the corner of the paper where Jack's note was tucked.

It was still early.

Too early, probably.

But the kind of early that hummed with potential.

She stood, pulled on her boots, and decided she'd walk into the village.

She told herself it was for more tea bags.

But the sketchbook under her arm told a different story.

The village was already beginning to stir.

Frances was sweeping the steps of the town hall with dramatic flair, as though the leaves had personally offended her. Mags was rearranging the outside display at the bakery, though Claire suspected it was less about symmetry and more about staying near the cinnamon swirls while they cooled.

Lily was nowhere to be seen, which meant she was either still asleep or inventing a dance routine for the Harvest Ball in secret.

Claire walked slowly.

Not because she didn't know where she was going—but because she did.

And something about that felt… good.

Like the first time you realised you didn't need to check the map. That you knew where the creaky step was, where the postman turned, where the sunlight fell just right between the butcher's and the flower stall.

She reached the green a few minutes later.

Jack was already there.

He was crouched near the corner, one of the wooden boards balanced across his knees, a small toolkit beside him, and a pencil tucked behind one ear.

He looked up as she approached.

And smiled.

Not wide.

Not expectant.

Just… glad.

Claire hesitated for a second, then held up the sketchbook like a peace offering.

"You asked for it," she said.

Jack stood slowly, took it from her, and opened to the bench page.

He didn't say anything at first.

Just looked.

Then: "You gave it a curve."

Claire shrugged. "Looked better that way."

He nodded. "It does."

He flipped the page—and paused when he saw the squirrel.

Claire felt her cheeks flush. "That wasn't for you."

Jack smiled. "You drew my squirrel."

"You named it, remember?"

He looked at the little fox-tailed menace, perched smugly on the edge of a bannister rail, and laughed.

Claire felt something uncoil in her chest at the sound.

He handed the book back carefully. "Think you've just inspired the armrest carving."

She rolled her eyes. "Don't you dare."

But her smile said something else entirely.

They stood there for a moment, just outside the shadow of the apple trees. The green stretched out before them, quiet, golden. A light breeze stirred the edge of the canvas Jack had propped against a bench—a rough outline of the proposed build.

Claire reached out without thinking, touched the corner.

"Still need paint," she murmured.

He looked sideways at her. "I was thinking something soft. Warm. Not too perfect."

Claire nodded.

Then: "Like the house."

Jack gave her a look—soft, unreadable.

Then, simply: "Exactly like the house."

Jack pulled a pencil from behind his ear and handed it to her.

"Draw it," he said.

Claire blinked. "Draw what?"

He crouched beside one of the boards again, bracing it gently with one boot. "The curve. Show me what you meant. I trust you."

Claire hesitated. Then knelt beside him in the grass, smoothing her skirt beneath her.

"Here?" she asked.

He nodded, shifting just slightly to give her space.

She bent forward, sketching a gentle line across the pale grain of the wood—nothing dramatic. Just a soft arch that followed the shape of the hill beyond the apple trees.

Jack watched without speaking.

When she sat back, she felt suddenly unsure. "Too subtle?"

He shook his head. "It's perfect."

He touched the pencil to the same spot and drew a mirror line on the opposite side. His fingers brushed hers once, lightly, as he steadied the board.

Claire ignored the spark that followed. Or at least, tried to.

They worked quietly after that.

Jack marking out cuts and notches. Claire sketching decorative ideas in the margins of her notebook. A squirrel. A fox pawprint. A loop of ivy twining into a heart that she immediately scribbled out before he could see it.

The green was quiet but not still—Bev passed by at one point with her flower buckets, giving them both a look that said *hmm*. Frances waved from the churchyard, then tripped over a paving stone and pretended she hadn't.

The world ticked on.

And Claire… didn't mind.

Not being here. Not kneeling in the grass beside a man who knew how to listen without interrupting. Not the way his voice sounded when he explained what a mitre joint was like it was something everyone should know.

She could almost forget the rest of her life for a moment. The flat she hadn't visited in weeks. The inbox she hadn't opened. The fact that she was now designing romantic bench installations for a village ball she had no intention of dancing at.

Almost.

She stood up finally, stretching, brushing grass from her knees. Jack stood too, walking around the board to eye her pencil line from the other side.

Then—"Claire!"

They both turned.

Lily was trotting across the green, balancing a takeaway coffee cup in one hand and a basket in the other, wearing a shirt that read *I Glitter Bombed The Vicar And I'd Do It Again*.

Claire braced herself.

"I brought muffins!" Lily declared, holding out the basket like she was presenting treasure to royalty. "Also, guess what? The cider stall wants you and Jack to pose for a promotional flyer."

Claire made a noise somewhere between a laugh and a groan.

Jack just blinked. "Sorry—pose for what now?"

Lily grinned. "Apparently rustic romance sells beverages now. And you two are apparently 'the face of heritage flirtation.' Frances's words."

Jack looked at Claire.

Claire looked at the grass.

"Nope," she said. "Absolutely not."

"You get free cider," Lily offered.

Jack paused. "Maybe."

Claire elbowed him. "Don't encourage her."

Lily plopped down on the edge of the nearest bench and handed out muffins with the air of someone who had completely inserted herself into the narrative and had no plans of leaving.

"Anyway," she said, tearing into a muffin like a gremlin, "everyone thinks you're adorably slow-burn, by the way."

Claire nearly choked on hers. "Excuse me?"

"It's a good thing!" Lily said brightly. "Like Pride and Prejudice, but with sawdust and better snacks."

Jack coughed into his coffee.

Claire stared at the sky, considering starting a new life under a new name in a nearby hedgerow.

But then Jack looked at her. Just once. Just enough.

And smiled.

Not teasing.

Not smug.

Just... warm.

Like this didn't bother him.

Like she didn't have to run.

Like he was quite content to sit in the sun, eating muffins and building benches, and letting it all unfold at its own pace.

And somehow, that made her breathe again.

The muffins were good.

Suspiciously good, in fact.

Claire suspected Mags had made them and Lily had simply... redistributed them under her own chaotic brand. The texture was far too perfect for anything baked by someone who routinely measured flour using the "vibes" method.

Still, she didn't say anything.

It was peaceful now.

Lily had wandered off to interrogate someone about the status of hay bale seat covers, leaving her coffee cup behind like a tiny flag of conquest. Bev had packed up her flowers. Even the wind had softened, turning lazy and warm as the light shifted gold across the grass.

Jack was kneeling again, measuring out the final angle for the bench's backrest. His movements were steady, precise. There was a kind of quiet focus to him when he worked—nothing showy, just *present*. Like he was fully there with the wood, the grain, the moment.

Claire sat a few feet away, sketchbook open on her lap, not pretending to draw anymore. Just watching.

Not him—exactly.

Just... the way the shadows moved around him. The way the breeze tugged gently at his sleeves. The occasional crease of concentration between his brows when something didn't quite align.

He looked up suddenly and caught her staring.

She didn't look away fast enough.

Jack smiled. "All right?"

"Fine," she said, too fast. Then, trying to recover: "Just thinking."

He tilted his head. "Dangerous."

Claire gave a tight smile. "You've never even seen me dangerous."

Jack considered that. "True. But I have seen you wield ribbon under pressure."

She rolled her eyes, but the corner of her mouth tugged upward.

They worked in companionable silence for a while after that.

Jack adjusted a frame, marked a line. Claire traced the curve of the backrest again, checking the slope.

Every so often their hands brushed.

And every so often, neither of them moved away quite fast enough.

The shadows had lengthened noticeably by the time Jack stood back and dusted off his hands.

"That's it for today," he said. "Boards are marked. Cuts are prepped. Tomorrow we start building."

Claire nodded, brushing wood shavings from her lap. "Do I get safety goggles?"

Jack looked amused. "Do you want safety goggles?"

"I want the aesthetic of someone who knows what they're doing."

He stepped closer, gently plucked a small shaving of sawdust from her hair, and held it up like evidence.

"You'll need more than goggles," he said, deadpan.

She laughed, startled by the warmth that rose in her chest. By how easily he did that—**disarmed her**.

Jack stepped back again, not far. Just enough.

"I'll be here at ten tomorrow," he said. "With coffee. And possibly goggles."

Claire nodded. "Right. Ten."

Jack gave her a look then—one of those calm, grounding glances he did so well. The kind that said *I see you,* without asking for anything in return.

Then he turned, toolkit in hand, and walked slowly back across the green toward the lane.

Claire watched him go, heart ticking a little faster than she liked to admit.

Then she looked down at the bench frame lying in the grass.

It didn't look like much yet.

But she could see it now.

Could see how it might become something.

And maybe, just maybe, so could she.

The next morning arrived wrapped in that soft, pearly kind of light that made everything in the cottage feel freshly dusted—even if it wasn't.

Claire came downstairs to find the radio already murmuring on low, her favourite mug clean and waiting beside the kettle, and her boots sitting just inside the back door as if they knew she wouldn't be staying in long.

She stood in the kitchen for a while, sipping her tea, half-dressed and barefoot, watching the trees sway outside like they were stretching before a dance.

She wasn't nervous.

She told herself that twice.

It was just Jack.

Just a bench.

Just… a thing they were doing. Together. In public. Where people could see them. Possibly with muffins involved.

She burned her tongue on the tea.

By the time she got to the green, Jack was already there.

Of course he was.

He was setting up a small saw horse and a neat array of tools that looked far too competent for a village installation about bunting and cider. He wore the same rolled sleeves, the same easy stillness—but there was something else too. Something open. Like he wasn't trying to hide that he was happy to see her.

Claire raised a hand as she approached.

Jack straightened. "Morning."

She glanced at the setup. "This feels unnecessarily official."

"I brought backup," he said, lifting a takeout tray.

Claire took the offered cup with a mock-grave nod. "Well, if there's coffee, I suppose I'll stay."

He grinned, handed her a muffin from a paper bag, and gestured toward the pile of pre-marked timber.

"First up: cutting."

Claire's eyes widened. "You're letting me use power tools?"

He gave her a look. "Absolutely not."

"Smart man."

He showed her instead how to brace the planks while he cut, how to line up the joints and check the grain. It was rhythmic, meditative—something she hadn't expected to enjoy but found herself easing into without even realising it.

They worked in sync. He'd cut; she'd collect. He'd measure; she'd mark.

At one point she smudged pencil across her cheek without noticing, and Jack gently reached over with the cuff of his sleeve to wipe it away—his fingers warm and steady against her skin.

Neither of them said anything.

They didn't need to.

By late morning the bench frame had begun to take shape.

Nothing grand yet—just the bones of it. The sense of structure.

Claire stood back, hands on her hips, a smear of sawdust on her jeans.

"I didn't expect it to look like a real bench," she said. "I thought it would be… less benchy."

Jack glanced sideways. "High praise."

She smirked. "I mean, structurally speaking, this might hold actual people. I'm shocked."

He shook his head, smiling. "Remind me never to help you move house."

"You wouldn't," she said before she could stop herself.

Jack paused.

Claire bit her lip. "I mean. I wouldn't ask. Obviously."

He didn't push. Just picked up the drill again, handing her the next screw. "Next brace."

They worked in silence again—but this time, it buzzed a little. Not awkward. Not tense.

Just aware.

Like they'd said something without saying it.

Around noon, Lily wandered past carrying a crate of felt and a length of bunting that was somehow already tangled around her elbow.

"Oooh," she said, stopping short. "Look at you two! Actual bench progress. I'm not saying the villagers are placing bets, but… there's a clipboard."

Claire didn't even look up. "Is there an option that involves you minding your own business?"

"Nope," Lily said brightly. "Also, Ellie wants to know if you're registering this build as a metaphor."

Claire turned slowly. "What."

"You know. Foundations. Support. Emotional stability. Good wood grain."

Claire blinked.

Jack tried—very hard—not to laugh.

Lily grinned. "Anyway. If this ends in a public declaration and/or a bunting-themed wedding, I want a front row seat and control of the playlist."

And with that, she vanished into the hedgerow like a very colourful gremlin.

Claire exhaled, turned back to the bench. "I'm going to staple something to her."

Jack chuckled softly beside her. "Wouldn't help. She'd just bedazzle it."

Claire gave him a look, but couldn't help the smile pulling at her mouth.

They went back to work.

Side by side.

Quiet. Warm. Unfolding.

The bench came together in fits and starts.

One piece didn't fit quite right. Another had to be sanded down. Jack measured everything twice, then muttered something under his breath and measured again.

Claire, to her own surprise, found herself not minding at all.

There was something deeply calming about the method of it—the way each piece had to find its place, the small clink of tools, the grain of the wood under her fingers. It felt grounded. Honest. Nothing to overthink.

Jack barely spoke unless he needed to.

He worked the way he lived: practical, thoughtful, with the kind of quiet certainty that didn't ask for attention. He didn't try to impress. He didn't comment when Claire accidentally glued her sleeve to the clamp. He just handed her a new one and offered a spare jumper from his bag without making a thing of it.

By the time the backrest was finally attached and the frame stood upright on its own, Claire felt oddly… proud.

Not because it was beautiful—though it was shaping into something quite lovely—but because she'd helped. Because something she'd touched was now standing in the world in a way it hadn't been before.

Jack straightened slowly, brushing sawdust from his jeans. "Want to try it?"

Claire looked at the bench. Then at him.

"You first. You built the thing."

Jack smiled, but instead of sitting, he stepped aside and gestured with a little nod.

Claire rolled her eyes, but stepped forward and sat gingerly on the newly placed wood.

It held.

More than that—it welcomed.

The angle of the back was perfect. The seat wide enough. The view looked out over the curve of the green, the line of trees, the corner of the bakery roof just beyond the church spire.

Claire exhaled.

Jack sat beside her.

Not close. Not far.

Just… there.

They didn't talk for a long moment.

And then Jack said quietly, "I'm glad you stayed."

She turned to look at him.

His eyes didn't leave the trees.

"I mean," he said, more quickly now, "when the bannister broke and everything was still a mess—I wasn't sure you would."

Claire hesitated.

"I wasn't sure I would either," she said softly.

They sat in silence again, the wind brushing the tops of the trees, the sky just starting to shift toward afternoon gold.

Claire thought about saying more.

About the sketch. The letter. The way he always seemed to know when to leave a room—and when to stay.

But the words stayed caught somewhere behind her ribs.

So instead, she said, "We'll need to varnish it."

Jack smiled. "Tomorrow?"

She nodded.

He stood. "I'll bring lunch."

She walked home slowly.

Not because she was tired—but because she didn't want to rush the feeling still curling gently inside her chest.

By the time she reached the cottage, the sun had dropped behind the tallest trees and the air had taken on that early evening hush that made things feel softer somehow.

She let herself in, toed off her boots, and padded into the kitchen.

The radio clicked on with a gentle hum.

The apple from the windowsill was gone—finally turned into a small jar of compote she'd made the night before on a whim. It sat on the counter now, slightly crooked, labelled with masking tape that read: *probably edible.*

She smiled to herself, filled the kettle, and stood with her hands wrapped around her mug as it boiled.

The bench image was still open in her sketchbook. But beside it now were notes: a swirl of vines, a lantern idea, a small scrawl that read *bring cushion?*

She added one more line, quietly, before closing the book.

Maybe ask him about the squirrel's name.

That night, she made toast again, because it was easy and warm and reminded her of the first week in the cottage when everything had felt upside down.

Now it felt... less so.

Not fixed.

Not certain.

But full.

And that, for tonight, was enough.

Claire curled up on the sofa with a blanket over her legs and her hair still faintly smelling of sawdust and outside. The lamp on the side table cast a soft glow across the room, picking out the uneven walls and the shelf of cookbooks she still hadn't opened.

The bench sketch sat beside her, closed now.

She didn't need to look at it again.

She could see it in her head. Every line. Every brush of grain. Every place her hand had passed beside his.

She sipped her tea slowly, letting it warm her from the inside out.

Outside, the wind was picking up just enough to rattle the old trellis by the back gate. It made the house feel alive somehow—like it was stretching its bones. Settling in for the night.

She glanced at her phone, then at the window, then back again.

Did she expect a message?

She told herself no.

Told herself she didn't want one.

But when there wasn't a ping, or a knock, or a note slid under the door… she felt it.

That flicker of something.

Not quite disappointment.

Not quite longing.

Something between.

She tucked her knees closer under the blanket.

Maybe she wasn't ready to say it.

Maybe he wasn't either.

But still.

She picked up the notebook again and, without really thinking, flipped to the back page.

There, in the smallest handwriting she had, she wrote:

*Things I didn't expect to want:

- Benches
- Muffins
- Someone who waits until I'm ready*

She stared at it for a long time.

Then closed the book.

And went to bed smiling.

Chapter Thirteen

"Bunting, Benches, and the Invasion of the Women"

Claire had only just sat down with her second cup of tea when the knock came at the door.

Not the polite kind.

The kind that said *I've brought something I'm calling a snack and also I've possibly made decisions on your behalf.*

Claire opened the door to find **Ellie** standing on the front step, hair up in a messy knot, cheeks pink from the morning air, and a carrier bag hanging from one arm with the enthusiasm of someone delivering either baked goods or mild emotional sabotage.

"I brought croissants," Ellie said, breezing past her into the hall. "Also, we have a problem."

Claire blinked. "Good morning?"

"Oh right, yes, good morning, you look charmingly dishevelled, now make more tea."

Claire followed her into the kitchen, slightly dazed. "What kind of problem?"

"The bunting committee has split into factions," Ellie said, dropping the bag on the table and pulling out a box of still-warm pastries. "One side wants traditional village tartan. The other wants a Regency theme in honour of the bench."

Claire paused, kettle in hand. "The bench has a theme now?"

"Oh, you've started something," Ellie said with a smirk. "Lily's drawing up blueprints for a 'vignette moment.' There's talk of a flower arch. Frances has ordered mood lighting. We're dangerously close to interpretive dance."

Claire groaned.

Ellie handed her a croissant. "It's not your fault. You just exist in a way that makes people want to embroider things."

Claire muttered something unprintable and took a bite.

The croissant was excellent. Buttery. Possibly laced with subtle peer pressure.

"I just wanted to build a bench," Claire said.

"You wanted to build it with *Jack*," Ellie pointed out. "Which, around here, is basically the same as announcing an engagement at the cheese counter."

Claire choked. "We're not—! I mean, it's not like that. He's… we're… building things."

"You're adorable when you're defensive," Ellie said, standing to poke around Claire's mug cupboard like she lived there. "Also, Lily's on her way."

Claire closed her eyes. "Why?"

"To measure you for a cape."

"Absolutely not."

"She's calling it 'whimsical rural drapery.'"

Claire dropped her forehead to the table. "I'm going to move into the shed."

Ellie sipped her tea, unbothered. "Too late. That's where she's setting up the embroidery loom."

They reached the green an hour later, croissant crumbs in their pockets, travel mugs in hand, and Lily already spinning in circles with a length of velvet and a clipboard.

"The curve is *sublime*," Lily declared, stopping short in front of the bench and clutching the air like a theatre director moved to tears. "It's giving longing. It's giving repose. It's giving Keira Knightley on a windy moor."

Claire glanced at Ellie. "Make it stop."

"I can't," Ellie said. "She's in phase three. There's bunting math."

Jack was already there, of course.

Measuring angles. Checking alignment. Wearing the same worn jumper and that maddening calm that made Claire want to both hug and hex him.

He looked up when he saw her.

Not with surprise.

With quiet certainty.

"Morning," he said.

"Apparently we're in a Regency romance now," Claire replied.

Jack nodded slowly. "Do I need a cravat?"

Lily beamed. "We're working on it."

The day passed in slow layers.

They varnished the wood—soft strokes, golden finish, the scent of polish filling the air. Jack showed her how to brush with the grain. Claire tried not to care how nice his voice sounded when he explained things. Ellie and Lily alternated between helpful commentary and wild speculation about harvest bouquets and proposal lighting.

Bev dropped off biscuits. Mags offered ribbon samples. Someone brought cider and forgot to take it away again.

The village moved around them like weather.

And Claire found herself smiling more than she meant to.

Not just because of the bench.

Not even because of Jack.

But because this—this moment, this rhythm, this *life*—was starting to feel like hers.

She didn't say it.

But she felt it.

Settling in her bones like something warm and inevitable.

By late afternoon, the crowd had thinned.

Lily had twirled off to an emergency Harvest Ball subcommittee session involving lantern colours and "symbolic vegetables." Ellie was last seen muttering something about bunting elasticity and gin. The air had cooled a little, the sky beginning to pink at the edges, and the green was scattered with the remnants of the day—empty coffee cups, rogue petals, and one lonely clipboard with a sketch of Claire wearing a cape that definitely hadn't been authorised.

Claire stood beside the finished bench, one hand on the newly varnished backrest.

It was dry now. Smooth. The colour a warm golden brown that caught the late sun beautifully.

It looked… real.

Permanent.

Like something that would last.

Jack was quietly packing up tools nearby, stacking boards, wiping down the last of the brushes with an old cloth that looked suspiciously like it had once been a shirt.

Claire watched him for a second, then bent to gather the stray scraps of ribbon Lily had somehow left draped across the grass like clues in a treasure hunt.

"Sorry about all the bunting chaos," she said, brushing past him to toss the ribbons into a paper bag.

He looked up, smiling slightly. "I like it."

Claire raised an eyebrow. "You like the bunting?"

"No," he said. "I like… this. People laughing. Making things. You, cursing at glue."

"I didn't curse," she lied.

"You absolutely did."

She tried not to smile.

They worked in silence a bit longer, clearing the green slowly, each in their own rhythm.

When she stooped to pick up a dropped cloth and stood too fast, her shoulder brushed against his—just briefly.

Jack didn't move away.

Neither did she.

He glanced down at her, and something passed between them then. Not dramatic. Not cinematic.

Just… *true*.

The kind of moment that Jenny Colgan writes with a pause instead of a kiss. A breath instead of a declaration.

"I kept thinking," Claire said, still looking at the bench, "that I'd only stay for a few weeks. That the house was just a detour."

Jack was quiet beside her.

"But now," she went on, "I've made jam. I've varnished furniture. There's a squirrel in my sketchbook. And apparently, I have a signature curve."

Jack smiled. "You do."

Claire turned to him. "It's ridiculous."

"It suits you."

She rolled her eyes. "Don't start."

But he was already smiling wider now, that quiet, steady smile that made her chest do unreasonable things.

They stood side by side for another long moment, watching the sun begin to slip behind the trees.

Jack lifted the last bag of tools and looked at her, soft and certain.

"Same time tomorrow?"

Claire nodded. "I'll bring the tea."

He paused.

Then added, very gently, "And maybe stay a little after?"

She looked up at him.

Met his gaze.

Felt it land somewhere low and unguarded in her chest.

"Maybe," she said.

He nodded once.

Then walked away across the green, his boots soft in the grass, the toolkit swinging lightly at his side.

Claire watched him go.

Then sat on the bench they'd built together, hands resting on her knees, and let the last of the day settle over her like a blanket.

She didn't look at her phone.

Didn't check the time.

Didn't rush.

She just sat.

And for the first time since she'd arrived in this village full of foxes and felt flowers and improbable muffins… she didn't feel like she was waiting for something else to begin.

She felt like she was already in it.

Lily was in full flight.

Not literally—though the velvet cape she'd borrowed from the community hall's costume bin did give her a certain wind resistance as she trotted purposefully down the lane, clipboard flapping like a wing and a half-peeled banana in her pocket for "nourishment."

She was late, again, for her meeting with Cynthia and Bev about the *Mood Zones* for the Harvest Ball. The last time she'd been late, they'd assigned her to *bin protocol*, and she had no intention of spending another year artistically arranging recycling bags around decorative gourds.

She took the shortcut through the churchyard.

This was a mistake.

Because halfway between the old elm and the questionable statue of Saint Elfrida holding a loaf of bread like a football, Lily's cape caught on a bramble—and her clipboard launched itself through the air, arcing gracefully toward the vicar's vegetable patch.

"NO!" Lily shouted, flailing after it.

The clipboard landed squarely in a basket of beetroots.

Which would have been fine.

Except that **Ellie** was standing next to them, arms folded, eyebrow already raised.

"Well," Ellie said calmly, "you've finally done it. You've assaulted the vicar's root vegetables."

Lily untangled herself, panting. "They looked judgy."

"They're beets."

"They were glaring at me."

Ellie bent to retrieve the clipboard, flipping it open. "You've changed the dress code from 'village rustic' to 'late period Georgian romance meets rustic bardcore.'"

"It tested well on Pinterest," Lily said with dignity.

Ellie gave her a long look. "You're not *on* Pinterest."

"No, but I channel it spiritually."

She reached for the clipboard. Ellie held it back.

"Did you actually talk to Claire and Jack before assigning them a 'slow-burn spotlight moment during the cider toast'?"

Lily blinked. "Define 'talk.'"

"You're unbelievable."

"You say that" Lily said, plucking a beet from the basket and sniffing it as though it might tell her a secret, "but when this ball is the talk of Gloucestershire, you'll thank me."

Ellie handed her the clipboard. "When this ball is reported in *The Guardian* as the event where the cider caught fire and someone proposed on a bench made of meringue, I'm denying I ever knew you."

Lily's eyes sparkled. "Meringue…"

"No," Ellie said flatly.

"But structurally—"

"No."

Lily sighed and tucked the beet into her bag. "Fine. Back to the original plan."

"Which was?"

"Subtlety. Drama. Apple-scented fog."

Ellie pinched the bridge of her nose. "I'm going to need gin."

The sun was starting to slip low when Claire finally got home.

The kind of soft golden dusk that made the cottage look like it belonged in a storybook. The ivy on the porch glowed green. The windows caught the last of the light and bounced it back with a kind of quiet pride.

She let herself in, toeing off her boots and hanging her jacket over the hook that still wobbled if you breathed near it.

The kitchen smelled faintly of rosemary and wood polish and something sweet she couldn't place—possibly the ghost of a jam tart.

She didn't go straight to the kettle this time.

She stood a moment in the doorway, breathing.

The day had pressed in gently but completely. Not just the bench. Not just Jack.

The whole thing.

The laughter. The varnish. The ridiculousness of bunting physics and Lily's velvet cape flapping like a bat in mating season.

Claire felt… full.

Not overwhelmed. Not spun out.

Just… like something was beginning to settle inside her, even if she hadn't agreed to it yet.

She crossed to the table and opened the back door, letting in the evening breeze and the faint, familiar sound of the village closing down for the night.

Birds. Distant voices. One lone laugh from someone outside the pub.

Then, her phone buzzed.

She checked it with the mild dread of someone half-expecting a work email from a life she hadn't lived in weeks.

It was a message from Ellie.

You're officially a subplot. Just thought you should know.
Lily says "spotlight moment during cider toast."
I say buy blackout sunglasses and run.

Claire stared at the screen.

Then it buzzed again.

This time: a photo.

A blurry shot of Lily holding a clipboard, a sprig of lavender, and what looked suspiciously like a theatrical fog machine.

Claire exhaled through her nose.

Then laughed.

Properly.

The kind of laugh that slipped out before she could stop it, and made her feel—just for a second—like herself again. The version of herself who wasn't pretending, or waiting, or trying to figure out what came next.

She texted back.

If I get fogged during cider, I'm suing.

Ellie replied instantly.

Already making the T-shirts.
"Bench. Bunting. Betrayal."

Claire dropped the phone onto the table and shook her head.

The ridiculousness of this place.

The sweetness of it.

The mess.

The people.

Her people, apparently.

She crossed to the cupboard, pulled down a box of biscuits, and poured herself a small glass of something that claimed to be elderflower and may or may not contain actual flowers.

Then, as the light faded to gold and the cottage wrapped around her like the softest, safest cardigan, Claire sat back in her chair, looked out through the open door…

And smiled.

Because chaos was coming.

Because Lily was unstoppable.

And because, for once in her life—

She wasn't trying to stop it.

The next morning arrived with suspicious brightness.

The kind of yellow, optimistic sunlight that usually meant something was about to go wrong—or at least get *very* over-organised.

Claire came downstairs to find a note had been pushed through her letterbox.

Folded once.

Tied with twine.

Sprinkled—yes, actually *sprinkled*—with lavender petals and what might have been a hint of glitter.

She picked it up like it might explode.

Unfolded it.

Read the handwriting.

And sighed.

Dearest Claire,

Due to unforeseen musical developments (aka Bev's ukulele group pulling out after last year's cider incident), you are now—CONGRATULATIONS!—in charge of finalising the Harvest Ball evening entertainment.

A shortlist of approved themes is enclosed. You are *welcome.*

Yours in anticipation and questionable artistic vision,
Lily x

Claire turned the page.

There was, indeed, a shortlist.

It included:

- "Folkloric romance: With flutes."
- "Harvest Disco: Glitter pumpkins encouraged."
- "Hay Bale Ballet."
- "Claire's Choice: Whatever feels right to your soul. Don't overthink it. But also don't ruin it."

Claire stared at the paper.

Then out the window.

Then back at the paper.

She made toast. Poured tea. Ate in silence.

The letter sat smugly in the centre of the table like it had done something clever.

By the time she'd finished breakfast, a second note had been posted.

This one was from Frances. It read:

Please confirm the playlist by noon. I refuse to dance to anything that includes animal sounds or synthesised flute.

Claire placed her head gently against the table.

Then reached for her phone.

To: Ellie
Subject: The Fall of Western Civilisation
Message: I'm now in charge of musical programming. Please send gin.**

Claire stood in her kitchen, a half-buttered crumpet in one hand and two competing lists of folk songs in the other. One had been annotated in pink glitter pen with "✨ energy!" scrawled next to every third item. The other contained a formal rejection of tracks "involving excessive fiddling," signed by Frances and underlined three times.

The toast had gone cold.

The tea was lukewarm.

Her brain was somewhere in the middle of composing a polite resignation letter to the entire county of Gloucestershire.

She glanced at the clock. It was 9:47.

At 9:02, Lily had sent her a Pinterest board titled *"Rustic Romance: Sounds to Swoon To."*
At 9:21, Ellie had texted: *"Lily just tried to hire a wind chime ensemble. I talked her down to interpretive morris dancing. You're welcome."*

Claire dropped the toast, wiped her hands, and dragged the kitchen chair over to the sideboard where she'd hidden her emergency biscuits. She ate one dry, leaning against the counter, staring out the window like a woman preparing to face a firing squad made entirely of bunting and emotional projection.

Then, without fanfare, the doorbell rang.

She opened it to find **Jack** standing there.

He held two takeaway cups and a paper bag, and wore an expression that suggested he'd seen something in the stars that morning and decided to intervene before the planets fully misaligned.

"Morning," he said. "You looked like you might need this."

Claire blinked. "Is it gin?"

"Better," he said, holding up the bag. "Warm cinnamon buns. And coffee that could wake the dead."

She stared at him.

Then stepped back wordlessly and gestured him inside.

He walked past her like he belonged there. Set the coffee down. Handed her the bag.

Claire sat slowly at the table, opened the top of the pastry bag, inhaled, and groaned.

"I may never love another human as much as I love this cinnamon bun," she said.

Jack sat down opposite her. "I'll take that as a compliment."

Claire tore off a corner, chewed, and exhaled. "I'm in charge of music now."

He raised an eyebrow. "You play anything?"

"Only emotionally."

He sipped his coffee. "Want help?"

"With the music?"

"With the meltdown."

Claire paused.

Then handed him the Frances-approved list. "You can start by decoding her annotation system. I think three asterisks means *do not* include. But it might also mean 'play only during cider toast while facing due north.'"

Jack studied it for a moment. "You know what you need?"

"Professional help?"

He stood, rummaged in her drawer until he found a pencil, then returned to the table and circled three tracks. "These. Play these. Easy tempo. Danceable. One mentions autumn leaves. No synthesised flute."

Claire stared at him. "Are you secretly in a ceilidh band?"

"No," he said. "But my nan was banned from one."

By mid-morning, they'd narrowed the list to something resembling functional. Claire was still vaguely panicked, but the edge had softened. Something about Jack's presence calmed the air around her—as if, by standing still long enough, he gave her permission to breathe again.

They drifted naturally from music talk to bench varnish checks to cider logistics. He offered to help move the benches to the hall later. She mumbled something about not trusting anyone else with the curves. He didn't comment, but his mouth twitched at the corners like he'd saved the thought for later.

The morning light filtered across the table, warm and dusty, and for a moment the cottage felt like it was exactly what it claimed to be: safe, lived-in, hers.

Until—

BANG.

A loud clatter from the garden. Followed by a very familiar, chaotic voice shouting, "It's FINE! I meant to fall that way!"

Claire closed her eyes.

Jack sipped his coffee. "And there's Lily."

Claire stood and opened the back door to find Lily halfway through her own obstacle course of dropped sketchbooks, a folding stool, and a large wicker basket of what looked like pumpkins in tiny wigs.

"Artistic concept planning," Lily called cheerfully, brushing mud off her trousers. "Also, I brought inspiration snacks."

"What does that even mean?" Claire asked, helping her upright.

"Cheese cubes shaped like moons," Lily said proudly. "For the Moonlight Market."

She spotted Jack, beamed, and shouted over Claire's shoulder: "Oh good, you're here. I need a strong male back."

Jack choked slightly on his coffee.

Claire turned slowly. "You're not lifting anything."

"No, but I need him to model for the cider stall signage. Shirt optional."

Claire muttered something that sounded suspiciously like *"I'm moving into the attic,"* and went back inside.

The rest of the morning passed in an escalating swirl of *Colgan-style* countryside absurdity.

Lily made three mood boards. Ellie sent a photo of Bev holding a pumpkin with googly eyes. Jack stayed, quietly helpful, quietly watching.

Claire found herself smiling more often than not. Not because the chaos had slowed. But because she'd stopped fighting it.

And maybe—just maybe—because something in the middle of it all was starting to feel like home.

Even if it had glitter on it.

The afternoon arrived in a tumble of too many lists and not nearly enough extension cords.

Claire found herself somehow volunteered to help run three different stalls, source "harvest-appropriate twinkle lights," and mediate a disagreement about whether the jam tasting table should feature scones or crumpets (Frances was firmly in the "scones are tradition" camp; Lily was arguing for crumpet innovation).

Jack, to his credit, stayed nearby for most of it—ostensibly to help move the benches into place outside the village hall, but in practice acting as a kind of quiet, grounding shadow to Claire's increasingly erratic orbit.

By two o'clock, the green was a flurry of activity.

Pop-up tents unfolded like origami under duress. Hay bales arrived via Bev's cousin's trailer, which was also inexplicably full of papier-mâché mushrooms. The cider stall was up, decorated with twine and honesty box signs and a giant wooden spoon someone had carved last year and forgotten to take home.

Claire stood with her clipboard—she now had one too; Ellie had given it to her with a smirk and a "welcome to the club"—and tried to look like she had control over any of it.

She didn't.

But no one seemed to mind.

There was a kind of joy in the chaos, in the small failures and ridiculous victories. The way Bev shouted across the green for someone to "fetch the decorative gourd netting." The way Lily dragged a miniature maypole into place and declared it a symbol of seasonal rebirth. The way Frances muttered about fire safety while stringing fairy lights with the kind of expertise only achieved by someone who'd once rewired her own oven.

Claire tried to help. She really did.

But every time she finished one task, someone appeared with another.

"Claire! Can you test the bunting tension?"

"Claire! Lily says we need three kinds of chutney now!"

"Claire! Where's the speaker jack for the folky Spotify playlist that doesn't make Frances cry?"

She lost count of how many times she said "one second" and forgot what she was doing halfway through a sentence.

Jack found her around three, crouched beneath the jam table trying to un-knot an extension cord that had formed what appeared to be a sentient tangle.

"You all right under there?" he asked.

Claire sighed. "Do you have wire cutters?"

Jack peered at the mess. "No, but I have patience and long fingers."

She handed him the cable and flopped backwards onto the grass.

"I think the pumpkin display is judging me."

Jack glanced toward the table where Lily had arranged several pumpkins with carefully carved faces, each bearing a different emotional expression.

"They *are* expressive," he said diplomatically.

Claire covered her eyes with her forearm. "I have no idea what I'm doing."

Jack didn't answer.

She peeked at him through her fingers.

He was still unwinding the cable—calm, methodical, not laughing at her.

"You don't have to stay," she said quietly.

"I know," he replied.

"But you are."

He met her eyes then. "You looked like you were trying to do everything yourself. Figured I'd rather be here than watch you fall over carrying six crates of jam."

Claire didn't say thank you. Didn't need to.

The moment sat between them like a settled stone.

By late afternoon, things were coming together—imperfectly, brilliantly, Maple Hollow-style.

The cider stall was positioned beside the bench, now draped with a plaid throw and two very unnecessary velvet cushions (Lily's doing). The maypole stood proudly near the apple bobbing trough. The food tables were groaning under the weight of pies, pasties, pickled things in jars, and a surprising amount of toffee.

Claire found herself, clipboard still in hand, watching it all from a short distance.

The sun was beginning to dip, casting everything in that golden sheen that made even the bramble hedge look cinematic.

She saw Ellie waving someone over with her wine bottle. Frances marching with purpose toward the speaker setup, clearly determined to eliminate every last banjo track. Lily was adjusting the pumpkins again, muttering to them like a stage manager prepping temperamental actors.

And Jack—

Jack was leaning against the side of the cider stall, arms crossed, watching her with quiet amusement.

Not interfering.

Just there.

Solid.

Present.

It did something strange to her ribcage.

"Claire!"

She turned.

Lily was bounding across the green with purpose.

Claire immediately tensed. "No. Whatever it is, no."

Lily beamed. "They want you to open the Market tomorrow. Say a few words. Welcome everyone."

Claire blinked. "Why me?"

"Because you're the heart of it this year," Lily said without irony. "You built the bench. You kept the playlist flute-free. You made Mags cry with your blackberry sponge."

"I didn't mean to!"

Lily winked. "That's when it's most effective."

Claire groaned. "I can't do speeches."

"Sure you can," Lily said, already handing her a sheet of scribbled notes that included the phrase *'autumnal romance is not just for books'*. "It's just talking. With sincerity. While probably holding cider."

Claire looked at the notes. "Is this… are these your vows from the Harvest Ball dream wedding scenario?"

"Adaptable," Lily said proudly.

Claire looked over Lily's shoulder to see Jack watching them still, his face unreadable now, the expression softer.

She folded the notes.

Put them in her pocket.

And said, "Fine. But no fog machine."

Lily grinned. "What about dry ice?"

Claire walked away.

But she didn't say no.

The crowd was thinning as the light deepened.

A few of the older volunteers peeled away first, nodding at Claire and murmuring things like "well done, dear" and "that bunting's the best we've ever had, if you ignore the glitter." Mags herded the last of the jam jars off the table with military precision, muttering under her breath about "custard proximity protocols." Ellie had taken Lily home under the guise of checking lantern stock, but Claire suspected it was just an excuse to stop her from ordering a fog machine online.

The green had settled into that golden-hour hush—*still*, but not *silent*.

The kind of moment where breath felt deeper, colours felt warmer, and everything seemed briefly in balance.

Claire stood near the bench, her fingers brushing the edge of its varnished back.

It still surprised her how much she liked the way it turned out.

There was a pride in it—not loud, not boastful. Just something *settled*. Something earned.

And maybe that was the difference here.

She hadn't planned it.

Hadn't aimed for it.

But the bench had happened. The ball was happening. This whole… *life* seemed to be slowly unfurling itself around her, stitch by stitch, like someone had picked up a thread she didn't even realise she'd dropped.

"Looks good," came Jack's voice from just behind her.

Claire turned to find him watching the scene with a quiet satisfaction that made her chest ache in a way she wasn't ready to admit.

"Suspiciously good," she said, folding her arms.

He raised an eyebrow. "You think something's going to catch fire?"

"I think the pumpkins might unionise."

Jack gave a soft laugh, then sat on the bench, patting the space beside him.

Claire hesitated for only a second before joining him.

They sat without speaking.

The bench creaked just slightly under them, settling into its place as if it had always been there.

Jack's arm brushed hers.

Not deliberately.

Not obviously.

But he didn't move it.

And neither did she.

Across the green, Bev was arguing with someone about apple tart slicing protocol. Children darted between hay bales. The cider barrel glinted slightly in the amber light.

And for a moment, it all felt far too much like home.

Claire stared out over the green, her fingers grazing the edge of the seat.

"I don't know how I ended up here," she said quietly.

Jack didn't turn to look at her. Just sat, steady beside her.

"But," she added, "I think… I'm glad I did."

There was a pause.

Then, softly: "Me too."

He didn't say more.

Didn't need to.

His arm stayed where it was.

And she let it.

The light slipped lower.

The village murmured around them.

And for the first time in a long time, Claire didn't feel like she had to fix or plan or prove anything.

She just had to sit.

And stay.

Chapter Fourteen

"Tea, Threats, and a Basket of Bribery"

Claire woke to the distinct sound of optimism.

Birdsong.

Kettle rumble.

And, beneath it all, the faintest echo of accordion music wafting in from somewhere she couldn't quite place.

She blinked at the ceiling, blanket wrapped half around her leg, hair aggressively misbehaving, and muttered, "No one warned me this village had a musical phase."

The cottage was warm. Cosy, even. The kind of temperature that made it easy to stay in bed and pretend she didn't have a thousand things to do, a speech to fake confidence through, and a bench that now doubled as a backdrop for community-level matchmaking.

Still, she swung her legs over the side of the bed and padded downstairs.

The kitchen greeted her like an old friend: slightly chaotic, faintly flour-dusted, with the unmistakable presence of a half-finished scone and a mug from yesterday that she still hadn't washed.

She flicked on the kettle and opened the door to let in the morning air.

And there it was.

A basket.

Sitting squarely on the doormat like a gift from a well-meaning cult.

It was wrapped in cellophane. Tied with gingham. A tiny tag attached with twine read:

Claire –
For courage, charisma, and distraction from your irrational fear of public speaking.
– Lily
(P.S. Please wear something whimsical.)

Inside the basket were:

- Two lavender shortbreads
- A miniature bottle of something fizzy
- A ribboned hair clip in the shape of a fox
- A playlist scribbled on paper titled *"Claire's Ball of Calm"* which included, curiously, *Celine Dion* and something called "Ye Olde Disco Lament"

Claire picked it up, turned in a slow circle, and said aloud to no one, "It's not too late to emigrate."

The postman, passing at that precise moment, tipped his cap and said, "Canada's nice this time of year."

She went back inside.

By ten o'clock, she was fully dressed, toast-adjacent, and holding her speech notes like they were nuclear codes. She'd rewritten them five times. At one point, she'd considered faking laryngitis. At another, she'd genuinely tried to outsource the entire task to Ellie, who'd laughed so hard she'd pulled a muscle.

Now the notes were scrawled in the back of her sketchbook, somewhere between a doodle of the bench and an emergency cider recipe Lily had handed her during "contingency hour."

The Market started at noon.

She had two hours to panic.

Claire made another cup of tea.

Burned her toast slightly.

And opened the door again just as someone knocked.

It was Jack.

Wearing his usual calm like a second jumper, holding a thermos and what looked like two wrapped bacon rolls.

"You look," he said, pausing just enough to make her nervous, "ready."

Claire snorted. "I'm three seconds from hiding behind the compost bin."

He handed her a roll. "Then you'll give a wonderful speech. From behind a bin."

She stepped aside to let him in, grateful for the warmth in his voice. He didn't try to fix her nerves. Just sat quietly at the kitchen table, drinking tea, letting her exist.

She handed him the playlist.

He raised an eyebrow. "Ye Olde Disco Lament?"

Claire shrugged. "Lily."

"Obviously."

They walked together to the green just before noon, past the now-legendary bench, past the lanterns being lit early "for mood," past the cider barrels now decorated with autumn leaves and inexplicably—googly eyes.

Claire felt the buzz of the village all around her. The rustle of stalls. The laughter of children. The smell of pastry and roasted apples and one slightly burnt toffee stand that might have been manned by Barry.

She felt it rise inside her.

Not fear, exactly.

Just *more*.

And Jack, walking beside her, said softly, "They're all here because of you, you know."

Claire looked at him.

"No one else could've pulled this together," he added. "Bench. Ball. All of it."

She looked away, smiling at the grass.

"Thanks," she said.

And then, as the crowd parted and Frances waved her toward the mic—still fiddling with the dials, muttering about "decibel dignity"—Claire stepped forward.

Not entirely confident.

But no longer hiding.

And that, in Maple Hollow, was more than enough.

The crowd was thicker than Claire expected.

Not packed, exactly. Not bustling like a festival. But full—*comfortably*, unavoidably full. Every bench taken. Blankets on the grass. A group of children halfway into an unofficial game of "Pumpkin Heist." Bev had somehow roped in a brass quartet from a neighbouring village, and Lily was already circulating with a clipboard and a woven crown of something floral and probably flammable.

Claire stood at the edge of it all, holding a microphone with clammy hands, and wondering—not for the first time—how a simple cottage renovation had somehow landed her in the middle of a community-wide celebration of squash.

Frances stepped forward, nodded crisply, and tapped the mic.

"Welcome, everyone, to the seventy-sixth Annual Maple Hollow Harvest Market," she announced, her voice ringing out across the green like the Queen's cousin had decided to open a raffle.

Muted applause.

Claire's stomach lurched.

"And now," Frances went on, "we begin with a few words from the woman responsible for the most attractive seating arrangement we've had since 1994—Claire Sutton!"

The applause picked up.

Claire blinked. Swallowed.

And stepped forward.

The mic squeaked once.

She cleared her throat. "Um. Hi."

A few scattered chuckles. Lily gave her two thumbs up from behind a hay bale.

"I didn't really plan to say anything," Claire continued. "Which will surprise absolutely no one who knows Lily."

More laughter this time.

"But I did want to say thank you. For… this. For welcoming me. For pretending not to notice when I painted myself into a corner. Literally. That hallway still smells like lavender regret."

Ellie barked a laugh.

Claire smiled, just a little.

"I came here to fix a house. And maybe—maybe find some space to breathe again. What I found instead was bunting, and baked goods, and more unsolicited advice than I knew what to do with."

Pause. Soft laughter. She glanced sideways and caught Jack watching her—arms folded, smile crooked, not blinking.

"But more than that," she said quietly, "I found something I didn't expect. A community. A group of people who show up. With muffins. And saws. And questionable taste in playlist names."

Lily blew her a kiss.

"And now I have a bench. And friends. And a deep suspicion that one of the pumpkins is haunted."

Louder laughter.

Claire took a breath. "So… thank you. For letting me be part of it. Even when I wasn't sure I wanted to be."

She looked down.

Then up again.

"And now, apparently, there's cider and interpretive dancing. So—good luck to us all."

The crowd cheered.

Lily whooped.

Someone somewhere shouted "Play the fiddle one!"

Claire stepped back, cheeks hot, heart hammering.

Jack was there in an instant. Didn't say anything. Just handed her a cup of cider and nudged her gently toward the edge of the green where the music was starting up.

The brass quartet was trying their best.

So were the speakers.

Between the occasional mic feedback and what might have been the ghost of a bagpipe solo, the music eventually settled into something vaguely folky and pleasingly off-kilter.

People began to move. Groups formed. Laughter spilled across the lawn like glitter no one would ever sweep up.

Claire stayed back for a while. Watching.

Drinking her cider slowly. Letting the hum of the evening soak into her bones.

Then she heard the bench creak.

Jack had sat down, hands resting loosely between his knees, gaze fixed forward.

She sat beside him.

"You didn't run," he said.

"Tempting," she replied.

He glanced at her. "You were brilliant."

Claire made a face. "Ellie says I looked like a deer giving a TED Talk."

"She's not wrong," Jack said. "But still brilliant."

They sat in silence for a moment.

Around them, the market buzzed. Lights twinkled. Someone dropped a tray of toffee apples and blamed the lantern placement.

Then Jack said—softly, too casually—"So when do we start the next project?"

Claire blinked. "What next project?"

He shrugged. "Dunno. You seem like someone who doesn't stop."

"I was hoping for a nap."

He smiled, slow and warm.

"You'll get bored," he said. "You're not really the sitting-still type."

She considered that. "Maybe."

Then, quieter: "But sometimes… sitting still with the right person doesn't feel like stopping."

That caught his attention.

He turned to look at her properly now, one hand shifting on the bench, brushing against hers.

He didn't speak.

Didn't push.

Just left the moment open, like a doorway she could step through if she wanted.

And Claire—

Claire was still deciding.

Because in that moment, with cider in her hand and fairy lights blinking above and a bench they'd built beneath them… she wasn't sure if she wanted the next thing.

Or if she wanted this one to last just a little longer.

The music changed.

Gently at first—so slowly that most people didn't notice. A few bars of something softer, older, threaded through the sound system, until the lanterns seemed to sway a little with it, until the whole green seemed to draw in a breath.

Jack shifted beside her. "You know this one?"

Claire tilted her head. "My nan used to hum it when she was baking. Something about late harvests and second chances. It's one of those songs that only works when the night's warm and cider's involved."

He stood, casually brushing crumbs from his sleeve.

Then held out a hand.

Claire stared at it.

"I don't dance," she said.

"You gave a speech," Jack replied.

"That was different."

"It really wasn't."

She hesitated. Looked around.

A few couples were already swaying awkwardly under the lights. Frances and Bev were arguing softly near the speaker, clearly disagreeing about tempo. Lily had stolen someone's shawl and was now spinning in slow circles, possibly choreographing a tragic bunting ballet in her head.

Jack's hand was still out.

Still patient.

Still offering, not asking.

Claire took it.

He led her gently toward the edge of the green, just near the bench but far enough from the food tables that no one would mistake their dance for a queue.

The first few steps were clumsy. Claire didn't quite know where to look. Jack didn't seem in any hurry to lead. But then the rhythm found them—slow, unshowy, just movement for the sake of being near.

She felt the tension in her shoulders ease.

Felt the cider, the music, the ridiculous magic of the night settle between them like an old coat pulled over two people.

Jack's hand was warm against her back. His other folded lightly around hers. His eyes stayed mostly on the trees, on the glow of the lights, on the shifting of the crowd.

But she caught him looking once.

Just once.

And in that look was a question she wasn't ready to answer.

Yet.

"Claire?"

They pulled apart at the voice—gently, naturally, but fast enough that the moment snapped like thread.

It was **Thomas**, the builder from the next village over. Older than Jack. Always crisply dressed, full of facts no one had asked for. Claire had met him once during a supplier mix-up over paint samples and a narrow miss involving limewash.

"Hi," Claire said, stepping slightly back, brushing her fringe from her eyes. "Didn't know you were coming."

"Got dragged in by Bev," Thomas said, smiling broadly. "She said something about strategic hay bales. And I heard you'd done some *serious craftsmanship*."

He glanced at Jack. Not hostile. Just *aware*.

Claire's stomach did something sideways.

"Ah—yes, the bench," she said, half-laughing. "It's become sort of a village mascot."

"It's bloody gorgeous," Thomas said, nodding toward it. "That curved backrest? Proper joinery. You do that yourself?"

"She helped," Jack said, calmly.

Claire looked between them.

"Jack did the technical work," she said. "I just—varnished it. And provided biscuits."

"She drew it," Jack said. "Designed the whole thing. Measured the curve herself."

Claire flushed.

Thomas smiled. "Impressive. Really."

There was a beat too long.

A space too open.

"Listen," Thomas went on, pulling something from his jacket pocket, "I've actually got a little job cropping up in Fairborough. Small cottage front. Nothing huge, but tricky layout. I could use someone with design sense."

Claire blinked.

Jack was still. Not stiff. Just *still*.

"I'm not—" she began.

"Think about it," Thomas said. "I've seen your sketchbook. Bev showed me. Got an eye, you do."

He handed her a folded slip of paper with his card inside.

Nodded once. Then walked off toward the cider stand.

Claire stared at the paper in her hand.

Didn't open it.

Didn't tuck it away, either.

Jack didn't speak.

Not right away.

Then he said, quietly, "Nice offer."

She looked up. "I wasn't—"

"I know," he said.

She hesitated. "It's not what I came here for."

"I know that too."

They stood for a moment in the middle of a crowd that wasn't watching.

And Claire thought—

There it is.

The thing she'd been afraid of. The thing she hadn't wanted to name.

A choice.

And the terrifying possibility that, for the first time in a long time, her life might contain *more than one.*

Claire didn't move.

The music had changed again—something faster now, fiddly and full of rhythm—and couples were forming a loose circle on the green, pulled into the beginning of what Bev optimistically referred to as the "inclusive group dance segment" and what Ellie, earlier, had called "the stage before cider regret."

Jack stayed where he was, hands tucked into his jacket pockets, gaze flicking once toward the dancers, then back to Claire.

She folded the card once. Slipped it into her jacket.

And didn't say a word.

Instead, she turned slightly and asked, "Want to get another cider?"

Jack gave the tiniest smile. "Rescuing me from square dancing?"

"I'm rescuing myself."

He followed her to the cider tent, where Bev was presiding over the taps like a benevolent monarch and arguing with a man in a tweed hat about whether last year's mulled version had, in fact, included cloves or just aggressively festive marketing.

Claire ordered two. Jack paid. They stood side by side, sipping quietly.

The green around them swirled with the soft blur of community joy.

Laughter. Lanterns. Small children with sticky faces and suspiciously few adults supervising them.

Lily had reappeared—somehow now in a cape again—staging a photobooth in front of the bench and trying to coax couples into romantic poses while handing out hand-carved carrot props. Ellie was beside her, arms crossed, clearly there only to prevent actual chaos and, occasionally, to roll her eyes for dramatic effect.

Claire and Jack stayed just outside of it.

On the periphery.

Together.

But not *quite*.

Later, as the dancing began to wind down and someone lit a small bonfire near the edge of the green, Claire found herself perched on the low stone wall beside the old wishing well. Jack had gone to return the cider mugs. Lily had drifted away in search of her "mood harp." The night had taken on that lovely, hazy softness where everything felt a little unreal.

A child tripped past in a puff of glitter and laughter.

Someone's dog barked three times in triumph and stole a biscuit.

Claire rested her chin in her hand and watched the flames flicker.

It was all so *much*.

Too much.

But not in the way that used to make her bolt.

In a way that made her ache.

Because the problem wasn't that she didn't want this.

The problem was that she might want it too much.

"Here," said Jack's voice, low behind her.

She turned to find him holding two toasted marshmallows on skewers, one slightly charred.

"Guess which one's yours," he said.

Claire took the burnt one and bit into it.

"You know," she said, "I think this might be the first village event I've ever made it through without crying in a toilet."

Jack blinked. "That's… quite the benchmark."

Claire laughed.

And then quiet fell between them again, but not awkwardly.

Comfortably.

He sat beside her, elbow brushing hers again.

They watched the fire. The stars.

The bench, still perfectly curved in the middle of the green, lit gently by the last of the fairy lights.

Claire exhaled slowly. "He caught me off guard, that's all."

Jack didn't respond right away.

Then: "You don't have to explain anything."

"I know," she said. "But I want to."

She turned to face him. "I didn't come here to find work. Or… anything, really. I came here to run away for a bit."

Jack nodded once. Still not looking at her.

"But the thing is…" she went on, her voice quieter now, "somewhere along the way, I stopped running."

Now he turned.

Met her eyes.

And something in his face softened, like a breath let out after being held too long.

They didn't kiss.

They didn't need to.

But Claire's hand found his. Barely touching.

Just enough.

Somewhere near the bonfire, Lily launched into a dramatic reading of cider-based haikus.

Claire and Jack didn't move.

Didn't laugh.

Just sat there together, still and warm and open, while the rest of the village spun around them like stars they'd only just started to see.

The house was quiet when Claire stepped through the front door.

The kind of quiet that only comes after a day soaked in people. That made the silence feel not lonely, but earned.

She kicked off her boots by the door, set her keys in the little dish she still hadn't decided if she liked, and padded into the kitchen. There was confetti in her hair—she found a piece shaped like an acorn clinging to her fringe and placed it gently on the windowsill like a shrine to the ridiculousness of the evening.

The air smelled faintly of cinnamon. Maybe from the bunting. Maybe from her jumper. Maybe from some moment she'd missed entirely because she'd been too busy not kissing Jack under the lanterns.

She paused.

Then said it out loud. Just once.

"Jack."

The name sounded different in the stillness.

He hadn't pressed her.

Hadn't reached.

Hadn't asked for more than she could give.

And yet—he'd been there. In every small moment. The kind of presence that didn't demand anything but made room for everything.

Claire turned the kettle on, almost automatically. Poured the water. Left the teabag steeping far too long while she opened the back door and stood looking out into the garden.

The moonlight touched the ivy climbing up the stone. The bench—*their* bench—wasn't visible from here, but she could still feel it. Still sense the weight of that last conversation. The hand that hadn't quite held hers but somehow had anyway.

She sat down at the kitchen table, cupped her mug, and stared at the steam curling upward like it might give her an answer.

Instead, it gave her a memory.

His voice.

That quiet smile.

The warmth of the night.

And Thomas—offering something real. Tangible. Sensible.

It wasn't just the offer. It was what it represented.

A return. A decision.

A step back into the version of herself that made plans and followed schedules and never stayed too long.

But now…

She looked around the kitchen.

At the slightly wonky shelf she'd installed. The tea towel that still had a splash of paint on it. The sketchbook left open on the counter with a half-finished doodle of a cider barrel shaped suspiciously like a cat.

This was no longer a pause.

This was a beginning.

And beginnings, she was learning, weren't always announced with fanfare or certainty.

Sometimes they crept in during a folk song. Sometimes they handed you marshmallows.

And sometimes… they sat beside you in the dark and didn't say a word.

Claire exhaled slowly. Got up. Crossed to the sideboard and opened the drawer where she kept scraps of paper, ideas, half-drawn plans.

She took out her sketchbook.

Flipped past the bench.

Past the flowers.

Past the little thumbnail drawings of Jack's hands holding tools.

And on a fresh page, she began to draw something new.

Not for Thomas.

Not for anyone else.

Just for herself.

A garden gate. Half-open. Vines spilling over. Light coming through from the other side.

Something unfinished.

Something waiting.

And when she closed the book and turned off the lights, the cottage didn't feel like a stopgap anymore.

It felt like part of the map.

The morning after the Harvest Market, the village was still wearing its hangover like a badge of honour.

Not the *alcoholic* kind, necessarily—though Frances was rumoured to have challenged a brass quartet member to a cider shot-off—but more the emotional kind. The slow, slightly off-kilter mood of a place that had **felt too much joy in one sitting** and now didn't know quite what to do with itself.

The bunting drooped.

A lone paper lantern had escaped and was drifting, ghost-like, along the high street.

Claire walked through it all with her scarf tucked around her chin and the strong suspicion that everyone she passed knew exactly how close she'd come to kissing someone by the fire.

"Morning!" called Bev from the bakery, holding a tray of apology croissants.

"Brilliant speech," said someone else, possibly the man who once yelled at her for parking too near his hydrangeas.

Even Frances, standing outside the village hall with a clipboard and a steaming mug, gave her a regal nod and said, "Could've projected more, but solid sentiment."

Claire smiled. Thanked them. Kept walking.

But underneath it all, there was **a hum**.

Not overt. Not malicious.

Just… *present*.

The kind of hum that vibrates through a small village after something slightly romantic has happened within walking distance of three separate jam stalls.

By the time she reached the greengrocer's, she'd already passed three conversations that paused mid-sentence as she approached and one actual wink from Mr Jenkins, who hadn't moved more than six feet in a decade.

Claire ducked inside the shop mostly for cover.

Ellie was already there.

Naturally.

Leaning against a stack of parsnips and texting with her usual expression of dry disapproval.

Claire tried to slip past.

"You did a twirl," Ellie said, not looking up.

"I did no such thing."

"In the dance. There was twirling. Lily has a sketch."

Claire groaned. "She was *drawing* during the dance?"

"She's claiming it's part of a community mural project. She used the phrase 'commemorative swish.'"

Claire dropped a head of broccoli into her basket and sighed. "Is there a plan for how long this will go on?"

"The mural? The gossip? Or your slow-burn collapse into emotional vulnerability?"

Claire narrowed her eyes.

Ellie finally looked up. "It was a good night. Don't ruin it by overthinking."

"I'm *not*—"

"You *are*. You have your panic scarf on."

Claire tugged the scarf looser. "I just… I don't know what happens now."

Ellie shrugged. "That's the point. You don't have to know. You just have to not run."

Claire paused at the apple bin.

Picked one up.

Then said, "Thomas offered me work."

Ellie blinked once.

Then raised an eyebrow. "Did Jack hear?"

Claire gave a non-committal sound. "He was there."

"And?"

"And nothing. He didn't react."

"Hmm."

"Don't 'hmm' at me."

"I'm not," Ellie said, completely 'hmm'ing her. "I'm just… considering the emotional implications."

Claire turned back toward the carrots. "Maybe I need to talk to him."

"Maybe," Ellie said. "Or maybe you need to stop waiting for someone to give you permission to feel what you already feel."

Claire looked at her. "Which is what, exactly?"

But Ellie had already wandered off toward the beetroot.

Outside, the air was crisp and edged with the smell of apples and leftover woodsmoke. The bench was still there, clean now, a few petals scattered across it like nature was trying to say *nice job*.

Claire sat for a moment.

Not long.

Just enough.

And she didn't notice until a full minute had passed—

—Jack wasn't the one watching this time.

Thomas was.

Across the green. Talking with Bev. Glancing over once.

And smiling.

Claire didn't go straight home.

She wandered a little.

Past the post office with its cheerful notice board full of lost gloves and jam jars wanted. Past the pub, where a man in a puffer jacket was still trying to extract glitter from his beard. Past the little churchyard, where the gravestones leaned conspiratorially toward one another like old women sharing secrets.

And then, without thinking, her feet took her the long way—up the lane toward the cottage, past the hedgerow, where the trees thinned just enough to let the sky through in quiet strips of pale blue and gold.

He was there.

Of course he was.

Jack, crouched on one knee beside the stone planter just beyond her gate, gently pressing soil around the base of a newly placed plant—one of the sad-looking dahlias she'd bought three weeks ago and never got round to planting.

He didn't look up straight away.

Just finished what he was doing.

Then stood, brushing his palms on his jeans, and said, "You keep walking past them like they'll do it themselves."

Claire folded her arms. "I was giving them time to self-actualise."

Jack smiled faintly. "They were halfway to compost."

She leaned against the gatepost. "You always show up like this?"

"Only when there's passive-aggressive plant neglect involved."

A pause.

The wind picked up slightly, rustling the hedge behind them.

Then Claire said, without quite meaning to, "He offered me a job."

Jack nodded once. No flicker. No surprise. "I figured."

She looked at him.

Really looked.

But he didn't shift. Didn't close up. Just stood there in the quiet, steady way of someone who knew storms and didn't fear them.

"And I don't know what to do about it," she said finally. "Or about anything, really. Which is new for me."

Jack glanced toward the cottage.

Then back at her.

"You don't have to know," he said. "You just have to be honest."

Claire pressed her lips together. "I am."

He didn't reply.

Not right away.

Then, very quietly: "Are you?"

She froze.

Not defensively.

Not in anger.

Just stilled.

Because it was a fair question.

She looked at the dahlia.

At the soil.

At the hand trowel still resting by his knee.

Then, quietly, sat down on the low wall beside the gate.

"I like it here," she said. "The cottage. The village. You."

Jack's mouth didn't move, but something in his face softened—so slightly that it might've been missed by anyone who wasn't watching carefully.

"I didn't expect to," Claire added. "I thought I was just… passing through. Healing something. Distracting myself with woodwork and jam."

"You're good at distractions," Jack said.

It wasn't a criticism.

Just true.

Claire folded her hands in her lap. "But I think I want more than that now."

Another pause.

The air held it for them.

"I don't know what it looks like," she went on. "Staying. Starting again. Letting it be real."

Jack didn't interrupt.

Didn't fill the space.

When she looked up, he was still watching her—steadily, like someone waiting for her to hear her own words.

And she did.

She did.

After a long moment, Jack moved to sit beside her.

Not too close.

Just enough.

Their arms didn't touch.

But they didn't need to.

"You don't have to decide today," he said gently.

Claire stared down the lane.

"No," she said. "But I think… I'm starting to."

They sat there a while longer.

The wind tugged at the trees.

A bird called once, sharply, from the hedgerow.

And when she finally stood, brushing dirt from her coat, Jack stood too.

He didn't reach for her.

Didn't ask for more.

But he walked her to the door.

And when she turned the key, stepped inside, and looked back at him—he was still there.

Still steady.

Still waiting.

And for the first time, Claire didn't feel like she was being asked to run.

She felt like she was being asked to stay.

Chapter Fifteen

"Unexpected Visitors and Inconvenient Optimism"

Claire was halfway through buttering a piece of toast when the doorbell rang.

Which wouldn't have been particularly strange—except it was **7:42 in the morning**, and the only people awake in Maple Hollow at that hour were farmers, bakery staff, and Lily during **"moonlight manifestation cleanses"** (which, thankfully, only happened during full moons and strong crosswinds).

She froze.

Listened.

Hoped it had been her imagination or perhaps the wind delivering the ghost of a social obligation.

Then it rang again.

Twice.

With the kind of cheerful insistence that suggested someone was either **very optimistic** or had already had three coffees.

Claire sighed, set the knife down, and padded toward the door still in slippers, hair scraped into something ambitious but uncooperative.

When she opened it—

There stood her **mother**.

Holding a suitcase.

Wearing cashmere.

And smiling like she'd *absolutely planned none of this and also everything about this*.

"Surprise!" her mum said, in the same tone one might use to announce a pregnancy or a free spa weekend.

Claire stared.

Tried to form words.

Failed.

Her mother leaned in for a brisk hug, scented faintly of Chanel and judgment, then breezed past into the hallway, pulling the suitcase behind her like it had travelled first-class on its own.

"I thought I'd pop down," she said brightly. "See how the renovation's going. Take in a bit of country air. You know how stuffy Cheltenham can get in autumn."

Claire closed the door slowly.

Still staring.

"You don't like country air," she said finally.

"I like the *idea* of it," her mother replied, stepping into the kitchen and immediately inspecting the windowsill. "Is this real ivy?"

Claire blinked. "Mum—what are you *doing* here?"

Her mother opened the fridge. "The market photos were lovely. That bench! Very tasteful. You should be proud. I wanted to see it in person."

Claire crossed her arms. "So you got in a car, before 7am, and drove three hours for… *tasteful bench appreciation*?"

"And to check you're still alive," her mum added. "You know I worry."

Claire rubbed her forehead. "I text you every day."

"Yes. Once. Usually in lowercase."

"Because I'm not a *regency debutante*, Mum."

Her mother poured herself a glass of water, took a delicate sip, and said, "Well. I suppose now that I'm here, we can finally get that guest room sorted."

Claire stared.

Then muttered something about divine punishment and made a second cup of tea.

By 9am, the entire village knew.

Of course they did.

Ellie texted *"Your mother is wearing white trousers. She is not emotionally prepared for Bev."*
Lily texted *"Claire! There's an aura clash happening. I felt it from the bakery. Also I saw your mum. Is she single?"*
Frances did not text. She just walked past the cottage slowly, twice, with her dog and a narrowed expression that suggested she'd already assumed Claire was being evicted.

Jack, of course, didn't text either.

But Claire was fairly sure he'd heard.

Maple Hollow didn't need internet.

It *was* the internet.

By mid-morning, her mother had "popped in" to meet Bev, "dropped by" the village hall, and asked six increasingly probing questions about Jack, including "Does he own *all* his tools or just the performative ones?" and "Is that his natural beard or something men do now to look competent?"

Claire fled to the garden.

She sat on the back step, mug in hand, staring at the lawn like it might open and swallow her.

When Jack appeared—quietly, as ever—carrying a rolled-up measuring tape and a fresh packet of screws, she wasn't even surprised.

She just groaned.

"I didn't tell her to come."

"I know," Jack said, settling onto the grass.

"She just… materialised."

"Like a glitter bomb in human form?"

Claire snorted.

They sat in silence for a moment.

Then he added, "She asked me if I'd ever considered a career in bespoke garden furniture design."

Claire covered her face.

"She also said," he continued casually, "that the bench was 'surprisingly understated,' and that you always had an eye for proportion, even as a child."

Claire peeked at him through her fingers. "She liked it?"

Jack shrugged. "She admired it. Possibly to weaponise it later in a family anecdote."

Claire groaned again.

Jack smiled.

Then, a beat later: "You're doing okay."

She looked at him.

Frowned. "With what?"

He didn't answer right away.

Just tapped the measuring tape against his knee.

"All of it," he said. "This. The village. Her. The staying."

Claire blinked.

Then—very quietly—nodded.

Just once.

Then reached for the second mug she'd made without realising and handed it to him.

He took it.

And together, they sat on the step in the early light, the air soft and full of new things trying to root.

They'd barely finished their mugs when the back door creaked open and her mother's voice floated out like a scented candle on a warpath.

"Claire, darling, do you know there are *three* different types of preserves in your cupboard, but not one single linen napkin?"

Claire closed her eyes.

Jack took another sip of tea.

"Also," her mother added, stepping into view, holding a jar of plum chutney at arm's length like it might detonate, "did you know this expired in 2021?"

"It's chutney, Mum. That's practically its prime."

Her mother tilted her head at Jack. "And *you* must be the infamous carpenter."

"Jack," he said calmly, standing to shake her hand.

Her mother glanced at the toolbelt, nodded with faint approval, and said, "Nice lines on that bench. You did the dovetail joins by hand?"

Jack smiled. "Claire did."

Her mother blinked.

Once.

Then turned to her daughter. "Oh. Well. That's… unexpected."

Claire muttered something about digging a second compost bin to hide inside.

By noon, her mother had:

- Suggested the front garden "would look less like an abandoned hedgerow with some low boxwood edging"
- Asked Bev if the pub could add a wine flight to the Harvest menu "for variety"
- Corrected Lily on the French spelling of *macaron* during a community baking circle
- Invited herself to *"just sit in"* on a planning meeting for the Winter Fête

Claire followed her around like a reluctant tour guide to an endangered species.

"She's not usually like this," she whispered to Ellie, who raised one eyebrow and said, "She once asked the vicar if his cassock came in navy. She's *exactly* like this."

And yet—

There were moments.

Small ones.

Where her mother looked around with something like *wonder* in her face.

She ran a hand over the bench and smiled—genuinely, quietly.

She accepted a paper cup of cider with only minimal commentary.

She stood in front of the post office bulletin board for a full five minutes reading every note, then muttered, "I think I envy this."

Claire wasn't sure what to do with that.

So she didn't do anything.

She just watched.

And tried not to notice the way Jack stood slightly further away that day. Not far. Just… enough. Still present. Still kind. But distant in that way people get when they're trying to let you choose something without swaying it themselves.

That unsettled her more than her mother ever could.

Later, back at the cottage, Claire found her mother standing in the kitchen flipping through her sketchbook.

She froze.

The kettle whistled behind her.

Her mother didn't look up.

"These are good," she said softly.

Claire moved slowly. "They're just ideas."

"They're more than that." Her mother turned a page. "This one—the window seat—you remember your gran's flat in Edinburgh?"

Claire nodded. "Of course."

"This has the same lines. The same shape in the corners."

Claire peered over her shoulder.

She hadn't realised.

Her mother closed the book gently.

"I think I always hoped you'd do something with your hands," she said. "You were never very good at sitting still."

Claire leaned against the counter.

"And yet," she said, "you sent me to accounting camp."

"Accountants can have active lives."

Claire snorted.

Then, softer: "I didn't think you liked what I was doing here."

Her mother looked at her. "I didn't understand it."

A pause.

"But I'm trying."

Claire didn't speak.

She didn't need to.

Her mother put the sketchbook down. Stepped back.

And for once, didn't try to offer a solution.

Just tea.

And a seat.

The day drifted on gently from there. A light rain. A quiet dinner. A short walk to the green where the petals still lingered on the bench like a secret no one had dared sweep away.

Jack didn't stop by.

But Claire noticed fresh varnish on one of the side panels.

No note.

No announcement.

Just presence.

In absence.

The rain had passed by early evening, leaving the village washed and glowing, the cobbles gleaming like old silver and the leaves plastered to the pavement in crisp, crunchy mosaics.

Claire had escaped upstairs after dinner.

Her mother had offered to "reorganise the spice rack by emotional tone," and that had felt like a good cue to retreat.

Now, wrapped in a blanket and propped up against her pillows, she sipped tea from the mug Jack had left behind last week. It still had the faintest chip on the rim, the kind that always seemed to find her lip.

The cottage was quiet.

Not the awkward kind.

The settled kind.

The kind that lets your thoughts wander without supervision.

She'd just reached for her sketchbook when her phone buzzed against the quilt.

A number she didn't recognise.

But something in her stomach sank before she even answered.

She swiped to pick up.

"Hello?"

"Claire? It's Thomas."
The voice was warm. Clear. Slightly smug by default, but never unkind.

"Oh—hi," she said, straightening instinctively. "Sorry, didn't have your number saved."

"No worries," he said. "Bev gave me your details. I hope that's okay."

Claire glanced toward the window where the last light was slipping past the glass like an afterthought. "Yeah, sure. Everything all right?"

"Better than," Thomas replied. "Listen, I've just spoken with the owners of the Fairborough cottage—the one I mentioned. They've greenlit the budget, and I told them I had someone perfect in mind."

Claire froze.

"I know you said you weren't sure," he went on, "but I think this could be a brilliant fit. It's not full-on architectural work—just spatial design, layout tweaks, fittings. You'd be free to interpret a lot of it."

She said nothing.

"I can send over the plans," Thomas added. "No pressure. Just thought you should see them. They've got another designer in mind if you pass, but I wanted to ask you first."

Another pause.

Then, more gently: "You're good, Claire. I saw it the moment I looked at that bench."

Claire swallowed.

"Can I think about it?"

"Of course," Thomas said easily. "No rush. Just wanted you to know it's real. And waiting."

She nodded, even though he couldn't see it.

"Thanks."

"Anytime. Speak soon?"

"Yeah. Speak soon."

The call ended.

And Claire sat there, the screen now dark in her hand, the room dim around her.

It was real.

A real offer.

With real stakes.

Not dramatic. Not urgent. Just… present.

And it unsettled her in ways she didn't have names for yet.

Downstairs, she could hear the faint rattle of her mother putting mugs in the dishwasher—probably in an order Claire would never understand.

Outside, the rain had begun again. Soft. Almost comforting.

She stood, tugged her cardigan tighter, and crossed to the window.

Somewhere in the distance, she knew the bench was still there. Damp now. Quiet.

But holding things it shouldn't have to.

She pressed her palm lightly to the glass.

Not cold.

Just cool enough to feel like something was shifting.

Then, before she could think too hard, she opened her sketchbook.

Turned past the gate drawing.

Past the soft pencil sketch of the lanterns on the green.

And began a new one.

She didn't know what it would become.

Not yet.

But the page didn't feel so blank anymore.

Claire didn't hear her mother enter the room.

But a moment later, there was the soft shuffle of slippers on the carpet, and then a clink—her mother setting down a cup of tea on the bedside table with a precision that suggested it had taken years of practice to make it seem casual.

"You weren't asleep," she said simply.

"I was drawing," Claire replied.

Her mother sat on the edge of the bed without asking. She was wearing one of Claire's jumpers—far too big for her but clearly adopted with the same breezy entitlement she used when "borrowing" restaurant salt shakers.

"You used to draw all the time," her mother said after a moment. "On the backs of envelopes. Napkins. School newsletters."

Claire smiled faintly. "I still do."

"I know," her mother said, tapping the sketchbook. "I've seen the pages."

Claire looked at her.

Her mother didn't flinch. "They're good."

"Thanks."

They sat quietly for a moment.

Then her mother added, "You're more like your grandmother than you think."

Claire blinked. "Nan?"

"She was always making something out of nothing. Clipping things from catalogues. Rearranging the living room at two a.m. She once painted a mural on the garden shed and told the neighbours it was modernist."

Claire laughed. "That sounds about right."

"She wanted you to build things," her mother said softly. "She said you had the hands for it."

Claire looked down at her fingers. "You never said that."

"I didn't know how," her mum replied. "You were so good at numbers. So... tidy. I thought that would keep you safe."

Claire's throat tightened unexpectedly.

"She'd be proud of you," her mother said. "The cottage. The bench. The way you look when you're talking about something you care about."

Claire looked over at her.

Her mother gave her a tired smile and patted her leg. "I'm sorry it took me this long to see it."

Claire didn't answer.

But she reached over and gave her hand a quick, awkward squeeze before pulling the blanket tighter around her shoulders.

Her mother left a minute later, trailing a faint scent of rose and responsibility.

The room was quiet again.

Not heavy. Just... full.

Claire picked up her phone, checked the time, and saw a new message waiting.

From Jack.

She hesitated.

Then tapped.

Still raining. Bench looks moody. Would probably write poetry about the lanterns if it could.

(Also I varnished the side panel. Sorry. It was driving me mad.)

Hope you're okay. Let me know if you want a distraction. I make excellent toast.

Claire smiled, in spite of herself.

Then typed back:

The bench deserves a book deal.

Also, toast sounds dangerously tempting. Might need to trade for a sketch.

The typing bubble popped up almost immediately.

Deal. I'll bring butter.

Claire set the phone down, heart a little lighter, sketchbook still open in her lap.

She wasn't ready for decisions.

But maybe she didn't have to be.

Not tonight.

Claire tossed her phone onto the bedside table—not dramatically, just enough to let it land with a soft thunk that matched the fog in her chest.

She sat there for a few seconds longer in the lamplight. The walls of the cottage had taken on their evening glow: warm shadows, low ceilings, the comforting scent of rain-dampened earth coming in through the half-open window.

She'd meant to sketch. Or maybe journal. Or maybe just sit and digest everything that had been said, offered, or silently implied since sunrise.

But instead, she did what she always did when the world became too big to contain: she got up, shoved her feet into her slippers, and padded downstairs in search of clarity, or toast, or both.

The kitchen was dark save for the under-cabinet glow left on to "guide the kettle," as Lily had once dramatically insisted. Her mother had gone to bed already—after polishing off a second slice of apple tart and declaring that Claire's mattress was "a little peasanty, but charming in its own way."

Claire pulled the cardigan tighter around her shoulders, reached into the bread tin, and blinked when a knock came at the back door.

Not loud.

Not urgent.

Just… there.

She crossed to the door cautiously, still half-expecting it to be a confused badger or a neighbour with strong opinions about bin rotation.

It wasn't.

It was Jack.

Holding a slice of toast already buttered, and a folded napkin over his arm like a budget butler.

"Thought I'd save time," he said, raising the plate.

Claire stared at him.

Then laughed—tired, genuine, and grateful all at once.

She stepped back without a word.

He came in like it was the most natural thing in the world.

He set the toast down carefully, grabbed two mugs from the rack without asking, and filled the kettle as though he lived there. And in a way, he sort of did—not in fact, but in rhythm. In the way he moved through the cottage like someone who *knew it*. Not just the space, but the person who lived in it.

They didn't talk straight away.

Claire buttered another piece of toast and handed it over.

He found honey in the cupboard, despite it having migrated twice during the spice rack saga.

When they finally sat down, side by side at the kitchen table, Claire spoke first.

"Did you mean what you said earlier?"

Jack didn't look up right away. "About the bench?"

"About everything."

He nodded once. "I don't tend to say things I don't mean."

Claire stared at her tea.

Then: "It's all getting a bit... real."

Jack's voice was quiet, even. "That's usually when it starts mattering."

She looked at him. "I didn't ask for this."

"I know."

"I didn't even think I *wanted* this."

"I know that too."

He finally looked at her then, eyes steady, and added: "But that doesn't mean you don't."

Claire felt the words settle somewhere behind her ribs.

Then she said, in a voice smaller than she intended, "He offered me the job. It's real now. The money. The contract. The hours. The deadlines."

Jack didn't flinch.

But he didn't smile either.

"He's a good guy," he said eventually. "Solid work. Decent kit. Pays on time."

Claire blinked. "You know him?"

"Worked with him on a remodel in Fairborough two years ago. He's not flashy, just efficient. Clients like that."

"Oh."

Jack took a sip of tea. "You'd be brilliant at it."

Claire stared at the tabletop.

And then, almost whispering: "I think I'd miss this."

Jack didn't answer immediately.

Then, carefully: "The toast?"

Claire laughed again, startled by it. "No. Well. Yes. But also… all of it. This house. This kitchen. You."

The words hung there.

Unrushed.

Unapologetic.

Jack looked at her for a long moment.

Then said, "You don't have to pick yet, Claire."

"I know."

"But when you do," he added, voice low and certain, "don't pick safe. Pick true."

They sat in silence for a long time after that. Just the tick of the clock, the soft hum of the kettle winding down, and the rain misting against the windows like an old lullaby.

He didn't try to kiss her.

She didn't try to stop him.

Because neither of them moved.

They just stayed.

Together.

Claire was already awake when she heard the kettle start to boil.

Which would've been comforting—if she'd been the one to turn it on.

She rolled over and groaned into her pillow.

Of course her mother was up early.

And probably rearranging the spice rack again. Or alphabetising the tea by emotional benefit.

By the time she padded into the kitchen in leggings, hoodie, and a sleep-induced squint, her mother was already seated at the table with a folded napkin, a poached egg that looked like it had been carved with a laser, and the **Financial Times weekend supplement**, spread across three placemats like she was hosting a solo breakfast summit.

"Morning, darling," she said, without looking up. "Did you sleep well?"

"Moderately," Claire muttered, heading straight for the kettle.

"I assumed as much," her mother replied. "The water pressure in your shower is like being blessed by a reluctant saint."

Claire groaned, reaching for a mug.

Then—another sound.

A knock.

Low. Familiar.

She froze.

Her mother didn't.

She rose briskly, smoothing her robe as if it were a diplomatic uniform, and opened the door.

Jack stood there, mug in one hand, tool belt slung casually low on his hip, and the same crooked smile that had utterly disarmed Claire the night before.

"Morning," he said.

"Ah," her mother replied, with the same tone she might use upon discovering unexpected paprika. "It's the carpenter."

"Jack," he corrected, stepping inside without hesitation.

Claire stared at him, wide-eyed over the rim of her tea.

He nodded once. "Morning."

"Hi," she said, more to her mug than to him.

He crossed to the worktop like it was routine, and placed a roll of sandpaper and a small wrapped packet on the counter. "You left this in the shed," he said simply, tapping the wrapped object.

She glanced over.

It was her sketchbook.

Not the working one—the one with the messy lines and ketchup stains—but the clean one. The one she'd started sketching in the day she arrived. The one that held *ideas*, not instructions.

"Oh," she said. "Thanks."

Her mother cleared her throat gently and said, "Would you like some coffee, Jack?"

"Only if it's strong enough to resurface a countertop."

Claire choked on her tea.

Her mother arched an eyebrow. "You'll find the roast rather refined."

"Good," Jack replied. "I brought my own mug. It's dented but loyal."

Claire sat down, slowly.

Her mother poured coffee like she was measuring out truce terms.

Jack sat.

Opposite her.

And the kitchen was suddenly far too small.

Claire picked at the edge of her toast.

Her mother took a delicate bite of her egg and said, "Claire's always been very precise. She once reorganised the Lego drawer by architectural period."

Jack smiled. "Explains the dovetail joints."

Claire looked between them. "Are you two… bonding?"

"No," they said in unison.

A silence followed.

Jack took a sip of coffee. "This is very good."

Her mother beamed. "It's single origin."

Claire's voice was flat. "I want to die."

Another silence.

Then Jack set his mug down and said, "I should get started on the porch frame. If I don't reinforce it this week, it'll sag through winter."

Her mother nodded once. "Sagging structures are the enemy of civilisation."

Jack gave Claire a sideways look. "I'll be out back."

He left with a nod—and the door clicked shut behind him.

Claire turned to her mother, who was buttering toast like it was a form of diplomacy.

"You like him," she said.

Her mother shrugged. "He's competent. And mildly amusing."

"Mildly?"

"That's my highest rating before breakfast."

Claire rubbed her temples.

Her mother sipped her coffee, then added: "You smile more when he's around."

Claire blinked.

"Also," she went on, "you talk faster. Your eyes do that *thing*."

Claire frowned. "What thing?"

Her mother waved a hand. "They sparkle like you've just solved a Rubik's cube. You used to get it when you talked about design. Or strawberries."

Claire didn't answer.

Not because she disagreed.

But because suddenly, she wasn't quite sure if she wanted to laugh, cry, or grab her sketchbook and disappear for a year.

"I'm just saying," her mother added, finishing her toast with regal finality, "he seems to know which version of you he's talking to."

Claire stared at her.

Her mother smiled.

And got up to do the washing up—like she hadn't just dismantled her daughter with three sentences and a poached egg.

Claire found him crouched by the porch steps, tape measure hooked to his jeans and a box of screws balanced on the wooden railing. He didn't look up when she stepped outside, but she could tell he'd heard her.

He was sanding a strip of timber, long smooth motions, rhythmical and unhurried. The kind of action that made you forget what time it was.

She stood for a moment in the doorway, arms crossed against the morning chill.

Then: "So you met the dragon."

Jack gave a soft grunt that might've been a laugh. "She's not a dragon."

"She categorised my spice rack by geopolitical relevance."

"She's sharp," he said, glancing up. "And proud of you."

Claire raised an eyebrow. "You got all that from one awkward coffee?"

He set the sander down. "I've been around long enough to recognise the look."

Claire stepped forward. The wood beneath her slippered feet creaked faintly—one of the boards he'd marked for replacement.

"Sorry she ambushed you."

"She didn't."

Claire tilted her head. "You brought your own mug."

Jack shrugged. "I don't go unarmed."

That made her smile.

He wiped a hand on his jeans, then nodded toward the exposed framework beside the steps. "This bit's going to need a new beam. The old one's bowed—wasn't installed right to begin with."

She crouched down beside him.

"Should I be worried it's going to collapse?"

"Nah. Not yet. Just… needs care."

She ran her fingers lightly along the grain of the wood, tracing the dip where time and pressure had done their work.

"Funny," she murmured. "Sometimes the things that look solidest are the ones most likely to give way."

Jack glanced at her.

But didn't say anything.

They stayed like that for a minute—crouched beside the bones of a house that was slowly becoming a home, breathing in the scent of sawdust and damp earth and something else neither of them wanted to name yet.

Claire broke the silence first.

"She says I smile more when you're around."

Jack looked over. "Do you?"

"I hadn't noticed," she said. "But then again… I hadn't really noticed I'd stopped."

That landed between them like a dropped nail—small, unassuming, but carrying weight.

Jack nodded once. "Well. That's something, isn't it?"

Claire watched him.

There was something in his face she hadn't quite let herself see before.

Not just patience.

Not just warmth.

But **choice**.

Like he'd already made his.

"I'm not going to ask you to stay," he said quietly.

Claire swallowed. "Why not?"

"Because if you did," he replied, eyes steady, "I'd want it to be for the right reason. Not because I made it easier."

She felt that like a breeze under her ribs.

Then, gently: "But I'm glad you're here. Even if it's not forever."

Claire didn't know what to say to that.

So she didn't.

She just sat with it.

With him.

And the sunlight on the porch, spilling gold across the planks.

The sander lay between them.

Unfinished.

Like everything else.

Chapter Sixteen

"Ladders, Lattes and Light Panic"

The day began with a ladder.

Specifically, a ladder wedged diagonally across the pavement outside the village hall, propped against the old noticeboard that had been unofficially declared "Frances's Domain" and was now draped with bunting, laminated health and safety diagrams, and one photograph of a hedgehog in a crown.

Claire arrived mid-morning, tugged along by Ellie who claimed she *desperately* needed her opinion on the aesthetic merits of biodegradable glitter, only to find herself roped into a community brainstorming session that had clearly started hours ago and shown no signs of ending.

"I just think the fairy lights should be colour-coded by emotional tone," Lily was saying from the top of the ladder, arms full of cable. "You wouldn't want regret tangled with nostalgia. That's just basic energy hygiene."

Frances, holding a clipboard and a visible eye twitch, replied, "I want the regret lights *removed*."

"You can't just erase regret, Frances. That's how people get blocked chakras."

Claire, who had only come for a quiet coffee and a possible muffin, turned to Ellie. "Why am I here?"

"Because you're the only one who can talk Lily down without causing a full moon incident."

Claire sighed and looked up. "Lily, please. Can you at least—"

But Lily had already climbed three more rungs and was now straddling the top of the ladder like a circus act, fairy lights in one hand, a strand of ivy in the other, and an expression that could only be described as *determined chaos*.

Claire reached for the base to steady it. "You know this isn't even *your* ladder?"

"It's borrowed from the vicar," Lily called down. "He said I could use it if I promised to bring back the 'vibe of 1993.'"

"I think he meant the *actual ladder,* not the existential dread."

But Lily was humming now, completely lost in her own plan, so Claire let go and took a step back.

"Do you ever feel," she said to Ellie, "like the village is just one minor health code violation away from becoming performance art?"

Ellie, holding a takeaway latte she hadn't paid for and wearing her usual look of benign exasperation, shrugged. "That's the charm."

Claire watched Lily lasso herself with the ivy and muttered, "That's not the word I'd use."

By lunchtime, the ladder had been retracted, Lily had declared the noticeboard "emotionally aligned," and Frances had gone home muttering about bylaws and anti-anxiety tea.

Claire sat on the bench with her sandwich, feet stretched out, sunlight warming the back of her neck.

Across the green, the cottage roofline peeked out through the trees. Familiar now. Hers.

It was strange, she thought. She'd arrived looking for a project—and somewhere along the way, **she** had become the project.

"You're thinking again," Ellie said, sitting beside her.

"I never stopped."

Ellie handed her the extra biscuit from her lunchbox. "You should. It's bad for the complexion."

Claire accepted the biscuit.

Then, tentatively: "What if I did stay?"

Ellie blinked. "You've stayed this long."

"I mean *properly* stayed. As in—didn't go back."

"Didn't you already sort of decide that last week when you helped sand the banister at midnight while quoting Jane Austen?"

Claire gave her a look. "That was one time."

Ellie shrugged. "The village has absorbed you. Resistance is futile."

Claire smiled, biting into the biscuit.

Then: "Thomas called again."

Ellie didn't say anything.

Claire glanced sideways. "He's sending over the contract."

"You going to sign it?"

Claire picked at a crumb on her jeans.

"I don't know. It's... everything I wanted. Or used to want. Or thought I was supposed to want."

"Sounds like a 'no' in a 'maybe' dress."

Claire snorted.

But Ellie just looked at her, calm and unreadable. "Jack doesn't know, does he?"

"No."

"Why not?"

"Because I don't want him to think he's a reason I'm not leaving."

Ellie tilted her head. "Isn't he?"

Claire didn't answer.

But her silence said plenty.

The village bell rang twice.

Not for church.

Just someone tugging it out of boredom or victory.

Claire looked over her shoulder toward the post office, where Lily was now handing out flyers and claiming the moon had changed its course.

Something about the day felt different.

Like someone had tilted the world just slightly while no one was looking.

Not dramatic.

Not defining.

Just... **new**.

By the time Claire got home, the light was already beginning to slant golden through the trees.

She kicked her shoes off at the door, tucked her curls behind one ear, and dropped her tote bag on the hall table with the distinct air of someone who *might never leave the house again.*

The cottage smelled faintly of rosemary.

Which was odd, because she hadn't cooked in two days and was pretty sure the rosemary bush outside had given up on her after one too many half-promises.

She found the answer in the kitchen.

A note.

Folded in half and propped against the sugar jar like it had been left with care. The handwriting was neat. Familiar.

*"Didn't want to interrupt. You looked happy on the green. Fixed the cupboard hinge. The rosemary was looking at me funny, so I used some in the lentils. Hope that's okay.
—J"*

Claire read it twice.

Then three more times.

The kettle clicked on out of habit, even though she hadn't touched it.

She stood there a moment longer, hands on the edge of the worktop, heart doing that uncomfortable thing where it tried to pretend it wasn't racing.

He'd been here.

Again.

Not asking for anything.

Just… there.

And somehow that presence was louder than a thousand voiced intentions.

She wandered into the sitting room, curling into the corner of the sofa with the note still in her hand, and tried to tell herself it wasn't significant.

That people fixed hinges for their friends.

That lentils weren't romantic.

That notes signed with just an initial weren't *possibly* the most devastatingly gentle thing anyone had ever left her.

But even as she thought it, she knew she was lying to herself.

And to make matters worse—

Her phone buzzed again.

Thomas.

Claire hesitated.

Then tapped.

Plans arriving tonight. Should hit your inbox by 6. Big job. Lots of trust. I hope you say yes. T.

She closed the message.

Didn't reply.

Just tucked the phone into the throw blanket beside her like it might warm up into something softer.

She could feel the choice forming around her.

Like fog.

Not threatening. Not sudden.

But enclosing, all the same.

Outside, the cottage walls glowed.

The ivy shifted gently in the breeze.

And the bench—Jack's bench—sat quietly in its place like a secret she hadn't said aloud yet.

Lovely. We'll stay exactly where we are—**mid-chapter, mid-thought**, no changes to pacing or flow—slipping naturally into a **quiet porch moment**, where Claire lets herself respond to Jack.

This scene will remain **unrushed**, layered with *Jenny Colgan's tone*: tender without sentimentality, thoughtful without overexplanation, and always grounded in the small domestic moments that say more than grand gestures ever could.

Let's continue.

The sky had started to turn that particular kind of blue-grey that meant the rain might come back later, but not just yet.

Claire wrapped a cardigan around her shoulders and stepped out onto the porch.

The bench at the far end of the garden caught the last of the light. The rosemary bush looked suspiciously pruned.

She carried her phone in one hand, Jack's note in the other, and leaned against the porch post—the one he'd reinforced last week without a word, as if he'd always known she'd lean there eventually.

The air smelled of damp earth and something herbal—probably the lentils he'd made, because apparently now he fixed kitchens *and* left you stealth dinners when you weren't looking.

She looked down at the note again. Read the last line slowly.

"Hope that's okay."

It was more than okay.

It was too much.

But she couldn't bring herself to say that.

Not yet.

Instead, she opened her phone.

Typed.

Deleted.

Typed again.

Finally, she landed on something simple. Something *true*.

Thanks for the rosemary intervention. And the hinge. And the note. Especially the note.

Also: yes. The lentils were oddly emotional.

She stared at the message.

Then sent it before she could overthink.

Set the phone down on the porch rail.

And waited.

Not because she expected an answer right away, but because some part of her needed to know she'd *said something*. That she'd pushed back, however gently, against the silence she'd wrapped herself in since this all began.

The wind stirred.

Somewhere across the village, a dog barked, and someone slammed a boot in a doorway.

Claire folded her arms around herself and let her eyes wander down the garden path, where the late-summer roses were stubbornly blooming for no one in particular.

Then her phone buzzed once.

She blinked.

Picked it up.

Jack's reply was immediate.

Glad the lentils made an impression. Thought I overdid the rosemary.

Also… you looked happy today. I didn't want to interrupt. Just wanted you to know I saw it.

It suits you.

He's lucky, if you say yes. But so am I, if you stay.

Claire read it once.

Then again.

She didn't cry.

Not quite.

But she sat down slowly on the porch step, phone clutched tight, and let the moment fill her chest like a breath she'd been holding since the day she arrived.

Because somehow, even without asking, he knew exactly where she was in the middle of it all.

And he didn't push.

He just made sure she knew he was there.

The smell of lentils hadn't entirely left the house, which was unfortunate, because Claire's mother had a deeply specific opinion about pulses being "nutritionally noble but aromatically misguided."

Claire found her in the lounge, seated upright in the armchair with the cushion she'd repositioned for "lumbar integrity," reading one of Lily's wellness newsletters and muttering under her breath.

"You know she believes the moon has a marketing strategy?"

"She might not be wrong," Claire said, flopping onto the sofa.

Her mother looked up. "Darling. You're flushed. Were you outside?"

"Yes."

Her mum peered more closely. "On purpose?"

Claire rolled her eyes. "Yes. I sat on the porch."

"Alone?"

Claire hesitated. "Not exactly."

Her mother's expression didn't change. Not really. But her eyebrows did something vaguely triumphal.

"I see."

"You don't."

"You're emotionally affected by lentils. I see plenty."

Claire groaned into a cushion. "I hate that you're suddenly insightful."

"Years of practice," her mum said, not looking up. "Also, I used to be you."

There was a pause.

Claire lifted her head slightly. "What does that mean?"

Her mother folded the newsletter and placed it neatly on the coffee table.

"It means," she said, "that once upon a time I also stood in a doorway and pretended I hadn't already made a decision."

Claire blinked.

"You think I've decided?"

Her mum shrugged. "You will. One way or the other. But part of you already has."

Before Claire could form a reply—or an argument—the door flew open with a gust of wind and a flurry of floral scarf.

Ellie burst in, cheeks pink, holding a half-eaten croissant and three mismatched tote bags.

"Emergency!" she declared, dropping everything onto the rug. "And also hi."

Claire sat up. "What kind of emergency?"

"The good kind," Ellie said. "Frances is threatening to ban glitter again, Lily's talking about forming a Lantern Union, and someone needs to explain to Bev why we can't hold a wassail in September just because she found a discounted cider barrel."

Claire blinked. "You came to *me* for this?"

"I came," Ellie said, "because I needed somewhere with tea, emotional grounding, and at least one adult who can stop Lily from invoking solstice law."

Her eyes drifted to Claire's mother.

"Oh," she added, slightly more cautiously. "You're still here."

Claire's mum gave her a regal nod. "Always a pleasure, Ellie."

"Is it?" Ellie said, mostly to herself.

Claire sighed, motioned for her to sit, and got up to put the kettle on.

It was ridiculous, how natural it all felt. The three of them in the living room like some strange intergenerational sitcom—her mother with her bone china opinions, Ellie in paint-spattered leggings, and Claire herself standing in the middle with a heart full of unread messages and a sketchbook full of possibilities.

"Where's Jack?" Ellie asked, flopping onto the arm of the chair.

Claire blinked. "Why would I know?"

Ellie smirked. "Because your cheeks are still pink and there's a note on the table."

Claire spun. "Did you read it?"

Ellie snatched it up. "'Hope that's okay.' He signed it with a **J**. That's emotional vulnerability *and* calligraphic restraint."

Her mother smiled. "I quite like him."

Claire poured water into mugs and said nothing.

The kettle hissed, and for a moment the only sound was the low hum of conversation rising in the village outside.

Then her mother said—softly, but with steel—"Don't let your fear be louder than your instinct."

Claire froze.

Ellie looked up.

Her mum sipped her tea.

"Just saying," she added, too casually. "It'd be a shame if someone walked away from something good just because it wasn't on their original five-year plan."

Claire stared at her mother.

And then, quietly: "What if I get it wrong?"

"You will," Ellie said around her croissant. "That's how you know it's real."

They all sat in silence for a moment.

Three generations of opinion, love, and unsolicited advice steeping in a room scented with lentils and unresolved feelings.

Claire didn't speak.

But she sat a little straighter.

And held her mug like it might hold answers too.

Claire woke to the sound of birds.

And then, more tellingly, to the sound of **Jack's voice**—low, steady, speaking to someone just outside the kitchen window.

She sat up slowly, the familiar tug of muscles reminding her she'd fallen asleep on the sofa again. The phone still sat on the armrest, Jack's last message blinking silently on the lock screen like a secret that had fallen asleep with her.

Downstairs, she heard the faint clatter of something wooden being moved.

She padded down in bare feet, still in her oversized jumper, and paused at the kitchen door.

Jack stood just outside the back porch, his back to her, a long cedar plank resting across his shoulder like it weighed nothing. The early light caught the side of his neck, the curve of his jaw, the familiar grey T-shirt worn soft at the collar.

For a moment, she just watched.

He turned slightly—enough to see her through the glass.

A pause.

Then a slow smile that settled somewhere low in her chest.

Claire opened the door. The smell of **sawdust and rosemary** hit her at once—faint but recognisable now, like something her skin had started cataloguing without permission.

"Morning," she said, voice still thick with sleep.

He nodded. "Didn't mean to wake you."

"You didn't." She rubbed her eyes. "I just… heard birds. And then you. And then birds again. So many birds."

Jack chuckled and set the plank down gently against the wall.

"I was going to leave a note," he said.

Claire leaned against the doorframe. "You really like your notes."

He met her gaze, quiet. "Only for you."

She blinked.

Didn't move.

The moment hovered.

Then, to her relief and frustration, he broke it first—reaching into his tool bag and pulling out a folded paper.

"What's that?" she asked.

He held it out. "Frances's porch plan. She's decided she wants a veranda now. With latticework."

Claire took the sketch.

It was absurd. Full of curling scrolls and impossible lines that looked like they belonged on a Victorian wedding cake.

"She drew this on the back of a yoga leaflet?"

"Yeah. While eating a biscuit. Crumbs came free."

Claire laughed softly and tucked the paper under her arm. "You're doing it?"

Jack shrugged. "It's either me or the vicar, and he's still banned from power tools after the gazebo incident."

Claire bit her lip. "Do you ever say no to anyone?"

"I haven't said no to you yet."

That did something she wasn't prepared for.

Her hands tightened slightly around the sketch.

He didn't press.

Just said, "You want coffee?"

"God, yes."

A few minutes later, they sat on the back step, mugs warm in their hands, the early sun just beginning to stretch across the grass.

Claire sipped slowly, watching the steam curl.

Then: "Do you remember when you said… you'd want me to stay, but not if it wasn't the right reason?"

Jack nodded.

Claire stared into her mug. "What if I don't know what the right reason is yet?"

"You don't have to."

"I think people expect me to."

Jack ran a hand across the back of his neck—she noticed a faint mark of paint near his wrist. Probably from the Hall. Or Lily's latest banner.

"The people who love you," he said quietly, "will wait while you figure it out. Even if it's uncomfortable."

Claire looked over at him.

Really looked.

There was a piece of sawdust caught in his hair.

She reached out—without thinking—and brushed it away.

His eyes didn't leave hers.

"I think I'm scared of choosing wrong," she said.

Jack's voice didn't shift. "You're allowed to be."

They sat for a moment, the silence soft and full.

Then he nodded toward the garden gate. "I've got to drop some timber at Bev's."

Claire nodded, suddenly unsure what to do with her hands.

He stood.

Paused.

And then leaned down—not for a kiss, not yet—but just to touch his fingers lightly to the side of her hand.

Warm. Calloused. **Familiar**.

"I'll see you later," he said.

She nodded.

Watched him walk down the garden path.

And didn't realise she was still holding his mug until the sun reached it.

Claire walked back inside, still holding Jack's mug like it might tell her what to do if she tilted it just right.

The kitchen was warm now—sunlight trickling across the floor, the smell of toast rising faintly from the grill. She hadn't meant to stay out there that long.

She set the mug in the sink.

Then stood a moment longer, fingers resting on the counter, the quiet of the house settling around her like steam.

"Did you kiss him?"

Claire jumped.

Ellie was in the doorway, holding a teabag in one hand and a suspicious-looking croissant in the other.

"Ellie."

"What?" she said, utterly unrepentant. "You've got your 'I just emotionally tangled with a man who smells like timber and competence' face on."

"I do not."

"You do. You've had it since the lantern meeting."

Claire rolled her eyes and turned away, but not before Ellie caught the faintest blush on her cheeks.

"Also," Ellie went on, breezing past her to fill the kettle, "you're holding his mug again. I swear that thing's basically a stand-in boyfriend."

Claire dropped the mug into the sink with more force than necessary. "It's just a mug."

Ellie opened a cupboard. "Right. And I suppose you're also *not* rethinking your entire life plan one handwritten note at a time?"

Claire leaned against the counter, arms crossed. "He brought lentils."

"Wow," Ellie said, spinning. "That's it. Call off the search, you've found The One."

Claire bit back a smile. "It's not like that."

"Oh, no. Of course not," Ellie said, opening the fridge. "He just fixes your house, leaves you thoughtful notes, feeds you, and looks at you like you hung the moon."

Claire opened her mouth to reply, but Ellie held up a hand.

"Nope. I'm not done. He also doesn't flinch when your mother weaponises poached eggs, and he doesn't crowd you when you go quiet. And he built a bench. Who *builds a bench* anymore? It's like emotional Morse code for 'I would like to be in your life but I respect your boundaries.'"

Claire groaned and put her head on the counter. "Why are you like this?"

"Because you're bad at being in love, and someone has to narrate it for you."

There was a beat of silence, then:

"Wait," Ellie said, frowning slightly. "You are in love, right?"

Claire looked up slowly.

Didn't answer.

Ellie leaned back. "Oh."

Claire straightened, arms still crossed tightly. "It doesn't matter. I haven't decided anything."

"Right," Ellie said, slowly dunking her teabag. "So just to be clear: you're not in love, you haven't decided, and you definitely didn't linger on the porch this morning watching him like he was a well-seasoned Sunday roast?"

Claire covered her face with both hands.

Her mother chose that moment to enter, dressed in linen and smugness, holding a tray of perfectly arranged toast soldiers.

"Morning," she said sweetly. "Has she admitted it yet?"

Ellie pointed at Claire. "Cracked wide open."

Claire looked up. "Do either of you sleep? Or respect personal boundaries?"

Her mother sat primly. "Darling. You invited me."

"I didn't invite Ellie."

"I let myself in through the back," Ellie offered, sipping her tea. "Felt symbolic."

Claire sat down between them, feeling like the only sane person in a house being slowly repurposed into a female-led intervention.

Her mother passed her a slice of toast. "We're just saying, it's not often a man like that shows up and doesn't ask for anything."

Claire stared at the plate.

Then, softly: "He asked for honesty."

Ellie and her mother shared a look.

"And what are you giving him?" her mum asked gently.

Claire didn't answer.

But the truth settled like warm butter between them.

She didn't know yet.

Not really.

But she was getting closer.

Claire should have known something was up the moment Lily appeared at the front door in dungarees, holding a clipboard and wearing a flower crown.

"We're mobilising," she said breathlessly. "Emergency wellness market. Bev double-booked the cricket pavilion, the cheese fair pulled out, and we need to launch in ninety minutes before the weather turns on us and Frances has a complete chakra collapse."

Claire blinked. "Is that… a real sentence?"

"There's no time," Lily said, already stepping inside. "Ellie's on bunting, your mother's cornered the tea urn, and you've been elected Stall Wrangler."

"I didn't run."

"You never do," Lily said cheerfully. "But destiny doesn't wait."

Half an hour later, Claire was crouched beside a table of "energy-activated wax melts" trying to pin a plastic tablecloth to grass while Ellie tried to stop a toddler from ingesting a glitter crayon.

The "wellness market" had somehow taken over the edge of the green. There were tables, collapsible gazebos, a suspiciously psychic-looking dog wearing a neckerchief, and a vague promise of goat yoga that no one had quite verified.

Claire held a pot of beeswax candles in one hand and an unravelling banner in the other. "I swear Lily's events are just community therapy with props."

Ellie, wrestling with bunting, said, "It's either this or watching Frances steam her collection of heirloom teapots. Pick your chaos."

Claire was about to reply when someone shouted from the far end of the green.

Something sharp.

Then a *crack*.

Then a sound that could only be described as a communal gasp.

She looked up.

One of the folding tables had collapsed.

Directly underneath Lily's main candle display.

Scented wax was now oozing across the grass like a festive lava flow. The air smelled aggressively of lavender, bergamot, and something that might've been regret.

Lily shrieked. "My serenity candles!"

Claire sprinted forward without thinking, dodging bunting, stepping over fallen flyers.

She was halfway there when she saw **Jack**.

He was already at the table, trying to right one of the legs. His shirt was smudged with wax. His forehead lined, jaw set, fingers clenched slightly around the collapsed frame.

He looked—**not fine**.

Not the version of Jack she was used to.

Claire slowed.

She hadn't seen him flustered before. Not really. He was usually calm in the face of chaos, sardonic in the face of village nonsense.

But not now.

Not here.

He stood up slowly, wiping his hands on his jeans, exhaling like he'd been holding something back all morning.

Their eyes met.

Just for a second.

But in that second, she saw it all:

The tension in his shoulders. The pressure behind his usual ease. The effort it took to keep showing up—for everyone, for her—without asking for anything in return.

She moved closer.

"Jack…"

But he shook his head.

Just slightly.

Then said, loud enough for Lily to hear, "I'll fix it."

His voice was steady.

But not soft.

He crouched again, grabbing a new brace, and didn't look at her.

Claire hovered—unsure if she was meant to stay, help, or back away.

She chose silence.

She stepped back.

Let him breathe.

Even though every part of her wanted to reach in and ask what was wrong, what had happened, what he needed.

She didn't.

Because she knew that look.

It was the one she wore when she'd just crossed a line and didn't know how to uncross it.

Later, after the candles had been salvaged and the psychic dog had been banned for growling at the cheese substitute, Claire found herself back at the cottage, legs sore, shirt damp with accidental essential oil, mood unsettled.

She sat at the table with a glass of lemonade, staring at the pattern of sunlight on the tiles.

Her mother entered silently, set down her mug, and didn't sit.

"Something's shifted," she said.

Claire didn't answer.

"He was rattled today," her mother continued. "And you didn't reach for him."

Claire swallowed. "He didn't want me to."

Her mum sat slowly, folding her hands. "And when has that ever stopped you before? You're not someone who waits to be asked."

Claire didn't reply.

Her mother studied her. "He's not asking for anything, Claire. But that doesn't mean he doesn't need something."

Claire's throat tightened.

"He's shown up," her mother said. "Again and again. Not for credit. Just to be close."

"I know."

"So what are you waiting for?"

Claire stared at the table.

"I'm afraid," she said. "That if I say something… it'll change everything."

Her mum's voice was soft. "It already has."

Claire didn't change clothes.

She didn't fix her hair.

She didn't rehearse.

She just grabbed her jumper off the chair, stepped into her old trainers, and walked.

Across the green.

Down the path past the postbox and Frances's hydrangeas.

To his door.

The cottage looked the same as always. Clean lines, half-built planter boxes, that one shutter that refused to hang straight no matter how many times he adjusted it.

She stood at the gate for a full thirty seconds, gripping the top bar with fingers that wouldn't relax.

Then she stepped through and knocked.

One-two-three.

The kind of knock that didn't say urgent or casual.

Just… honest.

She waited.

Nothing.

She was about to step back when the door opened.

Jack stood there in a plain white T-shirt, tea towel in one hand, hair slightly damp like he'd just rinsed the day off and started again.

He looked surprised.

But not annoyed.

He didn't speak.

Neither did she.

So she held out the small parcel in her hand.

"I brought biscuits," she said.

He blinked. "You brought…?"

"They're the emotional kind," she said. "Chocolate Hobnobs. I panicked."

A pause.

Then something in his expression softened, and he stepped back.

"Come in."

The kitchen was warm.

Not because of the oven, but because he'd left the windows cracked just enough to let in the fading sun and the slow, steady smell of rosemary from the garden.

Claire stood in the doorway.

"About earlier…"

Jack wiped his hands on the towel, then set it down.

"You don't have to—"

"I want to."

He waited.

She took a breath.

"You were off," she said. "And I didn't know what to do. So I did nothing. And then I spent the whole afternoon being mad at myself for not doing something when I should've done *anything*."

Jack leaned back against the counter, arms crossed, watching her gently. "You don't have to fix everything."

"I don't want to fix you," she said. "I just want you to know… that I see it."

"See what?"

"That it's not easy. That you carry everything quietly. That sometimes you show up for people who don't even notice they needed you until you're already walking away."

Jack looked at her.

Long and still.

Then: "You noticed."

Claire nodded. "Too late. But I did."

The silence that followed wasn't awkward.

It was full.

"I'm not good at asking for help," he said finally.

"Me either."

Jack stepped forward, close enough that she could smell sawdust and soap.

"You didn't have to come."

"I know."

"But I'm glad you did."

Claire swallowed.

"Me too."

He didn't kiss her.

Not yet.

But his hand brushed hers when he reached for the biscuit tin.

And she didn't pull away.

Chapter Seventeen

"Teapots, Deadlines, and Other Quiet Explosions"

Claire woke to the smell of toast and not a single idea what day it was.

The sunlight hit the corner of her bedroom window in that unapologetic summer way—bold, deliberate, *cheering before coffee*—and for a moment, she lay there in the tangled sheets, blinking into the soft brightness and trying to sort dream from memory.

There had been a tin of biscuits.

A brush of hands.

A quiet kitchen that smelled of him.

Jack.

She turned over and pulled the blanket higher, letting the stillness settle a little longer than necessary. Her phone buzzed somewhere in the house, and she ignored it.

Let it wait.

For once, the day didn't start with a list.

Downstairs, her mother was already at the table in a crisp blouse, buttering toast with military precision and sipping tea that somehow never went cold.

"I made you a cup," she said without looking up. "I considered bringing it up with a marching band but decided against the theatre."

Claire shuffled in, barefoot and wrinkled. "How thoughtful."

"Lily's outside," her mum added. "Something about a table emergency. I didn't ask."

Claire poured tea, took a long sip, and didn't flinch when the front door opened with its usual creak.

Lily burst in wearing a knitted poncho, a belt made of string, and a face full of existential purpose.

"We're under siege."

Claire blinked. "By…?"

"The **Historical Preservation Society**. Frances tried to book the church hall for a wellness chakra rebalancing clinic and accidentally overlapped with the Quilting Guild. It's turned into a passive-aggressive bake-off. There's lemon drizzle everywhere."

Claire looked to her mother, who calmly bit into her toast.

"I told you not to leave the house," her mother said.

Lily dropped a clipboard onto the table. "I need support. Emotional and physical. You're both coming."

"I have a call at noon," Claire said quickly.

"With Thomas?" her mum asked, too smoothly.

Claire glared. "You're suddenly interested in my work schedule?"

"I'm interested in how you're going to justify a thousand-mile consultancy contract with your heart currently hiding in a biscuit tin two doors down."

Lily clapped once. "That's poetic, and also, we're late."

Claire downed the rest of her tea and followed them both out, shoes barely on, hair not even pretending to behave.

The church hall was, indeed, **bedlam**.

One side smelled of incense and vegan brownies; the other was a fortress of gingham tablecloths and Victoria sponge cakes that looked like they'd been judged by Mary Berry *and found wanting*. Bev stood in the middle with a mixing bowl and a face like a thundercloud.

Frances was trying to rebrand the event as a "shared energy exchange with flour."

Claire ducked behind a table.

Ellie appeared beside her with a clipboard and a slightly glazed expression.

"I told you not to come."

"I was dragged."

"Fair." She nodded toward the corner. "Jack's here."

Claire turned.

And there he was—kneeling beside the raffle table, trying to fix the broken ticket drum while Bev shouted about unlawful stapling.

His shoulders looked tight.

But when he glanced up and saw her, something shifted.

His eyes softened.

His jaw unclenched.

And without saying a word, he nodded.

Claire smiled.

Then got up and walked across the hall—**not for him**, not exactly.

But because **she didn't want to not be near him**.

And sometimes, that was all the decision she needed.

Claire wasn't sure whether the cake stand explosion or the flying custard was technically the beginning of the end.

But somewhere between Lily lighting incense next to a tray of lemon slices and Bev losing her footing on a rogue scone, it became **clear** that the wellness-bake-off-crossover had crossed a line from charming to cursed.

The moment of impact—custard, tray, Frances shrieking about "sacred chiffon boundaries"—was almost cinematic.

The silence afterward was not.

Claire froze, holding a tin of ginger snaps that had *not asked for this level of exposure*.

Jack, still crouched beside the raffle table, slowly wiped a splatter of custard off his sleeve.

Then looked at her.

There was a pause.

And then—quietly, gently—he laughed.

Not a big laugh.

Just the kind of chuckle that started in the chest and ended somewhere behind his eyes.

Claire blinked.

Then grinned.

It was ridiculous.

All of it.

But somehow—right then—it felt like the most grounded thing in the room.

They retreated behind the bunting.

Claire passed him a paper towel. "This may be the most traumatic thing I've seen in a church hall."

Jack wiped his hands. "And I fixed a ceiling here once during a ferret blessing ceremony."

Claire winced. "I remember. That was the week Lily tried to ordain a sheep."

They sat on a wooden bench behind the raffle table, legs stretched out, knees just barely brushing.

The hall bustled around them—someone mopping, someone shouting about pudding rights, someone attempting to realign Frances's aura with a harmonica.

But here, in the small shadow of the stall, it felt still.

Safe.

Claire leaned back. "I used to think the chaos was the problem."

Jack tilted his head.

"And now?"

"Now I think… it might be the point."

Jack looked at her for a long time.

Then quietly: "You're not running, are you?"

Claire hesitated.

"No."

He nodded.

Didn't say anything more.

And she was grateful for that.

Because if he had pushed, if he had asked for more than she could give today—she wasn't sure what she'd say.

But here, with scone crumbs at their feet and the faint smell of cinnamon in the air, she didn't have to be sure.

She just had to be *here*.

With him.

Outside, the clouds thickened.

Someone rang a bell for no discernible reason.

But inside, beneath the bunting and the buttercream, Claire stayed seated beside him.

Not to fix anything.

Just to be close.

The bell, as it turned out, had not been symbolic.

It was Bev.

And she was holding a **clipboard**.

Which, in Claire's experience, never meant anything good.

"We've had a dropout," Bev barked, waving the clipboard like a warning flag. "Two, actually. Colin's trifle has gone rogue and Angela's soufflé collapsed under pressure. So we need volunteers. Immediately."

Claire looked around in case someone else might stand up.

They didn't.

Everyone suddenly became *very interested* in napkin folding.

Bev's eyes landed on Claire. "You bake."

Claire blinked. "Occasionally."

"She's being modest," said Lily, who had reappeared beside the jam jars like a benevolent chaos sprite. "Her fig scones recalibrated my entire nervous system."

"I just followed a recipe."

Jack nudged her shoulder gently. "You should do it."

Claire turned. "Are you trying to get rid of me?"

He smiled. "Absolutely not. I just think someone should show Frances that real wellness starts with actual butter."

Claire stood slowly. "If I end up in a bake-off duel with a man who thinks beetroot is a personality trait, I'm blaming you."

Jack tipped his head. "Deal."

Twenty minutes later, Claire found herself behind a folding table with a borrowed apron, a tin of slightly misshapen shortbread, and a growing audience.

Frances stood at the judging table with her arms crossed and a frown that could curdle cream.

"Presentation?" she said, eyeing the shortbread like it had made personal life choices she didn't approve of.

"Rustic," Claire offered.

"Interpretive," Lily chimed in helpfully.

Bev, for her part, was eating hers unapologetically, nodding like it was a political statement.

And then—

The door creaked.

And someone unfamiliar stepped into the hall.

A man.

Tall, well dressed.

Holding a briefcase.

Claire froze.

Jack, still at the side of the room fixing the raffle board, also straightened.

The man looked around, eyes scanning the mayhem—custard streaks, glitter bunting, a clearly malfunctioning crystal healing corner—and landed on Claire.

"Claire Everley?"

Her throat dried instantly. "Yes?"

He smiled. "I'm with Thomas Rowe's office. He sent me ahead of schedule—thought we might touch base in person while I was nearby."

Claire blinked.

"Nearby?"

"I was visiting our Devon clients. He said you'd be free for a few minutes."

Claire looked down at her apron. Her flour-dusted fingers. The shortbread crumbs on her shoes.

Around her, the village paused.

Then, all at once, tried to look like it wasn't listening.

She turned slightly.

Caught Jack's expression.

Neutral.

Careful.

And that—*that*—was worse than anything.

Because it meant he was bracing.

For what she might say.

For what she might choose.

For who she might still be.

The man cleared his throat. "If this is a bad time…"

Claire smiled, tight. "Give me five minutes."

She stepped out from behind the table.

But not before Jack said—softly, and only to her—

"Don't forget your biscuit."

She turned back.

Picked up the least wonky shortbread.

And held it like a talisman.

As Claire followed the man out of the church hall, her biscuit held like a peace offering, Jack didn't move.

Didn't call after her.

Didn't ask who he was or why she'd gone.

He just kept his hands in his pockets and stared at the place she'd been standing a moment before—like something might still echo there if he looked long enough.

Around him, the bustle resumed.

Bev had launched into a tirade about cinnamon theft.

Frances was claiming her meringue had been sabotaged.

But it all blurred for a moment.

Until Lily appeared.

Still in her poncho. Still barefoot for some reason. Holding two mugs of lukewarm herbal tea and wearing that expression she got when she was *pretending* to be breezy.

She handed him a mug.

"You okay?"

Jack took it. "Fine."

Lily tilted her head. "Hmm."

"What?"

"It's just… I've known you a long time."

Jack raised an eyebrow. "And?"

"And that's your emotional-silence voice."

He smiled faintly. "I didn't know I had one."

"Oh, you do," she said, sitting beside him on the edge of the raffle table. "It's somewhere between 'I'm coping' and 'I may sand down a doorframe just to feel something.'"

Jack huffed a laugh but didn't answer.

Lily let the silence settle.

Then: "She didn't look happy to see him."

Jack didn't speak.

Lily took a sip of her tea. "You think she's leaving?"

"I think," he said finally, "that she's still deciding."

Lily nodded. "And you're not going to try and convince her?"

Jack stared down into his mug.

"No."

"Why not?"

"Because she's not something you convince. She's someone you wait for."

That earned a pause.

And then, softly: "You're in love with her."

Jack didn't look at Lily.

But he didn't deny it either.

Across the hall, Ellie knocked over a jar of chia seeds.

Bev shrieked.

Frances muttered something about sabotage.

Lily smiled and bumped his shoulder. "Just so you know," she said, "if she doesn't pick you, I will never speak to her again."

Jack looked over. "Bit harsh."

"She'd deserve it."

Jack chuckled. "You're very loyal."

"I'm very nosy," Lily said. "But in this case, they overlap."

They sat there for another moment.

The kind of moment Colgan characters live for—the ones where nothing is said, but *everything* is understood.

Outside, the clouds were breaking up.

A bit of sunlight slipped through the stained glass, landing in a puddle of light at Jack's feet.

He didn't notice.

He was still looking at the door.

The rest of the day passed in a sort of gentle blur.

Claire managed to navigate the brief meeting with Thomas's assistant without dropping her shortbread or her temper—though the way the man had looked around the church hall, eyebrows arched at the bunting and biscuit chaos, had made her itch. He hadn't understood. Not the setting, not the people, not the life she was building between the chaos.

Not the choice she hadn't made yet—but was beginning to feel settle somewhere in her chest like a slowly turning tide.

By the time she slipped back into the hall, most of the stalls had packed up. Glitter dust clung to the corners of the floor. Someone had drawn a smiley face in the remaining custard puddle. Ellie was arguing with Bev about the ethical implications of raffling off foot scrubs, and Jack was nowhere to be seen.

Claire stood in the doorway for a moment longer than necessary.

She wasn't sure if she was disappointed, or relieved.

That evening, the cottage smelled faintly of wood polish and rosemary. The kettle clicked as it boiled, and the sky outside burned low with summer's end.

Claire sat at the kitchen table, legs curled beneath her, a notebook open in front of her and nothing written inside it.

Lily was upstairs—she'd bounded in earlier, wild-eyed from a group of children who had attempted, and failed, to build a lemonade-powered rocket. She'd only paused long enough to tell Claire, in great detail, why she believed oranges were "emotionally manipulative" before disappearing to her room with a poster tube and half a roll of masking tape.

Now the house was quiet again.

And that's when the knock came.

Not loud.

Just enough to break the stillness.

Claire opened the door to find Jack standing there with a mug in one hand and a small cardboard box in the other.

"She said I wasn't allowed to go to bed without delivering this," he said. "Apparently it's urgent."

Claire took the box and opened it.

Inside: two melted marshmallows, a hand-drawn map of the village (labelled 'MOST CHAOTIC PLACES'), and a note written in glitter pen:

"For Claire. Because you're brave and also really bad at ducking flying cupcakes. Love, Lily (age 11, in case you forgot)."

Claire laughed, something catching slightly in her chest.

"She's brilliant," she said softly.

"She is," Jack agreed. "She also thinks the cottage might be haunted, because you talk to the walls sometimes when you think no one's listening."

Claire flushed. "I—"

"I told her everyone does it," he added. "Especially when they're trying to figure out if they've accidentally fallen for someone in the middle of bunting season."

The silence stretched.

Then twisted softly.

"Have they?" Claire asked, without meeting his eyes.

Jack didn't answer.

But he smiled.

That small, sideways smile that never tried to be anything more than honest.

"I think," he said finally, "they might be trying not to."

Claire looked up.

And just like that—nothing else needed to be said.

Claire set the box on the counter and turned back to the kettle, pouring two mugs without asking. Jack stepped inside without being invited, which by now was its own sort of invitation.

They sat for a while, not saying much.

The marshmallows were gooey and slightly fused to the cardboard, but they ate them anyway. And when Jack left, he didn't say goodbye—just a soft, "See you tomorrow," like they'd always been meeting across a quiet threshold.

Claire locked the door, leaned back against it for a second, and let out a breath she didn't know she'd been holding.

The next morning began with birdsong and a text from Ellie.

Greenhouse emergency. Bring coffee. Possibly plasters.

Claire padded downstairs in Jack's oversized hoodie—which, if she was honest, had ended up on the coat hook after he'd left it during the shelf-fixing incident and never quite made its way back.

She made two travel mugs of coffee, grabbed a banana, and stepped outside into one of those bright mornings that looked lovely but still smelled like wet grass and minor regrets.

The village was already stirring. A man with a ladder was trying to reach a gutter that didn't want to be reached. Bev was arguing with someone about raffle ticket ethics (again). And the bakery had a chalkboard sign that simply read:

"SORRY ABOUT YESTERDAY. WE PANICKED."

Claire found Ellie standing behind the greenhouse, looking murderous and holding a trowel like it might double as a weapon.

"Slugs," she said by way of greeting. "In the spinach. The little bastards have unionised."

Claire handed her the coffee. "Commiseration, or encouragement?"

Ellie sipped. "Both. You look smug."

"I do not."

"You do. What happened?"

"Nothing."

Ellie raised an eyebrow. "Jack?"

Claire said nothing.

Ellie smirked. "Thought so."

They worked side by side for a while—Ellie swearing at invasive weeds, Claire gently relocating snails, both of them sweating mildly and pretending not to.

Eventually Ellie tossed down her gloves and leaned against the greenhouse wall.

"You know," she said, brushing dirt off her jeans, "the whole village has noticed."

"Noticed what?"

"Oh come on, Claire. You two orbit each other like a pair of socially awkward moons. It's adorable and agonising."

Claire flushed. "We're just—"

"Don't," Ellie said. "Don't say 'friends.' He doesn't look at friends the way he looks at you."

Claire didn't answer.

Because Ellie was right.

And maybe—just maybe—she was starting to look back the same way.

The cottage smelled like toast and pencil shavings.

Claire stepped inside, brushing flecks of soil from her sleeves, and was immediately greeted by a thud upstairs—followed by a muffled, "I meant to do that!"

She smiled, set down her mug, and climbed the stairs.

Lily's door was wide open, as usual, and the floor was strewn with what looked like a **papier-mâché diorama of the Moonlight Market**, complete with glitter pipe-cleaner villagers and a tiny model of Frances holding what might have once been a baguette.

Lily was lying on her stomach in the middle of it all, drawing furiously.

"Busy?" Claire asked.

Lily didn't look up. "Mildly. Frances is being difficult about the raffle tickets."

Claire stepped over a cardboard tree. "Naturally."

Lily flipped her pencil around and erased something with intense concentration.

"Did you know," she said, "that if you eat a marshmallow with your eyes closed, it's supposed to activate your trust chakra?"

Claire blinked. "I… didn't, no."

"Lily Snorklepuff on YouTube said so. She has six goats and a tiny house and one of those kitchens that folds into a shelf. I think she might be magic."

"I'll take your word for it."

Lily sat up suddenly. "Are you going to kiss my dad?"

Claire nearly dropped a glue stick.

"What?"

Lily looked entirely unbothered. "It's not a weird question. People kiss. It's all over telly."

Claire tried very hard not to laugh—or panic. "That's not… I mean, it's not something people just—announce."

"Why not?" Lily said. "He likes you. And you're not horrible."

Claire opened her mouth. Then closed it again.

Then sat down on the edge of the bed beside a marshmallow sculpture that might've been a dog.

"Your dad," she said slowly, "is a very kind man."

Lily grinned. "He used to burn toast a lot. Now he only does it on Tuesdays."

"I'll keep that in mind."

Lily leaned against her. "You make him less grumpy. And you don't get cross when I borrow your socks to make puppets."

Claire smiled. "High praise."

They sat like that for a few minutes.

No pressure. No expectations.

Just an 11-year-old girl with a craft knife in her ponytail and a woman trying to untangle a heart that had been quiet for too long.

Eventually, Lily said, "Do you want to help me build the market stage?"

Claire glanced at the box of matchsticks and glitter glue.

"I thought you'd never ask."

They were well into construction when Claire finally realised her socks had been turned into tiny market stall awnings.

Lily, for her part, had not asked permission—but she had, at least, used the clean ones.

The living room was a riot of paper scraps, glitter tubes, paintbrushes stuck upright in mugs, and the occasional marshmallow that had inexplicably rolled under the sofa. Claire's knees ached from kneeling on the floor, but she didn't move. Not yet. Not while Lily was still narrating the scene in her bright, sing-song voice.

"So this is the cider tent," Lily said, pointing to a cardboard tube with tiny flags taped around the top. "But it only sells fake cider because Bev said she wouldn't be responsible for sugar-high eleven-year-olds doing the conga."

Claire laughed, adjusting the tiny bunting so it didn't collapse inward. "A wise decision."

"And over here is the glitter station," Lily continued, "where children are invited to lose their dignity."

Claire raised an eyebrow. "That sounds suspiciously personal."

"I may have glued my elbow to the table last year," Lily said solemnly. "But only temporarily."

They both fell into giggles.

It was odd, Claire thought, how natural this felt. She had never considered herself particularly maternal—not in the way some women were—but there was something in the way Lily moved through the world that made space for you. Not demanding, but inclusive. She didn't just want Claire's company—she assumed it. As if Claire had always been part of this world of mislabelled glitter pots and emotional marshmallows.

It made something inside her soften.

"Did you ever build models with your mum?" Lily asked suddenly, adjusting a bottlecap she'd turned into a pretend chocolate fountain.

Claire stilled. "Not really," she said after a beat. "She was… busy."

"With work?"

"With everything. But mostly, I think, with not knowing what to do with me."

Lily tilted her head. "But you're easy to do stuff with."

Claire smiled. "Am I?"

"Yeah," Lily said with certainty. "You're good at pretending things matter."

Claire blinked. "What do you mean?"

"Like… you help me build this, even though it's a bit silly. But you don't laugh at it. You let it be real."

Claire reached over and tucked a strand of Lily's hair behind her ear. "That's because it is real. It matters because you care about it."

Lily beamed, then promptly leaned across her own cardboard stalls and whispered, "I think you're probably in love with my dad."

Claire almost snorted glitter.

"I'm not saying I am," she said carefully.

"But you might be."

"I might be... confused."

Lily nodded, utterly unbothered. "Love is always confusing. So are recipes. And long division."

Claire laughed, but there was a small lump in her throat now. One she couldn't quite swallow away.

Lily flopped back dramatically onto the rug. "Can we watch something now? I'm emotionally drained from managing an entire fictional marketplace."

Claire glanced at the clock. "Half an hour before dinner."

"Then I vote for the cooking show where everyone cries when their meringue collapses."

Claire flicked on the telly, and Lily wriggled into place beside her, head resting lightly on Claire's arm.

As the music began and a voiceover introduced "Trifle of Tears," Claire found herself exhaling—just a little—and letting the moment wrap itself around them like the oversized blanket Lily insisted was made from "the dreams of sleepy clouds."

And she thought: if this wasn't a kind of love, she didn't know what was.

The credits rolled in pastel cursive as the trifle on-screen imploded for dramatic effect. Lily gave a theatrical sigh and declared, "Justice for the lady with the lemon zest!" before stretching like a cat across the sofa.

Claire smiled, her fingers idly brushing a fleck of glitter off the hem of her jumper. The blanket was bunched between them, still warm from the shared stillness.

And then came the sound of a key turning in the door.

Jack stepped in, shrugging out of his jacket with that habitual quietness he always carried—like someone who didn't want to take up more space than necessary.

Lily bounced upright.

"You're late," she announced. "We already watched the emotional baking show."

"I can see I've missed something important," he said, stepping into the living room and pausing when he saw the glitter-blown chaos of the coffee table. "Should I be worried?"

"She's been helping me build the Moonlight Market," Lily said, with the casual pride of an architect unveiling a cathedral. "Claire says it's art."

"I said it's imaginative," Claire corrected.

"Same thing," Lily said breezily, already fishing around in her snack box for something crunchy.

Jack took in the sight—the mismatched models, the sofa fort barely holding together, the scattering of Claire's notebooks across the arm of the chair—and something in his expression softened.

"You've had a productive day, then," he said.

"She let me use her socks," Lily added.

Jack raised an eyebrow.

Claire held up a hand. "Voluntarily-ish."

He smiled. "Then I'm out of things to contribute. Shall I make tea?"

"Unless it's the sort of tea that comes with biscuits," Lily said, "I vote pasta. Claire said she likes dinner early, and also I'm starving and that makes me dramatic."

"You're dramatic anyway," Jack murmured, already heading for the kitchen.

Claire stood and started helping Lily gather the worst of the crafting debris, sliding markers back into their mismatched caps and brushing sequins into a pile that looked vaguely like a snowdrift. Lily narrated each item as it was lifted.

"Historic spoon. Legendary glue. Cursed glitter tube."

Claire paused. "Why cursed?"

"It explodes under pressure."

Claire peered at the lid, which was suspiciously taped shut.

"Fair enough."

In the kitchen, Jack moved with quiet efficiency. He didn't ask what had happened that day, didn't push, didn't pry. Just filled the pot, measured the pasta, stirred the sauce. And when Claire moved to help, he handed her the wooden spoon and nodded once, as if to say *stay, if you want to.*

She stayed.

Lily took over the dining table, now cleared enough to reveal its surface. She began sorting beads into colour-coded piles, humming a tune that might've been from the baking show or just something she made up.

"Did you always want to live in a place like this?" Claire asked, stirring gently.

Jack leaned on the counter, drying his hands on a tea towel. "Not always. Just once I realised what mattered."

Claire glanced at him.

He shrugged. "Noise never suited me. But this place… Lily likes it. And I like that she likes it."

Claire nodded. "It's growing on me."

He watched her for a second longer than necessary.

Then Lily called out, "Is it ready yet? Because I'm either going to faint or start eating beads."

"Almost," Jack said, pushing off the counter and reaching for the plates.

They ate together around the table, just the three of them.

Lily told stories with the full flair of a child who knew she had a captive audience. Claire smiled more than she spoke. Jack watched them both in the way of a man who never quite believed he deserved a moment like this—but knew enough to treasure it.

When the plates were cleared and Lily had finally yawned her way toward bed, dragging her bead box and a half-eaten biscuit, Claire stood in the kitchen doorway with Jack beside her, mugs in hand.

"She's good company," Claire said.

"She likes you."

Claire looked at him. "Do you?"

Jack didn't answer straight away.

He just turned to her, quiet as always, and said, "You make this place feel like more than just somewhere we landed."

Claire didn't know what to say to that.

So she didn't.

Not yet.

The house was still.

Claire stood at the kitchen sink, rinsing out mugs that didn't really need rinsing, just for something to do. The tap ran too long. The tea had long gone cold. Outside the window, the cottage garden was bathed in silver light, the overgrown lavender glowing pale in the moonlight, and somewhere, she was fairly certain, a hedgehog was rustling about under the hydrangeas.

She'd turned off the lights but hadn't yet convinced herself to go to bed. Her body was tired, but her thoughts were jumpy and knotted—an endless mental loop of Lily's words, Jack's half-smile, the familiar clink of plates shared between three people who didn't quite call themselves a family, but might as well have.

She wandered into the living room. The chaos of the day was still there, mostly tidied but not quite gone. Pipe cleaners curled on the edge of the rug. One of her socks was still acting as a canopy over a tiny lemonade stand. A single purple sequin sat on the windowsill like it had been placed there on purpose.

Claire picked it up, turned it between her fingers.

She didn't want to move it. Not yet.

She turned out the hall light and padded upstairs, the old wooden floor creaking in the way it always did—three creaks at the landing, one at the top step. She didn't even flinch anymore. The cottage had long since learned to welcome her back.

In her room, she changed into pyjamas and opened the window a little wider, letting the cool air wash through. Her notebook sat waiting on the bedside table, but she didn't open it.

Instead, she stood in front of the mirror, brushing out her hair slowly, as if that might help smooth the things inside her that still felt tangled.

She thought of Jack's face as he'd watched Lily talk.

The way his shoulders eased when he wasn't trying to be anything other than himself.

The way her own breath had caught when he'd looked at her—not with expectation or pressure, but with quiet familiarity. Like she was already part of something he didn't want to break.

She crawled under the covers and stared at the ceiling.

Lily had been so certain. Eleven-year-olds often were.

But what Lily didn't see—what maybe no one else could—was how fragile this was. How one wrong move, one misplaced hope, could undo it all. Claire had built her life carefully this time. She'd picked quiet. Chosen small.

And now?

Now she wasn't sure if her heart would let her stay tucked inside the lines she'd drawn.

The next morning began with a muffled thud from downstairs and the unmistakable scent of burning toast.

Claire groaned, rolled over, and checked the time. Too early. But also, exactly the time Lily tended to experiment with unsupervised breakfast ambitions.

She padded down the stairs in slippers, pulling her dressing gown tighter around her.

Lily was at the toaster, staring at it like it had betrayed her. There were crumbs everywhere and something slightly jam-adjacent smeared across the front of the fridge.

"I was going to make you breakfast," Lily said without turning around. "But the toast has... rebelled."

Claire peered at the blackened slices. "I see."

"I also may have confused balsamic glaze with treacle."

Claire blinked. "That's... an ambitious pairing."

"I'm developing a signature style," Lily said, as if this were perfectly reasonable. "Do you want the less-burnt one?"

"Tempting," Claire said, reaching for the kettle instead. "How about tea first?"

Lily bounced on her toes. "Deal. I'll plate the remains."

By the time Jack appeared in the doorway, freshly showered and already buttoning up a work shirt, Claire and Lily were seated at the table with two mugs, a pile of toast casualties, and a grapefruit that no one was brave enough to cut.

Jack stopped, took in the scene, and raised an eyebrow. "Is it safe?"

"No," Lily said brightly. "But we're committed now."

He grinned and stepped into the room, brushing a kiss onto Lily's head as he passed. "Your efforts are appreciated, even if they've confused my sense of smell."

Claire sipped her tea, trying not to watch the way Jack moved around the kitchen. He was light on his feet in the mornings. Efficient. Quiet. Like someone used to taking care of everything before anyone else woke up.

"I'm going to swing by the green this morning," he said, glancing out the window. "Apparently one of the new signs fell over during the night."

"That'll be the bunting curse," Lily said solemnly. "Frances broke the ceremony by shouting at a squirrel."

Jack gave her a look, then turned to Claire. "Do you want to come by later? We could do a materials check. If you're still planning to finish the front step."

Claire hesitated.

It was a small thing.

Just a repair. A plan. A reason to be in the same space again.

But the way he asked—not casually, not insistently, just... openly—made something inside her catch.

She looked at Lily, who was now carving faces into her toast crusts with the tip of a spoon.

Then she looked at Jack.

And nodded. "Sure. I'll bring biscuits."

He smiled, and for the first time that morning, Claire felt herself smile back without having to try.

Chapter Eighteen

"Biscuits, Bolts and Beginning Again"

The sun had already claimed the village green by the time Claire stepped outside, biscuit tin tucked under one arm and her scarf tied neatly at her neck. The air was the sort of early-autumn crisp that made everything feel sharper, more possible, and the sky above was a stretch of polite blue, dappled with hints of the weather that might change its mind by afternoon.

Claire crossed the lane with the familiar rhythm of someone who had, despite her own surprise, memorised the creak of every gate and the shape of every neighbour's morning routine. Bev's curtains were drawn but her kettle was whistling. The baker's son was loading trays into the van with the usual clatter. And on the corner, someone had once again attempted to fix the leaning sign for the antiques shop with what looked like chewing gum and hope.

She smiled to herself. The village never really changed. It simply adjusted.

Jack was already at the green, crouched near the fallen signpost, one hand braced against the wooden stake while the other worked a new bolt into place. His toolbox sat open beside him, and his hair was still damp from the shower, curling slightly at the back like it hadn't quite decided how presentable to be.

Claire approached quietly, her footsteps soft on the grass. "Your arch-nemesis strikes again."

Jack looked up with a wry smile. "If I ever meet the person who installed these things originally, I'm going to make them personally accountable for every loose screw in this parish."

She held up the biscuit tin. "Peace offering?"

"Always."

They sat on the edge of the green, the tin between them. Jack reached for one of the oat and cranberry ones, while Claire broke a shortbread in half and held it delicately between her fingers.

Nearby, Lily and two other kids were setting up a temporary chalk mural on the pavement. She waved at them with her foot, already mid-instruction, bossing around a slightly bewildered boy with a lopsided beret.

Jack watched her for a moment, quiet.

"She's grown more in the last year than I expected," he said. "Not just taller. Smarter. Braver. Sometimes I don't know where she gets it from."

Claire looked at him. "She gets it from you."

He smiled, eyes still on his daughter. "She gets the glitter from her mother."

There was a beat of stillness between them.

"I forget to ask sometimes," Claire said gently. "Do you want to talk about her?"

Jack didn't answer right away. He placed his biscuit down, wiped his palms on his jeans.

"She was brilliant," he said at last. "In the exhausting kind of way. You could never keep up. When Lily was born, I think we both panicked for a year straight. Then one day, she looked at me across the kitchen, hair full of baby food and mascara smudged to her ears, and said, 'We're doing it, aren't we?'"

Claire let the quiet settle between them.

"After she passed," he continued, voice softer, "I stopped laughing. Not deliberately. It just... slipped away."

Claire reached out, her fingers brushing his.

"It's okay to find it again."

He looked at her then. Not like he had before. Not just with appreciation or ease. But with the tentative gaze of someone who had kept a door closed for a very long time and was now, just maybe, leaning toward the handle.

The moment stretched. Not dramatic. Not rushed. Just quietly real.

And then Lily shouted something about needing emergency sparkle reinforcement, and the spell broke, but gently.

Jack stood first. "Duty calls."

Claire watched him jog over to the kids, handing over a mystery container from his coat pocket like a seasoned field operative. Lily grinned, already dragging him into a debate about the optimal angle for chalk stars.

Claire stayed on the grass, biscuit forgotten, heart oddly full.

Not everything had to be decided yet.

But some things were finally beginning to open.

Claire lingered on the green longer than she meant to, watching Jack with the kids. His sleeves were pushed up, revealing the faint mark of a long-healed scar across one forearm—something faintly industrial, possibly involving a shelf that had fallen over—or, knowing Jack, that he'd tried to catch. Lily had one hand tugging him in one direction, another child pulling his other sleeve toward the chalk star layout, and Jack, smiling despite the chaos, looked like a man who was right where he wanted to be.

And Claire—well, she wasn't sure what that meant for her.

She stood, brushed biscuit crumbs off her skirt, and started back toward the cottage. The warmth of the sun softened the bite of the wind, and the path home curved through the centre of the village like it had always known its way. Ellie spotted her just outside the post office.

"Oh good, you've survived," Ellie said, stepping into pace beside her with an envelope in one hand and a suspiciously squashed jam tart in the other. "I assumed either you'd melted under Jack's gaze or been conscripted into Lily's sparkle brigade."

"Both," Claire muttered.

Ellie smirked. "Ah. A double-whammy. Poor thing."

They passed Bev's front gate, where a small handwritten sign declared: *CLOSED DUE TO OVERWHELM*. Claire nodded at it. "That sums it up."

"You should see what's happening in the hall," Ellie said. "The committee's tried to reorganise the bake-off table according to 'spiritual pastry value'. Half the volunteers have staged a coup. I left when someone used the word 'authentic tart energy' in a non-ironic way."

Claire laughed, the sound easing something tight in her chest.

"Also," Ellie added, waving the crumpled envelope, "this came for you. Found it in the back room by accident. It's got that loopy handwriting I'd bet money belongs to your mother."

Claire accepted it with one brow raised. "Please tell me it's not another photocopied soup recipe with spiritual affirmations."

"No, I opened it. You're invited to a full moon release circle with ceremonial cacao and drumming."

"Oh joy."

They reached the cottage and Ellie followed her in without being asked, stepping over a stray sock Lily had flung into the hallway during one of her many spontaneous outfit revisions.

"I thought you were helping set up the Harvest Ball stalls today?" Claire asked.

"I was," Ellie said, collapsing into the armchair. "Then I remembered I'd rather stick cocktail sticks in my eyeballs than alphabetise bunting."

Claire peeled open the envelope. The handwriting inside was exactly as she remembered: energetic, slightly manic, a heavy swirl on every Y. Her mother had signed it "Moonlight and Marmalade" and included a flyer for a mindfulness retreat in Devon.

"I should've guessed it would involve tents," she said aloud.

"Tents, crystals, and at least one woman called River who sells herbal suppositories."

Claire shuddered. "God."

Ellie grinned. "Are you going?"

Claire gave her a look.

"Fair. But hey," Ellie continued, more gently now, "that thing on the green—Jack, Lily, you… It looked nice."

"It was," Claire admitted.

"And?"

"And… I don't know."

Ellie stood. "Maybe you don't need to know yet. Maybe it's allowed to just be nice."

Claire nodded slowly. She wasn't used to 'just nice'. Most things in her life had always been either fragile or chaotic, rarely steady. Rarely safe.

As Ellie left with a wave and a warning not to let Bev near anything involving icing sugar, Claire drifted toward the kitchen window.

Outside, a breeze lifted the edge of Lily's chalk mural, tugging the paper just enough to flip over the corner. Claire stepped out, crossed the garden, and tucked it back in place, smoothing the sheet as she did.

It wasn't until she looked closer that she noticed one of the chalk stars had her name in the middle.

Not 'Mum' or 'Claire'.

Just: **YOU ARE HERE**.

A child's doodle. A bright yellow shape with arms and legs and a lopsided heart inside.

Claire touched it gently. The chalk smeared under her fingertip.

Then she went back inside and didn't speak for a long time.

The knock came late in the afternoon, just as Claire was halfway through sorting the box of oddments she'd labelled "front room maybe?" sometime during the first week she'd moved in and then promptly abandoned.

She'd been holding a brass candlestick in one hand and a faded postcard from Scarborough in the other, debating which was more mysterious and whether either deserved space on the windowsill, when she heard the tap-tap—measured, solid, and unmistakably Jack.

Claire opened the door with a tug, not quite sure what her expression was doing.

Jack stood there holding a small wooden crate with "Greenvale Harvest" stamped along the edge. He had on his same battered coat and the sleeves were pushed up again, exposing his forearms to the wind like it hadn't even occurred to him to mind the cold.

"Delivery," he said, holding out the box.

Claire peered inside. "Plums and a potato?"

"I was told it was an essential emergency supply," he said. "Also, there's a scroll."

At the bottom of the crate, sure enough, was a rolled-up piece of brown paper tied with string.

Claire took it out and unfurled it slowly. There, in bright purple marker and suspiciously glittery ink, was a hastily drawn map with three oversized stars and the words "Secret Planning Council Emergency" underlined twice.

She sighed. "Lily?"

Jack nodded. "And possibly Bev. And someone with a laminator. I think they're calling it a 'pre-ball pre-meeting regroup'."

Claire blinked. "A what?"

"Your guess is as good as mine. But I think you're expected at the village hall in… well—" he pulled out his phone, squinting at a glitter-covered message, "—thirteen minutes."

Claire stared at him. "Is this an ambush?"

"Highly likely."

There was a pause. The kind of quiet where you pretend to think through options, even though you both already know you're going.

"I could stall them," Jack offered. "Show up alone and claim you've been taken hostage by your own wallpaper paste."

She gave him a look. "You really think that would stop Lily?"

He grinned. "Not even slightly."

Claire grabbed her coat, stuffed the scroll into her pocket, and locked the door behind her.

As they walked toward the hall, Jack glanced sideways at her. "You okay?"

"With what?"

"Whatever face you were making before you opened the door. You looked like you were in a staring contest with a ghost."

Claire considered that. "More like an identity crisis brought on by an unexpected postcard."

"Those'll get you."

When they reached the hall, the first thing Claire noticed was the music. Not classical. Not folk. But loud, thumping bass that vibrated the noticeboard and clashed magnificently with the scent of tea and jam.

Inside, the place looked like the backstage area of a school play, a bake sale, and a yoga retreat had all collided and agreed to disagree.

Ellie was stringing up bunting with garden twine and a look of deep regret. Bev was trying to secure a disco ball to the middle beam using a knitting needle and what looked like duct tape. And in the far corner, Lily was presenting a flip chart with great flourish to a semi-captive audience of three slightly alarmed pensioners.

"There you are!" she shouted, pointing at Claire as if she'd just summoned her with sheer willpower. "We're finalising the lighting grid!"

Claire raised a hand. "Hello."

"You've missed round one of sparkle testing," Ellie said, waving a clipboard. "Also round two. There was a fire hazard, but we've moved past it."

Claire looked at Jack. "This is your fault."

He didn't deny it.

Bev descended from the ladder like someone who'd just been denied a circus career and shoved a folded piece of paper into Claire's hand.

"Banner slogans. Pick your top three. We're narrowing them down for the entranceway."

Claire scanned them.

- "Let the Harvest Ball Begin!"
- "Magic, Mulled Wine, and Mayhem!"
- "One Night Only: Glamour and Root Vegetables!"

"I vote mayhem," she said.

Bev nodded. "Strong choice."

Somewhere behind her, a burst of glitter exploded from a makeshift cannon built from a repurposed Pringles tube.

Claire stepped further into the chaos, and despite herself, she smiled. There was something so deeply, wonderfully absurd about it all. The effort. The colour. The collective goodwill balanced precariously on a string of fairy lights and a very wonky disco ball.

"Right," Ellie said, clapping her hands. "We've got thirty-two hours, one functioning speaker, and a cake quota to hit. Let's make this madness beautiful."

Jack leaned in close, his voice low. "I think this counts as community bonding."

Claire looked at him, not moving away. "Do we get hazard pay?"

"Just bruised dignity and homemade pie."

He touched her elbow lightly as someone behind them dropped a box of glowsticks with a dramatic crash.

And in that moment—with the glitter, the music, the scent of mulled something beginning to bubble in the background—Claire felt something shift.

Nothing big.

Just enough.

Enough to remind her that sometimes, the village had a way of knowing what you needed before you did.

She blinked as a burst of gold sequins tumbled from a collapsing cardboard box near the stage. Ellie groaned audibly and kicked the box back into place with the grace of someone whose patience had clearly expired twenty minutes ago.

Claire glanced around the village hall again. The bunting was now half up, twisting like a festive DNA strand across the ceiling. A string of fairy lights blinked helpfully from one side and then gave up entirely on the other.

It was chaos. Glittery, mulled-wine-scented, deeply committed chaos.

"You know," Claire said, turning to Jack, "when I pictured a harvest ball, I thought… pumpkins. Rustic candles. Maybe a tasteful wheat sheaf."

Jack tilted his head. "We've got turnip disco balls and Bev threatening bodily harm with a glue gun. That's close enough, surely."

She smiled in spite of herself. "And why exactly are *you* here? I thought glitter was against your religion."

"Lily's helping with the decorations," he said, nodding toward the back of the hall. "Which apparently means I'm now on lightbulb-changing duty and emotional support for pensioners frightened by pyrotechnics."

Claire followed his gaze. Lily was still holding court by the flip chart, now debating whether silver or fuchsia fairy lights had more "emotional impact."

"She's good," Claire said softly.

Jack nodded. "She is."

Across the room, Ellie barked orders at a small group of teenagers trying to unravel a tangled mess of battery-powered candles. Mags and Bev were arguing about whether the band should open with ABBA or Fleetwood Mac. Someone—Claire suspected Tom—was testing the sound system by playing a remix of what might have once been classical music but was now mostly bass and regret.

And still, somehow, it was coming together.

Jack shifted beside her. "You alright?"

She nodded, but didn't say anything.

He didn't press.

Instead, he nudged a paper cup of something warm into her hands. Mulled cider. The good kind—fruity, spicy, sharp. Claire took a sip and let the warmth spread through her chest.

"It's weird," she said after a beat. "But this—this is the most settled I've felt in weeks. Months, probably."

Jack didn't reply immediately. Just watched the bunting twitch in the draught from an open window. "Could be the cider."

"Could be," she said. "But it isn't."

From the far end of the hall, Lily waved dramatically. "Dad! Claire! We need your opinions on the entrance tunnel!"

Jack grimaced. "I'm scared to ask."

Claire drained the last of her drink and handed him the empty cup. "Come on then. Let's go be tunnel consultants."

As they crossed the room, the music changed to something slower, slightly off-beat, and Ellie raised a triumphant fist. "Finally! It's not a rave!"

Claire stepped over a coil of extension cords and ducked under a half-hung banner. Jack held the ladder steady as Bev climbed up again, muttering darkly about "health and flaming safety."

Lily pointed at a crude sketch on the flip chart. "So the idea is: you enter through a curtain of ivy and fairy lights, like you're stepping into a secret woodland realm of agricultural wonder."

Claire blinked. "That's... surprisingly coherent."

Lily beamed. "I had help."

Jack raised an eyebrow. "From who?"

"Mrs Cartwright," Lily said, deadpan. "She says everything's better with ivy. And gin."

Claire let out a laugh that echoed gently through the rafters.

This wasn't what she'd planned. Not even close.

But somehow, it was starting to feel like exactly what she needed.

By the time Bev called a break—using a whistle she insisted was "left over from her brief but glorious tenure in the Brownies"—the hall was half-transformed. There were strings of twinkling lights where there had once been spiderwebs, and the battered trestle tables now bore actual cloths and an impressive array of biscuit tins acting as impromptu centrepieces.

Claire found herself sitting on the steps outside the hall, mug of lukewarm tea in one hand, a half-glittered pinecone in the other. Her fingers smelled like glue and cinnamon. She didn't mind.

Jack sat beside her without a word. Just lowered himself onto the step with a grunt and held out a packet of crisps he'd magicked from somewhere. She took one. They ate in companionable silence, broken only by the muffled thump of music behind them and someone yelling "We do *not* need more dry ice, Bev!"

Claire nudged his arm lightly. "So, do you do this every year?"

Jack shrugged. "Sort of. Last year I managed to dodge most of it. Claimed a plumbing emergency in Bramble Row."

"Was there a plumbing emergency?"

"No," he said, unapologetically. "But Bev believed me, and I slept very well that night."

Claire grinned. "So what's different this year?"

He didn't answer immediately. Instead, he leaned forward, arms braced on his knees. "Lily wanted to be involved. Properly involved. Not just watching. First time she's asked to be part of something like this since... everything."

Claire didn't press. She didn't need the details to understand the shape of what he meant.

"She's happier here," he added. "I can see it."

Claire looked down at the pinecone in her lap, at the flecks of glitter stuck in the creases of her palm. "I think I am too."

He glanced sideways at her. "Even with Bev and the glitter cannon?"

"Even with Bev and the glitter cannon," she echoed, smiling.

He was close. Not close enough to touch, but enough that if she shifted slightly to the right, their shoulders might brush.

She stayed where she was.

A breeze stirred the hedges at the edge of the car park, bringing with it the faintest scent of woodsmoke and damp leaves. Somewhere nearby, a dog barked. The village was slowing down, drawing in for the evening, but Claire felt no hurry to move.

Jack cleared his throat. "You're good with her."

"With Lily?"

He nodded.

"She makes it easy."

He hesitated, then said, "Not everyone does."

There it was again—that careful thing between them, like something being built without blueprints. Layer by layer. No rush. No shortcuts.

The door to the hall creaked open, and Lily poked her head out. "We need a ruling on the snack table layout. It's become... territorial."

Jack groaned. Claire stood, brushing glitter from her trousers.

"Coming," she called, and shot him a look. "And if there's another fight over the carrot cake, you're dealing with it this time."

He followed her inside, muttering, "I fear no man. But I do fear Bev with a serving knife."

The disco ball had finally been secured with three cable ties, one knitting needle, and a small prayer. Someone—probably Bev—had managed to angle it so the light bounced across the parquet floor like a hopeful meteor shower.

Claire stood near the side of the hall, paper cup in hand, watching as Lily darted between chairs, adjusting centrepieces with the focus of someone preparing for royalty. She had glitter on one eyebrow, her sleeves pushed up, and a clipboard that gave her an alarming air of authority.

"She's taking this seriously," Claire murmured.

"She always does," came Jack's voice beside her. He didn't step closer, but she could feel the shape of his presence in the way one does after becoming used to someone's shadow.

They watched as Lily conferred with Ellie over the placement of a table garland, then nodded, satisfied, and moved to instruct two teenagers in the art of chair arrangement. The boys looked vaguely traumatised.

"She's... really good at this," Claire said.

Jack made a quiet sound of agreement. "She hasn't done something like this in a long time. Not since... well."

Claire didn't ask. She didn't need to. There were lines on Jack's face that hinted at past things—things held quietly, the way men like him carried grief, like an old injury they didn't talk about but still limped from sometimes.

"I like how she bosses everyone around like a small CEO in sparkly trainers," Claire said lightly.

That earned the smallest of smiles. "She gets it from her gran."

A new track started—Fleetwood Mac this time—and Lily, having completed her decoration rounds, was now trying to teach Bev how to do a three-step turn without knocking over the tray of jam tarts.

"She's happy," Claire said. And then, without meaning to, "You're doing a good job."

Jack's head tilted slightly. "With the disco ball?"

"With her."

For a moment, he didn't reply. Just watched his daughter twirl under fairy lights with all the abandon of someone who hadn't yet learned to be afraid of looking silly.

"I try," he said finally. "It's not always easy. But... she makes it easier."

Claire nodded, something warm spreading in her chest like mulled cider on a cold night.

"You help too, you know," he added, quieter. "She looks up to you."

Claire blinked. "She looks up to the woman who almost glued her own sleeve to a cardboard hedgehog?"

A beat.

"Yes."

And suddenly the laugh bubbled out of her, short and sharp and surprised.

Across the room, Lily waved at them, a quick flap of her hand like she was catching their attention between tasks.

"Entrance tunnel's approved," she called. "I've drawn a schematic."

Jack groaned softly. "We're being managed."

Claire grinned. "I don't mind."

Neither of them moved for a moment. The room around them buzzed with voices, with the clatter of teacups and the low thrum of music. The kind of noise that made a person feel less alone without having to say a word.

Eventually, Jack said, "Come on, then. Let's go admire the schematic."

Claire didn't say it aloud, but as she followed him across the floor—fairy lights flickering overhead, warmth pooling at her collarbones—she felt it.

That soft, certain thing, still unspoken, but very much there.

The final biscuit tin was closed with a satisfying clunk, and the last paper streamer had been coaxed off the light fixture with a broom handle and a few muttered threats.

The village hall had thinned out. Ellie had left with her clipboard and the air of someone who would dream in bunting. Bev had gone to soak her feet in gin, or possibly drink it. Mags had wandered off muttering about sausage rolls and deadlines.

Only Jack and Claire remained.

She was sweeping glitter into a small, ever-growing constellation by the back door. Jack was folding chairs with military precision, stacking them neatly along the wall. Outside, the dark had deepened. Inside, the fairy lights glowed on, their warm little pulses casting golden halos on the walls.

Claire leaned on the broom. "You do know it's hopeless, right?"

Jack looked up. "The glitter?"

"It's become part of the building's structural DNA."

He surveyed the sparkling floor and gave a low grunt of resignation. "Guess we'll have to tell the next renters the place is cursed with festive cheer."

Claire smiled, brushing a speck of confetti from her sleeve. "Do you always stay this late?"

"Only when the company's tolerable."

She arched an eyebrow. "Flattery. Unexpected."

"I'm evolving."

She wasn't sure whether it was the lights, or the quiet, or the way his voice went softer when the room emptied—but something in her chest did a small, unexpected shift. A flutter, maybe. Or a loosening.

She crossed the room to where he was adjusting the last row of chairs. They stood together in the silence, the kind that only came after a long day's noise. She could hear the tick of the wall clock, the hum of the old radiator, the distant rustle of wind in the hedgerows outside.

"It looks good," she said finally, nodding at the room.

"It does," he agreed. "Thanks to Lily. And… you."

Claire shook her head lightly. "I mostly brought chaos and questionable paper flowers."

He looked at her, properly looked. "You brought more than that."

She met his eyes, and for once, didn't look away. The quiet pressed closer, a soft envelope around them.

"I like it here," she said quietly. "More than I thought I would."

Jack nodded, his gaze steady. "You belong."

The words caught her off guard—not because of what he said, but because of how much she wanted to believe it.

Before she could answer, the hall lights flickered once, dramatically, then settled into a low hum.

"Timer," Jack said, reaching for the switchboard. "We should lock up."

Claire nodded, stepping back, breaking the moment with the practiced ease of someone not quite ready to hold it.

He flipped the switches. One by one, the lights blinked out—over the stage, across the far tables, the entrance. But the fairy lights, strung up by Lily and Ellie, glowed on.

Jack turned to her in the soft gloom. "Want a lift home?"

Claire hesitated.

Then: "Only if you promise not to judge my parking job."

He held the door open. "No promises."

They stepped out into the crisp evening, the scent of bonfire smoke and wet leaves curling in the air behind them. Inside, the fairy lights twinkled on—steady, warm, waiting.

The drive back was mostly silent. Not uncomfortable. Just full of the kind of stillness that came when two people had used up all their small talk and were left only with the bigger things neither of them was quite ready to say.

The headlights swept gently over the hedgerows, picking out the silver glint of damp leaves and the occasional startled rabbit. Claire kept her hands tucked in her lap, her coat wrapped around her but left open at the front. She didn't feel cold.

Jack drove the way he did everything—steady, measured, as if he knew instinctively how to keep from startling her. Or himself.

When they reached the cottage, he pulled up just shy of the gate, engine idling low.

Claire turned to him. "You want to come in?"

It was casual. A simple question. But it wasn't.

Jack looked at her, and for a moment she saw something flicker behind his eyes—something uncertain, and maybe even a little hopeful.

He didn't answer straight away. Just let the silence stretch, not in avoidance, but in consideration.

"I should get back," he said eventually. "Lily's got school. And we've got that ivy tunnel to reinforce in the morning."

Claire nodded, trying not to feel anything about it. But she did.

She unbuckled her seatbelt. "Right. Of course."

He turned off the engine. The headlights faded, leaving them in the soft glow of the porch light and the faint wash of stars above the cottage roof.

Claire stepped out and closed the door gently behind her. The gravel crunched underfoot as she moved to the gate. She didn't look back at first. But something—curiosity or foolishness—made her glance over her shoulder.

Jack was still in the car. Still watching.

He raised a hand. A small wave. Not dramatic. Just there.

She smiled. Not big. Not wide. Just enough.

Then she went inside.

And though the door clicked closed behind her, and though she leaned her forehead briefly against the wood with a sigh she didn't quite understand, she couldn't shake the feeling that something had been left unsaid—but not unfinished.

Not yet.

The kettle took its time.

Claire leaned against the counter, arms folded, watching the steam begin to rise. She'd taken down two mugs out of habit. Jack's sat beside hers, empty and a little expectant, like it hadn't quite got the message.

She didn't put it back.

Instead, she filled hers, added too much milk, and sat at the little table in the corner of the kitchen with her hands wrapped around the warmth. The silence felt soft, not sharp. Like a blanket. Or an ellipsis.

On the windowsill, Gwen's old biscuit tin sat crooked, its lid slightly askew. Claire reached over and popped it open. Inside, beneath a few remaining shortbreads and a layer of greaseproof paper, was a folded scrap of handwritten paper. Familiar looping handwriting. Gwen's.

It wasn't anything dramatic. Just a line scribbled in the margin of a recipe:

"There's a kind of peace in doing something small properly."

Claire stared at it for a long time.

She didn't cry. Didn't smile, either. Just sat with it. Let it settle.

The wind rattled the old window latch gently, like it was asking permission to come in.

Claire took another sip of her tea. The mug was too hot, the lighting too dim, the floor still slightly gritty with the day's glitter fallout. But the chair beneath her was solid. The walls were hers. The silence didn't feel lonely.

Jack hadn't come in.

But maybe he hadn't needed to.

She reached for the other mug, rinsed it, and placed it upside-down on the draining rack.

Then, quietly, she turned out the light.

Chapter Nineteen

"The Banana Note and the Seating Plan Crisis"

Claire had just coaxed the toaster into cooperating — it had a particular button combination that reminded her vaguely of an arcade machine — when there was a knock at the front door.

Not the parcel sort. Not the Bev sort, either — which usually involved a double rap and a voice shouting through the letterbox before you'd even reached the hallway.

This knock was more... hopeful.

She wiped her hands on a tea towel and padded to the door in mismatched socks. When she opened it, Lily was standing there, hair half-pulled back with a glittery clip and a rolled-up poster tucked under one arm.

"Hi," Lily said, slightly out of breath.

Claire blinked. "Morning. Everything okay?"

Lily nodded. "I didn't tell Dad I was coming here. I mean — it's fine — he's at the workshop. But I was wondering—" she shifted the poster from one hand to the other "—if you could maybe... help me with something?"

Claire stepped aside without thinking. "Of course. Come in."

Lily headed straight for the kitchen like she'd been doing it for years. She sat at the little table, kicked her feet under it, and laid the poster flat. It was a seating chart — or at least it had ambitions of becoming one.

Claire poured two mugs of tea, pushing the sugar bowl toward her. "Is this an art emergency?"

Lily gave a half-smile. "Worse. It's a 'Mum usually helped with this but I don't want to ask her' emergency."

Claire paused, tea halfway to her lips.

"I mean," Lily added quickly, "she's fine, it's not a fight or anything. She's just... she makes everything look like a wedding. And I kind of want it to be..." she chewed her lip, "...not a wedding."

Claire sat down beside her, gently smoothing a curl of sellotape from the edge of the chart. "You want it to be yours."

Lily nodded. "I don't know what I'm doing. I just… thought maybe you'd get it."

Claire swallowed. "I think I do."

They spent the next hour rearranging names, sketching little sunflowers for the table numbers, and laughing over who absolutely *could not* sit near Bev if anyone expected to hear the speeches.

Claire found herself offering scissors, making tea again, and pulling down the biscuit tin without even thinking about it. The kind of tasks that were, she realised suddenly, *what Gwen used to do for her*. Without fuss. Without question. Just… done.

Lily leaned back in her chair, examining the poster.

"Thanks," she said. "You're good at this."

Claire shrugged, a little shy. "It's just paper and tape."

"No," Lily said firmly. "Not that part."

And for a second, it was like someone had opened a window somewhere deep inside her. Just a crack. But enough for fresh air to get in.

The front door creaked.

Jack stood in the doorway, paint flecks on his shirt, a folded tape measure in one hand. He looked at the scene — Claire pouring tea, Lily chattering about banner colours, the kitchen warm and full of light — and blinked like he wasn't sure he'd walked into the right life.

"I said you were probably here," Lily said breezily.

He looked at Claire, then back at Lily. "You didn't say you were leaving."

"I left a note," she said, unbothered.

He raised a brow. "It was on a banana."

Claire stifled a laugh behind her mug.

Jack looked at them both again, then gave the faintest shake of his head, like he was trying not to smile.

"Just checking you weren't kidnapped."

"I wasn't," Lily said. "But if I was, I'd ask Claire first."

Jack's eyes met Claire's over the rim of his tea. For a moment, everything felt a little too quiet. A little too warm.

Claire cleared her throat. "There's still some toast if you're hungry."

He hesitated.

And then — just like that — he sat down.

Jack sat with both hands wrapped around his mug, the sleeves of his paint-flecked jumper pushed halfway up his forearms. Claire noticed one of the cuffs had a frayed edge. She resisted the ridiculous urge to reach out and fix it.

The kitchen was still warm from the tea kettle, the smell of toast lingering like a hug someone hadn't quite let go of. Outside, through the slightly steamed-up window, Lily was wrestling a string of fairy lights with all the energy of someone preparing for battle.

Claire took a sip of her tea. "She's... determined."

Jack glanced toward the window and gave a small smile. "Always has been. Once, when she was six, she insisted on designing her own Halloween costume. Went to school dressed as a haunted sandwich."

Claire blinked. "A sandwich?"

"Complete with lettuce ruffles and a ghost sheet inside. No one got it, but she was thrilled."

Claire laughed softly, imagining it. "I like that."

He didn't answer straight away. Just kept his eyes on the window, watching Lily as she waved for approval from the garden.

"She likes you, you know."

Claire shrugged lightly. "We've done a lot of glitter-based trauma bonding."

Jack's mouth tilted, not quite a smile. "It's more than that."

The silence between them wasn't awkward, exactly. It was just... thick. Full of things they hadn't said, and maybe weren't ready to. Yet.

Claire traced the rim of her mug with one finger. "You don't mind her being here so much?"

He looked at her, properly. "No. Not at all."

Something inside her shifted again. Small. But real.

Jack leaned back slightly, stretching his legs under the table. His boot accidentally brushed hers — not hard, not obvious — just enough for both of them to notice.

Claire didn't move away.

"She's been different lately," he said, voice quieter now. "More open. Calmer. That's... since she's been spending time with you."

Claire looked down at the chipped ceramic in her hands. "That's sweet. But I'm just... here."

"No," Jack said. "You're not just anything."

And then — before it could get too serious, before either of them could panic or ruin it by naming what it was — Lily burst back through the back door, cheeks flushed, fairy lights tangled like a crown in her hair.

"I need an extension cable," she announced. "And possibly divine intervention."

Jack stood with a mock sigh. "I'll get the cable. Claire's got a direct line to divine intervention."

Claire raised her eyebrows. "I'm not sure the divine appreciates bunting."

Jack paused at the door, glanced back once. "Maybe not. But you make it look good."

Then he was gone, and Claire sat there, blinking at the sudden stillness.

And smiling, just a little, into her tea.

By the time Jack and Lily had left — with the fairy lights, an emergency packet of Hobnobs, and Bev's cake stand on loan under strict conditions — the cottage felt unusually quiet again.

Not empty. Just... paused.

Claire wandered into the front room, brushing biscuit crumbs from her jumper. One of Gwen's old blankets had been draped haphazardly over the arm of the sofa, and she found herself tidying it without thinking, folding the corners in just the way Gwen had always insisted — "no raggedy ends, dear, it's not a student bedsit."

She smiled to herself and turned on the little radio in the corner. The reception was patchy as ever, the presenter's voice fading in and out like he couldn't quite make up his mind about the weather. It was comforting, in its own wonky way.

The stack of to-do lists on the sideboard caught her eye.

Claire had started writing them weeks ago — practical things at first. Paint the skirting boards. Fix the bedroom curtain rod. Don't eat cereal for dinner three nights in a row. But somewhere along the way, the lists had become... stranger.

One, half-tucked beneath a coaster, read:

- Call Mum back.
- Learn how to poach an egg properly.
- Stop pretending this is temporary.

She folded it up quickly and slid it into the drawer before she could overthink it.

The kettle clicked on again — muscle memory — and she rummaged through the cupboard for the fancy teabags Ellie had insisted she try. Something with lavender and rosehips that smelled like a garden centre.

The knock at the door came just as she was pouring.

It wasn't urgent. Not Bev-style. Not even Mags-with-news-style.

Claire opened it to find a paper bag hanging from the gate latch. No note. But inside were three apples, a handful of cinnamon sticks, and a card with a drawing of a pie and the words *"Just in case. – Gwen"* scribbled underneath in faded ink.

She turned it over, half-laughing. Of course it was Gwen's. The card had probably been stuck in a drawer somewhere for years, and now someone — Mags, probably — had decided it was exactly the thing Claire needed.

And maybe it was.

She carried the bag inside, set it carefully on the counter, and looked at the apples for a long moment.

Then she tied up her hair, rolled up her sleeves, and reached for the flour jar.

Because there was a kind of peace — Gwen was right — in doing something small properly.

By the time Claire arrived at the village hall, the air inside had taken on a sort of urgent stickiness — like the walls themselves were starting to sweat with anticipation.

The main room was filled with the scent of polish, cinnamon, and vague panic. Someone had sprayed too much air freshener by the cloakroom and now it smelled like a very floral accident.

"Watch the bunting!" Ellie barked from the stage, as Claire ducked through the doorway and narrowly avoided decapitation by a trailing ribbon.

"I thought we finished that yesterday?" Claire asked.

"We did," Ellie said, frazzled. "But then Bev decided to 'refresh the palette' and now it's gone all... sorbet."

Claire looked up. It had indeed gone sorbet — pale pinks, peaches, and a disconcerting amount of mint green. It looked oddly beautiful. Like the inside of a very stylish meringue.

At the far end of the room, Jack was standing on a stepladder, muttering at a paper lantern that refused to hang straight. Lily was holding the ladder steady, sipping a juice box and issuing instructions like a foreman.

Claire gave her a small wave, and Lily beamed, giving a thumbs-up that was mostly juice-straw.

Mags appeared beside her with two mugs of tea. "You're not late," she said, "but you are underdressed."

"I thought this was prep day," Claire said, eyeing her sensible boots and very much-not-sparkly jumper.

"It is," Mags said, "but Bev's wearing sequins, and we're pretending not to notice."

Claire laughed, took the mug gratefully, and surveyed the room. Streamers, fairy lights, jam jars with tealights, handwritten signs pointing to "Cloakroom" and "Emergency Biscuit Tin." The community had truly outdone itself.

"Do you need me anywhere in particular?" Claire asked.

Ellie materialised with a clipboard and a look of barely restrained gratitude. "Yes. Table centrepieces. Immediately. And possibly crowd control if Bev starts moving the cake stands again."

Claire got to work folding napkins and fussing with fake ivy garlands. It was the kind of fiddly, meaningless task she'd once dismissed as filler — but here, now, it felt like part of something real. Tangible. A shared rhythm. Like breathing, but as a group.

Bev swept past with a tray of vol-au-vents and a wild look in her eye. "Don't touch the flan," she warned no one in particular.

Jack had finished wrestling the lantern and was now adjusting a cable by the stage. Claire caught his eye across the room — not an intense stare, just a quiet glance. The kind that said, *Still here?*
She gave him the tiniest nod. *Still here.*

The doors at the back burst open suddenly and Mags rolled in a crate of what looked suspiciously like sparklers.

"No," Ellie called, without even looking up.

"But—"

"No."

Claire smiled into her tea. There was no place she was supposed to be but here. And she hadn't planned that. Hadn't plotted it on any of her carefully numbered lists.

But here she was, anyway.

The fairy lights buzzed above them. The bunting swayed slightly in the draught from the open doors. Lily tripped over an extension cord, swore, then apologised loudly to the vicar. And somewhere beneath the chaos, the music system began to hum to life with a slow, jazzy version of *Dancing Queen*.

Everything was nearly ready.

And for the first time in a long while, so was Claire.

By the time Claire arrived at the village hall, the air inside had taken on a sort of urgent stickiness — like the walls themselves were starting to sweat with anticipation.

The main room was filled with the scent of polish, cinnamon, and vague panic. Someone had sprayed too much air freshener by the cloakroom and now it smelled like a very floral accident.

"Watch the bunting!" Ellie barked from the stage, as Claire ducked through the doorway and narrowly avoided decapitation by a trailing ribbon.

"I thought we finished that yesterday?" Claire asked.

"We did," Ellie said, frazzled. "But then Bev decided to 'refresh the palette' and now it's gone all... sorbet."

Claire looked up. It had indeed gone sorbet — pale pinks, peaches, and a disconcerting amount of mint green. It looked oddly beautiful. Like the inside of a very stylish meringue.

At the far end of the room, Jack was standing on a stepladder, muttering at a paper lantern that refused to hang straight. Lily was holding the ladder steady, sipping a juice box and issuing instructions like a foreman.

Claire gave her a small wave, and Lily beamed, giving a thumbs-up that was mostly juice-straw.

Mags appeared beside her with two mugs of tea. "You're not late," she said, "but you are underdressed."

"I thought this was prep day," Claire said, eyeing her sensible boots and very much-not-sparkly jumper.

"It is," Mags said, "but Bev's wearing sequins, and we're pretending not to notice."

Claire laughed, took the mug gratefully, and surveyed the room. Streamers, fairy lights, jam jars with tealights, handwritten signs pointing to "Cloakroom" and "Emergency Biscuit Tin." The community had truly outdone itself.

"Do you need me anywhere in particular?" Claire asked.

Ellie materialised with a clipboard and a look of barely restrained gratitude. "Yes. Table centrepieces. Immediately. And possibly crowd control if Bev starts moving the cake stands again."

Claire got to work folding napkins and fussing with fake ivy garlands. It was the kind of fiddly, meaningless task she'd once dismissed as filler — but here, now, it felt like part of something real. Tangible. A shared rhythm. Like breathing, but as a group.

Bev swept past with a tray of vol-au-vents and a wild look in her eye. "Don't touch the flan," she warned no one in particular.

Jack had finished wrestling the lantern and was now adjusting a cable by the stage. Claire caught his eye across the room — not an intense stare, just a quiet glance. The kind that said, *Still here?*
She gave him the tiniest nod. *Still here.*

The doors at the back burst open suddenly and Mags rolled in a crate of what looked suspiciously like sparklers.

"No," Ellie called, without even looking up.

"But—"

"No."

Claire smiled into her tea. There was no place she was supposed to be but here. And she hadn't planned that. Hadn't plotted it on any of her carefully numbered lists.

But here she was, anyway.

The fairy lights buzzed above them. The bunting swayed slightly in the draught from the open doors. Lily tripped over an extension cord, flailed, then loudly declared, "I'm fine! Totally fine! That was planned," before giving the vicar a dignified thumbs-up and marching on. And somewhere beneath the chaos, the music system began to hum to life with a slow, jazzy version of *Dancing Queen*.

Everything was nearly ready.

And for the first time in a long while, so was Claire.

The cottage was quiet again.

Claire stood at the mirror in the front room, hair half-pinned and makeup still somewhere between "understated autumn glow" and "lightly flustered commuter."

She held up two dresses. One was the practical navy wrap she'd worn to Gwen's funeral, neat and inoffensive. The other was soft green with slightly puffed sleeves and a waistband that didn't entirely trust her. Gwen had left it in the wardrobe. Claire had never tried it on.

She stared at them both for a long moment.

Then, slowly, she hung up the navy one.

The green one fit better than she expected. Not perfect — nothing ever was — but it had a bit of a swish when she turned in it, and she liked the way the sleeves made her feel like she might belong in a painting. Or a story.

The wind fluttered against the windows. Somewhere in the distance, bells rang the half-hour. She glanced at the clock. Still time.

She padded to the kitchen, checking the oven out of habit, even though there was nothing inside. Old routines, carried forward.

On the counter sat a folded note — one she hadn't seen before.

Just a scrap of paper with Gwen's handwriting, tucked under the biscuit tin like it had always been there.

"A good party doesn't need everything to go right. It just needs everyone to turn up with their heart open."

Claire exhaled softly. "Alright then," she said to the empty kitchen.

She slipped on her coat, checked the clasp on her bag, and paused only once at the doorway — fingers resting lightly on the frame — before stepping into the night.

The cottage was quiet again.

Claire stood at the mirror in the front room, hair half-pinned and makeup still somewhere between "understated autumn glow" and "lightly flustered commuter."

She held up two dresses. One was the practical navy wrap she'd worn to Gwen's funeral, neat and inoffensive. The other was soft green with slightly puffed sleeves and a waistband that didn't entirely trust her. Claire had never tried it on.

She stared at them both for a long moment.

Then, slowly, she hung up the navy one.

The green one fit better than she expected. Not perfect — nothing ever was — but it had a bit of a swish when she turned in it, and she liked the way the sleeves made her feel like she might belong in a painting. Or a story.

The wind fluttered against the windows. Somewhere in the distance, bells rang the half-hour. She glanced at the clock. Still time.

She padded to the kitchen, checking the oven out of habit, even though there was nothing inside. Old routines, carried forward.

Claire exhaled softly. "Alright then," she said to the empty kitchen.

She slipped on her coat, checked the clasp on her bag, and paused only once at the doorway — fingers resting lightly on the frame — before stepping into the night.

The village hall had transformed.

Gone were the folding chairs and trailing cables. In their place: candles in jam jars, streamers that somehow hadn't caught fire, and a low golden light that made everything — and everyone — look just a bit softer around the edges.

Claire stood just inside the doorway, taking it all in. The bunting still looked slightly crooked on the left side, but it worked. In fact, it all worked — in that perfectly imperfect village way, where nothing matched and everything sparkled slightly too much.

A wave of warmth rolled over her. And it wasn't just the mulled cider near the buffet.

Ellie swept past in a navy velvet dress, hair piled high like she'd mugged a 1950s film star. "You made it!" she called. "Quick, grab a table before Bev turns the raffle into musical chairs."

Claire made her way in slowly, smiling as she passed neighbours she now actually knew — Mrs Cartwright in sequins, the vicar in suspiciously shiny shoes, Tom and his partner laughing at a table by the punch bowl.

Music floated from the stage — a gentle folk trio warming up, the kind that made you sway before you even realised you were doing it. Someone had lit little lanterns by the windows, and they flickered like fireflies against the glass.

"Claire!" Lily's voice rang out from near the stage.

She turned just in time to see Lily come bounding over in a silver dress with a crown of ivy perched lopsidedly in her hair.

"You look amazing," Claire said honestly.

Lily twirled once. "Ellie did my hair. It took three clips, a prayer, and a bit of cake frosting."

Claire laughed. "Very on brand."

Lily leaned in. "Dad's here. Somewhere. Pretending to fix the lighting but mostly avoiding conversation."

Claire scanned the room. And there he was — standing near the edge of the dance floor, adjusting something on the wall that didn't seem to need adjusting at all.

He hadn't spotted her yet.

She wasn't sure if she wanted him to.

Lily pulled her toward the tables. "Sit with us? You're on the cool team."

Claire let herself be led.

Jack arrived a few minutes later, somehow managing to look both scruffy and smart in a navy shirt she hadn't seen before. He nodded to her across the table — nothing dramatic, just a slight lift of the chin — but there was something behind it. A warmth. A yes.

The music picked up. People were starting to dance. Bev had already declared herself Mistress of the Dance Floor and was doing something dangerous with a tambourine.

Ellie passed Claire a small glass of something vaguely fizzy.

"You alright?" she asked, gently.

Claire looked around — at the lights, the music, the laughter, Lily dancing with the vicar, Jack pretending not to smile.

"I think I am," she said.

And for once, she didn't mean "for now." She meant it.

The music shifted.

One of the trio on stage swapped instruments, and a soft, lilting melody floated out into the room — something slower, older. The sort of tune that made you remember things you hadn't meant to remember.

Claire stood by the edge of the dance floor, a cup of something spiced and suspicious in her hand, watching as couples paired off. The vicar twirled Mrs Cartwright with surprising grace. Ellie danced with one of the teenagers, all exaggerated spins and giggles. Lily, looking perfectly pleased with herself, had dragged Tom into a two-step they were inventing as they went.

She felt Jack before she saw him — that steady, quiet presence.

He didn't say anything at first. Just offered a hand.

Claire hesitated. Just for a second. Then took it.

He led her gently onto the floor. No fanfare. No grand gestures. Just two people finding the beat together.

Jack's hand settled lightly at her waist. Claire's rested on his shoulder. They moved slowly — not expertly, but in rhythm. It wasn't a dance, really. It was more like... a conversation where no one needed to speak.

Around them, the room blurred. Music. Laughter. Lights. It all softened into a hum.

She looked up once, met his eyes — and something quiet passed between them. Not a question. Not an answer either. Just *there*.

"I didn't think you danced," she said quietly.

"I don't," he said. "Usually."

The corners of her mouth tugged up.

They swayed together, the room turning gently with them. She could feel the warmth of his hand through the fabric of her dress. The way his thumb almost moved, but didn't. The way neither of them let go.

And then —

A shout.

A flicker.

A loud pop! from the side of the stage.

The fairy lights blinked once — twice — and then fizzled into darkness. Half the room gasped. The other half cheered.

Someone, probably Bev, shouted, "The flan! Save the flan!"

Jack groaned under his breath. "Knew we shouldn't have let her near extension cables."

The music stopped mid-note, replaced by a hiss and a confused yelp from the speakers.

Claire blinked in the sudden dark, still holding Jack's hand.

"Well," she said, "that was subtle."

He chuckled. "You alright?"

"I was mid-romantic moment. Now I'm worried about electrical safety and dessert casualties."

He didn't let go. "We'll rescue the flan together."

She rolled her eyes. "How gallant."

"Stick with me," he said. "I'm a dab hand with blown fuses and burnt pastry."

She didn't answer. Just squeezed his hand once before letting go.

The back corridor smelled like dust and forgotten church fetes.

Jack flicked on the small overhead light — the sort that buzzed for a second before giving in — and reached for the fuse box mounted slightly too high on the wall.

Claire stood beside him, arms crossed, trying not to look at the way the fabric of his shirt pulled slightly across his back as he stretched. Failing.

"You don't happen to carry a backup fairy light system, do you?" she asked lightly.

He glanced back over his shoulder. "What kind of amateur do you take me for?"

"Ah, so the flan-saving hero is also an electrician?"

"Jack of all trades," he said. "Pun not intended, but I'll take the credit."

He clicked a switch. A hum. Then nothing.

Claire stepped closer, peering at the tangle of wires. "What about that one?"

"That one is... possibly decorative."

She reached past him without thinking, her arm brushing his. Their shoulders touched — briefly, gently — and neither of them moved away.

Jack adjusted the final switch. A soft click.

From the hall, a distant cheer went up as the fairy lights blinked back to life, followed by a triumphant shout from Bev.

Claire exhaled. "The flan lives."

Jack turned, still close. "Never in doubt."

They stood there a moment longer than necessary. Not awkward. Just... full. Like the air had gone syrup-thick, like something might happen if they didn't step back soon.

Claire tilted her head, just slightly. "You're good at this."

"The fuse box?"

"Being... steady."

Jack's gaze held hers. "I don't always feel it."

She nodded. "I know."

The light above them flickered once, warningly.

Jack looked up. "We should probably get back before Bev installs pyrotechnics."

Claire smiled. "Or weaponises the trifle."

He stepped aside to let her pass first. As she did, her hand brushed his again — and this time, he didn't pull away.

Neither did she.

By the time Claire and Jack stepped back into the main hall, it was like the whole room had collectively decided to pretend the blackout had been part of the evening's entertainment.

Bev was holding court by the buffet table, brandishing a serving spoon like a conductor's baton and declaring that the sponge cake had "survived both war and faulty wiring." Someone had turned the music back on — not the gentle folk trio this time, but a cheerful swing number that made the floorboards tremble slightly with enthusiasm.

Claire spotted Lily in the middle of the crowd, spinning with one of Ellie's nephews, both laughing too hard to keep time with the music.

"There you are!" Mags swept over in a flurry of scarf and glitter. "We thought you'd eloped."

"We were rescuing electrics," Claire said, brushing imaginary dust from her sleeve.

Mags winked. "Very romantic. Nothing says courtship like a tripped fuse."

Before Claire could respond, Ellie clapped her hands from the edge of the stage. "Right, everyone! I know the schedule is already in tatters, but if we don't do the raffle now, Bev's going to burst."

"I'm emotionally invested," Bev called. "There's a foot spa up for grabs."

"Let's live dangerously," Ellie muttered, and held up a bowl of mismatched ticket stubs.

The next few minutes passed in a whirlwind of rustling paper, shrieks of victory, and mild outrage when it was discovered that Bev had somehow entered *under three different names*. ("The odds were still against me!")

Claire found herself pressed shoulder to shoulder with Jack near the side of the room as prizes were handed out. A packet of homemade chutney. A suspiciously heavy jigsaw. A calendar from 2019 that no one had the heart to discard.

At one point, Lily scurried over and slipped a toffee into Claire's hand without explanation, then disappeared again.

Jack watched her go, smiling faintly. "She likes you, you know."

Claire unwrapped the toffee. "I'm growing on people. Like moss."

"Nice moss," he said.

The lights above them glinted again, now firmly cooperative, and the band picked up a new tune — something slower, with a bit of swing and sway to it.

Ellie, back on the mic, called out, "Right, last dance of the evening, and I want to see *everyone* on the floor. Even the vicar."

"I have old knees!" the vicar protested cheerfully.

"No excuses!" Ellie shouted back. "God supports cardiovascular fitness!"

Laughter rippled through the room.

Claire felt a tug on her hand — Lily again.

"Come on," she said. "One more dance. Then we can call it a night and say we contributed to village history."

Claire glanced at Jack. He gave the tiniest shrug. "Better do as she says."

And so she did.

One last dance. Lights above, warmth all around, music that wrapped around them like a shared secret.

It didn't mean everything.

But it meant something.

The last of the fairy lights were being unplugged. Bev had declared the cake table "officially looted," and Mags was attempting to herd three elderly men out of the cloakroom, all arguing over whose flat cap belonged to whom.

Claire found herself near the back door, coat buttoned up, a slice of leftover sponge in a paper napkin tucked carefully into her pocket.

Jack appeared beside her, just as she reached for the handle.

"I'll walk you," he said, casual. No expectation. Just... there.

Claire nodded. "Thanks."

The night outside was cool and crisp, the kind of autumn evening that smelled faintly of leaves and woodsmoke. They walked in companionable silence, the gravel crunching softly beneath their shoes.

Claire glanced sideways. "You didn't dance the second time."

Jack's mouth tugged slightly. "Too much pressure. First dance was a triumph. Why risk the sequel?"

She laughed, quiet and warm. "A perfectionist. Who knew?"

They passed the old post box, its red paint dulled by time. A cat darted across the road ahead, pausing to glare at them before disappearing into a hedge.

Claire adjusted her scarf. "The Ball went well."

"It did," Jack agreed. "Despite explosions and flan panic."

She nodded. "It was... nice. All of it."

They reached her gate. Claire slowed, hand on the latch.

Jack didn't move to leave immediately. Just looked at the cottage, then at her.

"You did a good job," he said. "With all of it."

Claire met his gaze. "You too."

The moment stretched. Not charged. Not awkward. Just still.

"Right," she said, breaking the quiet gently. "I have half a sponge cake to eat and a very judgmental cat to ignore."

Jack gave a slow nod. "Night, Claire."

She opened the gate, turned once at the doorstep.

"Night, Jack."

And then she was inside, the door clicking shut behind her, the quiet settling in like a blanket.

Chapter Twenty

"Toast, Umbrellas, and Unwelcome Truths"

Claire had just managed to get the perfect toast-to-butter ratio — still warm enough to melt, not so hot it went soggy — when a sharp knock rattled the front window.

Not the door.
The **window**.

She turned, slice halfway to her mouth, and there was Mags, peering through the glass like a nosy neighbour in a sitcom. Which, to be fair, she was.

Claire opened the window a crack. "Is something on fire?"

"I can't find my umbrella," Mags said, as if this explained everything.

"I don't sell them."

Mags huffed. "It's not mine. I think it's Bev's. Or possibly the vicar's. Or Jack's? It's red. Or maroon. Possibly patterned. Anyway, it turned up in the cloakroom."

Claire blinked. "So naturally you've come to me."

"You're centrally located and morally responsible."

Claire stared at her. "I'm eating toast."

Mags leaned further in. "I won't come in. I just need to know if you think it's Jack's. It has that emotionally repressed quality, you know? Very upright. Functional."

Claire took a bite of toast and chewed, very deliberately. "How does one determine the emotional state of an umbrella?"

Mags grinned. "Ah, but that's where years of village life pay off. Anyway. Did he walk you home?"

Claire paused. "What?"

"Last night. Did he walk you home?"

Claire set her toast down. "Yes. Why?"

Mags shrugged, far too casually. "He used to do that with Lilys mum, you know."

Claire raised an eyebrow. "Are you implying there's a village tradition of emotionally significant chaperoning?"

"I'm implying," Mags said, "that the last time Jack walked someone home from the Harvest Ball, it ended in houseplants, three kitchen shelves, and Lily."

Claire opened her mouth, then closed it again.

Mags tapped the windowframe. "I'll leave you to your toast. Lovely swish on that dress last night, by the way. Green suits you."

And then she was gone, as suddenly as she'd arrived, striding off down the garden path with the confidence of someone who believed 9am was a perfectly reasonable time for emotional sabotage.

Claire stared out the window for a long moment.

Then picked up her toast.

And dropped it.

Butter-side down.

There was a knock at the door — this time, the normal kind — and Claire opened it to find Lily standing on the step, plait slightly askew, wearing a school jumper and a look of determined casualness.

"I was going to walk myself," she said, "but the cat ate Dad's shoelaces, so he's running late."

Claire blinked. "You live five doors away."

Lily shrugged. "It's called a scenic route."

Claire stepped back and let her in. "You've had breakfast?"

"Yes. But it was yoghurt. And yoghurt's not a real food."

Claire pushed a slice of toast toward her. "You're very focused on toast this morning."

"It's the great equaliser," Lily said, taking a bite. "Also, it makes people talk."

Claire raised an eyebrow. "Does it?"

"Yep," Lily said, around a mouthful. "People get weirdly honest over toast. It's like how grown-ups can't lie when they're carrying laundry or watering plants."

Claire leaned on the counter. "Is this a school project?"

"No. It's observational science."

They ate in silence for a moment — Lily working her way methodically through the toast, Claire stirring a cup of tea she hadn't yet touched.

Then Lily glanced up, casual. "You and Dad had fun last night?"

Claire kept her face neutral. "It was the Harvest Ball. Everyone had fun."

Lily picked a crumb off her sleeve. "He's not fun with everyone."

Claire tried very hard not to read into that. "Well, he was helpful. With the lighting and all."

"He likes you, you know."

Claire set the teaspoon down. "Lily—"

"It's fine," Lily said, too quickly. "I just… think he maybe forgets how to show it sometimes. Or thinks he's not allowed."

Claire said nothing. The kettle clicked off behind her, unnoticed.

Lily finished the toast and stood, brushing her hands together. "Anyway, thanks. For the breakfast. And the honesty-inducing carbs."

Claire managed a smile. "Anytime."

Lily headed to the door, then paused.

"You don't have to do anything, you know. Just… don't pretend it's nothing, either. That never works."

And then she was gone, backpack swinging behind her, off down the road in three long strides.

Claire stared at the space she'd left behind.

The tea had gone cold.

Jack stood in the workshop, holding a hammer he didn't need.

The job in front of him — fixing the cupboard door on Mrs Cartwright's sideboard — had taken twenty minutes. He'd now been standing here for nearly forty.

A sliver of sunlight angled through the dusty window, catching on the curled wood shavings scattered across the bench. Somewhere outside, someone was mowing a lawn. The kind of day you were supposed to *get on with things*.

He set the hammer down.

Picked it up again.

Set it down harder.

He wasn't avoiding anything. Obviously. He just… hadn't been sleeping that well, and the Ball had gone on late, and there were probably some mild electrical issues still to check at the hall. That was all.

He ran a hand through his hair and stared at the cupboard door. It stared back, smugly repaired.

Lily had been in a good mood this morning. She'd left for Claire's with one plait undone and toast crumbs on her jumper, humming something under her breath that sounded suspiciously like *Dancing Queen*.

She'd asked him if he was "going to say anything," and when he'd asked "about what," she'd just rolled her eyes and told him he was hopeless.

Which wasn't fair.

He wasn't hopeless. He was… careful.

Things with Claire were simple. Clean. Well, *they had been*. He helped her fix things, she made him tea. She understood silence. That was rare.

But then there'd been the walk. The dance. The hand that didn't quite let go. The way she'd said his name outside the cottage like it mattered.

And now the cupboard door was fixed, and he still hadn't stopped thinking about her hand in his.

He wiped down the bench, unnecessarily.

The thing was — and he wasn't being dramatic — he genuinely didn't know how to want something quietly. Not anymore. Not after everything. Wanting something meant eventually losing it. Or dropping it. Or watching it walk away.

He grabbed his jacket, paused, and checked the inside pocket.

There it was. Her hair tie.

She must've dropped it at the Ball. Mint green. Slightly stretched out. Smelled vaguely like vanilla and floor cleaner.

He stared at it.

Then put it back in the pocket and headed out.

Claire was halfway through reorganising the spice rack — not out of necessity, but because she needed to feel like something was under control — when there was a knock at the door.

She wiped her hands on a tea towel and opened it.

Jack stood there, one hand in his jacket pocket, the other already scratching the back of his neck.

"Hi," he said.

Claire blinked. "Hi."

There was a pause. The comfortable kind that didn't quite know what it was supposed to be anymore.

"I've, uh…" Jack cleared his throat. "I've got something of yours."

Claire raised an eyebrow. "Did I leave a shoe behind? Should I be worried about pumpkins?"

He blinked. "What?"

"Cinderella?"

He blinked again. "Right. No. Hair tie."

He fished it out of his pocket and held it up like a peace offering.

It was, indeed, hers. Mint green. Slightly stretched. Definitely not urgent.

Claire took it carefully. "Thank you. I was going to launch a search party."

Jack nodded. "Didn't want it to fall into the wrong hands."

A beat.

She opened the door a little wider. "You want tea?"

He hesitated. Then stepped inside. "Yeah. Just for a minute."

Claire moved to the kitchen, flicking the kettle on. "I'm reorganising."

Jack looked at the counter. "You alphabetising the herbs?"

"No," she said, far too defensively. "Maybe."

He leaned against the opposite counter. "You alright?"

She shrugged, focusing very hard on two mismatched mugs. "Mags turned up this morning. Something about umbrellas."

Jack exhaled through his nose. "Let me guess. She brought emotional clarity and an in-depth review of my walking habits?"

"She might have mentioned… a few things."

Claire passed him a mug, their fingers almost brushing.

He looked down. "She thinks she's subtle."

Claire smiled. "She's not."

They sipped in silence. The steam curled between them, softening the edges.

Jack finally set his mug down. "I didn't come here to make it weird."

"It's not weird," Claire said. "Not unless you're planning to return a single sock tomorrow."

Jack gave a quiet laugh. "No sock agenda."

"Good."

Another pause. Softer now.

Claire looked at him properly. "You didn't have to bring it back."

"I know."

"But you did."

"I did."

And that was it.

Nothing else. No grand moment. No music swell. Just two people standing in a quiet kitchen, holding warm mugs and something else between them neither quite knew what to do with.

Claire cleared her throat. "The oregano's in the wrong place."

Jack nodded seriously. "You should fix that."

"I'm going to."

"I'll get out of your way."

"Okay."

He walked to the door. Paused.

"See you later?"

Claire met his eyes. "Yeah. Later."

And then he was gone, and the kettle still hadn't cooled.

Claire had just settled onto the sofa with her tea and a half-hearted plan to *definitely not think about Jack anymore*, when her phone buzzed.

Ellie:

Are you decent?

Claire blinked.

Claire:

Why?

Ellie:

I'm outside. I have questions. And a Swiss roll.

Claire sighed, got up, and opened the door.

Ellie breezed in without waiting for an invitation, carrying a Tupperware box like it was an urgent delivery.

"I brought sugar," she said. "Because I have questions. And because I accidentally made two desserts last night and Mags said I wasn't allowed to eat them both."

Claire raised an eyebrow. "Do the questions relate to your sudden dessert surplus?"

Ellie flopped onto the sofa. "No. They relate to *you*. And a certain tall, brooding man with strong opinions about plug sockets."

Claire shut the door slowly. "Is this going to be another one of those village interrogations where you pretend you're just here to return a bowl?"

"I brought a Swiss roll," Ellie pointed out. "That's at least semi-honest."

Claire returned to her spot on the armchair, arms crossed. "I've already had Mags this morning. I don't need a follow-up inquisition."

"You say that," Ellie said, "but you have the look of someone who's had tea with emotional subtext."

Claire stared at her.

"I'm just saying," Ellie added, "Jack doesn't exactly make social visits. Unless something's leaking. Or collapsing. Or catching fire."

Claire exhaled. "He came to return a hair tie."

Ellie paused. "That's so mundane it might be the most romantic thing I've heard all week."

"It's not romantic."

"It's domestic," Ellie said. "That's worse."

Claire gave her a look.

Ellie unboxed the Swiss roll with great ceremony. "Look, I'm not trying to push. I'm just saying… if there's a thing happening, you're allowed to let it happen. You don't have to fix it before it's broken."

Claire stared at the jam swirl. "I liked it better when you were just awkward and full of cake."

"I'm still full of cake," Ellie said, through a mouthful. "But I'm also your friend. And we're all rooting for you, you know."

Claire blinked. "We?"

Ellie pointed vaguely toward the window. "The village. The women. Lily. Probably the cat."

Claire sighed. "Is there anywhere in this town where people *don't* talk about me?"

"Not since you alphabetised the herb shelf in the hall. That got people excited."

Claire laughed, despite herself. "Brilliant."

Ellie passed her a slice. "Eat the Swiss roll. Accept the goodwill. Maybe stop trying to fight things that feel good."

Claire took the plate. "You're very wise for someone who once got a spatula stuck in her hair."

Ellie grinned. "That was a phase."

They ate in comfortable silence, the kind that only existed between people who'd been through late-night set-ups, bunting crises, and shared cake-related trauma.

Outside, the wind rustled through the trees. Inside, the cottage held its quiet warmth.

Claire didn't say anything else.
But she didn't feel like fixing anything, either.

Jack was in the yard, trying to fix the wheelbarrow.

He didn't need to fix the wheelbarrow. It had been working fine for six months. Possibly longer. But this morning, when he'd spotted a small chip in the wood near the handle, it had suddenly become very important.

He tightened a bolt. Then loosened it. Then dropped the spanner and muttered something under his breath that wouldn't have passed Lily's language test.

The sky was a soft, indecisive grey. The kind that couldn't make up its mind between rain or apathy.

Jack stood, rubbed his hands on his jeans, and stared at the wheelbarrow like it might offer answers.

It didn't.

Claire had looked… good this morning. Not in the swishy-green-dress-from-the-Ball way. Just… warm. Comfortable. Tea in her hand. Barefoot on the kitchen tiles. Like someone who'd always been meant to fit there.

He hadn't said what he wanted to say.

Not that there was anything specific. Just… something. Something in the way she'd taken the hair tie. Not surprised. Not casual. Just quietly aware.

He checked his phone. No messages. Not that he was expecting one. But he checked again anyway.

From the window above, Lily's curtain twitched.

He frowned. She was supposed to be at school. Or at least pretending to be.

He headed inside.

Sure enough, Lily was perched at the kitchen table, doodling in the margins of a workbook with one sock missing.

"You're home early," Jack said, opening the fridge for no reason.

"I had a headache," Lily said. "And also I was bored. But mostly headache."

He gave her a look.

She gave him a sheepish one back.

"I didn't fake it," she added. "Not really. It was a small headache. Emotionally authentic."

Jack leaned against the counter. "You hungry?"

"There's leftover pie."

He nodded. "Pie, then."

He dished it up without fuss. They ate in silence for a bit — Lily chewing thoughtfully, Jack stabbing at a particularly thick crust.

Eventually, Lily said, "You saw her this morning, didn't you?"

Jack didn't look up. "She left a hair tie at the hall."

"That's not really an answer."

Jack shrugged.

"She looked happy when I passed her window."

He glanced at Lily. "You passed her window?"

"I walk by slowly. For updates."

Jack sighed.

Lily poked at her pie. "I like it when you talk to her."

Jack didn't reply.

"She makes the cottage smell like cinnamon."

Jack cleared his throat. "That's not a reason to date someone."

Lily gave him a look. "You're impossible."

He didn't disagree.

She stood up, put her plate in the sink, and headed for the stairs.

Before disappearing, she turned back. "You could just let yourself be happy, you know. It's not illegal."

Then she was gone.

Jack stared at the pie.

It didn't have any answers either.

Claire had only gone out for milk.

That was the plan. Milk. Possibly a loaf of bread if it looked like it hadn't been sat out since Tuesday. A quick walk to the shop, no drama.

She had made it as far as the corner before she heard the unmistakable sound of Bev arguing with a trestle table.

Claire slowed.

Bev was standing outside the community centre with a roll of crepe paper under one arm, a clipboard under the other, and a fold-up table that resolutely refused to unfold.

"Do I even want to know?" Claire asked cautiously.

Bev looked up, delighted. "You're just in time!"

"I'm really not."

"You've got hands. That qualifies you."

Claire stepped closer. "What's all this?"

"Post-Ball feedback," Bev said. "Anonymous. Totally optional. Unless they don't return it. Then we follow up."

"You're conducting a survey?"

"It's called event quality assurance," Bev said proudly. "Ellie's idea."

Claire raised a brow. "Ellie's idea?"

Bev hesitated. "Ellie's name. My idea."

The table gave a sudden lurch and collapsed with a thud. Bev sighed dramatically.

Claire knelt down. "Let me."

In a few practiced movements, she had the table upright and locked.

Bev watched, arms crossed. "You're useful, you are."

Claire stood, brushing her hands off. "Don't spread it around."

Bev narrowed her eyes. "You know, we're looking to reorganise the events team. We could use someone with a sensible brain and nice handwriting."

Claire blinked. "Is that a compliment?"

Bev ignored her. "You've got that calm energy. Like someone who knows how to say 'no' without shouting. We need that."

Claire stared at her.

Bev smiled, sweet as treacle. "Just think about it. No pressure. But also, there's a meeting Tuesday."

Claire shook her head, laughing softly. "You lot don't stop, do you?"

"We're the backbone of this village," Bev said, straightening the tablecloth. "And we've got a clipboard for everything."

Claire glanced at the clipboard, which was covered in doodles and a suspicious number of question marks.

Bev patted her shoulder. "Anyway, thank you. You're a good egg."

"I just fixed a table."

"Sometimes that's all it takes."

Claire walked away shaking her head.

But she was smiling.

Claire walked home slower than necessary.

Bev's clipboard pitch still echoed faintly in her ears, half-serious and half-comical — but it had landed in a place she didn't want to admit existed.

A few weeks ago, she wouldn't have known what to do with that kind of suggestion. She'd have laughed politely, made an excuse, and gone home to sit in the quiet and pretend she hadn't minded being left out.

But now? She knew where the community centre was. She'd folded flyers for it. She'd helped tie bunting to its radiators and had mild glue-gun trauma to show for it. People waved when she passed them. The woman at the bakery had started calling her "love."

It was only small stuff.

But it was becoming her life.

Back at the cottage, she put the milk in the fridge, stared at the inside for a bit longer than was strictly necessary, and shut the door again.

The quiet settled in quickly, but it wasn't heavy. Just... still.

She drifted into the living room, trailed a finger along the windowsill. The sun was sliding in sideways, picking up little dust motes and making them float like lazy snowflakes.

She curled up in the armchair, pulled a blanket over her knees, and let herself sit still.

That was new, too. She hadn't sat still in years, not without an agenda. Not without worrying about something just outside the edges of the moment.

Her phone buzzed. Just once.

A text from Lily.

Lily:

I gave Dad back his shoelace. We're pretending it never happened.
Also I may have told him your kitchen smells like cinnamon. He looked confused but not upset.

Claire smiled, thumbs hovering for a moment.

Claire:

Is that a compliment?

Lily:

In this house, yes.
Also there's still glitter on the cat. Dad says it's your fault.

Claire:

I regret nothing.

Lily:

We need more cinnamon.

Claire set the phone down.

She didn't need to text Jack. She wasn't going to. There wasn't anything to say, really.

Except she could still feel the warmth of the mug he'd held this morning. The quiet of him standing in her kitchen like it was a place he might return to. The hair tie, carefully kept. The way he hadn't tried to make it into anything — and somehow that had meant more.

She leaned her head back against the chair.

The cottage creaked softly around her.

She stayed like that for a long time — blanket pulled tight, cinnamon in the air, the world still enough to feel like hers.

Jack hadn't meant to walk this way.

He'd set out for the hardware shop. That was the plan. He needed more varnish, a new sanding block, and a particular kind of hinge that only Old Trevor stocked in a jam jar behind the till.

But somehow his feet had turned right instead of left. Past the bakery. Past the post box. Past the corner where Lily had once accidentally glued her shoe to a paving stone. And now…

He was standing near Claire's gate.

Not at it. Just near.

He hadn't texted. That would have made it a plan. This wasn't a plan. This was… a wandering. A check-in. Possibly an overstep. He wasn't sure.

The cottage looked peaceful. Curtains half-drawn, a small glow of lamplight inside. He could almost picture her curled on the sofa, wrapped in one of those blankets she always pretended weren't hers.

He checked his jacket pocket. The mint green hair tie was gone. Of course it was. He'd already given it back. That had been the excuse. There wasn't another one.

Unless—

Unless he'd left something else.

But he hadn't.

Still, he found himself opening the gate.

Just quietly. Just in case.

He reached the front step. Stood there. Hands in his pockets. Heart beating in a way that made no sense at all.

Then the door opened.

Claire stood there, wrapped in a cardigan that was about three sizes too big, a mug of something that smelled like cloves in her hand.

She didn't look surprised.

Jack cleared his throat. "I think I left… something."

She nodded slowly. "You did."

He blinked. "Oh?"

Claire stepped aside. "You can come in and look for it."

He hesitated.

She tilted her head. "Jack."

He looked at her then. Properly.

Something shifted. Nothing grand. Just a quiet falling into place.

"Alright," he said softly. "Just for a minute."

She stepped back, and he followed her in.

The door clicked shut behind him.

Inside, the cottage felt warmer than it should.

Jack stood just inside the doorway, hands in his pockets, pretending to look at the framed postcard on the wall — the one of the Cornish coast that might have come with the cottage, or might have been hers. He wasn't sure.

Claire disappeared into the kitchen, reappearing with a second mug and a questioning look.

"Tea?"

He nodded. "If it's no trouble."

She handed it over. The mug had a crack in the handle and a picture of a dancing turnip.

"I think this one's yours now," she said.

Jack looked at the turnip. "He seems confident."

"He's seen things."

They settled without discussion — Claire folding herself into the corner of the sofa, Jack on the armchair opposite, elbows resting on his knees. The silence wasn't heavy. Just... present.

Outside, the wind nudged the ivy against the windows. The faint clink of wind chimes down the lane drifted in, soft as breath.

Claire sipped her tea. "You really didn't leave anything."

Jack looked at his mug. "I know."

She waited.

He didn't elaborate.

After a long pause, she asked, "So... what did you come here for?"

Jack ran a thumb along the edge of the mug. "Honestly?"

Claire nodded once.

He exhaled. "I didn't want the day to end without... this."

"This?"

"This. Just..." He gestured vaguely between them. "Whatever this is."

Claire's gaze didn't move from his. "Okay."

He glanced up at her, surprised.

"That's all?" he said.

She gave a small shrug. "Sometimes it doesn't need a speech."

He nodded, slowly. "I'm not good at those anyway."

"I've noticed."

A smile tugged at the corner of her mouth. He almost smiled back.

They drank their tea in silence for a while after that.

At one point, she reached forward to grab a biscuit from the tin on the table, and their fingers brushed. Neither of them pulled away immediately.

Nothing else happened.

And yet, something had.

Later that evening, Claire still hadn't gone to bed.

The cottage glowed gently with lamplight — not bright, just enough to keep the corners from feeling like they were swallowing her whole. She'd lit a candle earlier without really thinking about it, and now its scent curled softly through the room: something vanilla-based, allegedly calming. It wasn't working.

She'd cleared the mugs Jack had used — both of them — and washed them under too-hot water, then dried them with the tea towel that always left bits of fluff behind. His mug, the one with the dancing turnip, sat clean and dry on the sideboard now. She wasn't sure whether to put it back in the cupboard or leave it there. She hadn't moved it.

Her book sat open beside her on the sofa, spine cracked and pages soft with too much re-reading. She wasn't reading. Hadn't read more than a page in the last hour. Her eyes kept wandering, drifting to the door, the window, the edge of her tea cup. She was warm enough, tucked under her favourite blanket, feet curled beneath her, but her thoughts were restless.

It wasn't that anything had happened. That was the maddening part. Jack had come in, sat down, drunk tea, and then left again, with nothing more said than thank you and see you later. And yet the cottage didn't feel the same now. He'd been in this room — quiet and present in that way only Jack could manage — and something about his absence left the air a little thinner.

She could still hear the soft scrape of his boots on the floorboards. The way he'd looked at her across the mug. The twitch of his fingers when they'd brushed over hers near the biscuit tin. None of it dramatic. None of it loud. But it clung to her now, like static — small, invisible, inescapable.

She got up and wandered to the window.

Outside, the village was still. The light from the lamppost by the green made the frost sparkle faintly on the grass. Somewhere in the distance, a fox barked. The post box stood sentry under the hedge, already crusted with white, and the gate creaked faintly in the breeze even though no one was walking past.

Claire pressed her fingers to the cold glass.

It had been a long time since someone made her feel... anything like this. Not swept away. Not giddy. Just... noticed. Steady. It was terrifying.

She wrapped the blanket tighter around her shoulders and went to put the kettle on again. She didn't need more tea. She just didn't want to be still. Stillness made room for things she wasn't sure she could hold yet.

As it boiled, she read Lily's text again:

He didn't say much when he got home. That's when you know something's up.

She hadn't replied again. But she didn't need to. Lily was clever — perceptive in the way kids were, especially when it came to their parents. She'd seen something in Jack's face that Claire hadn't dared to look for.

She poured the tea, this time without sugar. Sat back down on the sofa, this time without the book. She didn't reach for the radio, didn't turn on the TV. Just sat, tea cupped in both hands, the blanket draped over her shoulders like a shawl.

The fire in the hearth had burned down to embers, but she didn't bother stoking it. She liked the dimness. It felt true to the evening — not melancholy, but hushed. Like the cottage was holding its breath, waiting.

She thought about Jack's hand wrapped around the mug. His thumb resting lightly against the handle. The way he hadn't let go too quickly when their fingers brushed. The pause at the doorway. The way she hadn't wanted to ask him to stay but also hadn't wanted him to go.

If someone had asked her a month ago whether she could see herself here, like this — in a small cottage, in a smaller village, waiting for nothing in particular but thinking too much about a man who fixed things for a living and rarely spoke first — she'd have laughed.

But here she was.

And it wasn't waiting, exactly. It was more like... softening.

Letting the edges of her old life blur enough to make room for something she hadn't planned.

She didn't know what it was yet. Didn't know what Jack was thinking or what Lily had meant or what tomorrow would bring.

But for now, in the low hush of the evening, with the last bit of heat from the mug warming her palms and the candle flickering gently beside her, it was enough.

More than.

Claire had just finished her tea and was considering whether it was socially acceptable to eat toast again — purely for the comfort of it — when the knock came at the door.

It was too light to be Jack. Too fast to be Bev. And too rhythmically insistent to be anything other than...

She opened the door and there was Lily, in a hoodie that had clearly belonged to Jack at some point, sleeves rolled up three times and still too long, holding a shoebox under one arm like it contained state secrets.

"I brought biscuits," Lily said.

Claire stepped aside. "At ten o'clock?"

"They're mostly crumbs now. But it's the gesture."

Claire let her in, unsurprised. "Shouldn't you be asleep?"

"I did sleep. Briefly. But then I had a dream about frogs in waistcoats and woke up hungry."

Claire raised an eyebrow.

Lily dropped the shoebox on the table. "Also, Dad is being weird and mumbling and staring at your mug like it's giving him life advice."

Claire smiled despite herself. "Sounds about right."

Lily hopped up onto one of the kitchen chairs and helped herself to the remaining tea in the pot. No one had invited her to. She didn't need to be.

They sat in silence for a bit, Lily nibbling on what might have once been a digestive. Claire leaned her head against the cabinet, letting the warmth of Lily's presence settle in.

After a minute, Lily said, without looking up, "You make him more himself."

Claire blinked. "What?"

"My dad. He's always been good. He just forgets, sometimes. You remind him."

Claire stared at the girl across the table — this sharp, funny, slightly chaotic human who had somehow become the beating heart of two lives that had needed softening.

"I don't know what I'm doing," Claire admitted quietly.

Lily shrugged. "Nobody does. We're all winging it. Some people just wing it with better lighting and coordinated Tupperware."

Claire gave a soft laugh. "That sounds like something your dad would say."

"He probably did. I steal his best lines."

She reached into the box and handed Claire a slightly crushed biscuit.

"Take the last one," Lily said. "Symbolic and all that."

Claire accepted it. "Thanks."

They sat together like that for a long time. Not talking. Not needing to. The kind of quiet that only comes from earned comfort, not awkwardness.

Lily's head started to tilt after a while, her eyelids fluttering. Claire reached over without a word, and Lily leaned into her side, warm and slight and familiar now in a way that made Claire feel something at once terrifying and entirely right.

"You know," Lily murmured sleepily, "you smell like cinnamon and books and safety."

Claire blinked back a sudden, stupid welling behind her eyes.

"You smell like forgotten biscuits," she whispered.

Lily's breath evened out.

Claire sat with her like that, not moving. The clock ticked in the corner. The candle on the windowsill gave one final flicker and then blinked out.

She didn't need to know what was happening next. Not yet.

For now, this was enough.

Chapter Twenty One

"Proofing, Cinnamon, and the Trouble with Silence"

Claire was up before the sun.

Not on purpose. She hadn't set an alarm. But her eyes had opened sometime around five-thirty, and the idea of drifting back into sleep felt somehow more exhausting than just getting up.

The cottage was hushed and blue with early light. Her slippers were cold. The kitchen tiles colder. But there was something nice about moving through the silence while the rest of the village still slept.

She filled the kettle. Took the mixing bowl down from the high shelf. Pulled out the old flour jar that poofed a little when she opened it.

Baking wasn't a habit — not like Ellie's full-scale baking marathons, or Bev's aggressively scheduled jam sessions. But sometimes, like this morning, when her thoughts were too noisy and her heart too restless, it helped to make something *useful* with her hands.

Something warm. Predictable. Sweet.

She started with cinnamon buns. Proper ones, with the dough needing time to rise and proof. No shortcuts. She wanted the delay. Wanted the *process.*

As the yeast foamed in warm milk and sugar, Claire leaned on the counter and watched the sky pale.

She wasn't thinking about Jack. Except she was.

She wasn't replaying the way he'd stood in her hallway the night before, or how his hand had brushed hers twice, or the way he hadn't said anything significant — and yet somehow had said far too much.

She definitely wasn't wondering what he'd been doing awake at the same hour, if maybe he was lying in bed staring at the ceiling in the same way she had been, feeling exactly that same restless heat beneath the ribs.

Claire shaped the dough slowly, letting the stretch of it fill her hands. She'd never been good at sitting still, not really. Moving made more sense. Doing made more sense.

The cinnamon filled the cottage quickly, curling into the hall, the corners, under the doorways. She opened the window a crack to let the air out, then closed it again almost immediately. The cold rushed in like an overenthusiastic Labrador. Enough of that.

She'd just finished rolling the dough into neat, swirled spirals when she heard the knock.

She frowned. Too early for Mags. Ellie wouldn't be up yet unless her dog had thrown up on the rug again. Lily would've texted ahead with emojis.

Claire wiped her hands on a towel, crossed the kitchen, and opened the door.

Jack stood on the step.

Wool jumper. Ruffled hair. Holding two takeaway coffees in a cardboard tray and looking slightly out of breath, like he'd run the last part of the walk and was now deeply regretting it.

Claire blinked. "Good morning?"

He looked down at the tray. "I brought caffeine."

She tilted her head. "You're delivering coffee at six-thirty in the morning now?"

He exhaled. "I walked past the bakery van. They were setting up. I thought... it made sense at the time."

Claire opened the door wider. "Come in. You're going to spill those just from standing still."

Jack stepped in. The smell of cinnamon hit him immediately and his eyebrows lifted.

"I was baking," Claire said, unnecessarily.

"I can see that."

She took the coffee tray from him and set it on the counter, then passed him one without asking. He took it, nodded his thanks, then stood awkwardly in the middle of the kitchen like he didn't quite know what to do with himself.

Claire leaned on the counter. "Didn't sleep either?"

He shook his head. "Not really."

"Nightmares?"

"Just thinking."

She smiled faintly. "Dangerous habit."

He returned it. "You were on my mind."

It wasn't dramatic. He didn't say it like a confession. Just a fact. Like telling someone the forecast called for light rain.

Claire glanced down at the tray of buns.

"I made too many," she said.

Jack looked at the tray. "Convenient."

"They'll need another hour."

"I've got time."

They sat, this time in the living room, both with steaming mugs in hand, the air between them not exactly filled with words but with something else — not silence, but the kind of quiet that came when things were being felt, not spoken.

Claire drew her legs up onto the chair, one hand curled around her coffee. Jack leaned forward, elbows on knees, the same posture he always fell into when he wasn't sure whether to speak or wait.

Eventually, she asked, "Was it weird, yesterday? Us? Here?"

He shook his head. "No. I liked it."

"Me too."

She didn't say more. She didn't need to.

The scent of baking wrapped around them like a third person in the room — sweet, warm, nostalgic.

Jack glanced at the kitchen. "Can I help next time?"

Claire looked at him.

And smiled.

"Only if you agree to wear the ridiculous apron Ellie gave me."

He didn't even blink. "Deal."

And that was it.

No kiss. No declarations.

Just coffee, cinnamon, and the faint feeling that something, somewhere, was beginning to *settle*.

The kitchen timer let out a soft, insistent beep.

Claire moved without needing to check — already knowing by scent and instinct that the buns were ready. She pulled them out of the oven with the calm efficiency of someone who had done this before, even if she'd only just remembered how much she liked it.

The golden spirals puffed up perfectly in the tray, edges just catching with caramelised sugar. The scent doubled instantly, rich and clinging, filling the room with cinnamon, butter, and something harder to name — something like comfort.

Jack leaned forward slightly, still holding his coffee. "You're showing off now."

Claire smirked. "I absolutely am."

She set the tray down and reached for the icing she'd prepped earlier — just a quick drizzle, nothing fancy — when the front door opened.

Not knocked. Opened.

And in came Lily, hoodie askew, one sock missing, hair like she'd fought a pillow and lost.

"I smelled pastry," she announced, blinking at the light like a gremlin who'd been woken from a hundred-year nap.

Claire raised an eyebrow. "It's half seven."

"Time is a social construct," Lily muttered, dragging herself to the kitchen table and dropping into a chair like her bones had stopped working.

Jack grinned into his coffee. "Good morning to you too."

Lily glared at him. "I was asleep until someone slammed the front gate."

Jack looked mildly horrified. "I didn't—"

"You *always* slam it. You don't even know you're doing it."

Claire slid a plate in front of her with a warm bun. "Here. Soak up your attitude with cinnamon."

Lily sniffed it dramatically. "You *are* showing off."

Claire shrugged. "It's been that kind of morning."

Lily eyed her dad. Then Claire. Then the second coffee cup. Then the fact that her dad was in socks and hair that clearly hadn't met a brush yet today.

Her eyebrow arched in the way that was going to get her into serious trouble by the time she hit fifteen.

"So," she said, chewing, "should I be worried that there are no spoons left in the cutlery drawer? Or are you just emotionally repressing yourselves into a domestic routine?"

Jack choked slightly.

Claire gave Lily a look. "You're lucky that's a good bun."

"I know," Lily said, mouth full. "I'm a delight."

They ate in a kind of chaotic peace — Lily halfway awake but rapidly sharpening, Jack quieter than usual but not uncomfortable, Claire caught between laughter and a strange sense of ease that she didn't fully know what to do with.

After a minute, Lily said, "Dad, you're smiling. That's weird."

"I smile."

"Not like that."

He looked down at his plate. "It's the pastry."

Claire passed him another without comment.

The moment stretched, softened, settled. The sun had begun to creep through the window, touching the table with a soft line of gold.

Lily yawned, enormous and theatrical. "I'm going back to bed until school. I just wanted to make sure no one was being emotionally avoidant."

Claire raised a brow. "You woke up and thought *that*?"

Lily shrugged. "Welcome to my life."

She padded toward the stairs, then turned back at the bottom step. "You two should bake more often."

And then she was gone, leaving behind only one bitten bun, a mild sense of emotional whiplash, and the distinct scent of cinnamon and mischief.

Jack took a breath. "I think she's psychic."

Claire sipped her coffee. "She definitely keeps receipts."

They sat in silence for another minute.

This time, it wasn't heavy.
It felt, if anything, like the kind of quiet that comes *after* something has shifted — not during.

Like a page turning.

Claire wiped her hands on the corner of her apron and leaned back against the counter.

Jack was still seated, one hand around his coffee, the other idly tracing the rim of his empty plate with a finger. The sunlight through the window made him look softer somehow. Less guarded. Or maybe it was just the cinnamon.

"She's not wrong, you know," Claire said, quietly.

Jack looked up. "About what?"

"Baking. Fixes things."

He tilted his head. "Thought that was my job."

Claire smiled. "We can share."

For a second, she thought he might say something else — something heavier, or deeper — but instead, he stood, stretched, and nodded toward the still-warm buns.

"Reckon the village could use a few."

Claire blinked. "You want to walk them round?"

"Why not?"

"Because that sounds dangerously like a social gesture."

He raised a brow. "You're one to talk."

She grinned. "Let me grab a basket."

Five minutes later, they were walking down the lane with the scent of fresh pastry trailing behind them and a basket of still-warm cinnamon buns wrapped in a tea towel between them.

The village was just beginning to stir.

Curtains were twitching. A dog barked once, then seemed to think better of it. The bakery van was long gone, but the scent of bread still hung in the air like a promise. Somewhere, Mags was probably rearranging her spice rack or polishing her window ledge or reading tea leaves, badly.

Jack walked with one hand in his jacket pocket, the other holding the basket handle. Claire walked beside him, hands tucked into her sleeves, her breath visible in the cool morning air.

They didn't talk much.

They didn't need to.

It was the kind of silence that didn't feel empty — only full of things they weren't quite ready to say yet.

Outside the shop, Bev was unlocking the door, fumbling with her keychain and muttering something about how "these blasted locks weren't made for fingers that had worked with marzipan since 1983."

She turned and spotted them.

"Oho!" she called. "Is that pastry I smell? Or is it just the unmistakable aroma of emotional progress?"

Jack stopped. Claire stared.

Bev grinned. "I don't need to be subtle. I'm a widow."

Claire handed her a bun wordlessly.

Bev took it, looked at them both, and winked. "I'll be expecting wedding invitations printed on recycled napkins."

They walked on.

Two buns lighter.

Outside the community hall, they passed Ellie, who was crouched on the steps with a clipboard, a thermos, and the kind of expression that suggested she'd been out since dawn plotting some kind of seasonal bunting strategy.

She looked up, startled.

"Are those—are those real?"

Claire passed one down. "Fresh from the oven."

Ellie sniffed it. "You're dangerous."

Jack gave a slight nod. "We've been told."

They turned the corner at the end of the green, where the lane sloped gently toward the duck pond. The sun had properly risen now, turning the rooftops golden and making the frost sparkle like the village was trying just a little too hard to impress them.

Claire slowed, her hand brushing lightly against the basket handle next to Jack's.

"It's weird," she said, almost to herself. "How quickly this all started to feel... real."

Jack looked at her.

And for once, he didn't hesitate.

"It is real."

She met his eyes, surprised.

He held the gaze for a second longer than usual, then looked away. "I mean... it feels like it is."

Claire smiled. "Same."

They kept walking.

The basket was almost empty now. The morning was unfolding slowly around them. And for the first time in a long while, Claire didn't feel like she was chasing after anything.

She was just here. Walking beside someone who knew how to be quiet without making it awkward.

And maybe that was the beginning of something real.

As they rounded the last bend before the village green looped back toward the bakery, Claire spotted someone hunched on the low bench beside the bus stop, wrapped in a cardigan that might once have been beige and now defied categorisation.

Mags.

Naturally.

She was sipping something from a thermos mug shaped like a hedgehog, and wearing a hat that could only be described as "cabbage adjacent." A small knitted affair with multiple layers and an unfortunate shade of green that Claire was quite certain had never existed in nature.

Jack murmured, "We could turn back."

Claire smirked. "Coward."

Mags looked up before they had a chance to make an escape.

"Well, well," she said brightly. "Look who's wandering the village with domestic confidence and matching energy fields."

Jack blinked. "That sentence didn't make sense."

"It did if you'd had a proper breakfast," Mags said, peering over her mug. "And possibly a minor vision quest."

Claire handed her one of the final buns. "Here. It's warm. Eat before you start quoting the moon."

Mags took the bun like it was a peace offering, then held it in both hands, steam curling up into the cool air.

"You know," she said, breaking off a piece, "I remember when you first arrived. Looking like you were half ready to bolt, arms crossed like a fortress."

Claire chuckled softly. "Thanks."

"I don't mean it badly," Mags said, chewing. "You just looked like someone who hadn't been seen in a long time. Properly seen."

Claire glanced at Jack. He was pretending to study the cracked pavement.

Mags nodded, approvingly. "And now look at you. Early morning buns. Smelling like hope and cinnamon."

Jack coughed into his sleeve.

Claire said nothing.

Mags stood, dusting crumbs from her lap. "This is a good village. We don't always look like much, but we notice. People. Change. Love."

Claire raised an eyebrow. "Bit early for the 'L' word, don't you think?"

Mags shrugged. "I'm seventy-eight and I've outlived three husbands and one parrot. I say what I want."

She patted Claire's arm, then Jack's, and tottered off toward the corner shop muttering something about jam jars and fate.

Jack watched her go. "Does she just... appear like that?"

Claire nodded. "Like a fairy godmother, but with more cardigans and a lower tolerance for nonsense."

They stood there for a second, watching the morning continue without them. The village moved gently: the sound of a car door slamming, a dog barking somewhere by the green, a curtain twitching back into place.

Jack cleared his throat. "She's right, though."

Claire glanced at him. "About what?"

"You seem... more yourself. Lately."

Claire looked down at the basket — now empty except for one broken bun and a few soft crumbs.

"I think I am."

They didn't say more.

Didn't need to.

Instead, they turned back together, heading down the lane toward the cottage — warm fingers brushing once, not quite holding.

They reached the cottage just as the sun had properly stretched across the rooftops, dusting the lane with honeyed light.

Claire pushed open the door, the scent of cinnamon still hanging like a promise in the air.

Lily was already in the kitchen.

Not dressed. Not ready. Still wearing her duvet wrapped around her shoulders like a wizard's cloak. A half-eaten apple sat on the counter. She was scribbling something in a notebook with intensity and no regard for the laws of breakfast.

"I've had an idea," she said, without looking up.

Jack sighed as he stepped inside. "Do we need fire insurance?"

"No, but we might need ribbon. Possibly tinsel."

Claire raised an eyebrow. "That's not usually what people lead with after buns and sleep."

Lily looked up, eyes shining with the sort of expression that could only mean trouble disguised as creativity. "I think we should throw a surprise party."

Jack blinked. "For who?"

Lily grinned. "You."

He frowned. "Why would I want—"

Claire nudged him. "Don't ask. Just accept it's happening."

Lily continued, flipping a page in her notebook. "You've been grumpy all winter and now you're not. It's clearly cause for celebration. I've already made a list. It involves Mags, glitter glue, and a playlist Ellie refuses to approve."

Jack rubbed his face. "Please no glitter glue."

"Too late."

Claire passed him a mug of tea and took one herself, watching Lily out of the corner of her eye.

"She's been up to something," Claire said softly.

"I know that tone," Jack replied. "That's the *she's making a spreadsheet for emotional manipulation* tone."

Lily turned her notebook around. "I also have bun prototypes."

There were sketches. Actual sketches. Of pastries. With arrows pointing to where she thought more cinnamon could be "structurally incorporated."

Claire laughed. "This is what happens when you raise a child with access to both creativity and carbs."

Jack looked faintly proud. "She's always been advanced."

"I'm still in the room," Lily muttered, hiding a smile.

They moved around the kitchen easily, passing spoons and mugs without thinking. Jack sliced the last of the bread, Claire buttered it, Lily attempted to toast her apple under the grill for reasons unknown.

It felt like a family.

And it was just starting to feel normal when the post dropped through the door.

Just a soft clatter of envelopes on the mat — nothing special, no thunderclap.

Claire moved automatically to pick it up.

Gas bill. A flyer for windows she didn't need. A folded, handwritten envelope with no return address.

She stared at it for a beat too long.

Jack noticed. "What is it?"

She shook her head. "Probably nothing."

But it wasn't nothing.

The writing on the envelope was familiar in the way that made her skin tighten — curved letters with a slight left tilt, like someone had rushed but still cared how it looked.

She opened it carefully, pulse tick-ticking.

Lily, watching from her chair, quieted mid-sentence.

Claire unfolded the single sheet of paper inside.

Read it.

Read it again.

And sat down, the kettle still whistling behind her.

Jack took a step closer. "Claire?"

She looked up.

"It's from Jamie."

Jack blinked. "Jamie?"

Lily frowned. "Jamie as in... your ex-Jamie?"

Claire nodded slowly.

Jack said nothing.

Claire swallowed. "He's coming back. Just for a few days. Wants to talk."

The silence stretched.

Lily sat up straighter. "Do you want to?"

Claire folded the letter back along its worn crease. "I don't know."

Jack didn't move. His expression didn't change. But something in the room had.

Not shattered. Just... shifted.

Claire stood and placed the letter on the counter beside the cinnamon-smeared plate. She didn't say anything more. Just picked up the kettle, turned off the burner, and poured another cup of tea like it was the only thing she knew how to do just then.

Jack cleared his throat. "I should get going. I've got a thing in the next village."

Claire turned slightly. "Of course."

He lingered for a second. Long enough that she could feel the question hanging in the air — but not long enough for either of them to answer it.

Then he nodded once and left, the door closing softly behind him.

Claire stared at the mug in her hand.

Lily didn't speak. Just crossed the kitchen, opened the biscuit tin, and handed over the last shortbread.

"Emergency protocol," she said.

Claire took it.

And tried to breathe.

Jack didn't head straight to the next village.

He said he would — because it was something to say — but his feet carried him up toward the green instead, where the benches were always just slightly damp and the view stretched across the rooftops to the fields beyond.

He walked slowly.

Hands in his pockets. Shoulders hunched, though it wasn't cold enough to justify it. He wasn't sure what he was doing — only that walking felt better than standing still right now.

The letter.

He hadn't seen the words himself. Didn't need to. He'd seen Claire's face — the way her fingers tightened on the page, how she blinked twice like her brain needed time to rearrange itself.

Jamie.

That was a name he hadn't heard in months. Not since Claire had told him, in that careful, matter-of-fact tone she used for painful things, about the way it had ended. The distance. The unfinished-ness of it all. The way she'd never really had a proper goodbye.

And now the man was coming back.

Of course he was.

That was the trouble with beginnings — they so rarely arrived without dragging something else behind them.

Jack scuffed his boot along the edge of the path, watching a leaf tumble into the gutter. He wasn't angry. Not really. Not at Claire. She hadn't known. Hadn't asked for it. The letter had startled her more than him, and he could see she hadn't made any decisions yet.

But still, something inside him had pulled tight. Like a thread caught in a doorframe.

He reached the top of the green and sat down on the edge of the bench. The wood was cold, slightly damp, but he didn't move.

A dog barked in the distance. A jogger waved without making eye contact. Mags cycled past on a bicycle that creaked like an old man's knees, wrapped in a scarf that could've blanketed a small car.

Jack watched it all without really seeing it.

His hand drifted to the pocket of his coat where a receipt from this morning's coffee shop still lived — folded, nothing special. Just proof he'd been there. That the moment had been real.

The coffee, the buns, the morning walk with Claire.

The way her hand had brushed his, and she hadn't pulled away.

The way it had felt so simple.

And now... Jamie.

He didn't want to resent it. It wasn't Claire's fault. But some part of him — the quiet part, the part that never said things first — felt like maybe it had let itself hope too soon.

He stared out across the green, not moving.

He could fix broken hinges. Rewire lights. Replace floorboards.

But this — this uncertain, unfinished thing between them — this wasn't something he could build his way through.

Still, he hadn't misread it.

He was sure of that.

Claire had felt something. She still did. He knew her face now. Knew her silences. Knew what her half-smiles meant.

But Jamie's name had drawn a line in the sand.

And Jack didn't know yet if he was meant to step over it... or walk away.

The kettle clicked off again — Claire had forgotten she'd boiled it twice already.

Lily hadn't moved from the stool by the counter. She was perched awkwardly, knees drawn up under her hoodie, clutching the half-eaten shortbread with the kind of reverence she usually reserved for cinema popcorn or the last slice of pizza.

Claire poured the water anyway. Tea felt like something to do. Like scaffolding for the rest of the moment.

She slid a mug toward Lily, who took it without a word.

For a few minutes, the only sound in the cottage was the faint tick of the kitchen clock and the distant thrum of the fridge, like it was thinking hard about something.

Eventually, Lily broke the silence.

"So... Jamie."

Claire nodded, eyes fixed on the steam curling from her cup.

Lily tilted her head. "You okay?"

"I don't know yet."

Lily didn't push. She sipped her tea and stared at the edge of the table like it might provide some insight.

"I didn't expect it," Claire said finally, her voice lower than usual. "Not after all this time. It felt like... like that part of my life had gone quiet."

Lily twirled her spoon. "And now it's turned up with a handwritten letter."

Claire gave a soft snort. "Classic Jamie. Always had a flair for the dramatic."

She paused. "And the cowardly."

Lily didn't smile. "Did you love him?"

Claire blinked. She hadn't expected the question to come so directly. "I thought I did."

"That's not the same."

Claire met her gaze. "No. It's not."

Lily nodded, like she was filing something away.

Claire stood, wiped down a perfectly clean section of the counter, then leaned against it and crossed her arms.

"I spent years building a life that revolved around someone else's certainty. I thought that if I made myself useful — valuable — I'd be... safe. Wanted."

"And were you?"

Claire smiled sadly. "I was convenient. That's not the same either."

Lily looked down at her mug. "You're not convenient anymore."

Claire blinked. "Thanks?"

Lily shrugged. "You're cinnamon buns and boundary-setting now."

Claire laughed despite herself. "That sounds like a very complicated recipe."

"I'm working on it."

They sat quietly again.

Claire felt the heaviness starting to shift — not gone, but no longer stuck. The kind of movement that didn't fix anything, but made breathing easier.

Lily glanced toward the letter, still lying on the counter.

"You're not going to see him," she said — not as a question, but as a statement.

Claire didn't answer right away. "I might. Just to finish the sentence."

"But you're not going back."

It wasn't a question either.

Claire met her eyes. "No, I'm not."

Lily exhaled, sharp and relieved. "Good."

She stood and stretched, hoodie sleeves flapping.

"I've got maths homework," she said, with the grim resignation of someone about to face their nemesis. "But let me know if you need me to draft a strategic emotional takedown later."

Claire raised an eyebrow. "You're eleven."

"I contain multitudes."

She padded out of the kitchen and up the stairs, leaving Claire in the quiet again.

But this time, it didn't feel quite so heavy.

She turned the letter over once more. Read the opening line. Then folded it back and tucked it inside the drawer beneath the phone.

It didn't need to live on the counter anymore.

The day drifted.

Outside, the clouds moved in soft bands across a blue-grey sky, and the light through the front window shifted from warm gold to something cooler, softer, more diffused. The cottage settled into that particular kind of afternoon stillness — not silent, just content to breathe quietly.

Claire stood by the armchair with a laundry basket at her feet, folding clothes one by one.

A hoodie of Lily's — the one with paint stains on the cuff from last summer's school fair. A tea towel with a melted corner from the Great Microwave Disaster of April. One of her own cardigans, older than some of her regrets.

She smoothed each item automatically, her hands busy while her thoughts wandered. Not anxious. Just thoughtful. A kind of slow, reflective turning over of the day, like sifting flour through fingers.

The letter was still in the drawer.

It wasn't calling to her. Not anymore. She'd read it twice. That was enough. The words were there if she needed them, but they didn't get to dictate the rhythm of the house anymore.

She picked up a pair of socks — mismatched, naturally — and smiled faintly.

On the windowsill above the radiator, a small vase of dried lavender tilted toward the light. Outside, in the garden, the hydrangeas had started to fade to that bruised pink-blue they took on in late autumn. The grass was patchy. The rosemary bush needed trimming. A pigeon waddled indignantly along the fence.

Claire folded the last towel and placed it on top of the stack, then sat on the edge of the armchair, the sunlight catching in her hair, warm against her cheek.

She let herself breathe. Really breathe. Deep and full, like she hadn't for days.

There was something deeply ordinary about it — the laundry, the garden, the ticking clock — and yet it steadied her in a way no dramatic gesture ever could.

She didn't know what would happen next. Whether Jamie's return would rattle something loose, or if Jack would need space, or if Lily would try to start a spreadsheet titled *Reasons to Trust Mum's Instincts*.

But for now... she had folded towels and a warm house and the smell of cinnamon still faint in the air.

And for now, that was enough.

Chapter Twenty Two

"Interruptions, Intentions, and the Last Clean Fork"

The letter stayed in the drawer.

Claire hadn't looked at it again. She didn't need to. Its presence in the cottage was enough — like a painting turned to the wall, still there, but silent.

Sunday had rolled in slowly, all damp skies and quiet hours. The kind of day where time stretched like toffee and everything felt half-an-hour behind itself. Lily was still in her pyjamas. The toaster had started refusing to pop up on its own. And there was exactly one clean fork left in the drawer, which no one seemed inclined to wash anything else for.

Claire padded into the kitchen in thick socks and an oversized jumper, poured the last of the milk into her tea, and realised — too late — that someone had already left the carton empty in the fridge.

She sighed.

"Lily?"

No response.

Claire poked her head around the corner.

Lily was upside down on the sofa, legs draped over the back cushions, headphones in, mouth moving silently to whatever monologue was currently captivating her screen.

Claire smiled faintly, pulled on her boots, and reached for her coat.

She stepped outside just as the wind picked up — not wild, just blustery in that low-level inconvenient way that turned umbrellas inside out and stole napkins from outdoor tables. The village looked freshly rinsed: puddles along the gutters, windowpanes streaked, birds huddled in whatever bits of hedgerow still had leaves.

She crossed to the shop.

Bev was behind the counter, sorting receipts like they were personal insults.

Claire held up the empty milk carton. "Got anything resembling dairy?"

Bev snorted. "Just. Mags came in ten minutes ago and bought two full pints and a packet of marshmallows and then tried to pay in buttons."

Claire smiled. "Are we talking metaphorical buttons or actual ones?"

"Mixed currency," Bev muttered. "One had a ladybird on it."

She handed over a bottle. Claire paid with actual money.

As she turned to leave, Bev gave her a look — the kind of look that came with tea, a sofa, and maybe the kind of biscuit people saved for real conversations.

"You alright?"

Claire paused.

She could have said yes. Could have nodded, smiled, kept walking.

Instead, she said, "Mostly."

Bev nodded. "That's about as good as anyone gets, love."

Outside, the wind had changed direction. Claire pulled her coat tighter and began the walk back to the cottage, the bottle of milk swinging lightly in one hand.

She didn't notice the figure walking toward her until he was almost at the gate.

Jack.

He looked like he hadn't expected to see her either. Hair slightly windblown, jacket creased, and a paper bag in one hand that gave off the faint scent of sugar and butter.

They both stopped.

Claire lifted the bottle. "Emergency milk."

Jack held up the bag. "Emergency pastries."

They looked at each other for a moment, then both gave a soft, crooked smile — not quite apology, not quite explanation.

Claire shifted the bottle to her other hand. "Want to come in?"

Jack nodded. "Yeah. I do."

Claire stepped aside and let Jack in, brushing a few leaves off her coat as she closed the door behind them.

The cottage was warm, in that lived-in, slightly-cluttered way — the kind of warmth that came from half-dry laundry on the radiator, a forgotten candle flickering on the windowsill, and the smell of cinnamon still clinging faintly to the air from the day before.

Jack held out the paper bag. "Croissants. One of them might be almond, but I forgot which."

Claire took it with a smile and led him into the kitchen.

They sat at the little table by the window, each with a mug — hers tea, his coffee, both slightly too strong. Claire tore off a corner of her croissant, then another. Jack was already halfway through his.

Neither of them spoke for a while.

It wasn't uncomfortable.

It was the kind of silence that comes after something tentative but good — like both people were checking their emotional limbs for bruises but finding none.

Claire took a sip of tea. "I didn't sleep well."

Jack nodded. "Me neither."

She looked at him over the rim of her mug. "Are we allowed to talk about it?"

He shrugged, but there was something soft in it. "We can talk about anything. Or not talk about it."

Claire gave a faint smile. "You've got a real gift for ambiguity."

Jack chuckled. "Years of practice."

She set her cup down and leaned back slightly, watching him.

"I'm not going back to that life," she said. "Even if Jamie thinks there's something to 'revisit.' Even if he brings flowers or apologies or some newly discovered sense of perspective."

Jack nodded, slowly. "Okay."

"I just thought you should know."

He looked down at his plate, brushed away a few crumbs with one finger.

"I didn't ask," he said quietly, "because I didn't want to sound like I was asking you to choose."

Claire tilted her head. "But you were wondering."

"Of course I was."

She nodded once. "Thank you for not asking."

And that was it.

No declarations. No drama.

Just a small, shared truth, laid gently between them like a folded napkin.

The kitchen clock ticked. A bird tapped briefly at the window before deciding against whatever it had in mind. Somewhere in the house, a floorboard creaked.

Then—

Lily appeared in the doorway, hoodie sleeves trailing, hair an unbrushed riot of curls, holding a pair of glitter-covered cardboard cutouts in one hand and a roll of tape in the other.

"I need help," she said, with the urgency of someone launching a moon mission.

Claire blinked. "With...?"

"Operation Winter Ball Installation Strategy."

Jack sat back. "That sounds dangerous."

"It *is*," Lily said. "But it's also legally binding. Ellie gave me responsibility for decorating the stage and she said — and I quote — 'don't come crying to me if you mess it up.' Which is obviously a cry for help."

Claire smiled. "Do we need glue guns?"

"Three," Lily said. "And potentially Bev's stepladder."

Jack looked at the glittered shapes dangling from her fingers. "Are those... doves?"

"They're whatever they need to be," Lily said. "Symbolism is fluid."

She dropped the tape on the table and pointed at Jack. "You're tall. You're coming."

Jack raised a hand. "Why does no one ever ask nicely?"

Claire handed him the last bite of almond croissant. "This is your thank you."

He sighed, accepted it, and stood.

As Lily darted toward the hall to gather more supplies — muttering about snowflakes and Ellie's questionable taste in fairy lights — Jack glanced at Claire.

"Still not going back?"

Claire gave him a look — soft, sure.

"No. I'm going forward."

The village hall was already a mess when they arrived.

Not the usual kind — not dirty or neglected — but the kind of festive chaos that happens when half a dozen volunteers are given tinsel, authority, and vague artistic freedom.

Ellie was standing on a table in the centre of the hall, pointing dramatically toward the rafters while Bev unravelled a string of fairy lights with the grim determination of someone wrestling a python.

"Oh good," Ellie called as Claire, Jack, and Lily walked in. "You brought the tall one."

Jack blinked. "I do have a name."

"We'll stitch it into the bunting," Bev muttered. "Now hold the ladder."

Lily peeled off immediately, heading toward the back with her cardboard cutouts and a mouth full of strategic orders. Claire followed at a more reasonable pace, arms crossed, scanning the room.

The stage was half-dressed, one curtain hanging like it had lost the will to live. A pile of paper snowflakes spilled out of a Tesco bag onto the floor like a craft store had sneezed. Someone — probably Mags — had placed what appeared to be an ornamental goose on top of the piano.

Jack was pressed into duty almost immediately. Ellie handed him a tangled wreath and a hammer, pointed vaguely at the arch above the stage, and walked off muttering something about symmetry and "the tyranny of pastel palettes."

Claire set about rescuing a stack of candles from being wrapped in bubble wrap *and* foil, while Lily directed Bev toward the refreshment table with the air of a general marshaling troops.

It was chaos.

But good chaos.

The kind that smelled like mince pies and sounded like poorly timed Christmas playlists. The kind where glitter got everywhere and no one really minded.

Jack returned from the arch with pine needles in his hair and a piece of ribbon stuck to his jumper. Claire passed him a biscuit without a word.

"You look festive," she said.

"I feel violated by seasonal foliage."

She smiled.

They worked for another hour. Lights were strung. Paper stars were affixed to windows with dubious tape. Ellie tried to test the smoke machine and nearly set off the alarm. Mags appeared briefly, delivered a fruitcake no one had asked for, and disappeared again, humming.

Claire found herself laughing more than she expected.

Jack wasn't just helpful — he was easy in the space, joking with Bev, offering steady hands, always just where he needed to be without being asked. And Lily... Lily thrived. Directing adults like a benevolent dictator, cheering every small victory like it was structural engineering.

At one point, Claire stood back and just watched them.

Lily, her hoodie dusted with glitter, was arguing with Ellie about the optimal height for a hanging snowflake. Jack was crouched by the stage, reattaching a rogue garland. Bev was distributing lukewarm tea and half-smiling like she hated everyone slightly less than usual.

Claire felt it settle in her chest — that soft, spreading warmth.

This was her life now.

Not the glossy, polished one she'd once built around someone else's ambition. Not the carefully lit, brand-conscious future she'd imagined in a London flat.

But this.

A wonky wreath, mismatched fairy lights, a child with more ideas than time, a man who didn't say much but always noticed when she needed help lifting something — or breathing.

It wasn't perfect.

But it was real.

And real, she'd learned, was far better.

The hall emptied slowly.

Ellie left first, declaring she had to rewash all the mugs because "someone" — meaning Bev — had used fabric softener in the dishwasher again. Bev rolled her eyes, muttered about amateur dramatics, and followed, dragging a box of tangled tinsel behind her.

Lily lingered, adjusting a final snowflake with all the gravitas of an architect inspecting structural support.

Jack was helping coil the last of the fairy lights — slower now, movements unhurried.

Claire tucked a half-used roll of ribbon into the supply box and looked around.

The stage was still a little lopsided. The decorations were about 20% tasteful and 80% joyful chaos. Glitter floated in the air like festive dust. But it felt good. Not done — just ready enough.

Lily came over, smudged with silver sparkles and already halfway through a chocolate bar she claimed she'd earned by sheer creative labour.

"I'm heading home," she said through a mouthful. "My toes are tired."

Claire looked at her shoes. "That's because you wore slippers."

"They're festive-adjacent."

Jack smiled. "Want a lift?"

Lily shook her head. "Nope. I need to walk off the trauma of watching Bev glue sequins to a fire extinguisher."

She leaned in and kissed Claire's cheek — sticky, chocolate-scented — then gave Jack a suspiciously grown-up look.

"Play nice," she said, and wandered out into the dusk.

Claire and Jack stood in the middle of the now-quiet hall.

It always felt different once everyone had left — the air still full of laughter, but quieter now. Like a memory already forming.

Claire walked toward the stage and sat on the edge, feet swinging slightly.

Jack joined her a moment later, lowering himself onto the worn wood beside her with a slight groan.

"That garland attacked me," he said.

Claire glanced sideways. "It's hanging a bit to the left."

"Artistic choice."

They sat quietly for a minute.

Then Claire said, "I've been thinking about what Lily said."

Jack tilted his head. "Which part? The sequin trauma or the glue-stick dictatorship?"

She smiled. "No. The other part. About you."

Jack didn't answer.

Claire picked at a loose thread in her sleeve. "She notices everything, you know. Even the stuff I try to keep under wraps."

"Especially that stuff."

Claire looked up at him.

"I don't know what this is," she said quietly. "But I know what it's not."

Jack met her gaze. "What?"

"It's not temporary. It's not pretend. And it's not something I want to lose just because the past sent a letter."

He looked away, exhaled through his nose. "You're sure?"

She nodded. "More than I expected."

They didn't touch.

They didn't need to.

The space between them had changed — not closed, exactly, but filled with something new. Something soft, and slow, and *true*.

Jack leaned back on his hands. "Lily's going to take full credit for this."

Claire smiled. "She deserves at least partial rights."

The lights on the tree flickered once, a final sparkle in the growing dim. Outside, dusk had slipped in like a blanket — softening the edges of everything.

Claire stood and offered Jack a hand.

He took it without question.

And they left the hall side by side, the door swinging closed behind them with a gentle thud — like the story wasn't ending, just folding into its next page.

Lily walked slowly.

Not because she was tired — although her feet were vaguely offended by the existence of physical effort — but because the air smelled nice. Like cold earth and chimney smoke and something sweet that had escaped from Bev's pockets.

The village always changed a bit at dusk. It wasn't big enough for mystery, exactly, but it still held that feeling like anything could happen on the walk between the hall and home. Especially in winter. Especially when fairy lights had been switched on and everyone was pretending not to cry about baubles.

She pulled her hoodie tighter and kicked a leaf off the path.

Claire had smiled more today.

Not just the "I'm-fine-don't-ask" smile, or the "we're-late-for-school-again" one. But a real one. A quiet kind. The kind that sat in her face like it belonged there, not like it was just visiting.

And Jack had looked at her like he noticed.

Lily didn't trust a lot of adults — not really. They were too good at saying one thing and meaning another. But Jack was different. He didn't try too hard. He didn't pretend not to care when he obviously did. And he didn't make Claire shrink.

That was the important bit.

Claire had spent a long time being smaller than she really was. Lily didn't have the words for it exactly, but she'd seen it happen. Like someone had turned down her volume for years and only now realised the dial still worked.

She turned down the lane, breath puffing in little clouds.

She wasn't worried about Jamie. Not really. He might've written a letter, but Claire wasn't the same person who would've answered it last year. Or the year before that. She was different now. Stronger.

There was glitter on her cheek and flour in her hair and a man next to her who looked at her like she was a lighthouse.

Lily smiled to herself.

Things weren't perfect.

But they were better than they'd been.

And sometimes that was more than enough.

The cottage felt quieter than usual when they stepped inside.

Not silent — just still. The kind of stillness that welcomed you home rather than questioned your arrival.

Claire flicked on the side lamp in the living room, casting a soft glow across the floorboards. Jack toed off his boots at the door without being asked, and Claire padded into the kitchen, setting the kettle on as though it had been rehearsed.

"I don't think I've ever glittered that much in one afternoon," Jack said, pulling a stray silver star from the cuff of his jumper.

Claire smiled. "You'll find more in the morning. They multiply."

He wandered into the kitchen, leaning on the counter as the kettle clicked and hummed.

Claire pulled two mugs from the shelf. "Chamomile or classic builder's?"

"Dealer's choice."

She went for builder's. Something about the evening called for strong, simple things.

They carried the mugs into the living room, where Lily had clearly rearranged the cushions into some kind of teenage fortress earlier in the day. Claire swept a few to the side and dropped onto the sofa. Jack sat beside her, a little closer than before. Not pressing, just present.

They sipped quietly.

Outside, the wind had picked up — not fierce, just brushing past the windows in soft waves. The kind of sound that made you glad for thick socks and mugs with handles that didn't scald.

Claire glanced at him.

"You know," she said, "I don't think I've ever had this before."

Jack looked at her. "Tea?"

She gave a soft laugh. "No. This. Just... this. A house that feels like mine. A night that doesn't ache. Company that doesn't feel like performance art."

He didn't say anything, but he didn't look away either.

Claire traced a finger along the rim of her mug. "I used to be so good at pretending things were fine. At smiling just enough, nodding at the right moments, asking questions so I wouldn't have to answer any."

Jack's voice was quiet. "And now?"

"I think I'm getting tired of pretending."

He nodded once. "Good."

Another silence. But it wasn't empty.

He reached for her hand.

Just gently. Not clasping — just the backs of their fingers brushing on the cushion between them.

Claire didn't pull away.

After a while, she turned her hand palm-up and let his settle into it.

She didn't speak. Neither did he.

They just sat, together. The tea grew cooler. The cottage quieter.

And something between them began to *root* — not loudly, not suddenly — just steadily.

Like it had been growing all along, beneath the surface.

The room had taken on that late-night quiet — the kind that felt more like a blanket than an absence. The wind tapped lightly against the windowpanes, the radiator clicked as it cooled, and somewhere under the sofa, Claire was almost certain a rogue bauble from last year's Christmas had just rolled itself into a new hiding place.

She was warm.

That was the surprising thing — not just physically, but *emotionally*. The kind of warmth that came not from tea or thick socks or an extra layer, but from the absence of anything sharp.

Jack hadn't said much since taking her hand. He didn't need to.

He was still beside her on the sofa, one leg folded underneath him, his mug long forgotten on the coffee table, next to hers. His thumb brushed across her knuckles occasionally — not insistently, just... because he could.

Claire let her head drop gently to the side, resting it against the cushion. She could feel her body starting to settle, the kind of heaviness that meant she'd finally stopped bracing for something.

She blinked slowly. Then again.

The third time, her eyes stayed shut a little longer.

Jack glanced down.

"Tired?"

"Mmm," she murmured. "Just... still."

He smiled faintly. "Still is good."

Her head tipped sideways just a little more, and the cushion wasn't really a cushion anymore — it was his shoulder.

He didn't move.

Didn't shift or straighten or tease.

Just sat there, letting her lean.

Claire mumbled something he couldn't quite catch — maybe about the wreath on the hall door being crooked again, or maybe about the milk — and then she went quiet.

Jack tilted his head slightly, just enough to see the outline of her profile in the soft lamp light. Her breathing had deepened. One arm curled up under her chin. A small frown smoothed itself out across her brow as she drifted.

He didn't move.

Not for a while.

Outside, the wind dipped again. The fridge rattled once. A car drove past, slow and quiet.

Claire shifted slightly in her sleep and mumbled, "Don't forget the buns."

Jack smiled.

He sat there another twenty minutes, just... being. Letting the stillness hold.

When it became clear she wasn't waking any time soon, he carefully — slowly — leaned forward and picked up the extra blanket from the back of the sofa. Draped it over her. Took his time.

Then he stood, moving like the floor might squeak louder than it needed to.

He paused by the door.

Looked back at her — curled, peaceful, warm.

Then, very softly, he whispered, "Sleep well, Claire."

He let himself out into the quiet night and pulled the door shut behind him with the gentlest of clicks.

Inside, Claire didn't stir.

But the edge of her mouth turned up ever so slightly in her sleep.

The sunlight crept in softly.

Not the dramatic sort that spilled in with cinematic flair, but the kind that simply... arrived. Warm, low, dust-speckled. The kind that made the living room glow around the edges like someone had quietly painted light across the furniture.

Claire stirred on the sofa.

The blanket had slipped halfway down her legs. One sock was missing. Her hair was somehow doing two completely opposite things at once. And yet... she felt rested.

Not just in the physical sense — though that was part of it — but in a deeper, steadier way. Like her heart had been exhaling all night without asking permission.

She blinked a few times, the room slowly coming into focus.

The mugs were still on the table. The fairy lights on the mantelpiece were off now, but one of them blinked faintly — likely protesting retirement. The clock above the stove said 07:51.

And Jack was gone.

But in his place — or rather, left behind — was the folded blanket, tucked around her with quiet care. A mug had been rinsed and left on the draining board. His coat was no longer on the hook.

He'd left. Gently. Thoughtfully.

Claire sat up slowly, stretching her arms overhead and letting the blanket fall into her lap. She didn't move for a few minutes. Just sat there, letting morning settle around her.

There was no dramatic internal speech. No sudden moment of certainty. Just a soft, unfolding peace. Like the beginning of trust — in herself, in what she felt, in what might come next.

The kettle clicked once — as if remembering its duty — and Claire took that as a cue to get up.

She padded to the kitchen, reheated the last of the tea from the pot (ignoring the judgment of tea purists everywhere), and added a generous squeeze of honey.

It tasted like quiet.

She sipped, leaned against the counter, and smiled.

And that's when the sound came: a thump, a shuffle, and a faint groan of indignation from upstairs.

Lily.

Claire waited.

Sure enough, thirty seconds later, the staircase was filled with the sound of slippered feet and muttered commentary.

"Mum," Lily announced as she entered the kitchen, her hair in full Einstein mode and one slipper on the wrong foot, "you fell asleep on the sofa and I *knew* it."

Claire raised an eyebrow. "Good morning to you too."

Lily squinted at the tea. "Is there more of that?"

Claire poured her a mug.

Lily sniffed it. "Is this the wrong kind?"

"It's chamomile and honey. You'll survive."

Lily took a sip, made a dramatic face, and plopped onto the nearest chair with all the grace of a small goat.

Then: "So. Big day."

Claire blinked. "Is it?"

Lily gasped. "Mother. The Winter Ball. Have you forgotten the emotional climax of this entire season?"

Claire laughed. "You sound like you're narrating a Netflix trailer."

"I'm just saying," Lily said, swiping a piece of toast from the plate and chewing theatrically, "tonight is pivotal. There will be dresses. There will be cake. There will probably be Bev crying behind the stage curtain again."

Claire took another sip of tea. "Is she performing?"

"No, but she's bringing the sausage rolls. She gets emotional."

Claire leaned back against the counter. "I suppose you have a plan?"

Lily nodded solemnly. "Several."

"Do I want to know them?"

"Probably not."

Claire chuckled.

Lily stood, already animated. "Okay, we need: 1) hair prep, 2) clothes check, 3) decoration damage assessment — I heard a snowflake fell and Ellie's having an existential crisis — and 4) a playlist upgrade because Bev snuck three ABBA tracks onto the loop and it's not 2004 anymore."

Claire blinked. "What's wrong with ABBA?"

"Nothing. But she put them between two instrumental waltzes. You can't *emotionally pivot* like that, it's chaos."

Claire smiled. "You're terrifying."

"Thank you."

Lily turned, headed for the stairs, then paused. "Oh — and Jack's jumper is on the back of the sofa. Just in case you were wondering."

Claire followed her gaze. Sure enough, one dark grey jumper sat folded neatly on the cushion, like it had been placed there on purpose.

Lily gave her mother a pointed look. "Not saying anything. Just... observing."

And then she disappeared.

Claire looked at the jumper for a long moment.

Then reached out, gently touched the edge of the sleeve, and smiled.

Not a big smile.

Just the kind that said something in her life had quietly shifted — and, maybe for the first time in years, she wasn't scared of what came next.

The morning unspooled with the soft rhythm of a day not in a hurry.

Claire finished her tea, cleared away the breakfast things, and stood at the kitchen sink longer than necessary, her fingers trailing under the warm water.

It wasn't nerves, exactly.

More... awareness.

Everything in the cottage felt a little more *present* today. As if the walls themselves had perked up in anticipation. Even the radio, playing quietly in the background, seemed to have chosen a softer playlist — songs that didn't insist, just *accompanied*.

Lily had disappeared upstairs with a hairbrush, three safety pins, and a half-empty can of glitter spray. Claire didn't ask.

She moved slowly through her morning. A light tidy. A new candle lit. Her dress — simple navy with a soft neckline and a gentle sweep at the hem — hung from the wardrobe like it had been waiting all month.

Claire paused in the doorway, tea forgotten in hand.

It wasn't fancy.

But it was hers. And it felt like exactly the kind of dress you wore when you weren't trying to be impressive — just honest.

She stepped into the room, trailed her fingers along the fabric.

A soft knock at the front door made her start.

She glanced at the clock. Just gone eleven.

She wasn't expecting anyone.

Wiping her hands on a tea towel, she opened the door slowly.

No one there.

Just the cool breeze off the green, a faint scent of woodsmoke — and a brown paper package sitting on the doorstep.

No writing on it. Just twine. And a folded note tucked neatly under the string.

Claire bent to pick it up, heart ticking just a little faster.

She brought it inside and placed it on the kitchen table.

The note was short. No signature. But the handwriting was familiar — strong, neat, slightly slanted.

Claire,

Thought this might go with your dress.
No pressure. No expectations. Just in case.
—J

She stared at it for a second.

Then undid the twine with careful fingers.

Inside was a small, tissue-wrapped box. And in the box, nestled like something secret, was a necklace.

Not new. Not polished. Just... lovely. A fine chain with a silver charm — a small compass rose, simple and delicate.

Claire turned it over in her palm.

On the back, one word had been etched by hand: *Onward*.

She blinked once. Then again.

She didn't cry.

But she did sit down.

Not because she felt overwhelmed — but because something in her had just *settled*. Like a puzzle piece finally dropped into place.

After a moment, she stood, still holding the necklace, and crossed to the mirror.

It rested just below her collarbone. Light, sure. Like a promise you weren't being asked to make — just to believe in.

Upstairs, Lily called down, "Mum! I need help with something that might be glue-related!"

Claire smiled at her reflection.

"I'm coming."

She touched the charm once more, tucked it gently beneath her neckline, and turned toward the stairs.

The day was waiting.

And for the first time in a long time, so was she.

Claire was halfway up the stairs when Lily called again.

"Mum? Just—prepare yourself emotionally."

Claire paused. "For what?"

There was a pause. Then, solemnly: "The hair."

Claire stepped into Lily's room and blinked.

The glitter spray had won.

The floor was lightly dusted with shimmer, several hair ties had given their lives in service to the cause, and the small desk mirror was surrounded by a battalion of makeup items Claire didn't remember authorising.

Lily stood in the middle of it all, proudly holding what appeared to be a curling wand and a half-eaten biscuit.

"I'm a masterpiece," she declared.

Claire grinned. "You're something, that's for sure."

Lily twirled. "Do you think I look weird or whimsical?"

Claire considered. "A little of both. But in a good way."

Lily beamed. "Perfect."

She set down the biscuit and walked over, eyeing Claire with suspicion.

"Did you do your hair already?"

"I brushed it."

Lily gasped. "That's not a strategy."

She motioned for Claire to sit, which Claire did — more amused than compliant — as Lily reached for a comb and began fussing with her hair.

"You don't have to—"

"Shh. You're in the hands of an artiste."

Claire sighed and let her do her work.

It wasn't unpleasant — Lily was gentle, surprisingly so. And meticulous. She worked in near silence for a few minutes, tongue poking out slightly in concentration.

"Do you think I've changed?" Claire asked quietly, eyes drifting toward the mirror.

Lily didn't stop combing. "Since when?"

"Since we moved here."

Lily was quiet for a second.

Then: "You laugh more. You cook proper food. You let people in."

Claire swallowed. "That much, huh?"

Lily gave her a look in the mirror. "You were like a turtle when we got here."

Claire laughed. "Thanks."

"A chic turtle," Lily added. "With good taste in mugs. But yeah."

Claire turned slightly to look at her. "And that's okay with you?"

Lily shrugged. "It's better than okay. You're happier. And I get glitter and sausage rolls. So really, we're all winning."

Claire reached up and squeezed her hand.

They stayed like that for a moment — Lily behind her, both of them reflected in the mirror, the afternoon light softening their outlines.

Then Lily said, "Okay. Ready for your grand reveal?"

Claire stood. Turned toward the mirror.

Her hair had been twisted into a soft knot, pinned loosely at the side with a small clip that caught the light. A few strands framed her face. She looked... like herself.

But clearer.

Like someone had pulled her into focus.

She turned to Lily. "You did good."

Lily grinned. "I know."

Claire reached for her navy dress. Lily, already back at the glitter station, peeked over.

"You're going to wear the necklace, right?"

Claire hesitated only a second. "Yes."

Lily didn't ask where it came from. She just nodded, like she'd expected it all along.

And then — just as Claire slipped into the dress — Lily tilted her head and said:

"Do you think he'll tell you tonight?"

Claire blinked. "Tell me what?"

Lily smiled.

"That you're his favourite person."

Claire didn't answer.

She didn't need to.

Chapter Twenty Three

"The Ball, the Lights, and the Bit Where You're Braver Than You Thought"

The village hall had never looked better.

It probably *had* looked better, at some point in its hundred-year history — perhaps in the 1950s when people wore gloves to dinner and knew how to ballroom dance without YouTube tutorials — but tonight it shimmered.

Fairy lights cascaded from the rafters. The stage, miraculously upright, was now adorned with swags of velvet and paper stars. A Christmas tree stood by the piano like it was slightly too tall for the ceiling and proud of it. The whole space smelled like spiced biscuits and floor polish.

Claire paused just inside the doors, her fingers tightening slightly on Lily's hand.

People milled about — neighbours in their best shoes, friends wearing suits with mismatched ties, teenagers trying not to look like they'd actually made an effort.

There was music — something jazzy and upbeat — and Bev was already two mulled wines deep, narrating her scarf collection to an uninterested vicar.

Claire exhaled slowly. Not nervous. Just... aware.

She felt Lily squeeze her hand.

"You look good," Lily said simply.

Claire smiled. "So do you."

Lily twirled once, her tulle skirt catching the light. "Ellie says I'm what happens when a disco ball joins the drama club."

"She's not wrong."

They walked in together.

Claire's dress moved with her in soft waves. The necklace rested warm at her collarbone. And every few steps, someone said hello — a smile, a wave, a quick compliment that didn't feel like obligation.

She didn't see Jack right away.

She didn't need to.

It was enough to be here. In this space she'd helped hang stars in. With these people she'd slowly, stubbornly come to care for. Her village. Her evening. Her life, growing brighter at the edges.

"Claire!"

It was Ellie, dressed in what could only be described as Victorian glamour meets jazz age mischief.

"You have to come see the cake situation," she said, dragging her toward the refreshment table. "It's either a triumph or a structural hazard."

Claire laughed and let herself be pulled along.

Behind her, Lily had already found the DJ booth and was arguing about the playlist order again.

The next hour passed in warm blurs.

She spoke with Mags — who declared her dress "decently unsoul-crushing." She helped Ellie repair a fallen snowflake that had lost its will to remain suspended. She clinked glasses with Bev and promised not to judge if the sausage rolls went missing.

And somewhere, across the room, she caught sight of Jack.

Just for a second.

He was laughing at something Ellie had said. Jacket crisp, hair a little too windswept to be planned, one hand tucked casually in his pocket.

Their eyes met.

Not for long.

But long enough.

He didn't wave.

She didn't nod.

But the current between them changed — just a little.

Like they were in the same paragraph again.

Claire didn't see him approach.

She'd just finished rescuing Bev from a three-minute conversation with the headmaster about fundraising bylaws and was making her way toward the edge of the room, where the lighting was dimmer and the floor less sticky.

And then — Jack.

Standing just to the side of the makeshift dance floor, holding two glasses of something vaguely fizzy and definitely warm.

He held one out.

"Truce drink?"

Claire raised an eyebrow. "Were we at war?"

Jack shrugged. "Maybe a quiet one. One of those paper-cut ones where no one really bleeds but everyone flinches for a while."

She took the glass. "Sounds poetic."

"I had help."

They stood in companionable silence for a moment, watching Lily twirl dramatically at the edge of the floor with another Year Six glitter enthusiast. Claire took a sip.

"Warm elderflower?" she guessed.

Jack made a face. "Possibly. Or melted ginger beer. Either way, it's fizzy and non-lethal."

Claire smiled.

Across the room, someone hit the wrong button on the speaker system and a pan flute solo echoed awkwardly through the hall.

Jack looked sideways. "Do you dance?"

Claire blinked. "Not... well. Not with witnesses."

"That's not a no."

She hesitated.

The music shifted again — now something slower, smoother. The lights above the stage dimmed slightly, casting soft reflections off the fairy lights overhead.

Jack didn't move.

He just held out a hand.

Palm open. No pressure. No insistence. Just... a question.

Claire set her drink down.

And took it.

They stepped gently onto the edge of the dance floor. Not centre stage. Just close enough that the music wrapped around them like a scarf.

Jack placed his hand lightly at her waist. Claire rested hers on his shoulder. Their joined hands floated between them, uncertain but steady.

They moved.

Not gracefully. Not in time. But enough.

The kind of dancing where no one was watching — or if they were, it didn't matter.

Claire looked up at him. "I didn't think you'd come tonight."

Jack tilted his head. "And miss the chance to wear trousers that don't quite fit? Never."

She smiled.

His voice was lower when he added, "Also... I wasn't sure I could stay away."

Claire didn't look away.

"You left quietly," she said.

"I didn't want to wake you."

"You left your jumper."

"Wasn't an accident."

The music swelled, soft and mellow, wrapping around them.

Claire's voice barely above a whisper. "I wasn't pretending. Last night. This morning. Any of it."

Jack's reply was just as soft. "Me neither."

Another step. Another breath.

Then — not a kiss. Not a speech.

Just the press of her forehead gently against his chest, and the weight of his hand tightening slightly at her back.

They danced like that — quietly, awkwardly, perfectly — until the music faded into applause they barely noticed.

"CLAIRE!"

The shout broke through the soft post-dance hum like a trumpet in a library.

Claire turned just in time to see Lily hurtling across the floor, tulle skirt flaring, glitter trailing in her wake like a comet of mild panic.

"CLAIRE, CODE SNOWFLAKE!"

Jack blinked. "That sounds serious."

"It's either craft-related or deeply metaphorical," Claire muttered, stepping back as Lily skidded to a stop in front of them, cheeks flushed and crown of stars slipping off her head.

Lily panted. "Emergency. On stage. Snowflake fell. Possibly decapitated Bev's reindeer centrepiece."

Jack made a strangled noise.

Claire blinked. "Bev brought a reindeer?"

"A symbolic one," Lily said. "And now it's headless. Also the fairy lights shorted out and Ellie is singing a cappella because the mic went down and Bev is threatening to leave and take the sausage rolls with her."

Jack leaned closer. "This is incredible."

Claire sighed and handed him her glass. "Welcome to village life."

They followed Lily to the front of the hall, weaving between clusters of amused and mildly concerned villagers. Onstage, Ellie was indeed halfway through an impromptu rendition of *Walking in the Air*, sung with the vigour of someone who hadn't rehearsed and didn't care.

Bev stood off to the side, arms crossed, glaring at a now-decapitated tinsel reindeer while muttering about "craft terrorism."

Claire took one look and turned to Jack.

"Hold the ladder."

Jack nodded solemnly. "I've trained for this."

Claire climbed up onto the side of the stage, inspecting the fairy lights, which had become wrapped around a snowflake that had clearly had enough and given up on life.

"Got it," she said, untangling it carefully and rewiring the plug. The lights blinked once, then flickered into life.

A small cheer went up from the floor.

Lily, arms folded and nodding like a general whose troops had just won a minor but symbolic battle, turned to Jack.

"She's back."

Jack watched Claire descend from the stage, triumphant and slightly windswept, and smiled.

"Yes," he said. "She really is."

The hall had reached peak glow.

Now that the lights were functioning again — flickering only in that charming "vintage wiring" way — and Bev's reindeer had been ceremoniously laid to rest beneath the punch table, the energy had shifted.

People danced again. Laughed again. Moved like they weren't worried about the sausage rolls running out, even though Lily had definitely eaten three.

Claire stood near the piano, watching it all. She felt Jack's shoulder just brushing hers — not deliberate, just present. They hadn't danced again, not yet. But she felt it in the air. The *readiness* of it.

Then Ellie climbed onto the stage.

Which was rarely good news.

She tapped the mic (now mercifully operational), and the gentle hum of the hall quieted in waves.

"Right," Ellie said, in a voice that always sounded like it was late for a better offer. "I just wanted to say a quick something before Bev starts the conga line."

Bev shouted from the back: "I am not starting a conga line!"

Ellie ignored her. "I know we all moan about how nothing ever changes in this village — and how the lights don't work and the mice in the hall have a more effective community watch scheme than the actual council — but can I just say... this?"

She gestured around at the fairy lights, the music, the mismatched outfits, the sparkle and mess and laughter.

"This is bloody magic."

There was a soft, scattered wave of applause. Not thunderous, just real.

"And," Ellie added, eyes sweeping the room, "none of it would've happened without Claire."

Claire blinked.

Suddenly, every pair of eyes turned her way. Her stomach flipped.

Ellie kept going. "She fixed the lights. She saved the reindeer. She made actual cinnamon buns. And she reminded us all that starting again doesn't mean starting over. So — cheers to Claire."

The applause this time was louder. Not riotous. But long enough that Claire felt her ears go pink.

She smiled, slightly overwhelmed.

And then Lily shouted, "Also she's wearing lipstick and not even smudging it!"

More laughter.

Claire laughed too.

Jack leaned in and said quietly, "How do you feel about making a very slow exit?"

Claire turned toward him, her smile still soft.

"Are you offering me an escape route?"

"I'm offering you... air."

She glanced once more around the hall — the lights, the faces, the warmth of it all — and nodded.

"Yes," she said. "Let's."

Jack held out a hand, palm open.

Claire took it.

And together, they slipped out through the side door as Bev picked up a tambourine and someone — no one knows who — started the conga line anyway.

Outside, the air was crisp and velvet-dark.

The village hall's music pulsed faintly through the closed doors behind them, mingling with the faint rustle of trees and the scent of woodsmoke on the breeze.

Claire and Jack stood side by side beneath the low string of fairy lights someone had thought to loop across the front railings. They blinked slowly in the wind, casting little reflections across the ground like puddles of glow.

Neither of them spoke for a moment.

Claire wrapped her arms around herself, more from habit than cold.

Jack shrugged off his jacket.

She started to protest — "You don't have to—" — but he was already draping it over her shoulders.

"It's fine," he said. "It's not the kind of cold that bites."

Claire slipped her arms into the sleeves, inhaling the faint trace of cedar, sugar, and something unplaceably *Jack*.

They stood quietly, side by side.

"You know," Jack said, after a pause, "I didn't come back here to find anything."

Claire looked at him.

He wasn't watching her — just looking out at the green, where a few straggling villagers were heading home in groups of twos and threes.

"I just needed a break," he said. "From work. From noise. From... trying to be someone I didn't really like very much."

Claire nodded. "I know that feeling."

Jack turned to face her.

"But then I met a woman who made me laugh when she didn't mean to, who fought off a disgruntled pigeon with a recycling bin, and who makes the best cinnamon buns I've ever had in my life."

Claire smiled. "I think you're overselling the buns."

He stepped just a little closer.

"And somehow," he said, "I stopped trying to fix everything... and just started *being* here."

She tilted her head.

"With me?"

"With everything."

Claire looked up at him. The night was quiet. The sky clear. The stars showing up, finally, after days of hiding.

"I don't know what happens next," she said softly.

Jack nodded. "That makes two of us."

"But I'm not scared of it."

He met her eyes.

"I'm glad you're not."

Their hands found each other again — as if by muscle memory — fingers lacing without instruction.

Claire exhaled.

There was no kiss.

Not yet.

But there didn't need to be.

Because this? This was the moment that *mattered*. The moment that said:
We are here. We are still standing. And we are walking forward — maybe not fast, maybe not sure — but together.

The door creaked open behind them and Lily's voice rang out: "If either of you have any dignity left, you'll come back in for the finale!"

Claire laughed. Jack grinned.

They didn't move right away.

But they would.

Together.

Chapter Twenty Four

"Things That Stay and Things That Start"

The morning after the Ball came in slowly, like it had politely knocked first.

Sunlight spilled across the kitchen floor in long golden stripes, dust motes drifting lazily through the air as if even they weren't quite ready to start the day. Claire stood at the window, mug warm in her hands, watching two birds bicker over a crumb on the garden wall. The lilac bush outside had lost most of its flowers, but the stubborn few that remained swayed in the breeze like they hadn't got the memo.

The house was quiet, but not lonely.

Just still.

The kind of stillness that comes after something lovely has happened and the world is catching its breath.

She turned from the window and wandered slowly through the kitchen — barefoot, hair still vaguely party-shaped — and took stock. One of the fairy light strings from the Ball had made its way home with them, now draped haphazardly around the bannister. A few glitter specks clung to the hem of her jumper. On the table: a folded note from Ellie ("You left before the dancing got truly shameful — you're welcome") and a leftover mince pie wrapped in cling film with a passive-aggressive bow.

Claire smiled. She didn't remember bringing that home. But it was very Ellie.

She made coffee — real coffee, the good beans, the last spoonful she'd been saving for *a day that deserved it*. And this one did. She could feel it in her bones. Not in any dramatic, life-changing way — just in the small steadiness of her breath. The way her shoulders didn't ache from bracing against things. The way her heart hadn't fluttered with worry the second she'd woken up.

She was okay.

Maybe more than okay.

A creak on the stairs pulled her back, and a moment later, Lily appeared — blanket around her shoulders, one sock on, hair exploding in all directions like a celebratory firework.

Claire passed her the second mug without a word.

Lily took it with both hands and flopped into a chair.

"Morning," Claire said.

Lily groaned. "Who invented dancing?"

Claire sat down opposite her. "People who didn't know what back pain was."

"Or how shoes work," Lily muttered, flexing her foot dramatically. "I think I sprained dignity."

They sipped in silence for a while, the kitchen filling with the smell of toast someone *should* make but neither of them wanted to stand up for.

Claire tilted her head. "So... last night?"

Lily blinked. "Did you know Ellie did a cartwheel?"

"I did not."

"She shouldn't have."

Claire snorted.

Lily set her mug down carefully, then fixed her mother with a look — the kind that tried to look casual but had twelve questions hidden inside it.

"Okay," Lily said. "So. You and Jack."

Claire took a slow sip. "That's not a question."

Lily rolled her eyes. "Ugh, *fine*. Are you and Jack, like, a thing now?"

Claire tilted her head. "What does 'a thing' mean to you?"

Lily gave her a level look. "If this is going to be a birds and bees talk I will throw myself out the window."

Claire laughed. "It's not. I just... I don't know if we are anything yet. But we're not nothing."

Lily considered that. "You looked happy."

"I was."

Claire folded her hands around the mug. "It's strange. I don't think I realised how much I'd forgotten how to feel... safe. Until I started feeling it again."

Lily was quiet for a moment. Then: "You *do* look different here."

Claire raised an eyebrow. "Different how?"

"More colour. In your face. In your voice."

Claire blinked. "That's... very poetically specific."

Lily shrugged. "I've been reading the Christmas play script. There's a lot of metaphors."

Claire reached across the table and gently pushed Lily's hair back behind her ear.

"You always see more than you let on."

"I know," Lily said. Then added, "But don't tell Bev. She still thinks I'm mostly decorative."

They sat together a while longer, not needing to say much. The kind of silence that isn't uncomfortable — just shared.

Eventually Lily stretched and stood.

"Okay. Shower. Then toast. Then I'm watching The Holiday with snacks that are 80% sugar. That okay?"

Claire smiled. "Perfect."

Lily padded out of the room.

Claire stayed seated, fingers curled around the now-empty mug, eyes drifting again to the window.

Outside, the light was soft. The garden a little overgrown. The air looked cold, but kind.

She wasn't sure what came next.

But for once, that wasn't scary.

It was full of promise.

It was just past eleven when the knock came.

Not loud. Not rushed. Just... a presence. The kind of knock that didn't expect an answer right away, but hoped for one all the same.

Claire looked up from the kitchen table, where she was half-heartedly attempting a crossword and fully-heartedly ignoring the growing mountain of post-party laundry.

She crossed the room slowly, smoothing a hand over her jumper, and opened the door.

Jack stood there, one hand in his coat pocket, the other holding a brown paper bag.

He looked slightly sheepish. Hair windblown, cheeks a little pink from the cold. There was a scuff on his boot and a smudge of something that might've been flour on his sleeve.

"Morning," he said.

Claire blinked. "Hi."

Jack held out the bag. "I brought bread."

Claire stared at it. "Bread?"

He nodded. "Fresh. From the bakery. I figured... you'd probably have coffee and no carbs, and I didn't want that on my conscience."

She raised an eyebrow. "That's a very specific kind of guilt."

Jack smiled. "I was raised well."

Claire stepped aside. "Come in."

He did — slowly, carefully, like he didn't want to tread too heavily on the calm that lived in the room.

Claire closed the door behind him. The cottage instantly felt warmer. Not in temperature — just in energy.

Jack looked around. "Still standing?"

"Mostly."

He spotted the fairy lights wrapped around the banister. "Stealing decor now?"

"Ellie dared me."

Jack grinned.

Claire took the bread and set it on the counter. "Would you like coffee?"

"I'd love some."

They moved around each other easily, like two people who'd once been strangers but had since learned the geography of each other's kitchens.

Claire handed him a mug, filled it, added a splash of milk the way he liked. He passed her the butter from the fridge without asking. She sliced the bread, still warm, the crust crackling under the knife.

They sat at the kitchen table, across from each other. Steam curled from their mugs. Butter melted into the slices. The smell of yeast and toast filled the air.

Jack took a bite, chewed, swallowed, and said, "You saved the Ball."

Claire smiled. "I saved one reindeer and rewired some fairy lights. The real MVP is Bev's sausage rolls."

"She did threaten to throw them at Ellie."

"She does that every year."

They ate in silence for a few minutes, the kind that wasn't awkward. Just... domestic.

Claire looked up. "Did you sleep okay?"

Jack nodded. "Eventually."

There was something unspoken in that word, and she felt it settle between them.

"I kept thinking," he said, "how strange it is. To feel like you've lived somewhere for months, when it's only been weeks. Like the place already knows you."

Claire stirred her coffee. "Like it's been waiting for you."

Jack met her eyes.

"Exactly."

They sat with that for a moment.

Then Claire said softly, "I wasn't sure what last night meant."

Jack leaned back, not defensive — just open.

"It didn't mean pressure. Or expectation. Just... that I like being near you. And I'd like to keep being near you. If you're okay with that."

Claire didn't speak right away.

She reached for her coffee, took a sip, set it down.

Then she said, "I don't know where I'm going next. Or what I want long-term. I just know... this feels good."

Jack nodded. "Good's a great place to start."

Another pause.

Then — Claire reached across the table and took his hand.

Not with fanfare.

Just... quietly.

He let his fingers curve around hers.

And that was it.

Not a kiss. Not a speech. Not a dramatic promise.

Just warmth. And connection. And the kind of steadiness that said: *Yes. This. Let's see where this leads.*

From upstairs, there was a loud crash.

Jack blinked. "Should we be concerned?"

Claire sighed. "Only if you hear the words 'don't panic' next."

Jack laughed.

They stayed at the table another half hour. Talking about nothing and everything. The way people do when they've stopped trying to be interesting and started just being real.

Claire found Lily in the living room, surrounded by the aftermath of whatever teenage nesting instinct had overtaken her during the past hour.

There were pillows in strange places. A mug with three forgotten biscuits. A notepad covered in dramatic scribbles — "HOLIDAY PARTY PLAN, version 7" — and a crumpled packet of crisps balanced precariously on the armrest.

Claire stood in the doorway, quietly taking it all in.

"You realise," she said, "this looks like a small craft hurricane hit a Christmas market."

Lily glanced up from the blanket she was half-under, half-wearing. "It's an aesthetic."

Claire stepped further in. "Is it a survivable one?"

Lily shrugged. "Depends how you feel about crumbs."

Claire dropped onto the sofa beside her, curling one leg underneath her.

For a moment, neither of them said anything. Just the soft tick of the clock, the hum of something warming up in the pipes, and the gentle hush that lives in houses after something good has happened.

Then Lily said, "You seem... different."

Claire looked at her. "Different how?"

"I dunno." Lily twisted the edge of the blanket in her fingers. "Lighter."

Claire nodded slowly. "I feel it too."

"You don't flinch anymore. When your phone buzzes. When the door knocks. When I say 'can we talk.'"

Claire turned to face her fully, folding her hands in her lap.

"I didn't realise I was doing that," she said softly.

"I did," Lily said. Not accusing. Just honest.

Claire reached out, gently brushed Lily's hair back. "I'm sorry."

Lily didn't say anything for a second. Then: "I think I'm glad it happened."

Claire blinked. "The move?"

Lily nodded. "Even the messy bits. Even the weird, quiet mornings and the bit where you cried behind the kettle that one time and pretended it was onions."

Claire laughed. "I did no such thing."

"You held a red onion in the air like it was a defence mechanism."

Claire smiled. "Okay, fair."

Lily leaned her head against Claire's shoulder. "I just mean... we had to fall apart a bit, didn't we? To come back properly."

Claire wrapped her arm around her daughter. "Yeah," she said. "We did."

They sat like that for a long time.

Eventually, Lily said, "Do you think we'll stay?"

Claire didn't answer right away.

She looked out the window — the village green, the bare trees, the rooftops dusted with late frost. And further still, she could see the faint edge of the bakery sign, the line of cottages, the crooked chimney with the odd bird that always sat there.

She could see the whole shape of her life — not finished, but forming.

She smiled.

"I think," Claire said, "we already have."

Lily squeezed her arm. "Good."

Later that afternoon, Claire pulled on her coat — the soft navy one with the inside pocket that always surprised her — and stepped outside.

The village green was quiet, brushed in a silvery winter light that softened every edge. There was a hum to it, though — not noise, but *life*. The kind of small bustle you could miss if you didn't know what to listen for.

Snow clouds hung just out of reach, heavy and slow. The air smelled faintly of chimney smoke and cinnamon.

She made her way down the lane, passing Bev's house, where two new gnomes had appeared on the windowsill overnight. One was wearing sunglasses. The other appeared to be mid-yoga.

Claire smiled.

Further on, Ellie's front door was propped open with a bag of onions and the sound of musical theatre drifted out as if it had escaped captivity. A muffled shout rang through the hall — something about goose fat and emergency glitter.

Claire didn't stop. She didn't need to. The knowing nod from Ellie as she bustled past said it all.

Outside the bakery, Jack was chatting with Mags, who was wearing what appeared to be an enormous plaid scarf and a pair of snow boots that looked like they could survive a mountain expedition.

Claire approached slowly, her boots soft on the frosted path.

Jack saw her first. His smile wasn't wide. It was just... there. Constant. Easy.

Mags turned as Claire reached them. "Ah, the toast of the Ball," she said, examining Claire with the scrutiny of someone who knew exactly how many sausage rolls were consumed per capita last night. "Still glowing?"

"From Bev's fireworks or Ellie's singing?" Claire asked.

Mags snorted. "Neither were sanctioned."

Jack handed Claire a paper bag. "One almond croissant. It winked at me. I thought you'd want it."

Claire took it with a smile. "You're not wrong."

They stood there for a few minutes, just watching the village in motion. Nothing dramatic. Just people being people. A couple of kids kicking at frozen puddles. Bev's dog dressed like an elf. Someone wheeling a crate of what might've been wine or possibly just ambitious jam.

Mags eventually wandered off, muttering about cake rotations.

Claire and Jack walked slowly toward the green.

"Feels like home," Jack said.

Claire nodded. "It does."

She didn't say anything more. She didn't have to. He understood. That was the point.

They reached the bench by the noticeboard — the one with the wobbly slat and the tiny plaque that read: *For those who stayed when it mattered.* Neither of them had sat on it before, but now felt like the right time.

They did.

Claire unwrapped the croissant and tore it in half. Gave him the bigger piece without comment.

They ate in silence. Comfortable. Shared.

And when Jack brushed the crumbs from his hands and looked out across the green, he said, "I could stay a while."

Claire smiled softly. "Me too."

He stood a moment later. "I'll see you later?"

She nodded. "I'll be here."

He squeezed her hand — once, quick, and warm — and headed off down the lane, coat flapping slightly, steps light.

Claire stayed on the bench.

She looked out across the village — not scanning, not searching. Just seeing.

There were more layers to it now. More familiarity in the colours. In the sounds. The pace of things. The rhythm of a place that didn't need her to be anyone except *exactly who she was.*

She felt it in her chest — not a flutter, not a rush. Just a stillness.

And she knew, with absolute clarity, that this was what she'd been chasing.

Not the man. Not the success. Not the new life.

Just this.

Peace. Place. People.

She stood, slowly, and headed home.

Back at the cottage, Lily was curled in a nest of blankets and cheese crackers, watching something involving snowmen and questionable acting.

Claire ruffled her hair on the way past. Lily grumbled but smiled.

Claire made tea. The good kind. With the honey she liked. She lit the candle in the window that always smelled like warm sugar. And she sat down by the fire with her hands wrapped around the mug.

The cottage was quiet. The world outside was soft.

There was nothing missing.

Nothing waiting to be fixed.

Just a woman, a girl, a warm room.

And the sound of something — not beginning. Not ending.

Just... continuing.

Exactly as it should.

An Important Announcement from Lily

(Chief Cinnamon Bun Tester & Village Chaos Coordinator)

Right. Listen up.

If you enjoyed this book — the fairy lights, the cinnamon buns, the emotional growth (ugh) — then you officially owe me one. And by "one" I mean...

A review.
A short one.
With stars. Preferably five. But I'm not the boss of you.

(Except I kind of am. Ask Ellie. She fears me.)

Anyway — here's the deal:
If you leave a nice review, I'll save you a seat at the next Ball, sneak you extra cake, and **personally** prevent Bev from launching a glitter cannon in your general direction.

If you *don't* leave a review?

Let's just say I know where the glitter is kept.

So go on — be kind. Write the thing. Help Claires story reach more people. And maybe, just maybe, I'll let you borrow my emergency sausage roll stash.

Fair's fair.
– Lily
(Age: Eleven. Dangerous when over-caffeinated.)

Printed in Dunstable, United Kingdom

68057166R10178